B OF THE BANG

Andrew Shanahan

Copyright © 2024 by Andrew Shanahan

All rights reserved. No part of this book may be reproduced, distributed, or transmitted in any form or by any means, including photocopying, recording, or other electronic or mechanical methods, without the prior written permission of the publisher, except in the case of brief quotations embodied in critical reviews and certain other non-commercial uses permitted by copyright law.

This is a work of fiction. Names, characters, businesses, places, events, and incidents are either the products of the author's imagination or used in a fictitious manner. Any resemblance to actual persons, living or dead, or actual events is purely coincidental. The author and publisher are not responsible for any interpretations or conclusions drawn from this fictional work, and any resemblance to real persons, organisations, or events is unintended and entirely coincidental.

First paperback edition 1st November 2024

Book design by Michelle Lile

Cover design by Andrew Shanahan and Michelle Lile

For exclusive updates about this book and Andrew Shanahan visit
www.helloshan.co.uk

If you would like the chance to die (fictitiously) in a future book please visit
www.iwillliterarilykillyou.com

"I don't start running on the bang of the starter's pistol;
I start on the B of the Bang."
LINFORD CHRISTIE

"Your gold and silver are corroded. Their corrosion
will testify against you and eat your flesh like fire.
You have hoarded wealth in the last days."
JAMES 5:3

FOR MY FRIEND CRAIG

CONTENTS

PROLOGUE: NOW THAT'S WHAT I CALL TRICKLE DOWN ECONOMICS!	1
YOU THINK THAT BRADFORD IS GREAT	5
I'LL SETTLE FOR A PINT, SIR	23
THE CAT IS OUT OF THE BAG, BUT THE CATFLAP IS SHUT	32
SMILE AND WAVE BOYS, SMILE AND WAVE	42
LOBSTER ROCKED	50
RED OR GREEN?	62
THEY DIDN'T HAVE TO MOVE US TO SALFORD	74
NO ONE PANIC! EXCEPT MAYBE YOU.	83
HELLO, B OF THE BANG, HOW CAN I HELP YOU?	99
"LIVERPOOL LIME STREET"	109
SOME HELL BELOW US	121
DUCK SOUP AND A SANDWICH	129
HELLO MOTHER	136
LIKE ARMAGEDDON, BUT MADE OUT OF CARDBOARD	149
KEEP CALM, CARRY ON AND BE KIND	159
I'D MOVE THE CAPITAL TO BILLERICAY	174
LISTEN TO THE SAFETY LOBSTER, KIDS!	179
THAT IS LITERALLY A PRETTY PENNY	191
LONDON BRIDGE IS FOR FALLING DOWN	197
THE SOLUTION IS OBVIOUSLY TO STEAL A BOAT	204
THIRTY SECONDS TO MIDNIGHT (GMT)	211
CREAM RISES, SHIT FLOATS	221
DO YOU THINK WE CAN BLAME NICOTINE WITHDRAWAL?	235
ALL ABOARD!	241
THE DUCHESS OF BERMONDSEY	252
OH, NO! NO NO NO NO!	263
DANCE AND DRINK AND SCREW	273

THE KELLY CRITERION	280
PSSST...I HAVE A BUNKER	285
YOU GET A TRIDENT! YOU GET A TRIDENT! EVERYONE GETS A TRIDENT!	298
TIME GENTLEMEN, PLEASE	305
EPILOGUE: THE GREATEST TREASURES ARE FORMED UNDER THE HEAVIEST PRESSURES	315

PROLOGUE: NOW THAT'S WHAT I CALL TRICKLE DOWN ECONOMICS!

ANGELINA BIRD WAS fucked if she was going to let Etienne Lemoine fuck her like this. Some botoxed Frog who couldn't even finish half his shoe of absinthe at Davos? She was supposed to let that plastic-grinned croissant explode a dirty bomb *in her fucking London?* Her family *was* London. Her Dad. Her Nan. They owned the jewellery shops. The office buildings. The flimsy little flats. The Birds had been at it for centuries; they were more than…the thought exploded unfinished in a froth of rage.

What did he think this would do to rents? Who wanted to live in Chernobyl-by-Thames?

She had to take a second to let the fury pass through her.

She breathed deeply in the drizzly air of the grey, moist London morning. It all felt very *Monday*. The damp spattered against her face as she bent over and the water coalesced on the tip of her nose. She blew the droplets away with purpose and clamped the leg brace around her right thigh and clicked the buckle into place. This was going to mash these tights right up, but that was just more motivation for kicking Lemoine in his head until her Gucci was ankle-deep in the pulp. But she had to escape first. She clamped the left leg brace on, straightened up, and toggled the engine's jets. She felt the thrust immediately as a band of vibration across her back and down her arms. Woah, Daddy!

"Madam! Please! There's no access to the roof up here, you need to come down!"

Bird was vaguely aware of a security guard walking towards her, past the pipes and vents that punctuated the roof of the building.

"Piss off," she replied, while checking the monitors on her wrist display. Fuel wasn't optimal, but it would be enough to get her to the outskirts of London in the little time she had been given, and that was really all that mattered. She should have let her Nan know, but there wasn't really time. Lots of things wouldn't matter after today.

"Madam, now we don't want there to be any trouble here, do we?"

Bird remembered the guard and finally looked at the man, who was now five metres away. White polyester shirt. Black polyester trousers. Shiny patent leather shoes. Give him a run up and the right carpet and he could power the building single-handedly. There were weird epaulettes on his shoulder with two thin stripes of gold braid, like he'd been promoted. From what to what? A turd with one gold stripe to a turd with two gold stripes? Had his family gone out to dinner when he'd got the second gold braid? Bird recoiled; the man's teeth could have had their own documentary series. Non-playing characters like this infested her flats.

Lots of things wouldn't matter after today.

She raised one of her arms towards the man, who stopped approaching and took a moment to take in the weird exoskeleton that the woman was encased in. It looked like something out of Transformers. As he gawped, Bird levelled both her arms at the guard and briefly cycled the engine, causing the air at the end of her arms to shimmer. A concussive blast of power struck the security guard and shoved him back against the safety rail. He struggled to right himself, but the jets were relentless. He felt himself scrambling for purchase on the wet roof; his shiny shoes failed to get any traction against the blast. He felt the railing fall away. Then all he could see was a constantly revolving view of the top of the building and, increasingly, the ground. A bus. A tree. A surprised dog. He thought about the sausage bap cooling on his desk. Then there was just the ground.

"Blame Lemoine," Bird said over the railing.

She picked up the flight helmet at her feet and strapped it tight under her chin. She slung the hardshell briefcase across her front and felt a shiver of excitement about the value of what she was holding. Not just the Willy Wonka Golden Ticket that the case represented, but all of the diamonds nestled in the foam. Her Nan had always insisted that they had a stash of wealth "just in case" and everyone had nodded and gone along with it, but she'd been proven right. Bird couldn't imagine what the world would be like after the fallout settled, but she knew that five billion in diamonds would still be a good start. Maybe she would hire a hitman to bring her Lemoine's toes.

The head-up display on the helmet's visor relayed the power and fuel levels of the engines and gave her an overlay of her GPS position. There was a warning symbol flashing at the bottom, cautioning her that she was in a built-up urban area and that all jetpack flights had to be approved with the relevant authorities. Bird looked at the London that prostrated itself at the feet of the building. She felt confident that the 'relevant authorities' would have more pressing concerns than someone using a jetpack. She looked at London again. What had possessed Lemoine? It would mean war. None of it made sense.

Bird crouched slightly, braced her core and thighs as she angled the engines towards the roof and gradually let the power from the jets build. Her feet rose onto tiptoes and then with more power squeezed from the triggers in her hands, just the toenails of her tiptoes were touching the building. Then she took to the sky - one metre, ten metres, one hundred metres. She rose beyond the communication aerials and cooling vents. She felt her body being buffeted by the gusts of cold, misty wind. She blinked repeatedly behind the visor and shook the droplets of water that gathered on her chin.

She'd flown across London in a helicopter countless times, but to fly under her own power was a novel experience. Even the section of the Thames that she could see through the low clouds looked less caustic from up here. As she glanced down, she could practically hear the Eastenders theme tune as the city itself dissolved and the satellite view of the capital took its place. She picked out the various districts and zones of London. She saw the tourist spots, the dangerous places, the centres of power, the places she owned.

It wasn't beautiful exactly, but it was hers.

Yet somewhere down there, *right now,* radioactive material was billowing through the streets. She wondered where the bomb had gone off – she could see a few columns of smoke rising across the city and if she squinted, she thought she could see flashing lights, but that could be for anything. Bird tensed her core, repositioned the jets and watched the display showing her point towards the South, towards the promise of deliverance. As she spun through 180 degrees, she had a fraction of a second to see the giant black circle that burst through the cover of the clouds.

Her brain was just beginning to trace that the black circle was connected to a wing, and the wing to a fuselage, but by then she was at least two metres inside the engine, and in a flash her brain and body were ejected from the rear of the engine as a red, aerosolised mist. Angelina Bird was now only detectable as a faint metallic taste on the wind. Her hardshell case ricocheted around the blades of the engine, smashing it to pieces. The case's contents were spun around and blasted out, following her remnants into the sky. There was a slamming noise and long streaks of fire and a guff of dark black smoke emerged from the jet. It briefly let out another mechanical shriek, and then the only noise was a descending whine.

YOU THINK THAT BRADFORD IS GREAT

BRADFORD ALDERMAN VIIII – scion of the Alderman Retail Group – couldn't find a pose that looked rich, but disinterestedly so. He tried tipping himself back in his spotlessly white Arne Jacobson office chair, until his midriff jutted. It wasn't quite enough. He tried putting both feet on the desk, crossed at the ankles. As ever, his feet looked *too* big, absurd in their appalling size, more like kayaks than feet. Pops' jibe echoed in his ears from a decade past: "You want your mistress to be 18, not your feet."

But wait! He crossed to the bookshelves and retrieved a copy of *The Art of War 2*, a book he had written. Honestly, AI made writing so simple these days, anyone could fart out a book within a week. And Bradford had not only written the book, but he had also organised its bulk-buying to finesse the Amazon algorithm and hit the bestseller list. He had then shipped the thousands of unread copies to a pulping factory overseas. Now at just 32-years-old, he was a bestselling author, a master of the written form like whoever did the screenplay for *Fight Club*. He angled the book's cover towards the visitor's chair. Then he picked it up and considered if it was too cheesy to be caught reading it.

"Oh, you caught me brushing up on the classics. What is it? Oh nothing, it's a bestseller I wrote last summer. Sign a copy? Heh, yes, I suppose I could."

He decided it was too cheesy and swept the copy into the bin.

What if he was on the phone? That would imply a casual mastery of the business environment. It would also showcase that he was fitting this interview in, not that it had been his entire focal point for the last month; the subject of so many pre-meeting meetings, consultations, fittings, waxings, strainings, teeth whitenings and gum reddenings. He held his phone to his cheek and pretended someone was on the other end.

"Hola, hi, hey-hey. Yeah, tell Tokyo that I don't care if they think the Cransome deal is off, I say it's not."

As he tried to think of believable corp-waffle, he could see the opening lines of this stupid profile that he never should have agreed to, appear in front of his face like the words of an incantation.

Bradford Alderman VIIII, 32, scion of the Alderman Retail Group, greets me with his obscenely big loafers perched on the desk, babbling incoherently, ghostwritten books shamefully swept under the rug – instantly, his idiocy is as apparent and gargantuan as his sock bill…

One foot on the desk, chair tipped back? No, that was just weird, plus it made everything seem very *crotchy*. Arses! Why was this so hard? He should have asked his PR girl Alexandra how he should sit. She should have briefed him better. He'd only agreed to this whole thing because she thought it might help with Project Focus Pull, the ongoing plan to get attention away from Pops and to position at least one of Bradford's doll-like hands on the company's steering wheel.

Project Focus Pull had not been going well.

The Times Rich List profile seemed like a reasonable move. Alexandra had brought in a new stylist called Trent who had picked out a Brioni suit with Stefan Ricci silks to accessorise. He'd twinned those with snaffle toe Gucci loafers, silk socks and - after an hour of exquisitely timed discussion - a Richard Mille on his wrist. May Moloch continue to bless the Swiss.

The suit was cut with a lot of room and Bradford (*"As we shake hands, he insists I call him Brad…"*) had initially felt that the tailoring conveyed entirely the opposite message that they were hoping to put across. Namely, that it made him look like he was an 8-year-old wearing his dad's suit. This wasn't helped by the fact that the only plus-sized thing about Bradford was his feet. He stood at 5'5" and weighed slightly more than 50kg only after Christmas dinner. More than ten times in his life, he had been physically likened to a capital L.

Trent and Alexandra had overruled his objections and argued that it was more important that he broke cover and make his own statement. In many ways, they claimed, it didn't matter if it looked ridiculous, it was the fact that people would talk about it that was more important.

"This could be your meat dress," Trent had counselled.

Maybe he was right. Bradford had certainly started to feel rather chicken.

A muted knock on the door and Rozz appeared, followed by the *Times* reporter. Arses, what was her name? Jess? Jenna? Fortunately, Bradford had done a year of sessions with a celebrated telepath who had said that Bradford had an uncanny grip on what he called "the be-veiled world." Bradford focused his chi (which he had been surprised to learn was actually pronounced "*chaz*") and projected a thought into Rozz's head: "Say her name Rozz, say the journalist's name." Rozz looked at him curiously, smiled and backed out of the room. It didn't always work – Wi-Fi signals sometimes interfered with psychic messages. Forced to suddenly improvise on the perfect casual-yet-wealthy repose, Bradford picked up the grey metal bin that sat under his desk and rested it on his lap.

"Brad, great to meet you. Tabitha Wright from *The Times*, thank you so much for agreeing to meet with me," the reporter said and held out a manicured hand that nicely concluded the end of a toned, bronzed arm. Her watch was a bit of high street piffle, but that arm had potential. *Nice work, lady*. Bradford stopped his review of her body with the sudden panicked realisation that she'd called him Brad. He hadn't prepared anything else though, so he just ploughed on.

"I insist you call me Brad. Please excuse me, I'm just emptying my bin."

Bradford realised that he didn't know where the bin was emptied, so he simply lifted the bin to show her that it was empty, except for a single copy of *The Art of War 2*, which he hoped she didn't see and then put the bin back under his desk. Then he stood and shook Jess' hand. Firm, dry palm - nice. Hold for eight seconds. She has to initiate the disengagement, just like the handshake consultant had coached.

"<u>You like this man</u>. <u>He is handsome</u>." Bradford projected into her mind sphere.

Wait, she wasn't called Jess, was she? She'd literally just said her name, but he'd been worrying about the bin so he hadn't listened. No choice but to press on.

"Can I get you a drink…girl?"

"No, I'm fine thank you; I've got some water with me. Are you ok if I record the conversation? Alexandra asked for editorial approval of the final piece, which isn't the paper's normal policy, but my editor is happy to do it for the Aldermans."

"Yes, absolutely, record away."

"Okay, great – so my colleague Tim will be joining us in about thirty minutes to do photos, so that gives us plenty of time now to have a chat. Do you know where the Aldermans finished on the list this year?"

"I think Alexandra said we were plus-five from last year?"

Tabitha consulted her notebook. "No – plus-seven. There's been some last-minute shuffles because of the crypto market tanking." Bradford nodded sagely. Yes, crypto markets tanked, this was something he knew and understood. He steepled his fingers under his chin and kept nodding.

"So, we're what, 21st?"

"That's right. And I suppose my first question is – what does that mean to you *personally*? Is the *Rich List* something that takes up any mental space in Brad Alderman's brain, or is it all background noise to the important stuff of actually running the empire."

Finally, a moment Alexandra and Trent had prepped him for. He smiled – shining from teeth and eyes, just like the expression consultant had advised.

"I feel sorry for anyone who has money as their only metric."

He said the words clearly and aimed them at Tabitha's phone, hoping she would quote him accurately. They'd market tested the line and it had killed across all demographics. The feedback was that it sounded smart and intimated that he knew what a metric was, which 78% of respondents doubted was true.

"Interesting – so what metrics do you personally consider important?"

Before he could reply, a cupboard to his left began to vibrate. They both turned in alarm. The intense buzzing emanating from inside the squat grey unit made the metal doors quiver with a loud *GNRRR-RRRR - GNRRRRRRR*. The disruption intensified when a piercing alert noise sounded out. A klaxon rising in pitch, lasting two seconds and then repeating. It was so loud that Rozz opened the office door and peered in with concern, but Bradford waved her away.

"Wow! That is loud! What is that?" Tabitha asked with her palms pressed to her ears.

"I know! I don't…can you just excuse me a second?" Bradford said and Tabitha reached over to her phone which was recording the conversation and pretended to pause it.

Bradford got up from his seat and tentatively approached the cupboard. He opened the double doors and saw where the noise was originating from and felt his stomach drop. On the top shelf, behind stacks of post-it notes, was a black briefcase. As well as vibrating and emitting the ear-splitting klaxon there was also a red light pulsing from LEDs on its side. In the top right-hand corner of the case was a logo - a red triangle containing a large green eye, centred in which were the words B of the Bang.

Bradford's breathing grew shallow and fast. He felt frozen in fear. His bowels started to churn. He knew he had to touch it, but he was suddenly simply too scared to pick up this very fucking monumental thing.

"Brad, is everything ok?" Tabitha's question roused Bradford from the flight of fantasy he was engaged in, a fantasy where he was in a place exactly like this, but with the significant difference that this case wasn't doing what it was so obviously doing.

"Yes, yes, yes. It's fine. Everything is fine. Will you excuse me, I just need to go to the bathroom for a moment?" He couldn't look Tabitha in the eye, so he just detached the case from its mounting and speedwalked it to his office ensuite. He shut and locked the door and placed the case on the marble side. He still didn't dare open it. He looked up and saw himself in the mirror. His craven expression and the finger he was reflexively chewing on in fear disgusted him. He forced his features into an imperious expression instead. Another section of the profile appeared to him.

At the merest provocation, Alderman starts to peep like a little baby bird, desperate for its mother to return and regurgitate worm slurry into his mouth...

He didn't want that sort of press.

With trembling hands Bradford set his thumb onto the smooth black pad on top of the case. It flashed a green light and a panel slid back to reveal a numeric keypad. He tapped in his passcode: 8008135. Four locks on three sides of the case, two front and one each side, released with a *snap* and, after taking a deep gulp, he opened the case. Instantly, the alarms stopped and the case fell still.

Bradford had only seen inside the case once before, when it had been delivered to him by his B of the Bang on-boarding rep. The whole point was that ideally, he would never see the case again. It would sit on the shelf in the cupboard, plugged in and gathering dust. There were exactly four items in the case held in place by a dense bobbled grey foam. A Gerber 06 Auto knife in black with a 3.6-inch blade. Two Thuraya X5 Touch satellite phones, and a drawstring pouch containing £50,000 in gold coins.

The screens of both phones were flashing simultaneously with a large red notification. Bradford cancelled one and pressed OK on the other. Text and audio immediately erupted from the phone. Bradford sprang like he'd been stung and dropped the phone's volume.

"This is a message from B of the Bang for Platinum member… *Bradford Alderman vee-eye-eye-eye-eye*. If you are not…*Bradford Alderman vee-eye-eye-eye-eye*…then please close this notification and return the phone to the case, or you will open yourself up to…*severe*…legal consequences. If you are…*Bradford Alderman vee-eye-eye-eye-eye*… please confirm by entering your passcode immediately."

Bradford tapped in 8008135 again, there was a pause and then the message continued.

"This information is for…*Bradford Alderman vee-eye-eye-eye-eye*…only. Please consider this privileged and confidential. Seven Hwasong-17 intercontinental ballistic missiles have been launched from…*Hamhung, North Korea*. Three of these missiles were destroyed during the boost phase of the launch. The remaining four missiles are following steep trajectories and projections show they will impact targets around the world. We consider it very unlikely that these missiles will be stopped. The time until impact in…*London*…is 75 minutes."

Oh my God. The end. It was the shitting end.

Bradford clung onto the phone and leaned heavily on the counter. As the voice relayed more information there was grainy footage on the screens of missiles flying silently through the air.

"B of the Bang have issued immediate exfiltration plans for all members at…*Gold Level and higher*…your exfiltration will take place by…*fill this in later*…and you should immediately make your way to…*the pier nearest to the Savoy*…please acknowledge this by entering your passcode."

He numbly thumbed in his passcode again. A map appeared highlighting the location. Bradford knew the place, it was just next to Cleopatra's Needle. He could walk it from the office in twenty minutes, run it in ten, drive it in thirty.

"Once you reach…*the pier*…our extraction team will take you and…*one*…additional passenger of your choosing to a secure nuclear, biological, chemical bunker. Because of radiation it is *not* possible to shelter in place. At this stage it is not known how long it will be before this information is released to the general public. If you cannot make it to…*the Savoy*…or you are a…*Silver Member or below*… then we thank you for being a B of the Bang customer. If you need to ask additional questions then please press the Call button."

Bradford looked at the phone and hit *Call*. Additional questions!? His mind was tripping over itself to think of what to ask first. He also desperately wanted to hear another human voice, someone who could tell him this wasn't real. The phone rang three times before an automated voice answered: "Your call is important to B of the Bang. Please stay on the line and we will connect you to an operator. You are…*59th*…in line." A high-energy muzak version of *The Vengabus is Coming* started to play.

Bradford hung up and emitted a long groan. He wasn't going to explode listening to Europop. As he stood in his marbled toilet, he felt the terror draw a fingernail across the back of his neck. Nuclear strikes! On London! He pushed the heel of his palms into his eyes. He was conscious of his galloping heartbeat and when he looked at his reflection again, he could see his pulse hammering away in his neck. He felt like he should cry and he forced a few experimental sobs out, but they didn't quite take. Instead, he pulled his trousers down and waddled over to the Kohler Numi toilet whose lid automatically lifted as he approached, and he resolved to shit out all of his fear. The toilet's bidet system spritzed his bottom clean and released a pump of L'Eau d'Issey.

Bradford washed his hands and looked at his reflection one last time. He went to slap himself across the face but held back because it would have hurt. Instead, he pointed at himself.

"You have to survive, Bradford. The world will need leaders."

The thought struck him that this was probably the ultimate focus pull. Alexandra would be pleased, if an ex-human vapour could be pleased. He laughed at his little joke.

So, now what? Cocaine. That would be the best starting point. He'd been holding off for a month since he'd had a jet ski incident while he was high, but the end of the world and sniff seemed like an essential pairing.

He put one of the satellite phones in his trouser pocket and left the spare in the case. He slipped the knife into his jacket pocket and the pouch of coins into the other. He took a breath and tried to be strategic. He'd been on a Take Control Of Everything retreat once where a 12th Level Shaman had given him Ayahuasca and he'd learned, once he'd regained certainty of his own existence, that his brain was composed of different characters. Right now, he felt that The Donkey had reacted to the news, and The Chambermaid had also had her say – he was trying to summon up what The Wizard or The Quiz Master would suggest when his reverie was interrupted.

"Are you ok, Brad?"

The journalist was tapping lightly on the other side of the bathroom door.

"I heard you groaning and talking to yourself. If you're unwell we can reschedule the interview?"

"No, I'm good. I'm good. It's just toilet business. I'll be with you in a minute, I just need to make a call."

Despite the fact that he'd just used the phrase "toilet business" Bradford smiled at himself in the mirror. The Wizard had finally chipped in with an idea.

He took out his phone and called his wife. She answered sounding huffy, which had been her default state for more than a decade. Susie had always had Resting Bitch Face since Bradford had first met her, but it had gradually metastasised over the years, until it was more accurate to say that she had Resting Bitch Everything.

"What is it? I'm on my way to Kate's-"

Kate. Chris. Their girls. All gone in seventy-five minutes. Seventy-four minutes. Bradford nearly said something but caught himself in time. No point heading for the exit if it's blocked with other people. He'd joined B of the Bang precisely for that advanced warning and their expertise in being able to get customers out of the stickiest of situations. No Susies, Chrises or Kates allowed.

"Listen, where are the boys?"

There was a pause from Susie that belied her disbelief. "They're *at school.*"

Canterbury – about fifty or sixty miles - they might be ok. Bradford supposed it depended on the missile and the size of the explosion. Wind direction. Megatonnage. That sort of thing. He paused briefly to consider whether he could get a message to Toby to join him in the bunker in time, but knowing Toby, he'd probably try and bring Martin once he knew what was going on. Then they'd gang up on him to say that they should both get the places in the bunker at his expense. Twins were awkward for any number of reasons; this was just the latest in a long list. Susie's insistent voice jarred him back into reality.

"Bradford? What do you want?"

"Good. Look, Susie, you're an absolute horror show and I'm leaving you."

"*What?*"

"I'm leaving you. We had a good run for a few months, but it's been pretty miserable for the last couple of years and I'm going to shack up with a succession of hot yoga teachers and bone them all silly. Tit wanks, bum stuff, all of it."

"Bradford – what the fuck?"

"Just a point of clarification – the yoga teachers themselves will be hot, they're not "hot yoga" teachers. I mean some of them might be but, but I want you to hear me on that main point: they are *attractive* yoga teachers. I get that you've probably got a lot of questions and as it happens, I've got a bit of time opened up this afternoon, so why don't you pop into London and we can go over it all and get started on some of the paperwork. Can you meet me at the office in, say, seventy-three minutes?"

"You snivelling shit. I'll be there in forty minutes, with my lawyer *and my lover*. I am going to enjoy watching them take turns kicking you up your-"

Bradford hung up. Forty minutes might be a bit early, but he could get Rozz to delay her, then with a bit of blessing from London traffic Susie would be chewing on a Hwasong-17 while he was burrowing into his cosy little premium bomb-proof nest. Plus, he'd also accounted for her lover and her lawyer-cum-Rottweiler, Mitch – so this was very much a win-win-win. Bradford smiled. That was actually pretty clever. The new world would need clever leaders.

He coughed, checked his fly and exited the bathroom with the fake nonchalance of a twelve-year-old trying to get served in a pub, which in the suit was a fairly accurate depiction. A startling fact had just occurred to Bradford: he was in possession of the ultimate plus-one. He wasn't bringing Susie to the bunker. The twins would be fine, almost definitely. Pops would probably have his own membership to B of the Bang, or something even more exclusive. Rozz? No. So, who *was* getting the invite? As he emerged from the toilet, he looked at the journalist, who was stood over at the bookshelf. She was slinky. Blonde. She had those tennis player arms. If she got her teeth fixed, she would be seriously hot.

Bradford reminded himself that orthodontists might be hard to come by for the next few decades. Honestly – what was the point of all these people walking around with teeth like they'd just randomly rolled them into their mouths like dice? Was orthodontics a lost art to these people? Another more immediate positive in the journalist's favour was that she was physically there.

Was she plus-one material?

Tabitha appeared to be nosing through his book shelves, her keen journalistic senses suspecting that Bradford had never touched any of the books on the shelves, let alone read them. She was right, of course. Bradford had a book consultant who came in every month to add titles to the shelves, convincingly muss the spines of the ones he added and remove any books that were now deemed past it or cancel-worthy. If Tabitha had picked up any of the books, she would have found inside every front cover was a one sheet bluffer's guide, including an oven-ready opinion about each work. Bradford had never even seen any of the cheat sheets. For a while he'd got Rozz to write a round-up cheat sheet of the cheat sheets, but then he didn't read that either.

As Bradford emerged, two things struck Tabitha. Firstly, that this was a man in crisis. His colour was terrible and to make it worse, he was staring at her with a weird rictus grin. She could see that he'd sweated so much while he'd been in the loo that dark patches were appearing under the arms of his comically baggy suit. Who dressed him? Whatever that freak-out was about must have had something to do with the strange black briefcase he had clutched tightly by his side.

The second thing that struck her was an over-powering smell of shit, radiating from the recently vacated toilet. She tactfully switched to breathing through her mouth and tried to fight the impulse to gag. Meanwhile, Bradford was regarding her with something like lust.

"Is everything ok, Brad? I don't mean to be nosey, but it sort of comes with the job – what was the thing with the briefcase, I've never seen anything like that before."

"I'll tell you everything if you can answer one question for me."

"Shoot."

"In a hypothetical situation, would you drop everything and come away with me on a little break?"

"What?"

"It's as I said. I'm asking if you'd drop everything, as in right now and come away with me? I know I said it was, but it's not hypothetical, I'm actually asking you."

Tabitha paused and reassessed this odd little man.

"A little break to where?"

"I can't tell you that."

"What would I need to bring?"

"I can't tell you that, but you wouldn't have any time to pack, we'd need to leave immediately."

"Brad – this is scaring me a little – what was in that briefcase?"

"I need an answer."

"Would this be, like, a same-bed-sexual-activities sort of trip?"

He blinked slowly, just as the expression consultant had taught him. Capture the lust, magnify the lust, become the lust. "Yes." <u>I am good at sex</u>, he projected into her head to ram his point home.

Tabitha paused for a moment. She thought about the times she'd been sexually propositioned. A string of moments played in her mind, none of which sparked much joy. What was happening right now - being harassed by tiny David Byrne while the smell of his cloying diarrhoea filled the room - ranked close to the worst of those moments. But, as absurd as he was, Bradford Alderman VIIII did have several billion things going for him, even if the ability to correctly use Roman numerals wasn't one of them.

"No, I can't," she said, somewhat surprised by her own resolve.

"Can I persuade you?"

"Probably, but I'd rather you didn't," Tabitha replied.

"Right, thank you for your honesty. I need to go." He returned immediately to his desk, the briefcase now tucked under his arm.

He opened one of the desk doors and placed his thumb against a sensor pad. There was a beep and a small safe door swung open. Bradford started to pull items from the safe into the black case. Tabitha watched in amazement.

"Brad, seriously, what's going on? I'm officially scared now."

Bradford looked up from his task long enough to see the concern etched on her face.

"It's nothing," he said. "It's a shareholder issue. I just need to get it straightened out. I'll get Alexandra to reschedule."

He felt giddy with the power of his secret. He alone knew that in seventy-ish minutes this entire city, its buildings and its inhabitants would be turned into a giant novelty *I Love London* drinks coaster. He shrugged off his Richard Mille and handed it over to her.

"Here, take this as my way of apologising for skipping out on the interview."

Tabitha looked at the watch and held it up.

"This is a Richard Mille."

"It is."

"Aren't they about a quarter of a million pounds?"

"I think that one was about four-hundred thousand."

"Bradford, I can't take this."

"Your choice, leave it on the side if you don't want it."

While he was talking, he opened another drawer in his desk and pulled out twelve small glass vials filled to the top with white powder. He stowed some in the case and others in his pockets. Freed from the shame of consequences, he uncapped one and dipped the little spoon that was built into the vial's black screwcap. He held the tiny utensil under one nostril and cleared it in a single toot. He dipped it back in again and held it under the other nostril. Once he'd hoovered up a sufficient amount, he held the vial out to Tabitha.

"No, I don't. Wow, this interview really took a turn," she replied.

Bradford shrugged, smiled at her and refilled both nostrils twice more. He massaged the end of his nose between thumb and forefinger, twitched his nose like a rabbit and snorted loudly, dredging up some spicy phlegm from the back of his throat, which he spat into the bin and watched it hit the side and dribble down towards the carpet.

"Kobe!" he declared euphorically.

Tabitha watched and saw the corners of his mouth twitch up, and looking at him she imagined she could see his synapses switching on.

Suddenly, he stood up.

"I'm going," Bradford said and with the briefcase tucked under his arm he walked across his office. Tabitha found herself standing and trotting alongside him, pausing only to grab her phone from the desk and discreetly slip the Richard Mille into her pocket.

"Bradford, please just tell me, what is going on?"

"I said - it's a shareholder thing."

She stared at the briefcase he was holding and saw the B of the Bang logo. "What's B of the Bang?"

"It's a shareholder thing."

"Don't lie to me, is something bad happening?"

"You're the journalist, aren't you?"

"Bradford, *please*."

At the note of terror in her voice, Bradford turned and placed a comforting hand on her shoulder.

"Jess. Nothing is happening. It's just a shareholder thing. Look, if I'm lying to you then you can come and beat me up when we reschedule the interview, how about that? All good? Okay. Enjoy that Richard Mille."

Rozz looked at Bradford curiously as they walked past, but he just smiled and continued to the lifts.

"Oh Rozz – Susie should be on her way. Tell her I'll be with her soon and make sure you keep her here! Got it? Appreciate you!"

Rozz saluted. Tabitha and Bradford stood in a jittery silence as they waited for the lift to come. As it arrived, he turned to Tabitha and held out his hand.

"Great to meet you, a real pleasure, feel free to hang around as long as you want."

"Brad, what's B of the Bang?"

Bradford pressed the button to close the lift doors and raised his eyebrows in farewell. Tabitha gawped at him until the doors closed and swallowed him from view.

In the lift, Bradford turned and checked himself in another mirror, dabbing away a tiny crumb of coke from his nostril. He teased his hair and straightened the front of his suit.

His family may make clothes, but Bradford Alderman VIIII himself makes hearts race. I made a mistake Bradford, tongue me Bradford. Boom. Boom. Fuckety Boom.

That profile was really coming along.

The lift opened and spat him out onto the long ramp that led into the reception area. As he skipped lightly down the slope, Bradford spied the cracking little ginger Yank on sabbatical from the Chicago branch coming the other way. She was wearing a green skirt and blazer and a tight white shirt that really made her Bristols pop.

Bindy? Shit. Brandy? No. Brin! Brin! That was it. He stopped opposite her and waved his hand directly in her face, she pulled up short and looked at him.

"Brin! How are you?"

"Bradford! Ok, good to see you. I'm *great* thanks," she replied with a bright, wide, toothsome grin.

Look at those teeth. Americans really had perfected the art of dentistry. You could make a good case that it was actually their one positive contribution to the world. Bradford conducted a mental side-by-side comparison of Brin and Thingy's teeth. It was like holding a mint Tic Tac next to Stonehenge. These were precisely the sort of teeth that the new world would need. They were the teeth of an uber-woman. Uber-teeth. The ultimate plus-one teeth.

"Listen, I'm in a bit of a dash," he said and felt his accent becoming more plummy, which always happened when he spoke to an American. "Look, quick thought, I've got to bob out for a work thing, but do you know, I think it would really be good for your whole London experience to come with."

"Oh wow! That's kind, but it's sort of out of the blue! Is this something important?"

"Hmmm, bit of an embargo on it at the mo. All I can say is that it's from the very top," he replied with a knowing wink.

"Your dad?"

"*No*, this is from my desk."

"Oh, ok. Well, if it's important? I guess, sure! Should I cancel my afternoon meetings?"

"Ooh, good question. No, I don't think that will be necessary."

"Okay – well, it sounds intriguing!"

Bradford smiled at Brin and she treated him to another look at her pearly whites. The cocaine's bravery made him reach out his hand to her. She took it with a look of confusion. A feeling of absolute certainty gripped him, like a solid gold cock ring slipped over his Thumper: things were going to be okay. Better than okay. Things were going to be good. Not for everyone, but for him and maybe Brin if she played her teeth right, today could be a good day.

"Shall we?" he said and with his other hand he rolled out an over-the-top flourish to indicate that she should lead the way.

"What should I do with these?" Brin asked, indicating the fabric samples she had in her hands. Bradford took them off her with another flourish and placed them and his case on the reception desk that would be destroyed in a little over an hour. The very knowledge of this gave him the pulsing rumble of an erection that he knew would grow and grow until it loomed over the world like the Colossus of Rhodes. Oh, yes! Verily this engorgement would be a watch tower for generations. Weary sailors and superstitious farmers would come and tremble before this 300-metre-high golden Thumper!

The coke frothed away inside him like the rush of excitement five-year-olds get on Christmas morning. Bradford looked up into the office's vast atrium that, despite its grandeur, somehow always managed to smell faintly of urine. He spun around while he was looking up and belatedly realised Brin was still holding his hand. He held out his other hand and she took it, a curious expression playing across her face. He continued to spin, faster and faster. Then he shifted his weight to his heels and leaned back. She started to complain as she understood what was happening, but with both her hands gripped tightly, Brin shrieked as her feet were lifted off the ground and Bradford squeezed her hands even more and leant further and further back until the office, the reception desk, the vending machines and the visitor toilets were a nauseating blur. Bradford yodelled into the void. One of Brin's shoes flew off and his howls dissolved into laughter. He sped up and giggled with joy – this was all fucked. Fucked! The money! The company! The people! The world!

But not him.

I'LL SETTLE FOR A PINT, SIR

AMID THE GRATING cacophony of whooping alerts and warning sirens, Captain Chris Harlow was doing his best to follow a mental checklist of things to do. He knew that there was very little chance that they were walking away from this landing, but that knowledge remained in the background as he worked through his procedure.

"London Heathrow, this is Captain Chris Harlow, VIP Voyager, ZZ336. Repeat VIP Voyager, ZZ336. Bird strike. I repeat, bird strike. We are losing altitude."

"Understood ZZ336, we can clear a runway at City Airport, that's your closest."

"Negative Heathrow, we can't turn. Engine one is out and two is failing. We're falling short of Heathrow."

"Repeat ZZ336?"

"We're not going to make it to Heathrow. We're going to have to make an emergency landing."

"Confirmed."

Harlow looked to his right and saw his first officer Ryan Folds, holding onto the control stick, judders passing through the instrument to his arms which shook in response.

"Thoughts Ryan?"

Ryan glanced back, and his desperate expression told him everything Harlow needed to know. He reached to toggle a number of switches on the plane's sprawling dashboard.

"Two's dead."

"Ok, we're ditching in the Thames," Harlow said, and he immediately jettisoned his previous checklist of whether they could make it to a recognised runway and he started to work through the things that needed to be done to prepare the plane for a crash landing. The recent heavy rains meant that at least the Thames was exceptionally high and wide for the time of year – they'd have to hope that was enough. Harlow pushed his mic closer to his mouth; even Folds was impressed at the steel in the captain's voice as he addressed the plane.

"This is your captain speaking, we are unable to reach a standard landing field. Cabin crew, brace for impact, we are going to make an emergency landing. Passengers, please assume crash positions but be aware that this will be a water landing and we must prepare for a quick evacuation."

There was a pause as his voice caught in his throat, a vision of his wife's face intruding on the otherwise peerless professional setting of his mind.

"Ladies and gentlemen, if you pray, now is the time."

He joined Folds in starting to make the final adjustments. There was a procedure to follow and although they knew it off-by-heart, they still went through it thoroughly via the manual.

"Heathrow, we're taking her into the Thames at Richmond. Alert all emergency services."

"Understood ZZ336, the very best of British to you. God bless."

Back in the cabin, beyond the sealed cockpit door the atmosphere was eerily quiet. No one was screaming, although staff were frantically whispering to themselves and some passengers were clearly adhering to the Captain's advice to appeal to whichever deity they felt might favour them. Over everything, the cabin crew's calm repeated instructions came over and over again like a mantra.

"Brace! Brace! Brace! Heads down, stay down! Brace! Brace! Brace! Heads down, stay down!"

This request was assiduously followed by the majority of the passengers, formed largely of government staffers and the press corps. One ambitious member of the media had his phone recording in his lap and was streaming a play-by-play of what he was seeing, most of which was conjured from his imagination as the only thing he could actually see was his own shins. If he *had* looked over to the front of the plane, he would have seen a huddle of people, including two secretaries and seven close protection officers from the Special Protection Group. Rather than hunching over in their seats, they had massed around a bulky figure, whose thatch of blond hair immediately identified him amongst the fray as Prime Minister, Fenton Crossley. Crossley's gut was hampering his attempts to keep his head down, but the bodyguards around him were arrayed in such a way that they were all readied to take a poorly stowed piece of hand luggage for their leader.

Until the final moment, the cabin crew chanted their instructions, and the plane descended amid the grinding screech of the two failed engines. In the cockpit, Folds and Harlow wrestled the bucking plane into something resembling an approach vector and the passengers held their breath.

The plane struck the Thames at a sharper angle than intended. Immediately, the water's drag on the nose and the sudden deceleration flipped it over like a pancake, so the tail was at the front and pointing down in the water. Given the depth of the river, it meant that the tip of the tail ploughed a furrow in the river bed before snapping off with a loud metallic crunch. The plane's weight displaced a huge bow wave of water and it surged not just on the banks, but crashed over into the park beyond. Onwards the plane slid, momentum dispersing by the second, as first one wing dipped into the water and then the other - turning the plane laterally through ninety degrees. The wing trapped underneath ripped off in a brief explosion that was instantly doused by the river water.

The nose of the plane gradually turned and finally came to rest one metre away from a small sandy beach that led onto the green lushness of Richmond Park.

Folds and Harlow were assailed by even more shrieking alarms keen to point out that they had crashed. Folds was holding a hand to the side of his face, but otherwise they were miraculously unscathed. An alert started suggesting that they "Pull up." Harlow tried to call through to Heathrow to tell them of the successful crash landing, but the radio was dead. Folds unbuckled his seatbelt and started to fall toward the roof of the cockpit. He caught himself on the arms of his chair and by standing on the instrument panel and bracing himself on the side of Harlow's seat, he made his way to the back of the cockpit, which had turned enough so that the wall was now the floor.

"Any landing you walk away from…" he muttered.

Harlow momentarily marvelled at the brown water sloshing against the window before quickly unclipping his seatbelt and following Folds' path, until he too stood dazed on the roof of the cockpit. Between them, they kicked and heaved at the cockpit door which had buckled in the crash and managed to get it open. They stepped over the threshold and into the carnage behind them. The emergency lighting was on, but it was now in the ceiling and it cast a strange light on the scene, with the moving LED lights giving everything a sort of slow strobe effect.

"Calmly make your way to the emergency exit. If you are unable to then remain in your seat and we will help."

Harlow could see that the emergency exit that was on the ceiling was open and passengers were helping each other through the opening and presumably making their way onto the side of the plane. It was unnerving to see there was already half a metre of black water swilling around inside the plane. They couldn't tell where it was coming in from, but several of the passenger windows were under water.

"Are you ok? Any casualties?" Harlow asked as he reached Marcy, one of the lead cabin crew.

"Some cuts and breaks, but I think we're ok," she replied.
"Marcy – are you ok?"
"I'm good thanks, Chris."
"PM?"
"Alive and already out."
"Thank God."
"Chris?"
"Yes?"
"Great job."

He smiled in relief, then in a surging contentment. He didn't want to get ahead of himself, but he was fairly sure that he was an actual fucking hero. He internalised this as he took his time working through the cabin while the water continued to make its way into the plane. By the time he reached the back it was up to his waist. Despite the situation he was impressed by how politely everyone queued to make their way to the only emergency exit in operation. He assumed it was because everyone was in shock, or perhaps it was just the British DNA. He knew the drill, and waited until all of his passengers had made their way off his plane before he took his turn to stand on the seats and claim the outstretched hands that pulled him up and out of the downed jet, and into the welcoming pale light of South West London.

"Harlow, you turd! What did you do to my bloody plane?" came a booming Surrey accent. He found himself face-to-face with the Prime Minister. Crossley pulled Harlow into an embrace and as he squashed the air out of his lungs he leaned in close to his ear and said, "I'll make you a fucking Knight for this, you beautiful bastard. You'll bathe in totty, just don't tell the missus."

Chris smiled as he emerged from the bear hug and batted the compliment away with false modesty.

"I'll settle for a pint, Sir," he said. A line which he thought might just make it into his autobiography. Maybe even the title? No, that was a rubbish title for anything.

Then Fenton, ever the clown, hugged him again and buried his face in the pilot's chest, which made Harlow's ears tinge red with embarrassment. Then the Prime Minister kneeled in front of him and buried his face in his crotch. Some of the staff nearby smiled awkwardly at the humour. It was classic goofball Crossley.

"Just the pint is fine, Sir," Chris said in a stage whisper, eyeing the nearest Number 10 staffers and hoping that the japing would soon end. Then Fenton went further and actually grovelled, his face pressing hard into the top of Chris' soaking loafers and his hands curled around his heels as if he was in child's pose. The indulgent laughter went on for a few seconds, but then finally Chris realised that Prime Minister Fenton Crossley wasn't doing a bit after all. He was dead.

※ ※ ※ ※ ※

William McCartney pointed at the large rabbit in the book.

"Well, I suppose we have to assume that this is Bunnikins, then," he said, and several of the carefully selected children smiled weakly. Someone had done a decent job of hand-picking this lot for their ability to be telegenic and adhere to the head-teacher's instruction not to do anything stupid. Unfortunately, Year 2 didn't have a single ethnic minority student in the entire class, so one of the advisors had rummaged through Years 1 and 3 and come up with a wheelchair user and a child who had just returned from a fortnight in Egypt, who Barry the communications manager had put front row after it appeared that the cameras didn't just add ten pounds, they also made tanned skin look even darker.

"Although, as I've always said – let's not make assumptions, because they make an-" William paused as he realised he was about to say "arse" to a collection of pure-hearted children, but also because he noted that he'd got the gag wrong and he'd have had to say, "Don't make assumptions, because they make an ass out of you and -mptions." So instead of finishing his sentence he theatrically turned the page and growled loudly like a lion – an act of improvisation which seemed gratuitous enough to rouse Barry the Comms, who shifted in William's eyeline.

"Do you like lions?" William asked the children and hoped that one of them, hopefully the vaguely brown one, would respond with something adorable and pithy that could be clipped for the *News at Ten*.

"We did a project about lions in year one and our teacher said that one male lion can have as many as fifteen lionesses," this was from the wheelchair user, so William was forced to nod politely. He tried to think of a response that wasn't, "Lucky lion!" but instead he just nodded some more and wondered why Barry the Comms was walking onto the carpet, carefully picking his way through the children sat cross-legged on the storytime rug.

"Sorry children, I just need a moment of the Deputy Prime Minister's time."

Barry the Comms leant in close to William's ear and whispered, "Keep your expression very neutral. We need to go." McCartney held onto Barry's arm and pulled him in closer.

"Why? I can't just leave."

"Sir, the PM's dead, plane crash."

William McCartney reeled and tried to keep his facial features in check. He felt like he might fall off the tiny plastic chair that they'd perched him on. His sense of perspective shuddered and between the minuscule furniture and the teensy people at his feet, he momentarily imagined himself a giant. Two thoughts asserted themselves foremost in his mind.

Jenny. He had to tell Jenny.

And: it would finally happen. It would finally happen. Today.

"What do I do here?" William whispered.

"Tell them anything, I've got to get this call. Two minutes until the cars go wheels up."

Barry the Comms answered his phone as he retreated from the storytime carpet, only managing to tread on two children as he departed.

"Well…" William began, but realised that with the attendant news cameras – although they weren't live, this moment was very much being caught for posterity. Consequently, William made a big pantomime concerned face.

"Well, I am sad," he said. "That's not good news. My friend Barry has just told me something bad and now I'm going to have to go, children. I'm so sorry Mrs Townsley, I must pass on the opportunity to finish reading *See If You Can Guess How Much I Love You One More Time*, would you be okay to take over?"

"What was the bad news?" the wheelchair user asked, crystallising the thoughts of everyone in the room. William looked to the sidelines where Barry was conducting a frenetic conversation. Barry made an "I don't know what you should say, make up something, anything, just make it plausible" gesture, which somehow William managed to understand perfectly.

"Ok, hmmm well, you know, I was looking at your amazing artwork displays on the wall earlier and I saw that one of them was about the school's value of Always Being Totally And Completely Honest and I think that's very important too, so I will be totally and completely honest with you: the Prime Minister is dead."

The room burst into movement. Where there had been poise, calm and the weighted blanket of boredom, now there was shock, disbelief and the compression stockings of panic. Two of the children at his feet burst into tears. One got up and ran off in search of a supervising adult.

"How did he die?" the wheelchair user asked, seemingly unmoved. William was getting to quite like this young tyke, he was like Paxman with alloys.

"In a plane crash, that's why I have to go." Gasps met William's words.

"Are we at war?" the wheelchair user persisted.

"No, no, no. Well, I don't know. Maybe. If it's determined that he was killed, then yes of course we will assemble all means of response, including war."

William couldn't help but notice that he'd been de-facto leader of the country for approximately a minute and he was already starting his first war. Give him an hour and the galaxy would be ashes beneath his feet. The weeping contagion spread through the remaining children and William stood, crushing the fingers of another child. Honestly, what was wrong with these children? Did they enjoy being stepped on or something? He felt that the moment called for him to show that like Jesus he could bid the storms to cease. He subtly turned towards the television cameras.

"I'm going now, but I say this to you – and to anyone watching at home – you can be sure that as a proud member of this nation's highest chamber, I will rise to the challenge and take any blows that come my way. And I will, of course, listen to your demands to do something and share what I do with you, the great people of this land: our Great Britain."

Close enough. It got a little waffly and he worried he might have lifted a line from *Rasputin* which had been playing in the car earlier, but not bad for an extempore bit of poppycock. He strode from the carpet, breezing past the lesser figures of history who littered the room, into the idling car outside and onwards to London. He noticed as he looked out of the window that they were suddenly flanked by more police cars and motorbikes than they had been on the way to the school. He felt sure that there was a helicopter overhead too. They all seemed to have appeared out of thin air. So, finally, this was what real power looked like.

THE CAT IS OUT OF THE BAG, BUT THE CATFLAP IS SHUT

RASHID KHAN THREW the phone into the case and slammed it shut. He paused for a moment and then swept the case and everything on his desk onto the floor. As he stood trembling in his office, he felt the weight of this new knowledge settling on his shoulders, as significant as the garland of flowers Hema had hung around his neck on their wedding day. He wanted to weep, but instead he sighed deeply and made his decision.

Directly outside his office was the admin and sales floor, the hub of the packaging company that he had joined as an apprentice at sixteen, became CEO of at twenty-five as part of a management buyout, and spent his thirties expanding into a global empire until he stood there, a billionaire at 41. Although there were other more stately and imposing buildings in his property portfolio, he still felt that this room, with its portraits of smiling staff holding their products hanging from the walls, was the centre of his empire. On tours he liked to say that he could speak a handful of words here at morning stand-up and the impact would be felt across seven continents by lunchtime. That truth felt painful to acknowledge now.

Rashid had three secretaries - with Margaret's desk being the closest, it was hers that he climbed onto, causing her to jump back in alarm.

"What are you up to, Rash? You plonker!" she said, but he ignored her and waved his arms to the room at large.

"Everyone! Please may I have your attention immediately. Excuse me. Thank you, *everyone*! Please if you are on a call, hang up right now."

A flurry of noise and confusion followed. Colleagues stood in their cubicles to get a better look at the man the press called the Box King, but to his team he was always simply Rash – a leader who inspired not just loyalty, but a kind of feverish adoration. A newspaper profile had described him as the Jim Jones of Tupperware, and in his more honest moments he would admit that he enjoyed the power that he seemed to have over his people. He sold little plastic boxes for a living – it was nice to have something beyond that.

"Everyone, *please*!"

A scatter of shushes sounded out and anyone still on their phone uttered a quick word of explanation and hung up. One person suspected that something interesting was going on and started to film. Rashid knew that telling people what he had learned was not without danger, but he felt that he had a moral obligation to at least provide them the same insight that B of the Bang had given him. He knew that they wouldn't be able to get away in enough time, but maybe there was *something* they could do – a final chance to act, perhaps. Maybe just knowing was enough – he felt it was their right and therefore his onerous duty to tell them. He licked his suddenly dry lips.

"I need you all to listen very closely please, and I must insist that you listen in silence, because time is so crucial. After September 11th, I signed up to a very select service that gives me early warning about things that could be a threat to me or my family's safety. The company is called B of the Bang and they help people to get out of bad situations that might arise – whether it's a natural disaster or a terrorist attack – all these things. I joined because I was scared for my parents and Hema and the children. I wanted to have help… but as it turns out, it's not going to be enough. I have just received an alert that a nuclear missile is going to hit London in 60 minutes - please, please, friends…" A series of gasps went up and there was a scream, but they were quickly stifled and shushed into silence by those around them. "- Thank you. I needed to share this with you, because even though we will not be able to escape the blast and the fallout, I wanted you to know…"

"Is this a joke?" a man's incredulous voice called out from the office floor.

"It is no joke. I am so sorry. I am afraid that is all I know. It has been the honour of my life to build our company with you all and I wish you nothing but love, until the end. Thank you. Please, be with your families and friends. Take this time and use it. I am sorry to say it is all I have left to give you."

He climbed down from Margaret's desk as some of the early-adopters rushed to the door. Their movement sparked an exodus from everyone else and soon the entire floor was a mass of heaving bodies, pushing past each other to find their way to an unclogged exit. Those that remained had their phones pressed to their ears, reaching out to loved ones.

Some workers stopped to hug their colleagues tightly as freshly tear-streaked faces brushed hurriedly against each other. Others smashed their co-workers to the floor in their rush to get away. Rashid brushed the dust from his feet off Margaret's desk. He was surprised, but not entirely surprised, to find her still sat in her chair. He smiled at her. Margaret had been with him since the beginning and clichéd though it was, she was more a part of his family than a colleague, let alone a subordinate. Her cheeks and neck had flushed red and Rash noted that the spark of a smile, ever-present in the depths of her eyes, was absent. She was wearing a long white tunic with prints of ladybirds and black leggings, her neat brown bobbed hair tucked behind her ears and a silver crucifix at her neck. Even in the face of extinction, she appeared to Rashid as the sweetest woman, the auntie he had chosen and who had chosen him. There was so much that he wanted to say to her; he wanted to advise her, he wanted to praise her, he wanted to apologise for everything that he had not had time to do, but even that would take too much of the time that they no longer had.

"What do you need me to do, Rash?" she asked, sensing his confusion.

"Margaret, you are so sweet to ask. There is nothing I need. I need you to take this time and…I don't know. I *don't* know." Rash seemed lost in thought about what he did know. "Wait a moment."

He disappeared into his office and came back with a black velvet pouch. Margaret tentatively took it from him.

"What's this?"

"It's a bonus, Margaret. I'm not sure how much longer it will be useful for, but I want you to have it anyway. I should have given you so much more sooner than this. I should have given everyone more. That is a regret I will hold at the end."

Margaret looked in the pouch, "Is this gold?"

"To match your heart," Rashid said with sincerity.

"You don't have to do that, Rash!"

"It is done, there is no time to argue."

"Well, thank you then."

"No, thank you, Margaret."

"What are you going to do? What about Hema?"

"I am going to walk home and then I'm going to hold Sarina and Jaat and I'm going to read them *The Cat In The Hat*. The company…" He trailed off and looked as if he was about to burst into tears. "…They offered me two places in a bunker, but I wouldn't have time to go and get them and I couldn't…" He broke off and Margaret took his hand.

"I know, I know. Don't worry. You've got *The Cat In The Hat*," but even as she said it, she realised what a feeble consolation it was.

Rash smiled and composed himself enough to ask, "What will you do?"

"I don't know. I'd best ring Graham and ask him to get the cats in."

"You could have my place, you know? In the bunker."

Margaret looked shocked and then she smiled, the movement deepening the lines across her round face. The spark reappeared in her eyes.

"What would I do in a bunker? I'd go mad. No, the cats will need me more. Maybe Graham…" she left the thought unfinished.

Rash smiled. "Goodbye Margaret. See you soon?" He held out his hand and she shook it firmly.

"Ta-ra, Rash. I've loved every single minute of working for you, even when you were being an idiot. If it's okay to say so, you're my hero."

"Well, snap."

"Leave it out."

Rashid pulled her close and they hugged, an embrace that contained the entirety of their decades of work together; a hug that could only hint at the depths of love that their friendship held. Margaret wiped tears from her eyes as he walked away through the chaos of the recently vacated offices with its still-spinning office chairs. She dialled Graham's number and after several rings, he picked up: "Bermondsey 299, Graham speaking."

"Hi Graham, it's me. Can you put the cat flap on in-only? I'll be back soon."

"Hello, Me. POETs Day, is it?" he said with a chuckle in his voice.

"POETs Day?"

"Push Off Early Today!"

"I'll tell you when I get home. I won't be long. Graham?"

"Yes?"

"You need to know there's…I…I'll get some lunch for us on the way."

"Rightio, consider me told."

"I need to tell you…don't get bread out of the freezer, we can have fresh."

"Don't get bread out of the freezer."

"You don't need to make a note of that. Just don't get the bread out of the freezer."

She could picture him with such clarity. He would be sitting on the small stool in the hallway next to the phone, the corridor illuminated by the mottled glass panels of the front door. Graham didn't do mobiles, so the landline still reigned supreme in their house. She could picture the "Phone Memo" scratchpad that sat on the tiny console table with its stained wooden pot of pens, the small bowl of pot pourri, scentless for nearly a decade. Graham would have scribbled down, "Don't defrost bread." He would then follow the note's advice and proceed to not defrost the bread.

"I'll see you later then?"

"Yes," Margaret sighed. "See you later."

"A bien tot!"

"Graham…"

But he'd gone. She pictured him toddling through their little house in Bermondsey, his tartan slippers skidding over the carpet saver, across the lino, turning the dial on the cat flap and returning the same way, parom-pom-pomming back to his desk, back to the world of numbers he'd built in his never-ending Open University dissertation – a work that had taken so long he'd started to refer to it as his "dissertation and on and on."

The Colonel would barely raise his great tabby head to see what was happening. Mitsi would blink open one large green eye but she would not disturb the perfect 'O' she had created between her tail and nose. The familiarity of the vision swelled Margaret's heart and she found her courage returning. These special things hadn't stopped yet. There was still life to live and the missiles just made the time left even more important, even more beautiful. She closed her eyes and thanked God for what she had.

She stood and retrieved her long green overcoat from the rack outside Rash's office. She picked her bag up and hung it over the crook of her arm and placed the black velvet pouch into the pocket. She picked her way carefully through the office, ignoring the temptation to push people's chairs back into their cubicles – she was not going to spend her apocalypse tidying up.

The lifts were empty now, but as the doors opened on the ground level, she could tell that a panicking herd had recently passed through. One of the office doors was a spider web of broken glass, and a discarded cap lay in the middle of the steps. She shrugged on her coat to cope with the slight rain. A sign for the sandwich shop over the road had been tipped over and Margaret stooped to pick it up. It was heavier than she thought it would be. Margaret stood in indecision for a second. The reality of what was happening hit her anew. There was a missile coming for London. She wondered if they would shoot it down, or if that would just make matters worse. She was glad that the burden of these decisions lay with Fenton Crossley, rather than herself. Just for a second, she could feel the world diminish like plastic thrown onto a fire – she felt herself, her concerns, her impact shrinking, all of the significance and meaning collapsing into a dot, then into nothing at all. She reached out to the wall to steady herself and breathed a prayer. What would The Colonel think if he could see her swaying like this? She took a determined breath through her nose and stood under her own power. *Pull yourself together, girl.*

When Rash had offered her the spot in his bunker, she'd had the merest moment where she'd considered it. Forget Graham. Forget the cats. Maybe she could scrounge out a few more years in whatever passed for the world after a nuclear war. But why would she do that? And it was easy enough to say "Forget someone", but they wouldn't stay forgotten, would they? What if she was alone at the end of the world, with the ghosts of those she had left behind. She had a vision of a ghostly cat she couldn't stroke and shuddered at the horror.

To distract herself she reached into her pocket and took one of the fat, dense gold coins out of the velvet bag. She looked at it properly for the first time. It had been polished to a supernatural shine and etched on one side of the coin was the Queen. On the other side, Britannia was holding a trident and looking scathingly at the bearer, as if they weren't up to snuff. Margaret wondered if this was how all money looked at first, honest and present, before it became tarnished with the needs and desires of everyone who held it afterwards.

As she walked up the road to hail a taxi, she had a momentary impulse and dropped the coin in the tattered Costa cup of a man asking for spare change, who felt the unusual weight of her deposit and brought the cup to his face to examine it. Margaret had continued to walk onwards, but she heard an exclamation of "Fucking Hell!" and then the excited skitter of feet as the beggar caught up to her. He gently touched his hand to her shoulder. Margaret turned and saw that his neck was so thin that she could see the outline of each tendon.

"Did you drop this by mistake?"

"No, it's for you. God bless you. Well, God and Rashid."

"I don't understand."

"I mean it wasn't a mistake, I hope you can use it."

"This must be worth a hundred quid – maybe more. Why are you giving it to me?"

"If that *is* worth one hundred pounds, then it represents the one hundred times that you, or another homeless person asked me to buy a Big Issue, or lend you money for a bus ride home and I turned away. What you're holding is an apology, offered too late."

The man looked at the coin and smiled, unsure of what to say next.

"Well, cheers."

"You're very welcome, why don't you walk up the road with me."

"Yeah, alright."

"How long have you been homeless?"

"About a year."

"Sorry, I didn't ask your name. I'm Margaret."

"People call me Tone, but my real name is Sean."

"Do I detect a hint of an accent, Sean?"

"You can take the boy out of Birmingham, but you can't take the Birmingham out of the boy."

"I had my first holiday in Birmingham."

"That's…odd."

"Yes, I suppose it is. My father worked on the trains and he wanted to spend his week off in Crewe. My mother put her foot down and said that she wanted to go to Devon, so they compromised on Birmingham."

"I hope you didn't swim in the canal."

"Ha! No. We watched the Bullring being built and then my brother went to Crewe with my father to do a manual inventory of their rolling stock and I went to Devon with my mum. I don't know why they didn't think of that before we went to Birmingham. No offence."

"None taken, it's a shitheap. Margaret, don't take this the wrong way, but I'm freaking out a bit - why have you given me that coin? Is it dodgy?"

"No. The truth is I don't know if it means anything now. Someone gave them to me and I don't feel like they're meant for me, so I'm going to try and find them a good home. There's a taxi. Sean, will you do one thing for me?"

"Yeah."

"I want you to get on the next train and ride it to the end of the line. Then I want you to find the fastest mode of transport wherever you end up and keep going for as long as you can. Do you understand? I want you to get as far away from London as you can, just for today – treat it like a game."

"This is getting weirder by the second."

"I know it's strange but would you do it for me? Please?"

He held up the coin in front of her face: "You pay the piper; you call the tune. I'm just glad you didn't want rimming."

"What's r- I actually don't want to know. Sean, it's been a pleasure. Godspeed." She held out her hand at the top of the tube station stairs and Sean took it with his lanky fingers and gave it a feeble pumping.

"The Northern Line is calling, Sean."

"I'll answer that call. Thanks Margaret, be seeing you."

But Margaret was already opening the black cab's door and preparing to head home.

SMILE AND WAVE BOYS, SMILE AND WAVE

BEST WISHES? WHAT could she do with best wishes?

The phone started to play a message, letting her know that if she pressed "1" on her keypad, she could complete a short survey about her experience today. She squashed the red button to disconnect the call and screamed until her voice cracked, then she reached for the bottle. It had been a very long time since Her Royal Highness Princess Eulalia had heard the heartbreaking crunch of the little metal clips snapping on the cap of a bottle of vodka. There was a crescendo as the top was spun off by shaking hands and it fell still spinning onto the desk with an ambivalent swirl. It all felt so familiar.

Eulalia felt herself disassociating. There she sat, twenty-eight-years-old, alone; a wild, bitter and erratic alcoholic. Thirteenth in line to the throne. She was tall and slender, and dressed in jeans and an ancient Rage Against The Machine t-shirt. Her shoulder-length blonde hair was still damp from the shower. She forced her consciousness back into her body and watched the world through her own eyes for a moment. She muttered the word "Arseholes" then scrolled to the top of her contacts list, hit dial on a contact and listened to it ring until it automatically terminated.

Well, there it was.

Lally poured herself a large measure of vodka. Then she added another on top in case the first one didn't take. *If it were done when 'tis done, then 'twere well it were done quickly*, she thought and wondered where that came from. Then she caught herself, because of course it was Daddy reading to her from PG Wodehouse, tears of mirth snaking across his florid cheeks. She remembered lying on her pillow looking up at him. Staring at the odd words emerging from this lion's mouth, wondering why they debilitated him so; swearing that she would understand both the words and the titanic man before her. She never quite got round to that. She would be able to ask him herself soon, and she was buggered if she was going to go and see the old sod sober. She could already imagine the disappointment in his eyes. Oh, Lal. What was worse, he would know *everything* and she wouldn't be able to hide. She would stand in front of him as she really was – not as she'd wanted him to see.

No. It was definitely time to drink.

She looked out of the window. The day was grey but the lush canopy of Kensington Gardens and Hyde Park added a band of green to her view. Beyond the trees and the lakes, the jagged skyline of the city unsettled her. The clusters of points and glittering, bulbous facades looked like the start of a migraine. She held her drink up in front of her eyes and watched the panorama invert and blur through the prism of her glass. She could see the city, but would the city see her? Or would it see what it wanted from a minor royal: a body built for waving, a womb built for heiring, and a head built for feigning photogenic concern at the bedside of sick children.

Lally knew that she wouldn't trouble the top thousand richest in the city, unlike the Sheikh who owned this penthouse, but she had an inkling that she would be in the top ten most-loathed rich people. On a good day she'd probably even make the top five – and this wasn't a good day. The people never quite forgave her for not learning to do the stupid wave. She smiled at the frenzied vista of London and tipped the contents of the glass into her mouth.

Oh, mercy. The heat. That unmistakable nothing taste flooding her mouth. The neurons in her brain that knew what was happening but couldn't quite believe it. Booze! Actual real booze! So often dreamed of, but so rarely tasted. *Oh, Hot Damn!* The end of the world was worth it if it meant she could have this quicksilver plugged into her brain.

But not just this one. This one and this one and this one. More, more, more. Spend, spend, spend. Tomorrow and tomorrow and tomorrow. The words floated lithely in and out of her mind, twirling past each other in a sinuous dance. Lally knew why those words had always haunted her when it came to alcohol - because they hinted at the unending hunger in her for what was next. She'd sat in enough self-help meetings and in front of enough therapists that she knew her own failings like the back of her hand. She knew her problem was a biochemical glitch that meant that she was always thinking of the next thing. While she lay in the arms of one lover, she dreamed of the hands of the next touching her skin. While she was pouring one drink, she was tasting the next. While one relative sat on the throne, she fast-forwarded to thoughts of their heir. She didn't feel thirst, she *was* thirst. She felt the bile rising and blew the indigestion towards the ceiling.

Then she laughed. It broke forth as a gale of laughter. A machine-gun report of "Has" and "Hees" that tripped over each other in their eagerness to be free. She felt the warm tracks of tears making their way down her face as she saluted the infinite madness of it all. Today a missile from North Korea hits London! She would be vapourised, or irradiated, or toasted to a crisp. So be it. She wondered if Daddy was alive if he would have protected her. Could he have conjured up a bunker that she could shelter in? Would he have wrapped her in his arms and squashed the world away? Or would he have smiled sadly as he closed the hatch and turned the locking wheel? *Goodbye Daddy. Goodbye Lal.* She dispensed with the niceties of a glass and put the bottle to her lips and tipped. She briefly watched the gurgle of bubbles dance upwards towards the base of the upturned bottle and wondered if there was poetry in that. Probably not.

Silver member.

So, this is what it was like to be excluded. It felt fine, honestly. There was vodka for the excluded. There was the view. *We were all in it together.* She laughed, and then, in a moment of crooked inspiration, she jumped up, retrieved her laptop from the sofa and scurried back to the desk. When would the explosion come? She didn't know. The message had said something about 'within one-hundred minutes,' but she felt in her skin and her teeth that it was soon. What a beautiful place to see the end, with all of the other silver members. She remembered something, marched across the room and pulled the drawers out of her bedroom dresser, flinging them across the floor. At the back, she found her debutante gloves, white charmeuse silk fringed with silver thread, a beautiful gift from Mummy. Oh boy, she'd let her down. *You are not a lesbian – the end. I swear to you now that if you tell Daddy anything like that, he will jump off London Bridge – think on that.* She inched the glove onto her hand and with some effort she pulled it up beyond her elbow.

Lally sat back at her desk and flipped the laptop open, then tugged the lid back and forth positioning the camera so that she was framed squarely in front of the view of London. Perhaps this would be something that future sociologists would study. She opened YouTube, navigated through the different accounts she had linked to her email and found the one for the Royal Family, to which she'd got access for a series of ill-fated online Quiz Nights For The Nation they'd done through the lockdowns. Awful idea, simply awful. Why had they allowed comments? What did they think would happen? As the black sheep of the family Lally knew the reality of how the people actually felt, but the rest of the crew felt that they were untouchable – loved, even. The comments section of those videos was the closest Britain had come to revolution since Cromwell.

This account had the benefit of three hundred thousand subscribers, her own had only a handful. The website cast a ghoulish white light on her gaunt features, so she scrambled around behind her and clicked on a lamp. She looked at herself in the pre-live lounge and wondered who it was, and decided that it probably didn't matter anyway. She clicked "Go Live" and after labouring through numerous technical options, she saw a tiny dot of white light shine at the top of the screen to show her that she was live to the nation. *Lally, what do you want to say?*

She wanted to say sorry. She wanted to ask them all why they hated her. She wanted to ask if they knew that she agreed with them and hated herself too. She wanted to say that she was just a human and that she loved them, even though they didn't want her. She wanted to tell them that it would be all right. She wanted to ask for a friend. She wanted a lover. She wanted her Daddy back. She wanted to hold someone's hand as the missile landed.

Instead, she fixed her eyes on the white dot and started to wave. With her arm raised to the sky, her be-gloved fingers drew demure circles, just as she'd been taught by Granny. Her features remained neutral, as befitting a female royal, but the wave – she really put everything into that wave. It was the wave her family had hoped for. The wave that they'd had arguments over. In her teenage years, she'd felt so displaced from this gargantuan blob of power at the centre of the family, that she'd felt that a new wave was the innovation that she could bring to her role. She hoped it would be a wave which explained how she felt and that drew a direct line between her and the people. She wanted people to see that she was nothing special, she was just human. She would wave with her arm upraised, but with the hand tipping left to right, palm facing the people. A normal wave, no weirdo circles.

The people didn't like it. It's fair to say that the people hated it. She thought she'd been bringing the royals to the people, but as it turns out, the people didn't want the royals anywhere near them. Lally had noticed that you could see it on the faces of the people in a receiving line preparing to bow or curtsey – they were holding their breath until this fairy tale gargoyle shook their hand and fucked off. The public wanted the royals to be weird, distant, and fucked up. They wanted them rattling around in houses so big that they had other houses inside them. They wanted them shooting endangered animals. They wanted them made tiny and trapped on stamps and coins. They wanted emotionally-neutered waxworks.

When she'd debuted her wave at a royal wedding there had been a double-page spread in *The Telegraph* explaining why it was so important to maintain traditions and to wave like a royal. Thousands of words of vitriol expended on explaining why she had "cocked her snoot" at the people. From then she wasn't one of the people, but she wasn't one of the family either and her star fell lower and lower. Lally had always harboured a suspicion that it was Mummy briefing the press against her – keeping her and her quirky thoughts in the background. Lally could have personally lasered the cancer out of the Queen Mum live on TV and her obituary would still have led with that stupid wave.

So, give the people what they want! You want a wave? Here it is! A wave that could summon the Red Arrows! A wave that could muster an army of swans! A wave that was worth a mighty suckle on the emaciated teat of the sovereign grant. Lally managed to keep her eyes on the laptop's white dot for about a minute, before she became distracted by the movement at the edge of the screen, and glanced at the comments cycling past in the chat window. She didn't dare read them, but the speed of the tumbling vertical gallery suggested that there were a lot.

She closed the laptop and picked up the bottle. *No rush*, she thought, and poured a double into the glass. She suddenly remembered that she had cigarettes, real actual cigarettes that were hidden away in a memory box. She stood a little woozily and breathed until the world came into focus again. Then she paced across the flat's wooden floors into the master bedroom with its Turners and Kandinskys on the wall. She studiously ignored the B of the Bang case on the floor, where she'd thrown it when she discovered that she had once again not made the grade. By pulling a chair over to the wardrobe she could access the back of the top cupboard, where there was a large cedar box. She reached past the photographs and pulled out a packet of her Aunt's Benson and Hedges and a jade cigarette holder. She'd stolen them from her house at the bunfight after the funeral.

Back in the living room, she fitted the cigarette into the holder and used a long match from the log-burner to set the cigarette on fire. Her lungs revolted at the arrival of the smoke, but it felt right to have something destructive in her hand. Between the cigarette and the vodka, she felt impenetrable and doubted that the missile would even put a dent in her. She stepped onto the balcony and took in the skyline again. She wondered whether the missile would come from her side of the city, or the other. She'd quite like to see it. Would it be so quick that she wouldn't see it? Would the explosion reach her here, or would it be the radioactive particles that got her? The message had been clear – there was no point trying to outrun it. There was no place of shelter for her. What a mess.

She kept coming back to the thought of "what would Granny have done?" Granny would have been out there, with the people, driving a truck or rebuilding bombed houses single-handed. She would have leapt a mile in the air and batted the missile away with a gold croquet mallet. She would have been ashamed of Lally, sitting in a Sheik's £200 million-pound flat, half-cut and cowering from the world to end.

"If the world is going to end, then don't you think you should make the most of it?"

"I am you old sow. I'm getting drunk and smoking."

"Eulalia, your Daddy didn't hate you. Your Mummy sees your good points too."

"You don't think Daddy hates me?"

"No. You hate you."

Lally wafted the apparition away, she didn't need busybody spectres giving her cheap psychoanalysis. As she stared at London, she noticed a streak of black in the sky. Was this it? Had a hundred minutes gone by? If she squinted, she could just make out that it looked bigger than a missile. No – it was a plane, but it was so low! She watched for another few seconds, her mouth agape as she stared, then it dipped below the skyline and out of sight. What the fuck! A plane crash *and* a missile. Maybe the missile had hit the plane? Lally's mind raced through the possibilities. It was the end – that was the only explanation.

With a shaking hand she hit redial on her phone and looked at the display showing the words "Calling #1" The number rang out again.

Sod it.

Maybe Granny had a point. If it was the end, she shouldn't be separate from her people, even if they hated her. Maybe in some small way they might need her. Perhaps it would feel good to be needed. Perhaps this was important. She picked up her cigarettes, filled a hip flask with rum and looked briefly for her card key before realising that locks and doors and possessions really didn't mean anything anymore. She paused to take a small swig of the rum while she processed that thought. The rum promptly hit her chest with a reassuring prickle and convinced her that she was doing the right thing. Then she left the door hanging open as she descended the stairs, heading for the streets of Knightsbridge. Lally was going to help.

LOBSTER ROCKED

THE FOCUS FACTORY was a 'social selling space for entrepreneurs and influencers' in Shoreditch. It was an old textile factory with steep stone stairs, worn to such a shine by generations of feet that it made you grateful for the partial reassurance of the banister that clung to the wall like a milk tooth near a toffee. The walls themselves were all painted a shade called "White?" and there was an overbearing smell of cling film packaging and some kind of all-purpose, all-knowing cleaning solution that haunted the corridors. Yeah, The Focus Factory was a shithole.

Every floor of the old building was split up and rezoned with exhibition-hall temporary walls and ceilings, creating thousands of little spaces that could be amended simply by the lean of a fat man. Each of the cubbies were equipped with a bright white square light, a smaller ring light, a mixture of phones and tablets on an array of stands and moveable, mouldable tripods. All of the electronics were fed by a trail of cables which linked directly into the building's only truly modern convenience – a ten gigabits per second fibre optic connection that sucked the images and chat from The Focus Factory and delivered them around the world with barely a ping.

On most days a raucous jabber of sales patter emanated from the cubes; young, mostly female voices registered a degree of excitement that few humans would ever actually experience. There was cooing and swooning, squeals and gasps. The cubes mostly had simple décor, white or black walls and modest furnishings, but each was dressed in its own simple theme: sports, jewellery, clothes, accessories, foods, neon or ceramics. It was an open secret that an entire upper floor of the building was dedicated to women selling no products, except the writhing and cavorting that has done good business since Eve hid her shame with a fig leaf. At least it was a bit warmer up there.

Spread across the floors beneath, the marginally more dignified performers were hyper-focused on the cameras. They worked in shifts and somehow found angle upon angle upon angle to fawn about their products. They plucked things from the air to say about these tchotchkes and filled months of airtime with USPs, both real and imagined. They babbled in English, Japanese, Urdu, Mandarin and German. The Focus Factory was a nexus of postmodern capitalism, drop-shipping Eastern goods to Western audiences, working on an ever-declining margin as the East realised they could deal directly too. The factory had once creaked and shuddered with the effort of craft, but now it housed re-sellers who vied for eyes and clicks. It searched out the eyes waiting in the car for ballet to end. It wanted the eyes glazed over while walking the dog at the park. It yearned for the eyes drinking hot chocolate in a café and want-scrolling through social media.

The funny thing was that if you stared into the cameras hard enough, as some of these salespeople did, you could divine the eyes staring back. And you could feel their hunger, not for what the performers were selling – but for something beyond words, something that was maybe just one more scroll away. But what do you need when you've already bought the Ewok Russian Doll set? You have the dashboard Elvis bobblehead. You own the key tracking rape alarm and calculator gift set. You were already fulfilled.

Coco was in her late twenties and showed all the signs of accelerated exhaustion that London imbues in all its occupants, but especially on its lower-class inhabitants. She was as pretty as someone wearing a foam lobster costume can be. She had £9.98 in her bank account, a fact that she found galling because it meant she would have to spend £7 on buses to go to a bank to get access to that money, which she desperately needed for a variety of reasons – not least trivial things like food. Recently, she had been grateful for the bulky red costume because it hid the early signs of swelling around her belly. She wasn't ready for her mum to watch her on stream and start to ask questions that she had no easy answers to. Although the answers themselves were actually very straightforward: Yes. Twelve weeks. Intrauterine insemination. It means the sperm came from a clinic. A lot of money. Two separate credit cards and she'd paid more to get access to premium donors. It was a girl.

That last one wasn't confirmed yet, but Coco knew it down to the marrow of her bones. She was going to have a daughter and the knowledge filled her with the first excitement she'd felt in several years. To her it made no difference that she was an assisted conception baby. She was a baby and that was all that mattered. She was her baby. Coco already knew that she was going to bless her daughter with the dullest of names and spare her a lifetime of "Like the clown?" Yes. Like the clown. "Like the powder?" No. Not like the powder. "And what's your surname?" Let's move on.

Coco was on the food floor of the Focus Factory, but barely. She was at the very end of a corridor, where her nearest neighbour sold hot chocolate spoons. In times past, this is where one of the factory owners had his office, but in the time since he walked the floor it had been sub-divided into fractions of its former glory. There were thirty-four units now and only eight of them were allotted. Of those only six were staffed. People kept finding excuses not to be near the putrid wafts from Coco's section and reasons why they had to be housed at the other end of the floor. Red Steve, the section manager, had considered whether he should move Coco to the fuck floor. He had chatted to one of the section managers up there and he said that they weren't fussy about smells. "Maybe we should just make her do sex. Keep the lobster suit; furries like that," Red Steve had suggested semi-seriously.

"Time to pick another one," Coco said to the camera as she swirled her right hand among the tepid waters of the tank and stirred some life into the lobsters who were packed tighter than a rush hour tube train at Oxford Circus. There wasn't much movement, but there was enough to show the camera trained on the tank at her knees that these animals were technically alive. During her extensive seven-minute training Red Steve had been insistent about the swirling.

"Swirl the water when you get! Make them move. Look like dead, dead shits or else and dead shit doesn't sell!"

So, Coco pushed back the sleeves on her lobster costume and swirled the water. The lobsters sensed something other than the tightly-packed tedium and they moved just enough to appease Red Steve and keep Coco in work. She lifted a medium-sized male from the waters.

"Hello mate, how are you? Let's call him Ted. Alright Ted? He seems like a big Cockney lobster I reckon," Coco said and she held the lobster to her ear.

"What's that?" she said, positioning the lobster next to her ear as one of its massive antennae twiddled as if attempting to find a reception. *Tank too warm*, was what the lobster tried to tell Coco, but she didn't understand.

"Is that right? He says that he's ready to die. Don't worry, Ted, you won't even know about it. It'll be quick, but someone's got to buy you first. So, which one of you lucky viewers is having lobster for tea tomorrow?"

Coco lifted her head as she registered a scream further down the corridor, but she was streaming and Red Steve was monitoring her cube, so she ignored it like the professional that her one month of drama school training had made her into. She had a sudden flash of her bank balance taunting her. Nine hundred and ninety-eight pennies between her and financial oblivion.

"So, Ted is a French Blue lobster, he's probably about seven years of age and he's lived his life mostly terrified, squashed into a hidey-hole that's altogether too small for him, wondering if he dares to try and make a move for somewhere bigger. Same, Ted. Now, people often ask if it's true if lobsters mate for life and I hate to break it to you, but no, they don't. If I had a pound for every time someone has told me that factoid, I would have enough money not to be here telling you that fact about lobsters. I'd still do this job obviously though because I'm deeply, deeply committed to the groundbreaking and important work we're doing here."

Red Steve held up a warning finger and Coco returned to her spiel with a winning smile.

"No, the truth is that lobsters are basically loyal to their partner for about two days when they're courting, the sex lasts for about four minutes and then they start to play the field again. If the female is pregnant then she'll almost certainly never see her mate again and she'll be left to do the parenting on her own, terrified of the world and the predators outside of her dark, lonely micro-cave. Sorry Ted, it appears someone has accidentally swapped my script with my diary. Enough about me - what have you got to say for yourself?"

Coco held Ted the lobster up to the camera and took him in for a close-up – she panned across his crusher claws. His marble black eyes gleamed and his antennule moustache twitched in the eye of the camera. The gentle flecks on his carapace shone under the lights. Coco looked closely at the chitin galaxies hidden amongst the blue of his shell. There was another scream down the corridor and as Coco looked up, she thought she could hear running feet. Red Steve made a motion for her to keep going.

"Olright, me old china plates, if you're looking for a decent feast for the weekend, why not *snap* me up. Ha! Ha! Ha! Ahhhh, *you* kill me Ted! No, you kill me, Coco!"

While the feed was focused on Ted's face, Coco glanced at the comment feed that was streaming past her in large font on one of the tablets arrayed out of the camera's line of sight. Comments were coming in too fast to read, but if she squinted, she could pick out the occasional comment.

- *Lol, lonoon.* **jesusisking20209010**
- *LETTTTTTS GETTTT NYUUUUUUUKULEAR* **staring_at_at_at_theson**
- *Lonoon* **jesusisking20209010**
- *Rashid legend* **Ilovebeefsausages**
- *London* **jesusisking20209010**

It was the first time that she could remember that the comment wall wasn't focused exclusively on raping her or her getting her tits out.

- *GET UR TITS OUT* **tallpaulisonprozac**

"Cos frankly, if the choices are spending another facking minute in that tank, I'll gladly take the sweet oblivion of death. Let's get this thing done, buy me already, so I can die!"

Everything on the feed was suddenly interrupted with a large chyron that read *SOLD!* And the sound effects of party poppers and the whomp-whomp of a sad trombone. The username of Ted's purchaser rapidly flashed up (tokenidiot99) and, as had become a bleak tradition on the stream, the comments filled with messages asking Ted to take words to friends and relatives who had passed on. The graphic dropped from the screen and focused on Coco, who had positioned the Crustaystun wand behind the thick of Ted's neck. It tapped against the creature's carapace. A drumroll sound effect played and Coco waited until the *FINISH HIM!* graphic appeared, and then she solemnly intoned "Tokenidiot99" into the came ra and slid the wand under Ted's shell and into his brain.

She tapped a button on the wand and felt the lobster give a momentary kick and then as she released the button it went limp in her hand. She thought hard about the £9.98 and allowed the wave of nausea she always felt at this point to compete with the incongruous desire she had to eat Ted and all of the lobsters in the tank one after another.

A spurt of ichor drained from the puncture wound and over Coco's hand. Red Steve appeared by the camera and reached out for Ted's now limp body. He picked him up by the tail and threw his body in a plastic-lined cardboard box and scattered scoops of ice flakes over him. He pulled two pre-installed zip-ties on the side of the box and unstuck the mailing label from his arm and smoothed it over the front of the box. Once packaged he kicked it towards the other twenty boxes in the corner by the freight lift, while Coco swirled the tank and read more of the comments.

- *RIP TED, DEADER THAN ALL COCKNEYS* **samoan***legend**
- *All out noicula war* **jesusisking20209010**
- *What North Korea are doing is a crime against humanity, show your tits* **29lobsterapologist**

"We're taking a break, back soon," Coco said and she got up and dropped the "Back In 5" card across the lead camera. She unclipped her lapel mic and stretched her back out, then she reached for a towel and wiped the watery fluid from the back of her hands.

"Two minute is two minute, wee wee only, shit on your lunch."

Coco ignored Red Steve's comment. "Steve, what's with the comments about nuclear war and dead cockneys?"

"Some bullshit."

"Okay, what particular flavour of bullshit?"

"Just some bullshit billionaire saying Korea launched a nuclear missile at London."

"What the fuck? Are you serious?"

Coco scrabbled in the inside pocket of the lobster costume and found her own phone. She opened TikTok and saw the trending video under the hashtag #*nuclear* and hit play. In the video there was some jerky footage of a middle-aged Indian man jumping on a desk in an office. Coco watched transfixed as he relayed what he knew about missiles being launched towards London and offering a sincere appeal to his colleagues to leave and to spend their remaining time with loved ones.

The rest of the video was obscured by screams and a rush to the office door, the muttered cries and resounding echoes of steps in an office stairwell taken at speed. Coco's hand moved to her mouth as she returned to the trending #nuclear hashtag and found videos of people getting on bikes and packing TVs, suitcases, animals and children into cars. Another video showed traffic jams clogging up a road that she thought might have been near the Blackwall tunnel. In five seconds of scrolling, Coco could see that London was officially going batshit.

"Steve, is this for fucking real? There are missiles coming to London?"

"It's not on BBC."

"Where's everyone else?" Coco tuned into her surroundings and realised that for the first time the floor wasn't a buzz of sales patter. There was no one else there.

"Who fuck know, it's not on BBC. Go, take your precious shit, then come back and lobster. Now watching at 300,000."

"Steve! I'm not going to lobster - *there are nuclear missiles*. Don't you want to get to safety?!"

"IT NOT ON BBC! GET IN CUBE AND LOBSTER."

"I'm not going to sell lobsters while the apocalypse is happening! It's in my contract."

"This is in your contract – this!" Red Steve said and extended his middle finger to her. "Contract stipulate you sit on it. Half a million watching Coco! Get in and lobster or you don't get job! Be poor in apocalyptic wasteland. Work only in stupid escape room telling people stupid alien bullshit mystery. Boo hoo, no money for Coco. Ok Google, set timer hundred twenty second called "Coco sit down and lobster or no more job""

"Your timer called Coco sit down and less is more job has been set."

"Clock ticking Coco!"

Coco stared at Red Steve. Red Steve stared back. She regretted taking this job. She regretted the tiny flat it paid for. She mourned the succession of mentally unstable flatmates she had endured. She hated the two trains she had to take to get here and how much money it cost just to get to work. She loathed the fact that her mum kept telling people at church that she was on TV and working in theatre, when actually she live-streamed herself killing lobsters and, until four days ago, worked in the worst escape room in the UK hosted in a damp and abandoned tube station in Hammersmith. Coco didn't dare admit to Red Steve that the escape room had closed with immediate effect thanks to the nation belatedly catching on to the fact that escape rooms were shit; the power it would give him to know that this was her only gainful employment didn't bear thinking about. With dignity and poise, Coco cleared the fabric lobster antennae out of her face and stepped over the bundles of wires and sat in her chair and instinctively clipped the lapel mic on. What was she doing?

Red Steve smiled widely enough to reveal the yellow-grey dead canine tooth that lurked in his jaw and pulled the "Back in 5" card out of its slot and Coco saw the little green light appear above the main camera. She stared at it. She tried to process what was happening. She struggled to squeeze the enormity of what was going on into her head, to wring it through the neurones and devise something approaching a plan. Her colleagues had clearly done that and concluded that running was the correct procedure. She thought of her baby.

- *Do something bitch* ____----—**ConorMcChamp**—----____

"Fuck you, Conor," Coco replied.

Coco stared directly at the camera. The comment feed immediately descended into a frenzy because Coco never talked directly to them, the only people who got namechecked were the buyers – that was the golden rule. Acknowledging the insult was like kicking a hive of bees who had decided they were sick of making honey and were henceforth going to make shit instead. The viewers vied for her attention with ever-more graphic, libelous and biologically complicated insults.

Coco took a deep breath, whistling slightly as she blew out the panic she felt mounting in her throat. £9.98. Red Steve loomed by the camera gesturing angrily towards the tank. She reached forward and swirled the water. She reached right to the bottom of the tank this time, causing lobsters to scatter and flip as she searched for King Glen. She pulled her hand out and regarded the beautiful blue lobster in her hand. He was the biggest in the tank and his colouring was regal, even the expression on his tiny face seemed haughty.

"Your highness," she said, as the lobster cycled his legs in the air. "Viewers, we are honoured to once again be joined by lobster royalty. Please be upstanding for the lobster national anthem in honour of King Glen."

She put her clenched fist over her heart and blew several bars of an improvised mouth trumpet fanfare. Steve quickly moved to silence the Google timer that he had set. Coco took the opportunity to check the comments streaming past her.

- *We might actually get to see her explode. How is this website free?* **CTRLALTDELBOY**
- *Boooooomo* ***(*(*iliketrains)*)***
- *Last chance to get ur tits out* **arresteddevelopmentisagoodprogramme**
- *Newclear tites* **jesusisking20209010**
- *Nm* **jesusisking20209010**

- *Ted RIP* **saymyname__okbryancranstone**
- *MELTDOWN BITCH* ***(*(*iliketrains)*)***
- *If he's a king why are you killing him* **CTRLALTDELBOY**
- *It's spelled nuclear.* **arresteddevelopmentisagoodprogramme**
- *ur radioactive* **saymyname__bryancranstone**
- *bom in bombdon* **jesusisking20209010**

Coco could feel the panic pressing in on her. It was the grind. The fucking grind. She could feel that it had won. Since she moved to London, she had tried to rise and grind. She really had tried. She had listened to the podcasts and set her miracle morning routine. She had got up at 5am to give herself an extra hour of hustle. Ok, she'd got up twice at 5am and blithered around for an hour and then been exhausted for the rest of the day. She had worked so hard. Her side gigs had side gigs and her micro hustles were arrayed neatly under her macro hustles. But the grind had won. £9.98 had won.

"Do you know what, fuck you Steve," Coco said and gently placed King Glen back in the tank. She unclipped the Velcro strap at the back of her lobster head and flipped it off.

"I'm not going to wait here to explode. I just paid my rent for the month, so at least I've got somewhere to die. I refuse to work through Armageddon."

"Coco, 750,000 now watching. *Lobster*, or you're through in this town, I know people" Red Steve hissed.

"No Steve, I'm not going to fucking lobster. The fact that you want me to lobster at this point in time is actually the worst thing I've ever heard. Fuck you, fuck billionaires and fuck you virgin ghouls for watching me, yes you. Set your people free, Glen."

Coco braced herself against the back of her seat and placed both feet against the waist-high tank. She pushed and strained and felt the side of the tank start to move and then with a lack of ceremony, her chair screeched slightly backwards. She stood up with as much dignity as anyone wearing two-thirds of a cartoon lobster costume can.

"You know what, the lobsters are fine where they are. I'm not. Fuck this."

Coco stood up and gave the middle finger to each of the three cameras in turn. Red Steve stood with his arms folded behind the camera.

"900,000 now watching Coco have no job. I'm taking dry cleaning of suit out of your wage."

"What does it matter Steve?! There's a fucking missile coming for London. Where are you going to find a dry-cleaners that's even open? You're insane."

"It not on BBC. World Economic Forum false flag."

"That doesn't even – do you know what. Goodbye and fuck off."

Coco raised her hands above her head and threw the lobster head at him. He caught it cleanly, which annoyed her, but she felt that she'd made her point. She stalked down the corridor and took in the various empty cubes, tripods, and mic stands pushed to the floor in the occupiers' rush to exit. Coco decided she didn't have time to go up the three floors to the toilets to get changed if she was going to catch up with the people who had already left. She started to run, the Crustaystun banging against her leg as she went.

RED OR GREEN?

GREG TERDE, THE legal compliance officer for B of the Bang, was having a heart attack, and it was upsetting him. His fingers found an unconvincing pulse in his wrist as he sat at the front of Meeting Room B and counted the beats as he looked at the tops of the heads of his colleagues working through the training exercises he'd set them. As he pinched the skin at his wrist, he could discern ligaments and bone, but beyond that, he could feel that the pattern of his heartbeat was much jazzier than it should have been. He wasn't a cardiologist, but he knew that hearts were supposed to be ponderous Berlin deep house: *DUM-DUM-DUM-DUM-DUM*. As he followed the beat of his own heart, he was dismayed to find it was much more of a slippy, New Orleans-style *DUM-DUM-CHA-DUM...........DE-SKIDDLE-DE-BE-DUM*.

It was fitting that his doom was being accompanied by the syncopated rhythms of jazz, as he was reasonably sure that the final place he'd drunk last night had been a seedy jazz lounge populated with hipsters and shysters, all united in the myth that the music wasn't awful. This was well into the early morning, so he would have been on the wrong side of fifteen pints, on a well-worn stimulus-response autopilot, no longer a man but three monkeys stacked in an unconvincing human suit. If he shut his eyes and really tried to remember, he could *almost* recall singing something. Maybe on a stage, or on top of a bar. Possibly in a Japanese accent. There had definitely been booing and some angry people. An alleyway and some sick in a bin. Had he tried to coax a cat into his taxi? Yes, that sounded right and would explain the "Cat return" surcharge on his Uber receipt. Implausibly, there had then been a sort of romantic success in a low-end kebab shop, but he had sworn that he would never think about that again. Greg sighed a deep and heartfelt sigh which he imagined seeing as a green and fizzing mist coating the room. He considered the eternal question: why did every book club meeting he went to end up like this? He hadn't even read the book. No one had. It was almost like the book element of book clubs was just a convenient excuse for industrial-strength decadence.

And now his heart was giving up.

Greg wasn't sure he could blame it. It felt selfish to try and get his heart to engage in maintaining a project that Greg himself - and most unbiased observers - wasn't sure was worth the effort. Greg was a shambles of a man in every sense. His hair: black with strands of grey and hopelessly shambolic. His clothes: ruffled, bobbled, shambolic. His Matalan suit and tie: shiny, uncomfortable and shambolic. His finances: peak shambolic.

The last one was particularly impressive given that he was a legal compliance officer for a relatively successful business. He should have been comfortably lower middle-class. But each month his salary was hoovered up by an over-reliance on Ubers, subscriptions to a series of indispensable yet ultimately pointless services, commuting and a genetic inability to bring his lunch from home. He'd done the figures on the back of a number of beer mats and having a job was by far his biggest expense. Oh, and the pints. Money had reached new lows and his current shame was that he had hoodwinked his local sperm donation clinic into believing that he was an ex-Olympian, MENSA member who worked as a city lawyer and consequently his deposits attracted a premium fee which nearly cancelled out his Spotify, Amazon and Disney subscriptions.

Greg tried to guess at a prognosis. First his heart would go jazzy, then there would be a few ambient blips and, finally, the conductor would rest his baton and Greg would simply turn blue and die. Maybe his tongue would loll and his eyes would bug. That was depressing, but the one glimmer of positivity to his death was that he would never again have to train colleagues on the updated alert software. Never again would he have to stand in the supermarket aisle waiting for them to put out the yellow stickered items, casually snarling at all the other reduced offerings people. Never again would-

"Mr Terde, what should we do if we've finished?"

Greg was roused from his wallowing. He looked at the room to see who had spoken – Serge, one of the new in-take. Greg was aware - of course he was - that people loved saying, "Mr Terde" and that they would say it at any given opportunity. He could say, "Just Greg's fine" to them a thousand times, but they'd revert to "Mr Terde" whenever they could. If they had a public address system then they would find a reason to use it to say his name at a hundred-and-twenty decibels, forcing him to pantomime along with everyone else looking around for this comically named Mr Terde. They loved to snigger about it because Terde sounded like turd, which is another, more vernacular, way of saying a poo. He could have explained that it had a French heritage and could technically have been pronounced *T-air-d*, but really what was the point? It reaches a stage where you just have to own your Terdeness.

Greg released his pulse, perhaps for the last time, and approached the idiot who thought he'd finished the alert exercise. Of course it was Serge. Serge, mid-twenties, nephew of B of the Bang owner, Lee. Awful, brash, single-celled Lee. Horrible, cocky, nepobaby, Serge. Stupid cat return surcharge. Pitiful wonky heart. Serge was wearing a blue suit and a Guns 'N' Roses t-shirt and had a dramatic hair fade that made him look like Beaker from The Muppets, but the shit babies' version of The Muppets. Greg had a flash of fear that Serge might give him mouth-to-mouth when his heart finally stopped. That would not be ideal. He needed a living will that explicitly stated no mouth-to-mouth from Serge, stat.

"If you've finished then you've done something wrong, Serge," Greg managed to explain without vomiting directly onto the youth. "This exercise should take two hours, not a matter of minutes."

He looked at Serge's laptop to see what the cretin had done wrong and suddenly his heart was no longer arrhythmic. In fact, it was beating with a monstrous, speedy thump, a multi-hooved stampede that he could all but hear. The reason being that Serge's laptop displayed not the red learner system outline, but the green live system outline, as denoted by an apple-green L in the top corner with the word "Live" underneath it.

"But…you're on live? Why are you on live?"

Something about the high-pitched tone of terror in Greg's voice was infectious and even Serge's superhuman, my-uncle-owns-the-company confidence was rocked.

"You said to work on the green system!"

"No, no I didn't! I explicitly said you *absolutely shouldn't* work on the green system unless you were actually wanting to send out an alert. Remember? I said that you were all learners so you should have the red L? We laughed about it! I laughed about it."

"But this has a green L."

"Yes! For 'Live!'"

A blue-haired girl, who Greg vaguely thought might be one of the many Jennifers, raised her hand.

"So, we're *not* working on green?"

"Not you as well?" Greg shrieked.

"You said green!" she cried back, catching the fear from Greg's voice.

"I did not! *Red* Learner system. *Red* Learner. Like with cars — you get a *red* L."

"You get a *green* P when you've passed though," Possibly Jennifer noted.

"That's not relevant! There is no "P" is there? There is just a red L for Learner and a green L for Live! How could you confuse them?"

A calmer, more superior voice interjected: "Look, Greg – calm down. When you worked through the dirty bomb example earlier you were on the green L system. We just followed what you'd done."

Meg. Stupid team leader Meg with her 2:1 in Art History.

"Yes, *thank you* Meg."

Greg addressed the room with a spiralling dread.

"Listen. This is very important. Can everyone put your hand up if you're in the green Live system, so I can figure out precisely how many heart attacks I should have?"

He looked at the faces in the room. All but one of them gradually raised their hands. One of the slower girls at the front half-stood as if she was about to make a break from the room, instead she turned to the room with a gesture of pleading.

"Did I actually tell Princess Eulalia that the world was ending?" she asked, with little hope or expectation of an answer.

"I've sent loads out!" her neighbour Alan said, his face a ghostly bloodless mask.

Greg somehow made it back to his desk at the front. His mind was flooded with adrenaline, which allowed him to speedily calculate that these fuckwits (albeit fuckwits he was in charge of) had probably been able to message a very detailed apocalyptic alert to over 100 customers. 100 of the richest and most powerful people in London. People whose lawyers had lawyers, and whose lawyers' lawyers had lawyers, like Russian dolls, but with lawyers. These were the people with the means and the wherewithal to force Greg through a fine mesh and turn him into a legal compliance officer paste.

He sat at his chair and really concentrated on panicking. As a displacement activity he picked up the training sheets on his desk and flipped over the pages until he found the black and white photocopied reassurance that showed everyone should be in the red learner system.

"Look!" he held up the papers. "It even says it here! Did no one read this?"

"But that's black and white Greg, you can't see what colour it is!" Meg asserted rationally.

"And you were demonstrating on the green system!" Serge shouted.

"Not green! I SAID "NOT GREEN"!"

"Isn't there anything you can do?" Almost-definitely Jennifer asked.

"Not unless you possess the power to reverse time and unfuckwit fuckwits Jennifer? Can you do that? Can you unfuckwit fuckwits?"

"I don't think that sort of language is helpful Greg, we need to get a bird's eye view of what's happening and pinpoint an action timetable."

"Noted. *Thank you*, Meg."

The room fell silent, apart from one set of loud clacking keys.

"Who's typing? Is someone still typing?" Greg looked around the class and saw Gavin still tapping away. He made his way over and lifted Gavin's ear defenders away from his head.

"Gavin – are you working on the red or green system?"

"Green, why?"

"No reason," Greg said and let the ear defender slam back into place. He leant across and pushed Gavin's laptop onto the floor.

"Hey!"

Greg shakily walked to the door, he threw it open and stalked down the corridor, leaving the trainees staring dumbly at each other like crash test bellends. He realised something, turned on a swivel and ran back.

"Stay here and do not under any circumstances move," he commanded and shut the door. His fuckwits nodded at him mutely. He turned and ran back again down the corridor. Despite the day's mist and dullness, the heat somehow managed to be stifling in the office. The air was always close because of the building's design which was constructed from glass, chrome and incompetence. It was, Greg reflected, the very worst place to have the very worst hangover on the very worst day of his life.

Halfway down the hall he felt a strong nausea and sprinted onwards to the toilets, making it inside just in time to lean over the sink and hurl his guts into it. As his head lolled in the sink and he considered the chunks blocking the plughole, the automatic tap activated and water fell from the high hung appliance, soaking the back of his head.

"This is not ideal," he said. The water was obnoxiously cold, yet he let it fall over the back of his head and neck until he felt some form of reality returning. It wasn't a good reality, but it was marginally better than the psychotic break he had been verging on. He stood up and crossed to the wall and dipped his hands into the hand dryer. He tried to scoop some of the hot air onto his face, but it didn't work, so he settled for rubbing his hands over his head.

What was he going to do?

He looked out of the toilet's window just in time to watch a large white jet pass by only a handful of metres above the murk of the Thames. Flames and roiling black smoke were billowing from one of the engines. And then it was gone. In the time it took his mouth to drop open and for his finger to raise to point, the plane had vanished, leaving only a choppy wake in the waters and dispersing smoke.

"Ack…!" Greg shouted as he instinctively backed away from the window. At that point Greg's gratuitous hangover took the decision to hold all calls and reboot. Greg tipped backwards into unconsciousness, pausing in his descent only to crack his head on the corner of the sink, which started the automatic tap running again.

※ ※ ※ ※ ※

Greg was in the kebab shop again, it was 4am. He couldn't tell if he was a poorly animated replica of himself, or if he was just a smudge of consciousness in the corner of the room that anyone observant enough to spot, would just assume was heat haze from the cookers, or a free-floating grease spot. Regardless of how he was there, there he was. Greg took in the scene. A small radio in the kitchen was playing *Re-Rewind* by The Artful Dodger as the cook sweated over the kebab sticks, and another one folded pizza boxes with a casual dexterity and stacked them in towering piles behind the counter.

Greg saw real, actual Greg sitting on one of the implausibly delicate plastic stools that were placed next to the shop's plate glass windows. With the advantage of being corporeally disconnected, Greg watched horrified as he tipped his seat backwards and forwards, pitching himself repeatedly towards the large window. Greg stopped his health and safety assessment and watched himself devour a large donner kebab with pickled chillis, extra salad and mint sauce. He was shocked, but perhaps not surprised to see quite how feral he appeared. His arms were encircled around the unfolded paper and he looked furtively around the shop at the few other patrons, who Greg noted gratefully, were just as off their tits as he was. He was reminded of a nature documentary he'd seen where lions had feasted on a fallen zebra and their faces were stained red from the animal's innards.

Two girls leaning on the counter waiting for their food were Especially Drunk. They were passing a bottle of North Preston Cava back and forth and every time the song reached the point where Craig David was all over your BOINK, they cheered and necked more Cava. The disembodied Greg watched as drunk, actual Greg turned round when the two girls loudly shouted BOINK. Greg watched Greg watch the girls. He saw himself appraise the pair and wonder if maybe, *just maybe*, they could be interested in him. He saw the three monkeys piloting him lick his palm and swipe it across his hair, depositing a small shard of onion in his ramshackle quiff. Then, a minor miracle, as one of the girls, the tall, dark-haired girl who had unleashed the three-note belch a second ago, nudged her friend, motioned towards Greg and smiled. Greg gazed vacantly as she started to aim her shouts of BOINK towards Greg and gyrate if not at him, then at least in his vicinity.

Actual Greg finished the scraps of his kebab meat, licked every digit he possessed and wadded the various papers, chilli tops and shards of lettuce into a ball. He span on his stool, nearly tipped backwards through the window, but instead he raised the ball of rubbish over his head. He watched himself loudly and confidently slur the words: "EVERYONE WATCH THIS HAPPEN!" and then collect his poise as he held the makeshift ball like a basketball player readying himself for a three-pointer from Downtown. Greg saw the bin on the other side of the shop. A standard bin, waist high with an oval aperture approximately the width of the ball that Greg now held. Greg shouted "KOBE!" and then launched his papers.

Everyone in the shop seemed to be frozen as the paper ball traced a trajectory through the air and somehow sailed through the opening and directly into the bin. Greg saw the delight on the faces of the drunk customers, and even the appreciation of the kebab shop staff, but he definitely registered the spark of lust in the face of the tall girl who was now staring at Greg and rubbing the over-sized pickled gherkin she'd got with her fish and chips around her lips. She did this a number of times with her large mascara-clumped eyes blinking at Greg. As he failed to respond, she took to dipping the gherkin into her mouth and then out again. Greg finally noticed on her seventeenth fellation. Greg watched himself watch her suck at the gherkin and get progressively deeper with each pass until he thought he could see it bulge near her collarbone. He watched as she watched him watch her suck at the gherkin.

Then he saw her fingers fumble the gherkin and she started to cough. Then she started to panic. Then she clawed her friend's arm and pointed at her face. Ghostly Greg couldn't do anything other than stare as her friend started to scream as she registered that her friend was choking. Then real drunk Greg arrived on the scene and instinctively walloped the girl on the back. After three hits he looked at her face, which was starting to show hints of purple strain at the edges. She shook her head, and her eyes started to stretch into a widescreen rictus of grim acceptance. Then Greg was stretching his arms to their fullest and encircling as much of the girl as he could. Then he was jerking his arms together with all his might. Ghostly Greg couldn't help but notice that his Heimlich technique seemed to involve rather more pelvic thrust than might be considered standard. But there he was squeezing, thrusting and humping, squeezing, thrusting and humping, squeezing, thrusting and humping and then with a *blurp* noise, the gherkin emerged, sheathed in saliva and landed in the middle of one of the red Formica tables.

Everyone in the establishment turned to look at the gherkin, glistening on the laminated surface. The girl pushed her way out of Greg's embrace and without looking at anyone, grabbed her friend by the hand and jerked her out of the shop and onto the streets, where they sped away into the night. Everyone looked between Greg and the gherkin, the gherkin and Greg. Unconscious Greg, drenched in passive embarrassment, gratefully accepted the wormhole that brought him back to his earthly form.

※ ※ ※ ※ ※

Water from the sink was spilling over the side and splashing onto the floor and Greg. The soaking roused him and he woozily stood and waved vaguely at the sensor-activated tap until it shut off. His feet slipped in the puddles of water as he made his way across the bathroom.

The truth was that he had no idea what he should do. None. There was no precursor to this sort of event. Greg and Greg's hangover had accidentally unleashed a hypothetical apocalypse onto a small group of people, who were yet to discover that it was only hypothetical. He felt the heaviness in his soul – the realisation that his only true option was to own up. To get a message out to their customers that there had been a terrible, career-ending mistake. He would return to his parents' house and beg to live in his old bedroom and shoulder his father's barbed remarks. He would hold a pillow over his head as he listened to his mother practice the tuba. He would apologise again and again until eventually, perhaps in a millennia, this wasn't the biggest fuck-up that had ever occurred. That was what he had to do.

Given this realisation, Greg was surprised to see himself walk over to the fire alarm on the wall and jam his thumb hard onto the black dot at its centre. Immediately, a shrill mechanical whoop sounded out at a loud enough volume that Greg was forced to cover his ears. He slopped through the bathroom, found his way to the door and peered out into the corridor. He could see people looking curiously out of doorways, wondering if this was the real deal or an unannounced test. Some instinct propelled Greg into the small kitchenette next door, which was empty. Greg had to turn away from the gangway as a group of people scurried past following the fire evacuation plan. He searched in the drawers and came up with a number of serviettes left over from Christmas, which he jammed into each compartment of the toaster. He depressed the plunger and watched as the elements started to heat the paper.

At the first glimpse of fire, Greg turned and snuck out of the kitchenette, heading with purpose towards the customer service office. Like most of the building it was empty, with most of the normal occupants either currently in the training room wondering where Greg was or already heading to the stairwells. Greg found the B of the Bang duty phone, an ancient Nokia 3210, and ensured that it was charged, but it was a Nokia 3210 and was thus permanently charged and would be until the end of recorded time. He noticed that the phone's screen had topped out with its record of missed calls and the screen now simply said: "You have ^%%^ missed calls," as if the volume of calls could no longer be expressed by mere numbers. He tucked it into his pocket and was halfway down the corridor by the time the sprinklers kicked in and the entire office was showered with a serious, dense spray. He made his way into the back office, pushed through into the emergency stairwell, skipped down the stairs and blasted through an unused emergency door and into the end of the world.

THEY DIDN'T HAVE TO MOVE US TO SALFORD

CHARLOTTE THE PRODUCER bashed through the studio door the very second the show went to *It's The End of the World As We Know It (And I Feel Fine)*. Her show notes were scrunched in her hand and her nostrils were flared.

"What the fuck Martin – what the actual, ever-living fuck? You can't do this sort of shit. You'll get us all fired. Not to mention that it's actually immoral. It's *wrong*."

"Bullshit, I'm stating facts. Management moved us up to Salford – the anti-London. Did we want to go? No. Did they do it anyway and fuck us over with the relocation package? Yes. I'm not doing anything but telling the truth."

Charlotte leaned over the console and jabbed her finger at the DJ.

"You know precisely what you're doing – you're gloating. London is possibly being attacked and you're gloating. The fucking Prime Minister is dead and you're using time on the mic to mention a relocation that was done several years ago. It's pathetic and absurd, so I suppose it's very on-brand for you."

"If offering condolences to our upper management colleagues who remained working in London while we were shuffled off beyond the Wall to live with the Wildlings is pathetic, then I don't know what to say – maybe I am pathetic."

"There's no *maybe* about it, *you* are pathetic. *Arrghh!* Every time you try to stop smoking, you turn into the world's biggest twat."

"I'm fairly sure the man from Guinness gave that certificate to you, when the search party eventually found him."

"Why don't you just give in and have some nicotine, Martin? I'm begging you. No one will be mad. You can just pay me the £1 and admit on mic that you're weak. Then it'll all be over and a semblance of sanity can return."

"They will put me in a box before I give you the satisfaction."

"*Twenty seconds, and you're both pathetic,*" came the tinny voice of Sid the engineer, who was manning the booth while Charlotte berated Martin.

"Fine, I'm pathetic. I'm in Salford and I'm pathetic. Now if you'll excuse me, I'm preparing to give full play to the range of voices that listen to our show. Isn't that our programme brief? Isn't that the entire fucking reason for the existence of this show? That and to flog erectile dysfunction supplements."

"*Five seconds.*"

"Now, get back in your hutch and let me do my job."

"No Martin, I don't think I will. I think I'll take a seat on mic three." Charlotte dropped down into a chair and threw on the headphones attached to the mic. She glared at Martin and made a gesture to show that she was watching him.

"Fine, just make sure you're not day snoring like you normally do."

"Arsehole."

"Wank stain."

"Pedo."

"Fuc..." A light on the studio wall flicked to green and Martin hustled to the mic. "...King and country, that's who we are thinking of today. King and country. Speaking of whom, we are getting some confirmation that the royal family have been evacuated from London to an undisclosed location. A bleakly historic day. So, welcome back to your Big Talk show. We're with you all the way until 5pm today and we're going to be keeping you updated with what's going on. We'll make sure that all the voices that listen to this show are heard wherever they are in the country," he threw a middle finger towards Charlotte, who shook her fist at him in return. Through the soundproof window Martin could see Sid creasing up with laughter.

"So, I know we've been talking about this endlessly but if you're just joining us, it's a tough set of headlines to digest so I'd ask that you sit down. Tragically, Prime Minister Fenton Crossley has been killed after initially surviving his plane crashing into the Thames. I did warn you. And if that's not enough, you've almost certainly by now seen the viral video to end all viral videos, which is Billionaire Box King Rashid Khan explaining to his staff that missiles are due to fall on London from North Korea…now we have to be completely clear here and say that we still have received no verification about these claims although the government is obviously in a state of disarray, and we're hoping to hear from acting Prime Minister William McCartney in the next hour. What we do know is that the impact that it has had on London has been catastrophic, with what's being called the Great Panic causing people to fight for shelters and flooding the transport network, desperate to get to safety. Londoners, if you are able to and it's safe and appropriate to do so, we'd love to hear from you about what's going on from your perspective on this momentous day. I believe we have Dave from Twickenham."

"Martin, hello it's Dave. But can I just say that I'm actually from Ickenham. Common mistake, but worth correcting."

Martin made a wanker symbol at Sid who had screened the call.

"Sorry about that Dave, that's Sid's fault, I'm afraid he's still doing his phonics. So over in Ickenham are you struggling to take this in?"

"Honestly Martin, I'm not. It's what I always expected in a way."

"Right, how's that Dave?"

"Well, there was always something off about that Crossley and are you really surprised that the North Koreans have finally had enough with the repressive sanction regime that they live under and gone and shot off their missiles."

"Dave, I'm going to just be honest: I don't think this is something that you could say you expected. It's one of the most jaw-dropping and surprising days in the history of mankind."

"Not if you follow the logic, Martin. It's actually quite understandable. Kwon Hyun Gun isn't going to sit around and take it forever, is he? He wants to show his people that he's in charge. You can't back a rat into a corner and be surprised when it behaves in a rodential manner."

"Well Dave, all I'll say is that I wish you'd given the rest of us some warning. Line 5, you're on your Big Talk…"

Charlotte held up her scrunched-up notes above her head with both hands.

"…but before we do that, I do want to point out that your Big Talk show is brought to you in association with Invictus tablets. Men living with the shame of erectile dysfunction should remember that they don't need to hide it. Invictus, keep your head bloody but unbowed."

Charlotte gave a thumbs up. Martin pantomimed a stream of vomit coming from his mouth, eyes and ears.

"Line 5, take it away."

"Hello Martin, It's Mary from Stoke. But my husband is going to London for a convention next week and he said that there's nothing going on. No missiles, no panic or anything."

"Mary, you said he's in London next week?"

"Yes, for a conference. He's in double glazing."

"But that's next week?"

"Yes."

"And is he in Stoke now?"

"Yes, he's in the lounge. Hang on, he wants to say something – what's that? Oh, he can't find the remote."

"Mary, I'm just struggling to see why would he know that there's nothing going on today when he's in Stoke?"

"Because he's at a conference there next week."

"Mary that d- thanks for your call. We're going to take a quick break and come back after these words."

Charlotte stood up as soon as the light on the wall went to red.

"Thirty *seconds*."

"Sid, you've got to get me someone from London! What's the fucking point of all of us speculating when there must be millions of people actually there. Get me someone who can describe the crowds, I want someone who can smell the shit hitting the fan. Give me a Cockney Geezer who's kissing his ageing mother goodbye and doing the Lambeth Walk into the sunset, not braindead Marys from Stoke."

"Twickenham is in London," came Sid's reply through the studio speaker.

"So's Ickenham apparently. Aim for Stoke Newington, not Stoke-on-Trent."

Martin jumped up and pushed through the studio door. Sid looked up from whatever horrors he was browsing on his phone and Martin nodded at him. He ran into the bathroom and quickly force-pissed hard enough so that he could feel splashes against his hands and arms. One of the junior researchers came in and occupied the urinal directly next to Martin. He looked at the tall youth with irritation – there was an entire wall of urinals to choose from, why did he pick that one? The teenage gimp just smiled gormlessly back.

Martin finished urinating and went hands free. He rooted in his pockets for a tin of nicotine pouches. He popped the lid off and shook out two of the small white fabric bags into his other hand and put the tin back in his pocket. At the urinal he delicately retracted his foreskin and jammed the pouches against the unsheathed skin of his penis, then rolled it back to normal, although noticeably nobblier before. Martin looked up and saw the researcher slyly looking at him with horror.

"If I read about this on Popbitch, I'm coming for you" he snarled, and the researcher suddenly found the advert for car loans in front of him fascinating. By omitting to wash his hands, Martin was back at his mic as the light turned green.

"Ok, welcome back to your Big Talk show. We've got producer Charlotte in the studio with us who I believe can bring us up to date on a few items. Charlotte, what have you got for us?"

Charlotte was hastily adjusting her headphones and fiddling with the mic while glaring at Martin, but as she spoke, her voice sounded as smooth and professional as if she'd been perfectly prepared.

"Thanks Martin, it's been a momentous day so far and as we wait for confirmation on the missile story that's gripping the nation, we're really in a holding pattern about exactly what is going on today. One thing that I'm seeing on social media is a confirmation that both of the members of the over-70s rowing team who were on the Thames when the plane crash landed have been killed, which is obviously incredibly sad, but when you consider how dense the population of London can be at places it's something of a miracle that the death toll on the ground isn't much higher."

"Thanks Charlotte, our thoughts and prayers are with the friends and families of those rowers who lost their lives today. Tragic. Okay, let's speak to Paul, who I believe is on line three – Paul?"

"Yeah, hi Martin. Just mad, isn't it?"

"Absolutely. It's been hands-down the strangest news day in my distinguished career. What's on your mind?"

"Well, it's this video of the bloke on the desk, that is getting me mad."

"This would be the video of Rashid Khan?"

"That's right. You see, pardon my French, but it's total bollocks."

"Apologies to listeners for any bad language there – Paul, try and keep things P.G. please!"

"Sorry Martin, force of habit. My point though is that it's bang out of order. Just because he's some billionaire he gets to find out about all these things that are happening first? While your average bloke on the street just gets to find out when the fu-flipping missile hits him. It's bollocks."

"Paul!"

"Sorry Martin, but I'm wound up. Billionaires have ruined everything. They're scum. We all know it and I hope when the bomb does drop that it takes out as many of them as possible. But we all know that they'll be the ones that manage to come out of this shitstorm smelling of roses. It's just bloody unfair. Sorry, Martin. I get choked up about this."

"It's okay, Paul. Take your time. I know lots of people feel very strongly about this."

Martin could see that Charlotte was giving him a minute shake of the head. She mouthed the word "Careful" at him. He flicked the Vs at her.

"Seriously Paul. Take your time. I think that's one of the things that we need to be mindful of today is that we're going through something truly unprecedented and it's bound to be affecting us all."

"My head's in bits. I've got family in London and I know that they're not rich enough to get these warnings and I can't get hold of them. So, while you've got numpties like Rashid getting chauffeured to safety because they've got a few quid in the bank, everyone else is screwed. It's so unfair. And where's the bloody government? Eh? Appreciate that they've had a disaster today, but you can't just leave the country without leadership – can you? Madness."

"Thanks Paul. Appreciate your views and for sharing that emotion with us. To be clear we should point out that we don't know for sure what Rashid Khan has done with the information that he received. Anyone who has seen the video will know that he wanted to share it with his colleagues and I'm guessing here, but I would say that not all of them will have been billionaires. I don't know. But I can absolutely hear the frustration and the anger in Paul's voice. Can you hear that too Charlotte?"

He'd timed his question just as Charlotte was taking a sip of water and she started to cough as she answered.

"Ooh, say it don't spray it, Charlotte! You're supposed to speak into the mic, not eat it."

"*kof* – Oh, excuse me. Think something went down the wrong way."

"Something or someone?"

"It's probably not the day for that is it, Martin? But to answer your question, yes of course I can hear the frustration in Paul's voice. I think plenty of people feel the same. They want answers and guidance. We should say and be very clear that we still don't have any official communication about whether these reports of a missile from North Korea are true, so we need to keep a level head."

"Something that we're good at here in the North," Martin interjected. "Now, who have we got on line six – you're on your Big Talk show caller."

"Hi Martin, Hi Charlotte, first-time caller, long-time listener. I'm Ted and I just wanted to ask you if you've heard anything more about the Princess Eulalia weirdness?"

"Thanks Ted, good to have you with us. This would be the story where we've just seen her waving at the camera looking a little bit spooky. It's all over social media and has already been memed to the gills."

While Ted had been talking, Charlotte had speed-scrolled through Twitter and located a number of the popular memes, many of which were now well over a million views. She passed her phone across to Martin who squinted at the phone at arm's length.

"Yep, we've got all the standard things you could imagine here. Spongebob waving. 'This is fine' dog waving back at Eulalia. Two-button man trying to choose between "Explode with dignity" and "Make the day all about me." Could this day get any stranger Charlotte? We've got plane crashes, nuclear missiles and now waving royal memes."

Martin had kept hold of Charlotte's phone and was busily browsing through her camera roll. He kept pantomiming laughter at various photos as he swiped through and zoomed in on weird expressions.

"I don't think so. We're still not sure if that was a comment on the missile situation, a mistake, or as some people have commented, an indication that her battle with drink might have taken another turn. Obviously, everyone at The Big Talk Show wishes her all the best."

Martin had opened Tinder on Charlotte's phone and started to swipe indiscriminately, holding the phone up in the air so Charlotte could see what he was doing.

"That's right and once again we just want to reiterate our support for all our management colleagues down in London, we're sitting here around two hundred miles away from the capital, so we can only imagine the heartache and the terror that they must be feeling today. They must feel like they've got a target on their backs and it's awful, just awful. We hope that they know that our thoughts and prayers are most definitely with them. This is The Smiths and *Panic*."

NO ONE PANIC! EXCEPT MAYBE YOU.

COCO'S LOBSTER FEET hit the street, and she started to run towards Liverpool Street Station, which was her nearest tube. Shoreditch was technically closer but it had the disadvantage of being overground and therefore not much use as a bomb shelter. Within twenty metres she realised that the oversized lobster foam feet of her costume really weren't designed for speed, and five metres further on she tumbled forward, skinning her hands protecting her stomach as she fell. She jumped up, hissed curses through her teeth, wiped her bloody hands on either side of her arthropod torso, and started to run again.

As various people barged into her, she quickly noted that everyone was running in the opposite direction.

"Excuse me…hello…excuse…sorry…do you know…" Coco tried to get an answer from the people variously jogging and sprinting past her, but no one wanted to chat.

"Why is no one going to Liverpool Street?!" she screamed as loudly as she could.

"It's shut. All the tubes are," a young black man on an e-scooter said as he whizzed past, skipping off the kerb near where Coco was stood.

Well, shit.

She stopped and tucked herself and her large dangling legs in the calm behind a large industrial bin and tried to think. She felt like holding her head in order to stop the vibrations, like she'd morphed into an old-fashioned alarm clock that was going off. It put her in mind of a *Roadrunner* cartoon and she looked skyward to see if a ten-ton anvil was falling towards her. She shook the visual out of her thoughts and reached into the slit in the side of the lobster costume, plucking her phone from her back pocket. Ten missed calls. She took a deep breath, summoned all her restraint and called her mum.

"Coco?!" her mum gasped.

"Mum!" Coco suddenly felt tears spring to her eyes. She was so confused about what was going on, none of it felt real and suddenly hearing her mum's voice made everything come to life. "Mum, what's happening? They say that there's a missile in London? Is it true?"

"I tried calling you darling, but you weren't picking up your phone. I left a message but it will probably be alongside the ones I've left this week."

"I know mum, I was working and I've just found out about all this shit."

"Coco!"

"Mum, it is shit. Shit is the right word. I'm just outside work and the world's gone to shit. People are all running everywhere but I've got no idea where they're going. What should I do?"

"ITV aren't saying much other than about the prime minister dying."

"What!?"

"You didn't know?"

"No! Mum, I've been working! They wouldn't let – what happened? Oh, that's awful."

"His plane crashed in the Thames apparently and he died after the landing."

"What? That's insane. Mum, I can't think. What should I do? Should I go home? I started but everyone seems to be going towards Whitehall."

"They're saying that William McCartney is now the Prime Minister, but that doesn't seem right. They had footage of his wife sweeping out of their house into a white Land Rover. She had a huge pair of sunglasses on. That's not appropriate, is it?"

"I don't know, mum! Focus! I need your advice – where should I go? I feel like the people know something more than me, but I don't want to get stranded in town. Surely that's where the missiles are going to go? Wait, was the Prime Minister's plane shot by the missile?"

"They're saying that they think it was a bird strike. ITV are waiting for confirmation about the missile. Could you get a taxi?"

"Of course, I can't get a taxi mum! Imagine the surge pricing!"

"There's plenty in Canterbury, they have Uber now too. And Uber Eats, but I don't think that's starting until Autumn. Carol from pottery is getting-"

"Mum! Stop it! This isn't helpful! For once – I actually want you to tell me what to do – isn't this what you want? What should I do?"

Spotting a break in the flow of pedestrians, Coco edged out from behind her bin and looked up and down the road. A man in a business suit sprinted past and collided with her, sending her mum's voice wheeling through the air.

"What the fuck! Arsehole!" Coco shouted as she scrambled on the floor to retrieve her phone. The screen had splintered into pieces, but was fortunately prevented from falling out entirely by the plastic cover her dad had stuck on, which had permanently trapped a small bubble of air near the mouthpiece. She put the phone back to her ear.

"…and that's all you can do for now."

"Mum, I didn't hear that – what should I do – please just make it quick and easy to understand."

"Find a policeman!" her mum replied. "And make sure you call me later!"

Coco cradled the phone close to her mouth.

"Mum, I love you. Tell Dad."

"I know you do, sweetheart. Get moving!"

Coco looked both ways before heading out of the doorway, across the road and onto the opposite pavement where it was marginally quieter and there was a view of the murky Thames. She found her arms gravitating towards her waist and forming a protective bubble from the mayhem. She looked out onto the river and wondered what would happen to the water in a nuclear explosion. Would it be vapourised and scattered to the winds or would it curl into a tsunami? Coco sized up the concrete barriers that separated the pavement from the banks. Beneath lay a miserable mud beach. Could she swim away from London, or was her costume affecting her decision making? Coco filed it as an option, but felt she should get some sort of confirmation first – her mum was right, she needed to find a policeman and get the facts. For the sake of not pushing against the crowd, she started to run in the same direction that everyone was going.

Coco's adrenaline kept her moving for the next mile, despite her cardio deserting her by the time she got to the end of the street. She'd been meaning to do the *75 Hard* plan for a few months, but after starting it she was crestfallen to discover that it was both hard and lasted seventy-five days. She resolved to hold out for a *3 Easy* programme. She pushed herself through the low arch into Kings Bench Walk where all the barristers hung out; she remembered seeing them wearing their ornate wigs one morning, five of them leaving a building as if they'd just stepped out of the 1800s. Just as she got into the car park beyond, she saw a father with a young girl hurrying together as they held hands. Coco could see the fear etched on the man's face as he cajoled his daughter to go faster. Coco pulled alongside them and kept pace.

"Excuse me – where is everyone going?"

"I don't know, we're just heading the same way as everyone else. That's it Ruth, you're doing great!" His daughter pulled her hand from his and stooped to pick something up off the street which had caught her eye.

"Ruth! Come on!"

"My shiny!" Ruth shouted.

"Thanks," Coco said and resumed her run. She pulled alongside an older man who was trudging along as fast as he could, impeded by a bulging gut which wobbled as he toddled along.

"Why is everyone running this way?"

"Bomb shelter - Whitehall."

"Thank you!"

Coco's heart leapt. Of course, there was a bomb shelter! This was London! If you could get shrimp-fried rice at three in the morning then a citizen could surely get a bomb shelter for when the missiles started to fall. Go London! Coco panted lightly as she put her head down and found her stride again. She ran down the Strand and past the grandeur of King's College on her left. The absurdity of what was happening was softened slightly by the fact that everyone was moving in the same direction. Surely, if there was an issue, she would have seen more people moving in the other direction? Cars and buses had nearly all been abandoned. Oddly, there were few people panicking or crying, even though their faces were taut with urgency. People were too busy pushing themselves onwards to the safety that lay at the end of the journey.

The crowds started to congeal as Coco passed a Pizza Express just ahead of Trafalgar Square. She had to slow to a walk to keep the same pace as the throng pushing down the road. Voices were raised further along but she couldn't hear what the shouting was about, and the sound was just a mishmash of angry yelling and the occasional scream. The entire road now consisted of people making their way in the same direction. Thousands of people all wearing the same bleak expression of fear and concern. Desperate for a view of what was ahead, she strode out across the road, around a dark blue Amazon van and onto the central reservation. She found one of the old black lamp posts that was mounted on a wide plinth and pulled herself up it so that she was about a metre taller than the crowd. The sight ahead filled her with despair.

Around Trafalgar the crowds simply ground to a halt. All the way up to Nelson's Column, Coco could just see people making no forward progress. Across the crowd were shouts and scuffles as people tried to push their way onwards towards the shelters. Coco looked back and saw that more and more people were heading in the same direction clogging the road. Coco hugged herself to the thin column of the lamp post and despaired.

"What can you see?" an elderly woman who still had a shopping trolley with her asked.

"It's rammed," Coco said. "I don't think we can get through."

"I bet I can," the old woman said mystically.

Coco shimmied down the lamp post and shoved herself back to the pavement. Pushing sideways against the crowd took her back to a black wooden screen that ran the length of the block and was flanked by four red phone boxes. Coco stood in the eddy that the blockade caused and tried to think. Charing Cross station was across the road, but she could see that the barriers were down and she could hear the rhythmic banging as the crowd tried to force them open.

On nothing more than an instinct, she took the emptier right-hand spur of the road which led to the North of Trafalgar Square. She picked her way around the back of the crowd, looking for an opening where she might be able to force her way through and to the shelters that lay beyond. But there was nothing. All she could do was take streets that kept her moving in an orbit around Whitehall. At one point she spotted a policeman, but he seemed to be running away from the centre and was being chased by several members of the public, seemingly all as desperate as her for answers. She crabbed her way across the next mile, a stitch building in her side until she found herself hemmed into a narrow road lined with offices on one side and a three-storey car park on the other. She tried to turn back but found herself penned in by the constant flow of bodies. It was useless. The thin street meant that the crowd had become even more dense, with people now jostling shoulder-to-shoulder. She found herself carried by the crowd until it pinched in again and her hands instinctively came up to her chest to act as a buffer.

"Why can't we move!" she half-asked, half-shouted as she felt her feet lifting and she was swayed to the side of the street.

"Fuckin' police," a young woman about her own age said, as she too was squashed in between the surge of the crowd.

"What – why aren't they helping us?"

"They're not letting us go past."

"We're getting kettled? What about the missiles?"

The woman couldn't answer as a break of movement in the fray saw her lifted and deposited ten metres away. Coco was swept against the wall and for a moment she felt her body pinned against a brick wall and the swirl of the crowd pushed against her. She groaned as she was ground against the wall. She tucked her head down and pushed her elbows out to create the smallest bubble of space around her stomach.

"Help! I'm pregnant!" she cried aloud, feeling utterly useless, as once again she felt her feet leave the pavement.

Just as she was struggling to keep her feet on the floor, she passed a set of stairs that led into the rear of the car park that ran alongside the road. A pair of strong hands grabbed her under the shoulders and yanked her up into the void. The gate at the top of the steps was shut, but she was free from the carnage for now. She turned and managed a breathless smile of gratitude towards the large Caribbean lady who had hauled her into the temporary sanctuary. Alongside her, there were three other women and at the back of the stairs a huge workman bulging out of his hi-vis waistcoat.

She felt the rawness of a scrape along her arm to match her bloody palms. Suddenly, she felt like she might start to cry, not from the pain but from the frustration. "How are we supposed to get to the shelters if they're keeping us here?" she asked, but the other occupants of the stairs had no answer. Coco looked at the mass of people at her feet as they continued to push and scream with fury.

💎 💎 💎 💎 💎

Brin had struggled to get into the McLaren. Bradford had opened the door and she'd assumed he was being chivalrous and started to get in, when he stopped her to explain that in the McLaren the driver came first, otherwise he'd have to climb over her to take his seat. Once he'd moved her out of the way he stepped in and slid himself across to the central driving seat, placing the B of the Bang case carefully onto the right-hand passenger seat. He pulled the dual belts over his shoulders and fastened them at his waist. Brin was still marvelling at the car's dihedral doors, but he urged her to get in.

"Do I just slide in?" she asked with a nervous giggle.

Bradford thought it was blindingly obvious how you got in, which didn't speak wonders for her intelligence. If this had been an IQ test a squirrel would probably have cracked it before her. The McLaren had three seats, one for the driver in the very middle of the car – boss man, numero uno. The passengers tucked themselves into one of the two low-slung bucket seats to the left and right, in much the same way that in a normal car you might slip a banana into side pockets. Brin struggled as she squatted low to get in.

"This is my first time in a McLaren," she said with a grunt – *big whoop*, it normally was Bradford thought. "Yikes, I don't think it's designed with someone with arthritis in mind," she laughed as she winced and levered her way into position.

"You've got arthritis?" Bradford asked with barely-concealed dismay, an image of Tabitha's toned arms popping into his mind.

"Yep, it's genetic. I take so many pills I rattle," she said.

"Oh," Bradford said and chewed at his lip. Then he reminded himself of the superiority of Brin's teeth. "Let's go! Let's go!" he said.

"Go where though? It's all so exciting! I feel like I'm in a book!"

"Or a film," Bradford corrected. What manner of idiot would want to be in a book when they could be in a film?

"Sure," Brin agreed neutrally.

"Hold tight," Bradford said, trying not to imagine a subterranean future where a puffy-knuckled Brin was passing him every jar of gherkins that she needed opening. That would be depressing, especially when you factored in the apocalypse. He fired the McLaren into life and gunned the accelerator until the yearning of the 6.1 litre engine hit a resonant frequency with the cocaine leaching from his nasal passageways into his bloodstream. Bradford turned to Brin and growled in a similar pitch and held the car on the clutch until white smoke started to billow from the tyres. The smell of rubber melting onto the tarmac filled the air. Bradford cackled and dropped the car's tiny handbrake and instantly felt himself being thrust back into the seat. Brin screamed and reached with both hands for the "Oh Shit!" handle, whereupon she found that Bradford had intentionally specced the car so it didn't have any. She settled for simply holding her hands out towards the dash and saying, "Oh Shit!" repeatedly.

Bradford got up to fifty-six miles per hour by the time he left the car park and drifted out onto the road, narrowly missing a scaffolding van. A wicked spike of adrenaline coursed through his veins as the back end of the F1 fishtailed across the road and beeps and shouts sounded out around them. He whooped and the sudden proximity of death did something to annul the impact of the cocaine and the shock he felt. He slowed the car to thirty and took a moment to mentally calculate the route. Down Brook Street, head to the corner of Hyde Park, through Piccadilly, down to Trafalgar Square then onto the Embankment. He decided to see how many speeding tickets he could pick up in the course of the journey. He was beginning to see the benefits of there not being a tomorrow.

"Don't go to Hyde Park," Brin said.

"Why not?"

"I was there earlier, it's *ba-na-nas* because of the Smash Capitalism protest."

"Oh fuck, fuck, fuck, fuck, fuck, fuckity bum cock fuck it! Why do they have to smash capitalism today? Or at all?" Bradford's internal sat nav revised the journey time to thirty minutes. That was still well within the margin of error. It was fine.

"Hey – why not just go round?"

"No! That'll take even longer!" he shouted with force and smacked the steering wheel with the palm of his hand. "FUCK!" Brin became very still.

"Listen…Bradford, I wonder if this project is the sort of thing that you actually need me for? Is it easier to circle back to the office?"

"No! You're perfect for the project, we just need to get to The Savoy as soon as possible. I don't want us to miss our connection. We're ok. We've got time. We're fine." It was fine.

Bradford looked up and noticed that Duke Street, which led down to Grosvenor Square was full with protestors with banners and the sort of haircuts that suggested they had opinions and were keen to share them. He nosed the McLaren into Duke Street and then spun the wheel taking them past the No Entry signs into Weighhouse Street. The engine grumbled at being kept under 1,000 RPM but cheered slightly as Bradford stomped the accelerator to take them over the cross streets. An Ocado delivery man gestured to the No Entry sign with a furious expression and Bradford gave him the Vs as he mounted the kerb and found the smallest of gaps to break through. Brin shrieked.

The pavements were still heavy with protestors as the McLaren idled at the lights outside Bond Street. Bradford noticed that the crowd seemed to be split between those who had placards and typical antifa style gear, then the others who just seemed like an assortment of regular Joes and Josephines. What he also noticed was how many of the people crossing in front of them seemed to be eyeing up the car, not with the yearning that Bradford was used to, but with a different sort of expression. It almost felt like contempt. Perhaps this is what it felt like to drive a Range Rover, Bradford thought. Suddenly, something hit the F1's window with a sharp crack, and Brin's shrieks rose to an even higher pitch as two more eggs splatted across the windscreen.

"Oi! Sod off!" Bradford shouted at the hooligan or hooligans, without opening the window. The cocaine urged him to leap out and deck the twat who'd thrown the eggs, but even the cocaine didn't think that it could win against several hundred people. Instead, he casually leaned on the central locking for the doors and vaguely gave a middle finger in the general direction of the eggman or eggwoman, earning *him*, Bradford Alderman VIIII – scion of the Alderman Retail Group – actual boos. Who booed outside of a pantomime? These unemployed toerag cucks, that's who. The light changed and he dropped the clutch, exploding forwards while simultaneously running the windscreen wipers, which only succeeded in leaving dirty smears of yolk across the glass.

"I don't like this," Brin said, and it looked like she was getting a bit teary-eyed – all from some bloody eggs, scattered boos and a few hundred murderous looks! It was going to be a long apocalypse with Knuckles. Bradford momentarily considered stopping and cutting her loose, but he didn't know what quality of flange he would come across between now and the exfil. *Better the flange you know*, he counselled himself and put his foot down as much as he was able.

The next thirteen minutes of driving consisted of more reversing than Bradford had done in the entire time he'd owned the F1. It was not a fun car to reverse, given that there was no rear-view mirror and Bradford's neck cramped unhappily as he leaned right over and checked behind him in the split rear windows, to make yet another U-turn to avoid yet another plug of protestors or yet another abandoned car. They were everywhere! At every pedestrian crossing and traffic light, the McLaren had been spat at, keyed, kicked and egged to the point where it was now more of a hepatitis omelette than a vehicle. As they travelled, Bradford noted that the agitation and panic levels of the crowd seemed to suggest they were also desperate to get to safety, but that was impossible – how would anyone know? These plebs weren't B of the Bang customers.

"Why don't we just park somewhere and walk?" Brin suggested for the fiftieth time, and Bradford had to admit to himself that he should have taken this advice ten minutes ago. His reluctance to get out was largely because he felt so foolish in what he was wearing. The car may be attracting attention and hate, but at least it was metal. He didn't want to be out there, surrounded by pond life and shielded only by a comically large £10,000 suit. In a fashion photo shoot for *The Times Rich List*, an outrageously tailored suit was just the thing, but on the street in the middle of a protest, it made him stand out in the wrong way. If any of the shops had been open, he would have gone and bought a more utilitarian outfit, but as it was, he felt that they'd committed to driving there now and they should just stick with it. They still had time.

He'd somehow managed to navigate them to the top of Haymarket, near the National Gallery. He was hoping that he could follow it around and then drop down onto the Strand and then on to the Embankment and the Savoy. Part of his brain was trying to work out which of the streets around here were pedestrianised, when he noticed a small gap open up in the crowd ahead and he dashed the car forward onto Orange Street. He didn't recognise it, but he knew it ran South and that was good enough. He groaned out loud as he saw more people completely blocking the road ahead. He turned to see if he could back out and felt his neck spasm. Through a fleeting break in the people, he saw a cordon of yellow-jacketed police with linked arms at the end of the street, sealing it off.

Bradford heard the chants and the whistles of the people and suddenly the sheer scale of the crowd dawned on him. They were being penned in by the police, presumably in the hope of controlling the rate and direction of the march. Bradford really had no option other than to keep the car crawling forward towards them. The car gradually nudged up against people as they went.

"What are you doing?" Brin asked. "You're hitting people! Stop the car! We should walk!"

"What else can I do, you stupid arse? I can't just abandon the F1 in the middle of a riot!" he replied as he kept the lightest touch he could on the car's greedy accelerator.

"Bradford, stop running people over!"

"No!"

Bradford wafted the accelerator, but the unruly panther under his foot could contain itself no longer and, in a moment, it lurched forward, throwing a number of people over the bonnet and pushing others to the sides. Screams rang out and fists rained onto the chassis from all angles as the crowd's anger redirected itself towards the gaudy hypercar. Bradford leant on the car's peevish horn but it only seemed to encourage them. People ducked down to peer into the windows and pressed their horrid faces to the glass while others banged on the doors and bonnet. Brin tried to placate them with a smile featuring those legendary teeth, but in the finest tradition of the dentally-challenged Brits – it only seemed to make them angrier.

Disappointingly, the cocaine had peaked, leaving Bradford alone with his deepening public pariahdom. He briefly felt disconnected from his body. Something about the situation reminded him of the warmth and belonging of sitting in Pops' Rolls Royce, ordering the chauffeur to drive through the car wash at the local garage over and over again. Snuggling deep into his seat as the swishy rollers advanced, the muffled oblivion of the foam, the noise of the machine which blocked out the bad thoughts and left everything sparkling. He remembered begging the chauffeur to go through just one more time, but being told that Pops wanted him to go back to work.

Cherry Doc Martins, blue Vans and off-brand white trainers thumped across the bonnet of the car to assess its sturdiness and once it had been established – they flooded onto the roof and started to jump. It didn't take long before others saw the opportunity to treat a legendary automobile like a trampoline. Bradford looked at Brin and saw that she was screaming as she stared at the car's roof, which had started to buckle with each new reveller. Without warning, the airbag in front of Brin suddenly burst out of the dashboard and struck her in the face, her screams muted by the large balloon trying to insert itself into her mouth. She looked open-mouthed in horror at Bradford. He looked back at Brin, and saw that the impact had dislodged some of her front teeth. It was the last straw.

Bradford Alderman VIIII, large-footed yet tiny man of action - threw the car into reverse and backed up with a squeal of tyres. Screams and shouts rang out in the narrow road as the crowd of twenty spilled forward off the roof, tumbling over the bonnet like boulders. He would have kept going but something, quite possibly someone, was trapped under the rear wheels and the F1 didn't have the torque to overcome the blockage. People gathered around the car again, but they were singing a different song now.

"Tip it! Tip it! Tip it!"

More took up the chant and in seconds the car was rocking, and Bradford suddenly regretted the day at the McLaren factory when he'd said in a bold voice that he wasn't going to have "Oh Shit!" handles. He held fast to the steering wheel as they were bounced violently from side to side, and then gradually lifted onto the hands of the protestors on one side of the vehicle. Once the car was lifted to knee height, more people poured in to add their muscle to the cause. He found himself tipping towards Brin as the car crunched and toppled at last, and a cheer arose from the crowd. Blood was rushing to his head, and he felt the shoulder straps cut into his clavicle. The B of the Bang case fell onto the roof. Brin's anguish reached fever pitch and Bradford considered again that it would have been better to have walked.

Suddenly the screams filled the car with alarming clarity, as Bradford found the door near him yanked open and torn off its upper hinges.

"Get out!" someone was leaning in and screaming in his face and tearing at his hair. He fumbled at the buckle and released it, just in time for more hands to enter the car and drag him out into the street.

"No! Put me down! Stop it! I'm a haemophiliac! My case! It has my medicine!" Bradford commanded impotently as he was hoisted into the air.

He turned in time to see Brin hanging onto her seatbelt to prevent herself being extricated by the mob. There were cries as some of the people who had been trapped underneath the car were dragged out.

"I'm one of you! I'm a protestor!" Bradford cried as he was pushed to the ground.

"In a fucking McLaren?" someone asked.

"That's not my whip! I stole it!" Bradford said, whimpering in his best roadman accent.

"Bullshit!" yelled another sceptic.

"Honestly! Believe me! I'm here to riot and protest! I saw that car while the owner was having a slash in the garage and I boosted it."

"What a load of crap," one of the people around him said.

"Smack him in the face," another suggested.

"Look, I'm down to riot and protest and all of those things. Keen to."

Someone took the advice and punched Bradford in the face. He felt a hot surge of shame and self-pity well inside himself. He wanted to sit down and tell the chauffeur what had happened and get him to drive through the car wash again. This was all so unfair. The missiles. These stupid people in the way. The assault. If they'd just let him go then he could get to his evac and then this stupid city and these horrible people could explode already! Bradford's rat energy asserted itself and his inner-Wizard fed him a line.

"There's thirty thousand pounds of cocaine in that car!"

There was a swift lull in the fracas, and the people who were queueing up to offer him bodily harm suddenly found themselves more interested in checking if what he said was true. The stampede only created greater interest and, like flotsam in a rampaging river, Bradford found himself tossed aside and discarded into the foot of a stairwell where he landed at the feet of a rather beautiful lobster.

HELLO, B OF THE BANG, HOW CAN I HELP YOU?

GREG EMERGED FROM the fire and into the frying pan. He had anticipated that he might have to speedily sneak away from the office onto the streets of Millbank, so that his co-workers didn't spot him and make him answer tricky questions like, "Have you inadvertently started the apocalypse?" But as he was swallowed into the chaos on the streets, he realised he could have been wearing a hat that said, "I Am Greg, Harbinger of The End Times" and nobody would have noticed.

The duty phone vibrated constantly against his thigh as he took in the scenes of carnage on the usually quiet backwater of Erasmus Street. From where he stood, he could see three separate fires and flurries of papers blew through the streets. There was a harsh smell of burning oil from down the street that made his eyes feel gritty. He couldn't spot any of his colleagues near the B of the Bang building, which was now casually smouldering with a steady flow of white smoke billowing out of the windows. Given its normally molten temperature, Greg wasn't sure if it would even feel that much different in the corridors. He was sure it would all be fine. Meg, Serge and Jennifer were probably yomping their way to safety at that very instant. They were almost certainly not sitting around like vacant idiots, waiting for him to return while their architectural hair-dos and rock band t-shirts flambéed.

Despite his confidence that it would all be fine, Greg hid in an alley opposite the building and watched the entrance. He was beginning to wonder if arson had been a good choice. He would have run it through his sharp legal compliance mind, but Greg had realised close to the beginning of his career that his job was essentially pointless and he had allowed his brain to atrophy ever since. A legal compliance officer fulfilled much the same function as a fire blanket. There was a vague agreement by everyone that you ought to have one, but no one really wanted to think about it until there was a disaster. In that eventuality, the idea was to throw the fire blanket/legal compliance officer over the blaze and walk away as fast as possible. Essentially, his purpose was so that the organisation could claim that someone somewhere had read the instructions. It didn't matter if the legal compliance officer hadn't read the instructions, after all, no one else was going to know – his role was simply to exist and therefore show other organisations that they were the sort of organisation that had people who read instructions. Arson was by no means a conventional choice, but Greg was already probing the clauses around temporary insanity and arson played nicely into that. He also felt that fire was the primary instance of a reboot. If anything, what he had done was a service to architecture.

As he mused, Greg caught a shock of blue hair emerging from the office, followed by several other stupid haircuts, and he heaved a huge and unexpected sigh of relief. Damage to property Greg could forgive himself, but damage to person was a slightly different ballgame. Except Serge. He would gladly have murdered Serge. The band of idiots stood on the street looking back up at the building, they then turned with the flow of the crowd and followed Westward. Greg watched them dissolve into the tide of people flowing past and then pointed himself East towards Parliament.

The roads around Erasmus Street were gridlocked. Some drivers remained in their cars, leaning on their horns in the futile hope that traffic would clear, but Greg could see that many of the vehicles further down the road had been abandoned. A white Audi Q7 was left hastily on the kerb with the engine still running. He peered inside and saw a selection of bags spread across the back seat, alongside a large TV. Greg wondered whether or not to steal the car solely on the principle of the thing, but then realised that he'd only be able to escape a few metres before joining with the congealed traffic. Twenty metres down the road Greg passed an abandoned bus. He saw there was a solitary pensioner stubbornly sitting on the reserved seats at the front, his hands folded on top of a walking stick. Greg wondered briefly if he was dead, so he stepped onto the bus.

"Are you okay?"

"Don't make much difference to me if it is or it isn't," the old man said gnomically.

"Right. Do you need help?" Greg persisted.

"Do you?" the man replied and Greg was forced to concede that he may have a point.

He paused getting off the bus as a group of teenagers dressed in black surged past. He just caught a snippet of their chat, "…get to the East End…". A young Japanese family were hurrying along the street, the mother's face was drawn and the father kept a protective arm on his wife as they went. They were all dragging wheeled suitcases and the little girl in front was having trouble keeping hers from tipping from side-to-side as her mum and dad urged her onwards. Greg could feel his guilt mounting. A moped weaved between the stationary cars and Greg watched as a businessman stepped dangerously close, waving a thick stack of money in the face of the driver, who promptly swiped the notes from his hand and sped off.

It was all too much. Greg pushed himself into the cover of a jewellery shop window and panicked when he saw the shutters coming down, potentially trapping him inside. He dropped his head and skipped out from underneath. As another wave of people approached, Greg turned into a side road and saw an old man's pub called The Pheasant beckoning him like an oasis. He recalled having had a few in there after a work thing once, so he jogged up to the entrance and pushed at the heavy wooden doors.

He couldn't believe his luck when they opened to reveal a quiet and orderly pub, completely at odds with the anarchy going on just a few metres away. There was just one patron inside, an old man with the paper spread in front of him, geological sediment lines of froth marking his slowly nursed pint. Greg nodded at him as he looked up, but the man just went back to reading his paper with its outdated pre-apocalypse news. Behind the bar a middle-aged woman was leaning on the counter, craning her neck to look at the TV mounted above her station, which was showing aerial footage of a plane stranded in the Thames. She slowly panned around to face Greg, her head remaining cocked at the strange angle.

"I saw that," Greg said pointing at the TV, remembering the waves in the Thames.

"Saw it? It looked like it landed on you, love," the landlady said with a raucous guffaw, which she directed at the customer reading his paper. "Doesn't it Rob? I said it looked like the plane landed on him. You've got egg on your hair."

Rob nodded.

Greg was too busy reading the text splashed across the screen to worry about eggs in hair.

"Wait – so, the plane crashed in the Thames?"

"That's about the size of it."

"And it was the Prime Minister's plane? Wait! The Prime Minister is dead?"

"Nothing wrong with his reading, is there Rob?"

Rob nodded.

"So, is that why everyone out there is panicking?" Greg asked, a spring of hope bubbling in his soul.

"He's sharp, isn't he Rob? He wants to watch he doesn't cut himself! Rob?"

Rob nodded.

"Oh my God! That's...that's, well, it's really something." Greg said and lay his head on the cool wood of the bar. He was saved. By some outrageous quirk of fate, the Prime Minister's dramatic death had trumped Greg's minor faux pas. It was truly the greatest day to bury bad news about the world ending.

"That and the missiles," the landlady said.

"Sorry? Missiles?"

The landlady gestured at the screen and Greg watched a clip from TikTok play on screen. A handsome Asian man jumped on a desk and started to speak – with the sound off, it was easier to focus on his face which seemed pained. Greg could lip-read the word missiles, then the camera shook, bedlam erupted and the clip ended.

Missiles from North Korea. Hwasong-17s. Limited time to get across London. Upload the missile footage. Tell the customer where to meet for exfil. Training exercise number one.

"What can I get you, love?"

"How many lagers will forty pounds buy, please?" Greg replied.

"Three."

"Three lagers please. And I'm going to put my head on the bar again."

Greg returned his head to the bar and imagined that the bar towel was a smoothing cold compress being pressed against his head by a beautiful and sympathetic woman who understood the valour in Greg's complex and unique soul, a woman who hated Serge and was prepared to overlook arson.

"Forty-one pounds, please."

Greg retrieved two credit cards from his wallet and held them aloft.

"Can you put ten on the black one and thirty on the Aqua one?"

"Cash only I'm afraid. Machines aren't working. Wi-Fi's a bit widdly as well, if you want to get on it's just pheasantpluckercustomer – all one word - and then robsgotabigknob with a "k" for the password."

Down the bar, Rob chuckled. Greg pulled the only twenty-pound note from his wallet. He then took off his right shoe and under the insole removed another twenty. He rummaged amongst his pocket fluff for a pound, found a two-pound coin, passed that and the notes over and waved away the change.

"Much obliged."

Greg noticed stairs at the back of the room, and carried his triangle of pints carefully up the irregular steps and into a large and empty dining space. The walls were festooned with stuffed pheasants and above the fireplace there was a large decorative rifle which some wag had stuck a large "Bang" flag into the barrel. Greg took a seat at a table with a view of the stairs, a concern creeping in that *they* might be coming for him, although his paranoia hadn't identified precisely who *they* might be yet.

When he was sat down, he checked the walls for CCTV before leaning in to address the pints.

"Lads. I'm in deep shit. I could do with some inspiration. It would also be good if one of you could get my heart to be normal. Cheers."

He picked the right-most pint and sank nearly two thirds of it with a few gulps. It was cold and a bit flat, but the alcohol got to work. Greg shut his eyes hard. He finished the pint while his eyes were still shut. There was a moment of uncertainty where his innards threatened to quickly become outtards, but he breathed through the moment and when he opened his eyes, he had recaptured some of his equilibrium. His heartbeat was still being squirmy and melodramatic, but at least some of the fires inside his brain were doused. He felt in his suit jacket for his phone, but realised with a pang that it was currently melting on the desk in Meeting Room B.

After another thirty seconds of sitting with his eyes shut, he felt strong enough to look at the duty phone. He took it from his pocket and became mesmerised watching it vibrate. Every five seconds it would pause for a moment and then start to vibrate again, with another unknown number displayed on the screen. Greg waited for another pause and then hit the red telephone button. He watched as the phone returned to calm for a second, before it began to ring again. Greg lay the phone on the table and drank the second pint while he watched the phone buzz along the surface towards the cutlery pot. The number of missed calls moved from ^%%^ to $%^^. At the end of the second pint, Greg decided that thinking was getting him nowhere and it was time for action. He placed the phone next to his ear and answered it.

"B of the Bang, how can I help you?" he said in his politest voice.

"Hello?" said a woman's incredulous voice, "Is this a real person?"

"Yes, I'm Greg. Can I take your customer number please?"

"Oh wait, is it on the briefcase – wait, please hold on, don't go anywhere – it's 2984BA."

"Let me type that into the system, hold a second."

Greg mimed typing something into a computer.

"Can I take your name?"

"Yes, Eulalia Kent."

Greg realised why the name might have seemed familiar.

"Your Highness, how can I help?"

"Well, I want to get in the bunker, obviously! The message I got said that I was a Silver Member, but that can't be right. You can't expect the royal family to be Silver Members. It's not like we can't pay."

"Let me check our files," Greg said, and once again he mimed typing things into a keyboard.

"It would appear that Silver Member is the level that you selected when you registered. I'm sure you understand that no upgrades are allowed on the day of an alert."

"Well, no! Actually. I don't understand! You're telling a member of the royal family that you won't save them?"

Greg felt like he had a reasonable idea of what it was like to be shunned.

"I'm afraid there's nothing I can do – our system is locked now until the end of the alert."

"Who's your manager? Let me speak to the owner of the company."

"I'm afraid he's currently unavailable. Thank you for being a B of the Bang customer, our best wishes to you."

"Best wishes? What am I-"

Greg hung up. His heart was hammering in his chest. He picked up and drained half of the third pint. Before he could convince himself not to, he answered the phone again.

"Hello, B of the Bang – how can I help you?"

"Wait – there's someone there, finally! Right - is this a joke, or is this really happening?"

"Can I take your customer number please? You'll find it on your case or on the welcome email you received when you registered."

"Yes, my customer number is 4100SQ."

"And your name please?"

"Roland Barthe – B-A-R-T-H-E."

Greg fancied he knew the name, he'd probably seen it emblazoned on the side of cranes, or lighting up the sky over a building.

"Mr Barthe, yes, how can I help?"

"What do you think? Are you serious? I'm not calling for a chat, am I? Is this real – is there really a missile coming?"

Greg paused and really tried to think.

"Hello? Are you there? There's no one there."

He hadn't tried honesty yet. Bugger it.

"No. It's not real. My name is Greg Terde and I'm the legal compliance officer for B of the Bang. This morning, I was hosting training and rather than working on the red learner system, they were working on the green live system. I'm so, so, so sorry. Genuinely. I feel…awful and I am so sorry for the disruption and panic this must have caused. I can only offer you an apology, which must sound very weak, but I am. I am sorry."

Greg grimaced and waited for the explosion. He wasn't sure what he was expecting, but the catharsis given in return for his magnanimous honesty didn't seem to have materialised.

"Hello? Mr Barthe?"

All he could hear was a measured inhale and exhale of breath as Roland Barthe computed what he'd been told.

"Hello?"

"I'm here. You're trying to tell me that this whole thing isn't real?"

"Yes, it was a mistake."

"A *mistake*."

"A booboo. Of sorts. If you will."

"London is tearing itself to pieces, the Prime Minister is dead and you have taken over my entire morning…because of a booboo?"

"Yes. A snafu."

More silence. More breathing. Greg started to wish he'd just scream at him and get it over with. He suspected that he might have to get used to people screaming at him, so he may as well start now.

"Ok, *Mr Terde*. How much?"

"Sorry?" Greg replied.

"How much?"

"How much for what?"

"For the bunker, you chump. Do you know how much I'm worth? No? I'll tell you. I have a property portfolio worth more than three billion pounds. Three billion, Greg. Do you think I've got this far and not known a shakedown when I see one? So, I'll ask you one more time – how much do you now want for the spot in the bunker?"

"Shakedown?"

"How much?"

"It's not real. I goofed. The trainees technically, they did the goof."

"Greg – I'm not an idiot. It's all over TikTok. So, I'll ask you one final time - how much do you want?"

Greg hung up.

No one would believe him. For the next four calls he answered everything with searing honesty. No, it wasn't real. It was his own stupidity. He was hungover. He'd sung in a jazz club. He'd paid a cat return surcharge. He was pathetic. Choking on a gherkin. Sick in a sink. Stupid. Blithering. Wrong. Serge. No one believed him. They called him an extortionist. A blackmailer. They promised to find him and remove his entrails with a blunt stick, an axe, a P&O ferry. But when it came down to it, all of them wanted to know one thing: how much?

"Gold. Gold coins. There's fifty thousand pounds of gold in your case. I want that," Greg said and put his hands together in prayer to whatever low-rate deity would listen to a scourge such as himself.

"Done."

As the lager joined up with the remnants of the alcohol from Greg's Book Club night out, he formulated a plan. There was no forcing the genie back into the bottle. He would admit that he had played a minor role in the blooper that had led to the alerts being sent out, but *sent out they had been*. He couldn't unsend them. And even when he tried to tell people it was a mistake, no one believed him. They'd seen it on TikTok. They'd heard it on the radio. Their friend had sent them something on WhatsApp. The boulder was rolling down the hill and standing in the way would only result in an unpalatable Greg jam. And if the boulders were determined to go down the hill, then Greg felt his new role was to facilitate. This path even offered a small but viable chink of hope. With enough gold came possibilities. Gold was escape. Gold was hope. Gold was a legal defence fund. So, Greg decided to steal a boat.

"LIVERPOOL LIME STREET"

COBRA WAS BEING fumigated, so the first and most significant meeting of William McCartney's premiership was held next door in Cabinet Office Briefing Room B. No one in Whitehall ever called it COBRB, although that was technically its name. William fancied that he could taste the pungent insecticide from next door and it brought on a bout of sneezing. Six sneezes consecutively – not a record, but certainly not without merit, and he accorded himself three runs in a pinned note on his phone's Memos app. He noted with satisfaction that India's nasal run total – a number he would have previously said was unassailable – was now within sight. This had truly been an incredible series. He sneezed once more, but denied himself the single out of respect for the game.

In reality, COBRB was every bit as unimpressive as its alphabetically-advantaged neighbour – it was just a meeting room, marginally wider than the large central boardroom table inlaid with monitors, surrounded by twenty-five extra-wide leather chairs that left not an inch of space available. On the wall by the door, a bank of screens lay dormant awaiting input. On the screens an animated government seal bounced around the perimeter. William watched as the seal nearly slid neatly into the corner of the screens and wondered if he could ask for the remote. If he was going to wait, he may as well have the news on.

The chairs were so bulky, and the room so constricted, that anyone attempting to lean back in them would hit their head on the wood-panelled walls. Only the three chairs at the far end of the table could recline, a fact Fenton Crossley had made great play of during previous meetings. William remembered the unrelenting hours that he'd been forced to attend mind-numbing seminars on threats, real and imagined. Or worse, talks about the impact of tough economic times! Or blasted COVID and those germ nerds suddenly revelling in being able to explain what an R value was.

In those meetings, he had sat in one of the chairs pinned in on the opposite wall and was never asked to have any actual input. In fact, Crossley would often shush him like a child if he attempted to speak. This room seemed to always be cursed with stifling heat, regardless of the weather outside and, often, all he wanted to do was put his head on the table and enter a dreamless sleep, but he wasn't allowed. William's presence in the room always seemed like a procedural formality, like the arrival of the buffet at lunch. Well, they would hear him now. *I am McCartney, hear me roar!* He sneezed twice and noted the run on his app.

William tipped his chair back and then popped upright and the leather made a bassy ripping noise. William smiled at the security detail by the door, but he was immune to his presence. He'd asked the block-shaped man to wait outside the room but it appeared that he didn't march to William's beat. At least not yet. William marvelled at the frame of the man. The only logical conclusion was that he must have been brought in as a child and raised inside the room. Yes, he'd have to find out how to control men such as this, because it wasn't seemly for a Prime Minister to not be able to command those around him. There was a knock and the door-like security guard turned to the actual door and opened it a crack. Outside, another security guard whispered something and the door opened further to reveal a slash of red hair and a five-foot seven-inch scowl.

"Jenny! Oh darling, thank God!" William said, unaware until that point of how much emotion was sitting in his chest. The sight of his wife, who would have taken an axe to anyone who described her as a figure of comfort, brought an unfamiliar feeling to William's breast.

"Bill! Oh, sweet Bill! Poor Fenton! Dead!" she cried, as she edged her way around the room, mashing her voluminous handbag into every chair as she went, while William stood patiently with his arms outstretched awaiting her embrace. Finally, she reached him and pulled him into an iron hold. He felt the ripple of her fine muscular arms and his head fell to her chest.

"Cry if you must," she whispered.

"I mustn't. I'm fine. But, thank you." Jenny broke off and turned to the security guard.

"All right King Kong, off you fuck. The Prime Minister and I need to discuss matters in private."

"Protocol Ma'am, someone needs to be with the Prime Minister at all times while we're at Critical."

"Someone will be with him, you ridiculous clot."

"Someone on the security team, Ma'am."

"Who's he safer to be with than his wife? And, do tell me what your security clearance is? Because unless you're DV or higher then I suggest you either leave the room or pull your ears off and blind yourself with the chunks because what we're about to discuss is the hushest of the hush and I would so hate to have to get MI6 to pull you apart neuron by neuron to find out what you know. Although I suspect it wouldn't take long."

The guard beheld Jenny with a flat expression that managed to convey both his respect and his murderous intent.

"I'm going to step outside to the lavatory, Sir."

"Excellent choice, see if you can rustle up a cup of coffee as well. Try not to eat the kettle," Jenny suggested.

"Yes, very good, you have my permission," William said as the man somehow managed to wedge himself through the door.

William and Jenny left a pause for appearance's sake and then once they knew the door was properly shut, Jenny screamed and danced on the spot. William whirled around in his chair and jiggled his legs in the air, cooing with joy. Jenny threw herself on the boardroom table and writhed around, oblivious to the glasses she knocked over.

"We did it, Booby!"

"We only went and did it!" William agreed, joy splashed across his face. "Darling, I need to know: does that mean it will happen today?"

"We will have to see, but get me into Number 10 and I will honour our agreement."

"YES! YES! YES! We've only bloody gone and done it!" William shrieked with excitement.

"I don't remember saying you could shout like that. Why are you being like this? Is it because you're not turned on? It is, isn't it? Let's get you switched on," Jenny stood and held out her hand, William abashedly held out his left hand, which Jenny took in her own. She reached for his ring finger and gently rolled William's wedding ring around, so that the tiny inset diamond faced away from him and a minute black opal winked up at him instead. William's face became serious. Jenny turned his palm over and started to trace circles.

"Are you ready, Teddy?"

"Yes, Mummy."

"Round and round the garden, like a…"

"Teddy bear."

Jenny mimed her hand taking steps up William's arm and said, "One step, two step, and a tickly under there!"

Without pageantry, she drove her clenched fist into his genitals. He doubled over and exhaled a long high-pitched "Achh!" into the room. As he fell spluttering to all fours, Jenny located and stood on his left hand, lifting her other foot off the ground so that all of her weight was on the planted foot, and twisted delicately on a knuckle.

William's groans ran from simple pain to a strangulated pleasure.

"Fortunately, there's things I need you to do for me William, so you can be grateful that all of your precious little digits will make it through today unscathed. Tell your Goddess what happened – what do you know?"

"Can The Goddess get off my finger? I think it's broken."

"The Goddess will get off when she's good and ready, won't she Teddy?"

"Yes…Goddess. What do you want?"

"Oh, that's simple, William – I want the world. I want to step out from the wings and stand centre-stage in the spotlight. Now, tell me what you know."

Jenny hopped on the spot and William grunted again and in-between pained panting he outlined everything that he'd managed to glean. The plane that had ditched in the Thames was RAF Voyager, Crossley's jet, he'd survived the initial impact in part because of the brilliance of the pilots, but he'd then succumbed to a heart attack as they evacuated. The nation was at Critical threat level and they were convening an emergency meeting.

"That explains the queue of ministers and special advisers outside. And? Are you officially the Prime Minister?"

"Yes, Goddess. Interim."

"Ooh, interim. I like that. If you're a good boy today and give me *what I want*, then maybe I'll be interim later on. Would you like that?"

"Yes, Goddess."

"Oooh, so have you got to toddle up to the palace and see Pinky?"

"Not while we're at Critical, all bets are off, Goddess. Pinky and the rest of the Wibbles have all been evacuated to the Isle of Man." There was a pause while William sneezed six times, but he sensibly decided not to access his phone while the Goddess was on his hand, though he did make a mental note. Three more for England, the chase was on!

"But if and when things calm down, then you go and see Pinky and he gives you a dusting off?"

"It'll probably be an election."

"Interesting. What might stop the election?" she asked as she hopped again.

"Ahhhhh! Ow! Sorry Goddess, nothing democratic. Maybe something procedural?"

Jenny spun again on her heel, eliciting one more shriek of pain from the interim Prime Minister, before she buffeted her way past the chairs and back to the door, throwing it open.

"Come in."

She returned to William's side as an assortment of white men in varying degrees of decrepitude shuffled through the door and found a space around the table. Clearly, it didn't matter which chair they all took, but for these men, which chair they got mattered very much indeed, so there was a fair amount of covert jostling. The special advisors were easy to spot because they never stopped tapping furiously on phones, while squashing folders of indeterminate paper under their arms. They also opted to lean on the walls in case their importance saw them called out into another meeting more significant than this one. The members of the cabinet were even easier to spot because they all looked like they had been exhumed and reanimated by hobbyists.

By the time she took her seat next to William, Jenny was impressed to see that he had regained his composure, although from her vantage point she could see that he was sporting a full erection from her attentions. He reached gingerly with his right hand for a bottle of fizzy water which spumed everywhere when he clumsily opened it, cradled in his left arm. He dried most of it off with his suit sleeve before it could make its way into the table top consoles. He smiled shakily at her and took a sip, which went the wrong way and snorted out of his nostrils. This presaged a coughing fit which required Jenny to slap him on the back, although she didn't *need* to hit him quite as hard as she did.

"I'm fine…fine…*cup!*" William managed to exhale through hiccups, saliva and extravagant swallows of air, while the rest of the room looked on, rapidly calculating the next step in the chain of command.

The MP for Wirral South had been forced to stand due to a lack of chairs. He partially raised his hand and began, "Could I just ask why…"

"Gentlemen," Jenny interrupted. "I feel it would be appropriate to be upstanding and observe a minute's silence in memory of Fenton Crossley, a man we all knew, admired and loved. A man whose passing leaves our nation immeasurably poorer."

Several aggrieved looks were exchanged across the room, as chairs were once again batted back to allow everyone to stand. William subtly picked up a folder of papers to hold across his swollen crotch. When he stood, he did so with a hunch to his back. For one minute, the tiny room was silent apart from the sound of phones vibrating, day apnoea and the *hiccupping* of the nation's most powerful man. Jenny took her seat first and thanked the room. William sat quickly, his face red. Jenny reached under the table and squeezed his crotch.

"Ok, what do we know, Mike?" Jenny asked Mike Whittaker, Fenton Crossley's Chief of Staff, who looked up, initially at William for guidance.

"Well? *Hic!*" William said. Whittaker pursed his lips but he was politically astute enough to recognise that his only path to survival in the post-Crossley Number 10 was an acceptance of the new order, whatever that order turned out to be.

"What we're hearing is that the pilots believe that the plane was brought down by a bird strike. In short, we don't think it was terrorism, but equally we're not prepared to rule it out, yet. For a plane crash in London there were miraculously few injuries, couple of broken arms and legs, and a DM reporter live streamed the crash and managed to catch one of the *Times'* editors shitting himself. I've sent the footage onto you on Telegram. Oh, and the Richmond Rowing Club lost a boat with some members who were caught trying to row where a plane was trying to park."

"Tom, what are the populace saying?"

Tom Bachmann, head of communications for Number 10 was a quick study and realised that, for now at least, Jenny held the power.

"Social media sentiment on the crash is currently calm, surprisingly. Memes are mostly of the add-a-union-jack-to-your-profile sort of gash. 'RIP Crossley' is trending across most platforms. Florists on The Strand are price-gouging. Pretty predictably, people are leaving pork pies at the end of Downing Street, never mind that it was probably a pie that saw him off. The alt truthers and their conspiracy theories haven't floated to the surface yet, but they will. Remains to be seen what sort of panic that will cause."

"*Hiccup!*"

"What else?"

Several people across the room looked awkwardly from one to another, with most wordlessly nominating Mike as the one to deliver the information.

"Out with it," Jenny demanded.

"We're…we're getting some awkward questions from special interests," Mike said.

"Awkward how?"

"Some donors want to know what we know about this North Korean missile situation."

"And what do we know about it?" Jenny asked.

"Well, that's it – it's total bullshit. Some extraction company called B of the Bang sent out a series of alerts to their customers, but it looks like it's nonsense. They sent alerts to their customers saying things like the French have detonated a dirty bomb in London and that North Korea have lobbed a load of Hwasong-17s at the rest of the world. Toby Kitchener got an alert saying that there was a meteor headed for Peckham. It's all bollocks but the money is still panicking."

"That's probably what's keeping social media in line around Crossley," Tom chipped in. "Most people are sharing videos of a billionaire telling his staff to go home and wait for the end. Then there's another one with a woman dressed as a lobster who is getting traction from the C2DEs. Hashtag "I'm with the lobster" is trending. We should keep an eye on that."

"So, what's ruffling the donors' feathers?" Jenny asked.

"Well, *they* don't know that it's bollocks. Not yet. It will all come out obviously when London fails to explode."

"*Hiccup*! 'Scuse me."

"Okay, we need to weed out the room or I'm in danger of asphyxiating from Lynx Africa and halitosis. Honestly, we'd be better off in COBRA with the smell of you all. All advisors apart from Mike and Tom fuck off and all non-cabinet MPs can wait outside too."

There were murmurs of dissent, but gradually the non-combatants in the room picked up their stuff and made it seem like they had more important places to be. By the time they'd shuffled out, the council was reduced to seven. Tom, Mike and David from the special advisers, Colin Heed, Minister of Defence and Sam Worthington, Home Secretary. Then there was Jenny and William. As the door shut, Mike gamely tried to regain control of the room.

"Look, Jenny. I appreciate that you've always been active in William's political life, but we need to come to an understanding about who is playing what role here."

"Good idea Mike, should we discuss what your role is? You were Fenton's C.o.S., but it may not have escaped your attention that he's now being ground down into filling for a novelty gout-flavoured pie. Tom, same goes for you. David, I have no real idea who you are…"

"Well, my…"

"I didn't say I wanted to know," Jenny interrupted.

"*Hiccup!*"

"Or from you. Colin, Sam, I think we know each other well enough to say that you hate William and would stab him in the back at the first opportunity. Figuratively and metallically. But let's be clear, today – and only today - we have an opportunity. Mike, Tom, David - under William's leadership you'll have a job. Maybe not the job you have now, but a job. You'll be paid ridiculously well and you'll have access to power, by which I mean me. Colin, Sam – you know you don't have the backing to get to the top without shafting each other and all that's going to do is tear the party a new arsehole. And it's our great good fortune that we already have one of those…"

Jenny waited for a beat and William duly filled the silence with a hiccup, then she sat back while the others in the room calculated this shift in the possibilities. Could it happen? William McCartney a puppet PM with Jenny's hand up his arse?

"What is it you're trying to say, Jenny?" Colin asked. "William – what do you think?"

"He doesn't. Not unless I tell him to," Jenny answered and William micro-shrugged at Colin in agreement with Jenny and smiled.

"Fucking hell. Blink twice if you need rescuing mate," Colin said.

"What I'm trying to say Colin is that this nation has lost a beloved leader in extremely suspicious circumstances, possibly as a result of an enemy at our door. There may be missiles being launched that threaten our sovereign way of life. Our country has not been thus imperilled since the Nazis, Covid or the advent of the gender reveal party."

There was a silence as each of the men tried to establish precisely what was going on. Mike was the first to break.

"But…there is no threat. It looks like it's just going to end up being a very bad day at the B of the Bang office. What do you see as the opportunity exactly?"

"The opportunity is what we make it. The truth is as we need it to be. The thing about being in power is that the rules are what we make them. I'm offering you a historic moment. You can choose if your response is, "Russian warship, go fuck yourself" or "This looks like a bad day at the office"?"

"But you're not answering my question – I think I'm right in saying that we're all interested in being involved, but what is it that you're proposing?"

"Among other things: war."

"With who?"

"Fear."

Tom smirked. "Aren't we still fighting the war against their neighbour, Terror?"

"Tom, the War on Terror has been the single smartest war that anyone has ever started. It sharpens the public focus. It justifies any attack. It sanctions every expense. Plus, we can never lose. A phalanx of Fearites is unlikely to loom off the Surrey coast in the next decade."

"Surrey doesn't have a coast, you're thinking of Sussex," William interjected and then looked up and saw the molten fury on his wife's face and withered visibly. "You were right, the Surrey coast is correct."

"But what I don't get is: *who* is afraid?" Colin said.

"Everyone we want to be afraid. Look, I'm not suggesting anything improper or even anything that doesn't make sense. I'm simply saying that we respond to the situation we are facing with all due reverence. Our former Prime Minister is dead. Our shores are threatened with missiles. We would be doing the public a disservice if we reacted as if all of this wasn't real."

The room ground to a halt. Mike was thinking, if you squinted you could see a certain logic to what Lady Macbeth was saying. Tom was onboard and had been since he'd been told that he could keep his job. He had a mortgage he intended to pay and a dealer that he didn't want to disappoint. The MPs were calculating and positing, wondering which morals would need to be shredded to go along with this plan. Gradually, they each retreated into their shared political faith: it was always better to be on this side of the door than the other.

"We would need a slogan," Tom said as William hiccupped again.

"Shut up William. Go on."

"It's a Pavlovian thing, give them a three-word slogan and they go limp because they're so busy trying to keep the three important things in their head. Add a fourth thing and they forget how to breathe. Hands, Face, Space. Something like that," Tom said. Jenny nodded.

"Twist one they already know," Mike said. "See It, Say It, Sorted."

"Stop, Drop, Roll," Colin added.

"Catch It, Bin It, Kill It," Sam put in.

"No, that's too clinical. It really needs to drive the fear agenda home. Suspect. Dread. Alarm. That sort of thing. It doesn't matter if you tell them not to do those things, because all they'll hear is dread and alarm," Mike said.

"Keep Calm And Don't Explode," William ventured.

"Better Dread Than Dead," Jenny said.

"Yes. That could work, although it's four words and they won't breathe. But if we tell them that it's *good* to be afraid because it could keep them all alive, some version of Better Dread Than Dead could work," Tom said.

"We can workshop the details, are you in?" Jenny asked.

"Better Dread Than Dead," Mike replied.

"Everyone?" Jenny asked.

As one, the room intoned: "Better Dread Than Dead."

SOME HELL BELOW US

THE RESIDENTS OF Knightsbridge weren't panicking because panic implied that you were late to know about something, and that simply wouldn't do. Unfortunately for the Sloanes, the panic had found them. The Smash Capitalism protest in Hyde Park had split in two when the news of the plane crashing in the Thames came in. One rumour went through the crowd saying the plane had been shot down. Another rumour said someone was using the protest as a cover to launch missiles. Whichever rumour you heard; most people decided that today it was probably better to be somewhere other than London.

The police weren't expecting the crowd to move from the park and they initially tried to corral the protestors where they'd gathered, which made them even more determined to get out. Some protestors forced their way out of the eastern edge, demolishing Speakers' Corner as they went. The rest pushed south and headed into Knightsbridge. The panic only doubled as the crowd learned on the hoof that the downed plane belonged to the Prime Minister. Crossley wasn't beloved by any stretch, but after nearly ten years he was at least familiar – like the racist, handsy uncle who appeared only at weddings and funerals. Did you wish he was different? Of course. Did you wish him dead in a plane crash? Only occasionally.

With the kindling laid and the firelighters set, Rashid's video dropped like a lit match and the fire took hold instantly. Somehow it all seemed too credible, too aligned. Even the wait-and-seers took up the sprint when they heard that there was a missile heading for

London that only billionaires were being warned about. Wasn't that just fucking typical? Didn't an exclusive 4 Minute Warning just for the yacht-botherers make so much *sense*? In the crowd who had decided to head south there was an unspoken feeling that Westminster was where they would find answers - precisely the same hope that had disappointed millennia of Brits. From start to finish, the evacuation of the park and the genesis of the Great Panic took around eleven minutes and crushed thirteen people.

When she exited the lift on the ground floor of One Hyde Park, HRH Princess Eulalia was mildly surprised to find that she was wearing a blue New York baseball cap and a vast Barbour wax jacket that reached to just above her knees, covering a classic black Adidas tracksuit and her faithful Nike Vaporflys. The coat was one of her father's cast-offs, an heirloom of immeasurable sentimental value for Lally. It still had a Locket wrapper in the pocket, a pathetic scrap of connection worn to the width of an atom after too long of Lally running it between her fingers like a tiny comfort blanket.

She didn't remember getting changed to go out, so some muscle memory must have taken over. Paired with dark sunglasses and a focused don't-talk-to-me walk, it was an effective way of limiting gawping from the people on the street, but also perhaps hinting that, yes, she was someone special. She had Sennheiser HD 820 headphones perched on her head, with no music playing. She was grateful for the perfection of the noise-cancellation as she looked out into London and saw chaos swarming past her building. She thumbed her phone and dialled. She listened to the full complement of rings as #1 once again refused to take her call.

"Bugger," she said into the glass atrium of One Hyde Park. She peered out behind a giant fiddle-leaf fig and watched as people trampled each other through the pinch points of the gates by the building, forcing their way into Knightsbridge. A constant mucky stream of humanity – *Her People*, she reminded herself – fled past the windows to a soundtrack of sealed-off silence. She reached into the inner pocket of the Barbour, retrieved the hip flask and took half of its contents in one pull. The shock of seeing what was actually happening at ground level hit Lally hard, and she felt the shock of quite how pissed she had become from her recent drinking and felt the hunger of how much more drunk she wanted to become. She steeled herself for chaos. The headphones would take care of the sounds and the drink could take care of her heart.

Lally swiped her phone across the building's access pad and the doors parted before her. The melee appeared in greater clarity. She saw a young woman of about sixteen on the other side of the road trip and buckle under the stampede of people charging from behind. At the last moment, she thrust herself to her feet and sprawled into the road. The cars were at a standstill, but she was thrown across the bonnet of a taxi and fell heavily onto the floor. Lally felt her heart go out to this young woman in her 'KILL THE KING!' t-shirt, although on second thoughts, perhaps she wouldn't appreciate being the recipient of Lally's first saintly act. Lally turned instead towards the tube station and saw a middle-aged woman leaning a hand against the side of a shop for support. She had a cut running horizontally across her forehead, which she was tending with an old tissue.

"Are you okay?" Lally asked, her voice sounding warm and instant in her head. She then watched as the woman's lips moved with no sound. Lally pushed her headphones around her neck in time to hear the woman finish "…go fuck yourself."

Lally swallowed the disappointment, smiled sweetly at the lady and spotted a man with grey hair and a stuffed camping backpack being barged by the people pushing past him as he looked around, trying to get his bearings. Lally elbowed through the crowd and pulled alongside him.

"Sir? Sir – are you okay?"

The man turned to look at her as if she was speaking gibberish.

"You seemed to be struggling, I wondered if you needed help?"

"Who are you? Are you one of the organisers?" he asked, seemingly still confused about her role in things.

"I'm just someone who's helping. Do you need help?"

"I don't know where we're supposed to go. Some people are saying the Prime Minister is dead in a plane crash, is that true?"

"I'm afraid I don't know," Lally said, her mind casting back to the smoke trailing through the sky.

"Well, where are the police saying that we should go? What are people saying about a missile?"

That was a good question. Lally hadn't really thought about it. She'd just wanted to help; she hadn't really thought about how. The B of the Bang message had said that there was no point sheltering in place and that only the gold members would survive in the bunkers. But maybe they could get to a sort of shelter? For inspiration, she tried to remember what Granny had done during the war? Figurehead stuff mostly, but she'd been a driver or something hadn't she? It's hard to pay attention to history lessons when they're mostly talking about your relatives.

"There is a missile, I'm afraid. A nuclear one. I'm sorry to say that. I don't want to be the bearer of the worst possible news."

"So, what are we supposed to do – oof!" The man was rocked by a builder pushing against the crowd, bellowing the name "Katie!" Eulalia found her arm slipping around the man's shoulders. He seemed to tense against the intervention but remained under her support.

"We need to get you off the streets – let me take you somewhere."

She looked up and found that they had already worked their way across the road between the traffic and were now stood outside the Knightsbridge tube station. At the entrance to the building a Transport For London employee was arming the shutters with a key and shouting at the people trying to get past him.

"It's full! We've got to close, you've got to get out!"

He saw Eulalia and her passenger and stuck out his arm towards them as he depressed a green button and the shutters started to descend.

"No more room, sorry Miss, you have to go back."

Lally saw the shutters coming down on them and felt once more the sting of exclusion dropping on her head. The uselessness of Silver. She summoned up generations of breeding that had faced down actual guillotines and focused her will into a thousand-megawatt beam of hauteur.

"You *will* let my charge and I through."

The guard looked pained as he thought for a moment – a pause that Lally took advantage of to shove the man and his backpack roughly under the barrier and swoop through herself. The guard looked exasperated and regained his authority.

"Right, that's the last ones. Sorry everyone, try other stations – you've got South Ken and Sloane Square – sorry everyone."

Lally felt triumphant, but didn't dare to turn and look at the disappointed hordes behind them who started to thump on the shutters. She heard a shout of "There's children out here!" and kept her eyes facing forwards. She had made it, but others hadn't.

Lally found herself at the top of a packed flight of stairs that led down into the central concourse. The crowd didn't seem to be moving, so with the noise of the shutters rattling just behind them they waited their turn to edge down the stairs with the other harrowed faces seeking shelter. Her rescue project seemed to drift away and she had to work to keep him tucked under her arm.

"I don't even know your name," she said.

"Colin," came the terse reply.

"You can call me…Betty," Lally replied.

"Right," said Colin flatly. "You know, I'm fine you don't have to support me."

"I don't mind," Lally said.

"I'm not some doddering old man, I'm only fifty-one."

"Are you? Actually?"

"Yes. *Actually*. It's just that there's quite a powerful scent that you have and I'm not great with strong smells."

Wounded, Eulalia dropped her arm to her side and covertly licked the back of her hand and sniffed it. There was definitely a hint of something. She uncapped her hip flask and sank most of the rest of the container, leaving a mouthful for an emergency. She wasn't entirely surprised when she found that the emergency she was waiting for turned out to be boredom at the fact that they'd only gone down ten further steps in the next five minutes. The problem was that she had imagined that helping people might have come with a sense of purpose, but as she stood among the people she felt as lost as she had in her apartment. What the hell was she doing there?

As the slow trudge of the fortunate ones inside the station continued, by the time they reached the twelfth step she was upending the empty flask above her open mouth and grabbing at the solitary drip with her tongue and lips like she'd just crossed the Sahara. Colin eyed her from his side of the stair.

"It's ok to admit you're scared you know."

"What do you mean?"

"The alcohol – I could smell it on you when you first fell into me. It's okay, I used to drink…"

May The Saints Preserve Us From Recovering Alcoholics. Lally had experienced this exact discussion before and through her years of sobriety she had explored every variation of this conversation, so that it was like being a Chess Grandmaster who knew the inevitability of all the things that could possibly branch off from pawn to d4, pawn to d5.

"I see," she said.

"Whisky was my poison. I bet you're more of a vodka girl – am I right? I'm right, aren't I?"

"It's the end of the world, Colin. It's the one time we don't have to worry about hangovers."

"If you're a drinker, the world has already ended."

"That's patently untrue. Here I am drinking and the world has not already ended. Quod erat demonstrandum."

"You know the thing that helped me? To stop? I remember seeing a poster that said that as you drink from the bottle, at a certain point the bottle starts to drink from you. It reverses, see? Hit me hard that did. It's never too late to put it down you know."

"Colin, we're all just trying to find a way through today, okay?"

Lally physically bit her lip and closed her eyes. She felt the lip split and tasted the sweetness of her blood. She fought to bring her breathing under control and keep herself calm. She could feel anxiety spreading across her shoulders. Yes, from one perspective she was sheltered here, but from another viewpoint she was stuck there, with no option for escape. With Colin. And with all these people. Her people. So many people who obviously hated her. She found that she couldn't get her breath and Colin was eyeing her closely. She waved her hands in front of her face to cool down, and get some air in. A picture emerged in her head of this stairwell collapsed and ruined, her body laying rigid next to Colin forever. Then, across the solemnity of the people trudging down the stairs, a voice broke from somewhere further down.

"Imagine there's no…"

It was a woman's emotional soprano, boldly singing all on its own. There was a collective pricking of attention. The woman's singing continued. Then another voice closer to Lally joined in. A man's voice picked up the song. Then another woman. Soon, the song raised in volume and the plodding anthem was being earnestly bounced off the tiled walls by a hundred voices in communion. All harmonically wondering, *what if?*

Lally turned and ran back up the fifteen steps they'd managed to descend. Maybe Granny could have coped with twee choral singing in the underground as the bombs fell, but it turned out that Lally could not. As she reached street level she turned and addressed the stairwell beneath her. She had a nice line that she'd thought of as she ran: "Colin, I'd rather be drunk and dead out there, than in here listening to you recite the litany of sober cliches." But Colin wasn't even looking at her and he was singing along with the rest of the stairwell. As he hit the high note, Lally leapt up, and pressed the button to make the shutters rise. As soon as it was at knee height the people outside started to drop to the floor and roll underneath. Lally waited until it was waist high and then elbowed her way through, back to where she could breathe.

DUCK SOUP AND A SANDWICH

IN THE TAXI, Margaret laid the remaining coins from the pouch on the seat to distract herself from looking out of the window and finding her eyes drawn, inevitably, towards the sky. She knew Rash had been right to share the news, but part of her wondered if it was as much a curse as a blessing. What was she supposed to do with her time? Did it ultimately matter? Wasn't this moment in her life simply the punctuation at the end of a sentence? She admired the three gleaming coins she had left. She wondered where Sean had got to with his. Margaret ran her finger around the edge of one of them and had to think hard about if she'd ever actually touched real gold before. There was no wedding ring on her finger, no expensive necklace had deigned to grace her neck. She concluded the closest she'd been was Uncle Ray's tooth, but he'd swallowed that in the end, so she wasn't sure it counted.

What surprised her the most was the weight of it. The two bigger coins were about the same size if she made a closed circle with her thumb and forefinger, and its denseness seemed to proclaim its own importance. She thought momentarily about how that could be – what made something so relatively small, feel so heavy. Graham could explain it. It would be something to do with atoms. He would draw a picture on a napkin if she ever asked. He would probably do it even if she asked him not to. The smaller one was slightly bigger than a two-pound coin. The confidence the coins projected was an attractive illusion and as she looked to the skies once more, she decided that she would like to borrow some of that confidence.

Margaret had been staring at the coins so intently she hadn't even realised that she was crying. The first tear had collected on the rise of her cheek and dripped onto her hand and then onto the seat. Something in Margaret had finally ripped apart. She screwed her eyes tight and clenched her fists. She tried to swallow the sadness that ran through her body, but her cries wouldn't be stifled and soon she was weeping. The gold mutely accepted her tears. Margaret dried her eyes on her coat sleeve and tried to order her thoughts. She caught the taxi driver looking in his rear-view mirror, but he looked away and focused on the roads. It was the *frustration* more than anything else. It just wasn't fair! Rash and his family! As she thought of Sarina and Jaat and all the children everywhere, the tears mounted up behind her eyes again and she choked another round of sobs. Hema! *Poor Hema!*

Then there was Graham.

Her dad would have told her that worrying about a thing that had already happened had less value than coins you'd never get a chance to spend. She liked having them anyway, and she picked the coins up by the edges, unwilling to smudge them and carefully plinked them back into the velvet pouch and pulled the drawstring tight.

"Anywhere here, please," she said and handed over two twenty-pound notes to the driver and got out. If she had any time left to her, then she wanted to feed the ducks.

※ ※ ※ ※ ※

Margaret knew that you weren't supposed to feed the ducks bread, but in the little Tesco that she'd passed she'd seen a single large baguette in the bread holster and it had seemed to call out to her. In the duration of a single journey home, it seemed that word had spread about what was coming to London. She saw people moving quickly along the street and a couple of times she saw people throwing families and belongings into cars. This was modern life, Margaret thought – nothing travelled faster than bad news.

In Tesco too, it seemed like the talk of missiles had arrived. No one was overtly panicking, but the aisles were full of people with multiple trays of lager, loo roll and multipacks of crisps. Covid lockdowns had taught people what life's real essentials were. She managed to snag the baguette, which she tucked under her arm, and a Battenberg cake. She doubled back and got four tins of premium cat food and returned to the till. There was only one young girl on the checkouts. As she was scanning her items, she looked twitchy and kept looking around.

"Are you okay?" Margaret asked, and the young woman looked surprised to even be acknowledged.

"I honestly don't know what's going on. Do you? People keep saying something about missiles?"

"I heard about the missiles."

"Is it true then?"

"I'm afraid so. Do you have somewhere you can go?"

"I can't leave! All the managers went and said that we had to keep the tills open. If I go, there's no one else. Max was here, but he said he was going to check the stockroom and that was five minutes ago."

As she focused on her, Margaret noticed how round and watery the girl's eyes were. Poor child.

"Go home. It won't matter soon."

"I need this job," said the girl, and the bitterness in her admission was evident. Margaret reached into her pocket and removed the black velvet bag.

"No, you don't," she replied and handed the girl a coin.

"What's this?"

"It's gold. It's what your time looks like. Take it back."

"We can't take tips though," the girl said with uncertainty.

"If you don't tell, I won't," Margaret said and smiled.

The girl looked around and then reached out her hand and plucked the coin from Margaret's hand. She instantly stood and vacated her seat behind the till. She was out of the door before Margaret finished putting her shopping into her bag.

Two coins left.

Just up the road from the little Tesco there was a small rusty gate flecked with paint that led into a residents' park. Margaret wasn't *technically* a resident as she lived a few minutes' walk away, but she liked to apply a broader Bermondsey resident definition to the sign. Plus, she felt she had been coming here long enough that she had tenure. She pushed against the stiff gate and walked down to the little lake in the centre of the gardens. Well, it was more of a pond really. A beautiful weeping willow draped itself across the view of the water and fringed the scene perfectly, provided you could ignore the four illuminous yellow grit bins on the far shore. It had been damp and overcast earlier, but it seemed to be clearing up a bit. Margaret sat at the single bench and looked around for the ducks.

"I know I shouldn't give you bread," she explained to the ducks as the first of several waddled over to her side of the pond. "But you should know that all of this will be gone soon and so I think that being the case, it doesn't really matter if you feel a bit bloated."

She scattered small, pinched pieces of bread in front of her and watched as the ducks went to work hoovering them up. She adored the oil-slick iridescence of the males' feathers, but she felt a kinship with the dun females and ensured that she launched her bounty in such a way that no duck went without. Even to the pure white one, which tended to boss the others around.

"Give it a rest," Margaret scolded him as he pecked one of the males.

"Now listen, I know that you've got a good thing going here on the pond, but I want you to know that there is danger coming. It's a terrible thing, something you won't have seen before. There will be noise and fire and then a great darkness. You need to escape. Fly away as far as you can. Do you understand?" The ducks paid her no mind and started to dive for the little crumbs that had broken off. The braver ones came closer to inspect what was left in the wrapper. However, most of them simply returned to the pond and swam away once she'd outlived her usefulness. It was a very duck thing to do. Margaret sighed and folded over the plastic sheath of the bread and slid it into her coat pocket. Graham would like a sandwich. She wouldn't tell him it was second hand from the ducks.

Back on the street outside the park she noticed people moving around with armfuls of possessions, wheely suitcases trailing behind them as they ran along the pavement, hulking great sports bags hefted over each shoulder. In Bermondsey, lots of people seemed to be sheltering in place. In several houses, she could see families at work fixing things across the windows, either old boards, or stretched out Amazon boxes being fixed to the inside of the windows. She watched a young boy of about four standing next to his dad who was perched on a chair hammering a heavy purple cloth to the front of their bay window. It was difficult to imagine that it would make any difference.

It was funny, but she knew where she'd probably be when the bombs dropped. It was inevitable really. She would be sitting in the high-backed chair that she had from Nanna Owen. It had been reupholstered in a thick velvet material and she loved the height of it. It felt much more comfortable to get up from. But then, she wouldn't be getting up, would she? The missile would hit and there would just be the end. She hoped that Graham would be there with her. Maybe the cats would be there. Mitsi, she could pick up and settle if Margaret stroked her. Nothing could persuade The Colonel to do anything he didn't want to do. He'd give a warning hiss and then strike out. But then, that's why he was The Colonel. Maybe she would show Mitsi her gold.

While she sat with the ducks, Margaret had been considering the option of pills and whisky. She had sleeping pills, which were probably out of date now, but she was sure that they'd still work if she dosed them both in great enough quantities. That might be calmer, all things considered. She wondered if it would be doing Graham a favour if she crushed up the pills in his sandwich. He'd almost certainly eat anything she put in front of him, provided she slathered it with mayonnaise and mustard. She pursed her lips at the decision.

Her feet knew the way home. She'd walked the same route for nearly twenty years. The markers of her walk saluted her as she went past for the last time. The postbox where she sent her niece her birthday cards. The narrow alley where the buddleia grew through the fence and blossomed into purple, bee-heavy glory in July. The old BT exchange building that had fallen into disrepair with the mysterious word "SHARKLES" sprayed across the side. Margaret turned into her road. It too was mostly deserted but she could sense life behind the closed doors, like a spider who knows the twang of every strand of her web. She turned into the path that her small terraced house shared with next door and tapped on Terry's door with the knocker. She heard shuffling and waited patiently while three separate chains were removed from the door.

"Only me, Terry," she called through the door.

"I know it's you! It's always you!" came the irritated voice through the glass. Finally, the last bolt relented and the door swung back to reveal Terry in a wool cardigan, his face rough with stubble. He had two white dots of spittle glistening at the corner of his mouth, probably from the exertion of getting up.

"I'm back from work early, I wanted to check you were ok."

"I'm fine! I'm always fine! I was listening to the radio."

"Anything good?"

"Why do you want to know? It's just the radio!"

"Terry, I wanted to see if you've heard the news? About the missile?"

"They had a caller on the radio."

"Do you want to come to ours? We might be able to keep you safe."

"I'm as safe as I'll get. I'm not going to get any safer, two metres to the right or two metres to the left. The missile isn't that accurate."

"No, I suppose not. Well. I just wanted to check if you needed anything, before I get in."

"No! I've got the radio." He started to shut the door.

"Terry…"

"What!"

"I just wanted to say it was nice living next door to you. And Janet."

"Yes, yes." The door closed firmly and the rebolting began. Margaret remembered the Battenberg and knocked on again.

"What now!" Terry shouted through the door.

"I got a Battenberg. Do you want it?" There was a pause while Terry considered his options.

"Yes." A second later the letterbox opened and Margaret sighed and fed the cake through.

"Not the whole thing!" Terry shouted and let the letterbox go, allowing the keen hinges to scythe the cake in half. Margaret tugged at the mess of wrapping and the yellow and pink crumbs of the cake. She scooped it into her hand as best she could and turned to her own front door, and placed the familiar key in the familiar lock for the final time.

HELLO
MOTHER

COCO THE LOBSTER was the only member of the unhappy band crammed into the now-packed stairwell on Orange Street who seemed at all bothered by Bradford's plight. As he was unceremoniously dumped on the steps, his nose already turning a dark red from the punch, she reached down and half lifted, half dragged him to his comically large feet and held onto him to stop him from being swept away in the crowd. Just ahead of them, the street had been thrown into a frenzy as people searched the F1 for the Class A treasures Bradford had proclaimed it contained.

Fighting broke out around the car as a group of men tried to smash their way through to get to the precious powders. The F1 was jostled on all sides, shaking an already catatonic Brin inside the vehicle, who was now certain that this sabbatical year was not the opportunity for growth and nourishment that her dad back in Glenview had insisted it would be. The food was revolting, the weather was shocking and now she was going to be violently set upon by a horde of men with awful teeth.

"He-lp!" she screamed as the men fought for the right to get into the car first.

"Your wife!" Coco said with shock.

"She's not my wife! I boosted the car and she wanted a ride, so I picked her up," Bradford replied, deciding to stick to his persona of have-a-go streetwise Cockney hoodlum, despite the fact that the only role he was less qualified to play was Miss Marple.

"You should still help her," Coco said and pushed Bradford towards the car. He clung to one of her lobster arms and climbed back up into the stairwell before he could be swept away in the crowd.

"No, I can't I was assaulted and I think I'm haemorrhaging internally. Why are you dressed like a lobster? Is that for the protest?"

Despite the chaos, Coco still managed to be embarrassed at her outfit, as if she'd entirely forgotten that she was dressed as a lobster, which in many ways she had.

"It's Balenciaga," she said.

"Wow. It has a strong shellfish smell too."

"That's the design. It's swatch and sniff," Coco replied, deploying a business idea that she'd once seriously considered starting when she'd drank slightly under a litre of Ouzo.

"It's quite strong."

Brin's screams sounded out in the street again.

"You have to help her!" Coco said and shoved Bradford back into the street more forcefully.

"No! I'm not going out there…I need to get to the Savoy. My daughter is there. She's only one. Her school just threw all the children out on the street and told them to look after themselves." Bradford inwardly applauded his nimble improvisational mind, which could seemingly spew out imaginary children at will. This escapade was teaching him a lot about his capabilities.

"<u>You believe me, I am wonderful</u>," he broadcast into the local atmosphere for good measure.

"What? That's awful!" Coco said, before her face contorted in confusion. "Wait. Why is she at school at one? Did they kick her out because of the missiles?"

"Wait – *you* know about the missiles?"

Coco looked at him incredulously.

"Of course! What do you think everyone is here for?"

"The protest? Smash Capitalism, that bollocks."

"No! Everyone is trying to get to the bomb shelters in Whitehall."

Bradford was stunned. So much for the B of the Bang guarantee that he would be "First to know and first to go"! Another surge in the crowd forced all those on the steps to retreat even further up and lean hard into pushing people away. Bradford tried to ensure he was jostled towards the curious and demure lobster, but he ended up reluctantly pressed against a brick shithouse in a luminous electricity company jacket. Bradford's arms were pinned by his side, so his cheek could only rest against the man's chest. He smelled of chips and Bradford was so close he could see the minute specks of dirt on the jacket. Bradford's nose ached and he wanted the car wash more than ever.

"Stop pushing!" Bradford shouted into the man's chest as the crowd rose onto the step and then swayed back across Orange Street. The man's powerful arms pushed him away, and Bradford felt both sides of the crush.

"We're going to die if we don't get out of here!" Coco screamed and cast around the stairwell for some avenue of escape. About two metres above them the first floor of the car park opened up to allow the fumes out and the daylight in. A metal barrier ran around the wall.

"What's your name?" Coco asked the large man in the hi-viz.

"Cole," the man replied in a flat South West accent.

"Cole, can you get him up there?" Cole looked appraisingly at where she was pointing to and then without further ado, reached down and picked Bradford up, who squealed as Cole jerked him cleanly onto his shoulder in a single smooth motion.

"Why don't you pick her up!" Bradford yelped as he sat on the giant's shoulders and surveyed the swarm of humans in the street in front of him.

"You're the smallest!" Coco retorted, as Cole turned so Bradford was facing the building. He clawed at the wall for purchase and then held onto Cole's head and eyes for balance, as he placed one foot and then the other onto his shoulders. The barrier was just out of his reach.

"Get on your tiptoes!" Cole shouted.

Bradford stretched his giant feet and one of his fingers grazed the bar.

"Jump!" Coco screamed. Bradford hopped as high as he could and his fingertips curled around the top of the barrier. Cole reached up to his feet and boosted Bradford higher. He just managed to get an arm over the top and then with an effort he swung his right foot up, so that he was lying horizontally along the outside of the car park. The pebbledash exterior dug into his suit jacket and face. With a massive effort he heaved himself level and then rolled over the top of the barrier and landed on the car park floor with a grunt.

"The door at the top of the stairwell looks like it can be opened from inside. Go and open it!" Coco shouted as Bradford fell from view. She looked at the red door that was flush to the frame with no handle on her side. Surely there was some way of opening it inside? The crush returned and even the relative safety of the stairwell didn't help this time, and she was forced against the car park wall. Cole had crouched down and was using his arms as a buffer against the crush. She tried the same technique and felt how feeble her efforts were to protect the baby inside her. She was only the size of a plum. Coco tried to think of a less easily bruised comparison. She was the size of a hand-grenade.

Coco gritted her teeth and pushed against the mob as she felt her back grind into the stones of the wall.

"Hurry!" Coco shouted.

One floor above and with space to move, Bradford's shaking hands fumbled in his jacket pocket and he retrieved one broken vial of cocaine and then another, which he threw on the floor. As he checked his trouser pockets, he found one remaining vial intact and he abandoned the niceties of razor-sharp lines and tapped a healthily unhealthy amount of cocaine onto the back of his right thumbnail and, holding it steady with his left hand, he managed to keep it under his nose for long enough to bolt the cocaine down. He repeated the process with the other nostril and inhaled all the confidence in the world into himself.

Okay. Yes. That would work.

As he looked out of the car park onto the horrors of the crush below, he felt the euphoria coming on like a million sunrises overlaid on top of each other, while the trumpets of Jericho played the refrain from Primal Scream's *Loaded* and lasers split clouds of dry ice into green and red smiley faces. For a split second, the crowds below weren't groaning with pain and anger, they were an audience of adoring fans desperate to hear what Bradford would play.

"Open the door, Tiny Tears!" he heard Cole shout, and he remembered he was supposed to be saving people.

He looked around frantically and saw another stairwell in the corner of the car park. He ran over and skipped down the stairs, two at a time with the beat of cocaine certainty returning to his bloodstream. Bradford the Motherfucking Hero. DJ Bradford dropping the hottest saviour hits.

"Bradford is great and everyone thinks so," he projected into the surrounding environment as he ran out into the ground level of the car park.

He could see the other side of the red door in between a white Prius and a pink Mini with blinking eyelashes, forcing Bradford to wonder if the end of the world was such a bad thing after all. This side of the red door had a bar that he could push to access outside. He ran up to it and shouted through.

"Are you there?"

"Of course we're fucking here! Open the door!" came Coco's aggrieved voice.

"Hold on, I'm going to open the door."

Bradford started to push on the bar, but then stopped. He'd got too caught up in the moment. There were *missiles* coming to London. Saving these people now didn't make a big wet fart's worth of difference, they were all toast within the hour anyway. But *he* wasn't. He was the only one that mattered in this – and every other – situation. Once again, the cocaine had made a very valuable contribution to Bradford's survival. And his experience on the other side of this door had shown him there were other factors at play. Namely people who were happy to punch him in the nose and destroy his possessions. He needed some muscle to help him get to the extraction point. Just for a second, he revelled in the imbalance of power and luxuriated in the fact that it now favoured him.

"I'm going to open the door…*if* you help me," he called and pushed his head flat against the door to listen.

"Open the door!"

"I want Cole to help me get to the Savoy. My daughter needs me, remember?" he said, laying the emotion on with a trowel. People were so easy to control when you had the sort of insight into the human psyche that he had. He didn't hear a response.

"Promise me. Promise me for my daughter."

"All right!" came the man's gruff voice. Bradford wondered about the lobster. Could he make her come with him? He cursed himself that he couldn't remember what her teeth were like. He'd never had sex with a crustacean before, although he'd once come back with crabs after a season in St. Moritz.

"NOW OPEN THE FUCKING DOOR!" Coco screamed and such was her intensity that Bradford found himself doing what she said. The bar went down and the door sprung forward an inch and then jammed against the push of the people outside. Then the filthy tips of four large fingers rounded the side and Bradford watched as Cole prised the door backwards against the masses. Coco was the first to be ushered through and just behind her Cole forced himself through the gap. As Cole emerged, he swept Bradford up and dragged him round to the back of the Mini. Bradford sensed further violence and raised both hands to his face.

"Don't hit me! My daughter needs me!"

"You're pathetic! Your daughter is better off without you," Coco shouted, slapping at his shoulder. She stomped away across the car park.

More people were bowling through the doorway and Cole was buffeted on both sides as the crowd started to swarm into the car park with relief. Cole positioned himself in front of Bradford and moved his hands to either side of his head and started to push on his cheeks. Bradford's nose throbbed and he felt his jaw crack. It was like being held in a clammy vice.

"Please," Bradford said. "I have gold."

Bradford rummaged in his pockets and pulled out the black velvet pouch to make his point. "Look, this is gold. Real gold."

"I'll 'ave it when you're dead," Cole said and continued to mush Bradford's face together. Bradford's hands scrabbled helplessly at Cole's jacket.

"Pwee, mmh huf bunkuh."

Cole continued to crush.

"Bnnkuh! Bnnkuh! BNNKUH!"

<u>"I have a bunker, you ape."</u>

Bradford felt the vice-like grip on his face lessen minutely.

"A bunker?"

"Ymh, uh bnkhh."

"You have a bunker?" Cole all but removed his hands from Bradford's face whose lips had hyperextended into a ludicrous pout.

"Yhesh."

"Right then. Let's go."

💎 💎 💎 💎 💎

For his twenty-first birthday, Pops had hired an escort to shit on to a glass table while Bradford lay underneath. Bradford was currently experiencing that same sense of not being able to look away from the horror, but being piqued by a giddy curiosity. Cole had pushed him through the car park and out onto the street at the other side, while Bradford tried to mush his features back into place. Cole had then spent precious minutes leading them up and down roads staring at grids in the pavement until he apparently found what he was looking for. While he did this, Bradford had kept up a self-involved monologue about the perils that he had faced. Cole mostly just grunted in response, but after a while that stopped too.

Just as Bradford was wondering if he could make a break for it and leave the oaf to survey pavements on his own time, Cole pulled a metal T-shaped tool from his jacket and drove it into the ground, twisted it and lifted up a triangular metal flap, which he then repeated on the other side of the grid. A rectangular opening was revealed in the pavement. Bradford admired it, until he was brusquely told to climb down the ladder into the sewer. Bradford had started to object, but he realised that Cole was still holding the metal T and looking at his eyes as if he wondered what would happen if he drove the tool into his skull. So, Bradford sat on the edge of the entrance into the underworld and then reached out for the slippery top rung.

Since that point Bradford's main learning had been that snaffle toe Gucci loafers weren't the ideal sewer shoes.

Bradford had always thought that sewers would smell worse, but really it was more of a taste than a smell. A horrible, chewable taste that suggested farms and music festivals. As he breathed in the fetid and humid air in the passageways it seemed to leave a lasting impression on his lips, teeth and tongue. It reminded Bradford of cocaine, naturally – the way it searched out the pathways and spread a little numbing fun. This was similar but with stench and nausea.

Cole had set a frantic pace and Bradford had no choice but to scurry along behind his guide. At points they passed inlets where water from drains in the street came jetting into the sewer through metal flaps. He kept to the far wall when they passed these but the soiled water still splashed him. Within minutes of descending into the sewer he had been soaked to the skin, as it was impossible to keep your footing on the slimy ground beneath them. When he first slipped, Cole had helped him to his feet, but now when he fell Bradford simply righted himself and tried to keep his mouth closed. After ten minutes of travelling Bradford had made the choice to kick off his Gucci loafers and as his bare feet squished against the silt and weeds on the tunnel floor, he had to remind himself that Pops would be proud of him for not crying.

"<u>Yes, Bradford!</u>" he declared to boost his flagging morale.

Cole stalked ahead, his mobile phone in one hand illuminating the oval passageway. It seemed to be getting narrower, but that could have been a trick of the feeble torch's light – which made the next short stretch ahead of them bright, but quickly faded into blackness. The tunnels shrank down to around one and a half metres in height, and Bradford could imagine being squeezed down to a tinier dot and presented with a miniature bottle of sewer water to drink if he wanted to return to normal size. He licked his dry lips and regretted it as more of the sewer mist made its way into his mouth. Cole had to walk hunched over at the waist in order to make his way through these sections, but the constriction didn't seem to slow him down much.

"I take it you know the tunnels well?" Bradford asked.

"Well enough," came the curt reply.

Bradford's occasional questions about where they were resulted in single word answers like "Interceptor" and "Fleet" as if he should know what that meant. The seventh time he asked for an explanation, Cole stopped and Bradford walked straight into his hulking back. Cole somehow managed to turn around enough to eye Bradford.

"This isn't a chuffing Uber," Cole said and Bradford saw that the T tool was once again gripped in his hand. After that he trailed behind in silence.

"It gets shallower ahead," Cole finally said over the hustling rush of the water.

As they went further down into the sewer, Bradford noted that for the first time he could feel cold air against his face. Before then the tunnel had emitted an ungodly heat – as if it was warmed by some sinister, spectral source. As they rounded the corner, the passageway opened out into a large chamber with a number of other tunnels feeding into it. Their passageway came out several metres above the pool of water below. The roof of the space soared above them like a vaulted Cathedral ceiling. Several of the other passageways were blocked with metal shutters and Bradford saw the words "HAM BAKER" enigmatically embossed on the doors.

"How the hell are we supposed to get down there?" Bradford asked, tabling the question about HAM BAKER for now.

"There's a ladder, you gert lummox." Cole replied and stepped out of the tunnel and onto metal rungs that were embedded in the wall just to the right. Bradford watched him descend and suddenly felt a premonition of doom.

"And you're sure this leads to the Savoy?"

Cole stopped a few rungs down the ladder and looked at Bradford with disbelief.

"Didn't I tell you it did?"

"Yes, but it feels like we've been moving for a while. And I'm so terribly concerned for my son, I mean my daughter."

"We have to work our way down to the embankment and then across on the cable tunnels. It's not hard from here. So, if you want trouble-free access across London, this is it. Can't see any crush down here, can you?"

"No."

"Right then."

"How deep are we?" Bradford asked, suddenly wondering if the sewer wasn't the perfect place to see out the incoming missiles.

"Only about ten metres, you can see the grates on the streets if you look."

Cole dropped out of sight on the ladder and as soon as he was gone, Bradford fished in his jacket pocket for the vial of cocaine which he quickly spooned into each nostril twice. As he swatted the crumbs from his nose, a rat crossed the threshold of the sewer and Bradford flinched and flicked it out into the watery chamber beyond with his bare foot. He watched it arc out over the pool and plop into the black waters and carry on swimming as if this had been its plan all along. Adapt and overcome, Bradford thought – a salient lesson for his own situation.

He'd managed to submit this brute to his control, simply by luring him with the offer of a bunker. It wasn't an offer that Bradford planned to make good on because if they were caged in a bunker together then Bradford didn't like to extrapolate about how the situation would play out. As they'd made their way, he had been fingering the knife in his pocket and gauging their journey for the optimum point to literally stab his guide in the back. Bradford Alderman VIIII wasn't about to use his plus one on someone with the bearing and IQ of a phone box. He had to time it right though.

"Come on down," Cole called from below.

Bradford descended the ladder and found that the rungs finished a few metres above the water.

"Just jump; it's deep enough to catch you," Cole said. Bradford thought about the rat, took one hand off the rungs to pinch his nose shut and let himself drop backwards. The frigid water claimed him and he pushed his way up and broke the surface breathing deeply. He spat out the water that he'd swallowed upon impact.

"It's freezing! You could have told me!"

Cole had already waded most of the way across the room though, and was investigating the tunnels on the other side. Two were blocked off with HAM BAKER vents and so he was peering into the remaining one they could access. Bradford started to walk across the floor until his bare foot drove into something squelchy and a bubble of a noxious yellow gas rose to the surface. He squealed and doggy paddled frantically across the waters with his neck rigid so he could keep most of the water from getting on his face.

"This is the one," Cole said to himself and heaved himself up and started down the tunnel.

"Is it far?"

"No. Close now," Cole replied, and Bradford smiled. He slipped the knife from his breast pocket. In the dim light of the tunnel, Bradford could barely see it in his hand, but he could feel the quietly brutal weight of it. The metal handle was cold, and he could just make out the word "Gerber" on a clip on one side of the blade. He felt a thrill of wrongness at what he was about to do. But on today of all days – was murder really so very significant?

He pulled at the side of the blade and looked for the thumbnail divot that would help him to extract it from the handle. He turned slightly so he could get the benefit of the greater light behind him. He turned it over and over but he still couldn't find the divot. Where was it? He felt along the handle and noticed that there was a button – of course, it was a flippy one! He pushed the button and nothing happened. He quietly jammed his thumb harder onto the button, but it still wouldn't emerge. Stage fright! His murder weapon had stage fright!

"You have to slide the safety back," Cole muttered from the darkness, and Bradford looked up in time to see a giant fist coming towards him.

Thank God the chauffeur was here. He was picking Bradford up from a house party. He said he'd had beer, but it had been wine. He said it had been a glass, but it had been bottles. The chauffeur didn't seem to care. He just dragged Bradford back to the car.

"Car wash on the way home," Bradford said. The water was leaking into the footwell of the car. But it didn't matter, it wasn't his car or his problem.

Bradford woke and found himself slipping over the wet bricks at his feet. The chauffeur was here? That was nice. Cole pushed Bradford and he stumbled and fell into the shallow water in the tunnel. The splash roused him and he remembered where he was. He was in a sewer with a man who he'd evidently failed to stab.

All other considerations were put on hold as a gut punch of stench hit Bradford. It smelled like stale vomit on dog shit crackers. Cole aimed his phone torch in front of them and Bradford saw the tunnel was jammed from the floor to the ceiling with a grotesque off-white and black slug of fat and rubbish.

"What…on earth is that?" Bradford said unable to keep the horror from his voice.

Cole sounded awed as he said, "That's Mother."

Something about Cole's reverence caused Bradford to look closer and as it came into focus, he could see that this monstrosity was embedded with several once-familiar items, their colours faded in a symbolic gesture of hopelessness. He could make out a nappy and the faint blue circle of a brand logo caught his eye. There were globs of used make-up wipes and wadded tissues, all of it bound together with a stinking white putty that looked crumbly like Cheshire cheese. It looked like capitalism had taken a crap. As Cole brought the torch closer, the smell became too much for Bradford and his eyes watered and he bent over and gagged onto the foot of the beast blocking their way.

"We…we…have to go…go…back," he said between mouthfuls of bile.

"Oh, there's no going back," Cole said. "There's only going in."

LIKE ARMAGEDDON, BUT MADE OUT OF CARDBOARD

KWON HYUN GUN ducked a volley of laser blasts from his opponent's eyes, crouched momentarily behind an indestructible crate, then vaulted high in the air. As he flew effortlessly, he tucked and pivoted twice, meaning he was in the perfect position above Captain America to deliver the Woke Blast Ear Popper. Captain America's red-gloved hands came to the side of his masked face, blood trickling from both ears. With a final "CLANG!" he dropped his red, white and blue shield and fell to his knees in defeat.

Hyun Gun landed deftly, pushed his tortoiseshell glasses further up his nose and kicked the shield from his fallen foe. He paused briefly to execute a victory dance, wiggling his butt and trailing Vs across his pure hazel eyes. Then he dropped his knee onto the shield and a delighted smile played across his face as the iconic weapon shattered. Hyun Gun then pulled the spine out of Captain America. Then he did something to the spine that was anatomically complex but that he seemed to very much enjoy nevertheless. A caption extolling communism displayed on the room's massive screens, the game ended and returned to the menu screen.

In the auditorium, the crowd went wild.

That didn't surprise the North Korean leader. His entire life had been punctuated with crowds going wild. Either those within his borders who were mostly going wild with reverence, or those outside his borders who were nearly always going wild with outrage. What did surprise Hyun Gun as he rose from behind his large desk and raised a chubby hand to capture some of the adulation, was how happy he felt. He raised a second hand, the one holding his game controller and the crowd applauded even faster. He looked at some of the clapping hands and noticed that they were a blur.

The first twelve rows of the audience were military officials. Hyun Gun eyeballed Generals Lu and Jeong, who were keeping time with the rest of the seals. Hyun Gun made sure that they knew he was watching them. Jeong noticeably sped up his applause and Lu followed suit. Hyun Gun watched until he could see the effort of the ovation turn their faces a shade of beetroot. Then Hyun Gun turned his attention to the rest of the crowd – ordinary North Koreans who had been invited to watch the country's first livestream of *Kwon Hyun Gun's Quest: National Nemeses And Also Spine Cracking With Blood*, which after today would be available on the country's first gaming console – the Electron Theatre X, a pet project of Hyun Gun's. He was happy because this applause seemed almost genuine. He knew that they mostly only clapped him because the alternative was a beating or a re-education camp, but it was still possible that he had done something objectively good.

He milked the raptures for another eight minutes and then as he saw his lead assistant appear in the wings, he walked off stage.

"Play back the footage and see if Lu or Jeong slowed their clapping first – whoever it was, increase surveillance," Hyun Gun said to his cadre of assistants. He was passed a bottle of water, which he sipped from while another assistant held a cotton serviette under the bottle to prevent drips. Notes were made on several clipboards.

"Respected Marshal, if it pleases you to know, the power panel have convened in Mandatory Advice Module Booth B."

"Now? What do they want?"

"With deep apologies Delightful Chairman, they were silent on the matter of the subject."

"What's wrong with Mandatory Advice Module Booth A?"

"Regretfully, it is being fumigated Chairman Kwon."

The inklings of a fury landed on Hyun Gun like the first tickle of a sneeze. If he was to meet the power panel then it should be in MAMBA, not MAMBB, which as an abbreviation didn't even make sense. Hadn't he long ago tasked one of his assistants with renaming all of the Advice Module Booths? MAMBA, COPPERHEAD, PYTHON, etc?

"Comrade Cho – didn't I ask you to rename the Advice Module Booths?"

Comrade Cho, a conspicuously tall member of the group of assistants who tended to walk with a pronounced stoop to hide his unfortunate stature, paled under Hyun Gun's attention and looked earnest as he replied.

"No, Supreme Leader, but if you would like me to do so then I would be honoured."

A barely perceptible twitch passed through the assistants and the Hyun Gun turned more fully towards Cho.

"Are you saying I'm *wrong*, Comrade Cho?"

Angst played across Comrade Cho's face. He looked like he was trying to choose which testicle to extricate from a tiger's mouth.

"No- well, what I mean, Supreme Leader, is yes, you are of course correct that you tasked someone with this, but I must profess it wasn't me who was honoured with this assignment. I shall immediately consult the files and see who this was. If you would excuse me, Respected Marshal."

Cho flung himself forward in a gratifyingly deep bow and without turning his back, started to edge away. Hyun Gun's eyes met Comrade Park's malevolent yet dutiful stare. A deliberate blink was sufficient to communicate deadly intent to his head of personal security. Comrade Park withdrew.

The assistants swept into MAMBB ahead of Hyun Gun, and a security detail of twenty pressed into the room, interrogating the chairs, the curtains and monitoring tables, and checking behind the screens. The ten officials in the room stood up and applauded as Hyun Gun came into the room. His assistants and security detail also clapped feverishly. Hyun Gun stood for a minute out of formality and then took a seat. The assembled clappers didn't miss a beat and Hyun Gun was interested to see that no one had slowed at all. Maybe they were learning. Or maybe they just loved him more. Hyun Gun raised his hands for the end of the applause. Without looking in the leader's direction, Hero of the People Yoon addressed the room.

"We are proud and honoured that the Supreme Marshal has met with us and we thank him for his time and his presence…" Several minutes of adulation followed. "…we also would like to add to the joy of the rest of the party at the launch of *Kwon Hyun Gun's Quest: National Nemeses And Also Spine Cracking With Blood*. We all enjoyed the talented and skilled playthrough that Chairman Kwon treated the party to."

The fury sneeze whispered behind Hyun Gun's eyes. He was tired. He had put his heart, and several other people's organs, into the video game project. He wanted his nation to enjoy games and live streaming as much as any other nation, and hadn't he achieved that? When he was on the platform listening to people's applause, he could almost imagine that this was what normality was like. To put in work on something and then to receive the earned plaudits. This was how people should feel who had completed a project. But now here he was in MAMBB, where nothing but problems ever arose. An assistant passed him a note. *In the official edicts there has never been an instruction to change the name of the Advice Modules.*

Huh. Maybe he was wrong. Perhaps he should call Comrade Park off and stop him from attaching the electrodes to Comrade Cho. He would make it top of the list of things to do next.

"Hero Yoon, thank you for your acknowledgement and for assembling the power panel in the Advice Module. This is a great thing for us as a nation and for me as a leader…"

Hyun Gun continued talking, but his mind checked out. He watched the faces of all the assembled people, their eyes glassy with joy. Or fear? Probably the latter, but he couldn't avoid the fact that people were often joyful to see him. He didn't know what it was, he just seemed to have this impact on people. His mother had called it his Happiness Haze – she said it was a sort of cloud that followed him everywhere and when other people were in it, they were happy. That sounded nice; his mother had always had a nice way of explaining things.

"…how on this glorious day for the Republic can I be of assistance to my esteemed comrades?"

"Sir, I regret to inform you that there has been martial disturbance on a national scale."

Hyun Gun risked the abnormality of pinching his nose, in the hope that it would stave off the swelling fury.

"Could my friend and honoured citizen give more specific and detailed details?"

Hero Yoon looked deeply uncomfortable. "Respected Marshal, it would appear that the rest of the world thinks that we have launched a nuclear missile at London."

Hyun Gun raised a delicate eyebrow. This was new. This was something.

"And *why* would they think this?"

"We do not know, Great Successor. We believe it may be a mistake."

"Ours?"

"No, theirs," Hero Yoon added, very quickly.

Hyun Gun was now fully invested in the situation. He templed his hands and rested his chin on them, his eyes scanning the room.

"General Chen, your advice?"

A beautifully uniformed military man who was one gram of starch away from being a statue, stood and bowed as low as his crackling suit would allow. Hyun Gun nodded his head to acknowledge the etiquette.

"It is indeed a path that we were not expecting, Glorious Leader. On a global level we feel that this may be a positive thing because it shows that North Korea is a viable enemy of the West. On the other side, we must be wary that this may be a false flag operation – a ruse to enable the enemy to blame us for disruption."

"Indeed – and your advice?"

"We feel that it is imperative to remain neutral at this time Superior Director, if they are blaming us then we can still respond. However, if it is a mistake then we do not want to antagonise the West if they are already on high alert. This is the consensus of the Mandatory Advice Module, we trust that it meets with your considered appraisal."

Hyun Gun let the General finish and then he allowed a spell of silence to settle on the room. This was a tactic that his father had taught him. Silence was good, it raised the pressure in the immediate vicinity and allowed you to see who was twitchy and who was altogether too calm. "Both of these people you must watch closely, Honoured Son." Hyun Gun stood and as one the room got to its feet with much scraping of chairs.

Hyun Gun left them standing and walked over to the large windows that overlooked the thoroughly bleak skyline of Pyongyang. He could see the Juche tower and the looming sci-fi slash of the Ryugyong Hotel, which would definitely be finished very soon. From there, he could see where he had sat the last time that they had thrown a military parade in his honour, on the occasion of his thirtieth birthday. He had smiled and blessed his people with his favour as he watched the assembled might of the North Korean army march past him.

Like most of his countrymen, he knew *The Art of War 2* off by heart. It had been the most popular book in the country for a long time, especially since Hyun Gun had been photographed on holiday reading a copy. There was a line from the book that he was thinking of now: "If your enemy decides to take a big old dump in his own hands, why not invite him to clap?"

"We are a nation, yes?" Hyun Gun asked the gloomy landscape of the capital.

There was some confusion amongst the ranks – both at the question and who it had been directed towards. Eventually, General Chen, ventured an answer on behalf of the room.

"A glorious one, Discerning Master."

"I believe so," Hyun Gun agreed.

He turned to face the room and those closest to him couldn't help but notice that his chest seemed to have swelled. His trousers too maybe.

"I believe that our enemies are making mistakes. They are mistaking us if they believe that we will take this slight kindly. They are mistaking us, if they believe that we cannot capitalise on their mistakes. General Chen – there are missiles in the armoury?"

"Well – yes, of course Vaulted General."

"Launch one."

As one, the room swallowed, making a collective noise like a caterpillar emerging from a rotten apple.

"A missile?"

"Yes."

"Launch it at who, Principled Creative?"

"Why, London of course. My logic is simple: if we are to be blamed for something, why would we not take the advantage it is assumed we have taken? We have a window of opportunity to be who they are portraying. A glorious nation who cracks spines with blood."

"Yes, Righteous Commander. Your logic defies rebuttal. We will launch a missile at London because if they believe we have launched a missile – why would we not launch a missile?" Chen's voice cracked under the magnitude of what he was saying.

"Exactly – and if they are merely trying to portray us as missile-launching war-mongers – we also have nothing to lose by launching a missile. There is a phrase that they use in the West which applies to this situation: they have accorded us a freebie."

As one the room all applauded for several minutes.

"Would you have guidance on which missile we should send?" Chen asked.

"Of course – the biggest, one of the nuclear ones from the parade."

"Eminent Interrogator, may I be blessed with a conversation with you in private? There are military matters that should be more restricted."

Chen and Hyun Gun walked down to the end of the room, while the other attendees pretended not to be listening intently. Chen leaned in close to Hyun Gun.

"Perfect Sir, at your birthday parade you will have been told about the devastating impact that these weapons can have and I know that your ready intellect will have understood the ramifications of your command."

"Of course, Chen – what is it you want to say?"

"Sir, the weapons we have displayed to you before have a single factor that differentiates them from the full version of these weapons."

"Full version?"

"Indeed. The cost of creating an arsenal such as we paraded to you is something that we feel is viable, but only over the course of many decades. You know at Burger Comrade how the photos behind the counter do not necessarily reflect the meal that you are served? This is a similar thing."

"General – get to the point."

"The missiles are cardboard, Worshipful Majesty."

"Cardboard?"

"Yes. *Extremely* high-grade cardboard. Weapons-grade cardboard. They are exceptionally strong, but perhaps not ultimately as strong as the eventual metallic missiles."

When Hyun Gun spoke, it was with the venom of a mambb. "Our arsenal is pretend?"

"*No!* Not pretend. They launch, they fly, they may even explode, but the point I make is that they might not be as robust as the eventual metal weapons we will construct at a later point."

"You are telling me that instead of weapons of mass destruction we have an arsenal of…*pinatas*?"

"Well…"

The fury came then, it spilled from Hyun Gun's brain across his face and body in shuddering waves. He could feel the points of his teeth biting against each other with such force that he thought he heard a crack. His mother had referred to these moments as his Uh-Ohs. By nightfall he would watch as the General's innards were wound around a large spindle. But for now, he had work for him to do.

"Launch it."

"Sir?"

"The missile. The *cardboard* missile. Launch it. As *The Art of War 2* states: "Confusion is worth a million soldiers, sow it at will and reap the rewards with infinite pleasure." If the missile falls short, we will say that it was a warning. Elementary."

"Sir, the missile will launch and even fly, but it lacks some elements of a missile that are considered traditional. Namely, a guidance system, a detonation system. All things which are being implemented in the later, non-cardboard versions."

Hyun Gun's eyes were aflame with an expression that Chen couldn't read. He suspected it may be hunger.

"From what you say I hear that you need a volunteer to steer and detonate the missile. Someone who wants to prove his value to the Republic. I have the perfect person."

Hyun Gun smiled and walked back towards the room. "Comrades, prepare for an historic broadcast. We must tell the people of the glory we are to unleash. Today, there will be spine cracking, with blood!"

KEEP CALM, CARRY ON AND BE KIND

JENNY WAS ONLY a sex worker for a little more than two hours. That was how long it took for her advert to go live on the classified site and for William to see it and respond, asking if the Mistress would be interested in seeing: "A real wretch, a poor and suppurating wound on the face of humanity (my actual name is William)."

Jenny replied bluntly, saying that she would give him five minutes to make his case later that day. As she waited for him to arrive, she paced nervously in her cramped and charmless Croydon flat. She felt confident that she could embody the sort of Dominatrix that he was looking for, kink and cruelty were second nature to her, but there were details to the business side of sex work that she hadn't figured out. Did she ask for the money when he walked through the door? Was she in character all the time, or just when they were playing? Who was she when she wasn't in character? What if she hurt him, or if she didn't hurt him enough? What if he hurt her? Did she need a minder? Did he?

She was in the middle of Googling safeword suggestions when there was a gentle tatter-tat-tat on the door. She checked the spyhole and saw a fish-eye representation of William looking eager and sweaty on the landing outside. Suddenly and rather awkwardly, she was in love. It was precisely that quick and that emphatic. It stunned her. She had previously never loved a man, a woman or cuddly toy before, and those close to her would have declared themselves surprised that she had even remotely liked anyone.

Before that lightning moment at her front door, she would have said that love at first sight was a confection from romantic movies that had no place in real life. But then it happened to her and she was in love. She shut her eyes and sighed at the life-altering inconvenience of this happening to her on her very first day, with her very first client.

She released the security chain and pulled the door open, whilst she stood obscured behind it. William walked into the flat and turned to face the lithe, powerfully-structured woman lying in wait. His first thought on seeing her was that she was like the Angel of the North, or a Renault Trafic van, although he would be hard-pressed to say why on the latter. The confidence she projected made him entirely discombobulated and he found all manner of odd thoughts flitting through his head. She was dressed head-to-toe in a shiny vinyl material that made him think of those iridescent beetles who glimmer through different spectra of colours as they move. Her red hair fell in waves and the contrast against her white freckled skin and the sensual gloss of her outfit made William feel faint, but also more present than he'd ever been. She straightened her arm and slammed the door. William found he was momentarily without voice and simply held out the boxes of chocolates that he was holding in his arms.

"For me?" she asked.

He nodded meekly.

"I don't eat chocolates, but put them on that table for now. So, you're William?"

"Yes," William managed to say in a voice like air rushing from a recently unsealed tomb.

"And you think that I might be your Mistress?"

William burst into tears. Jenny watched as his face crumpled like an old hankie and he scrabbled in his pockets for an actual hankie, which he draped over his face like a shroud.

"You couldn't be my Mistress. You couldn't! You're too perfect. I'm a verminous, poisonous blight. I'd sooner kill myself than ask you to own me. I mean – how cou-"

With a sudden squeak of latex, the back of Jenny's hand ripped across the space between them and back-handed all thought from William's head, and the hankie from across his face. His head snapped to the side and they both stood still in the shelter of the silence that followed. William stopped crying. So, this was what peace felt like, he mused. He understood now why others spoke so highly of it.

"Follow me," she commanded and with a series of further rubbery squeaks she made her way to the leather sofa and settled herself in the corner with a diminuendo of rasps. She looked at this pathetic creature – a human being of sorts who seemed to have been constructed from off-cuts of limbs and the sweepings from an abattoir floor; he was handsome, but somehow misshapen. Above anything else – he was easily most pitiable figure Jenny had ever seen. He was like a cat after a bath and the disappointing true shape of the animal is revealed. She patted the sofa next to her.

"Come, sit here and tell me all about it," she said with honeyed tones.

William made his way over to her and joined her on the sofa.

"Tell me all about it," Jenny encouraged.

And he did. Between sobs he told her that he was the son of a vicar. When he was four, his mother died in a gas explosion that had levelled the vicarage, both killing her and cremating her in a feat of organisational efficiency that she would have approved of. Her life insurance had seen him attend decent prep and boarding schools. He'd orbited the rich children and been swept along with their passage. First to Oxford, then into the civil service. When his father had died, he had returned home and got into politics because of the local graveyard, which a developer wanted to build on. William had strenuously objected citing decorum, but he had been approached by the developer who had offered to bankroll William's nascent political ambitions on the condition that he pushed the church into agreeing on the graveyard issue – which William duly did.

He had risen through the ranks and now he was one of the younger politicians in the house and even though it had been months, he still didn't know what he was doing. He explained that in most sessions he discreetly picked someone and simply copied everything they did. After two weeks he twigged to the fact that everyone on his side of the room was in his party and that things were less confusing when he copied someone from his side. He had a speechwriter who handled most of his content and policy ideas and that left him with lots of time to himself. Time which he spent contemplating his awfulness, all of which he concluded stemmed from his penis, which was like a pink font of woe, and occasionally a pink font of *woah*.

As he wept on Jenny's glistening thigh, the rot expunged itself from his soul. He told her he was base like a beetle, gross like a gargoyle, as fun as a bunion. He deserved nothing but pain and humiliation, and his enjoyment and craving for that punishment and hurt made it all the naughtier and more delectable. If he was discovered with a sex worker, then his career would positively implode. But he needed his mistress to know the truth about him. The boring, ghastly truth. He suspected if left to his own devices that the path he was on would end in madness or murder. He needed someone he could outsource all of his feelings to; in return he would never stray, never falter in his devotion, he would deliver everything to his Mistress - but he didn't deserve that – did he? Finally, he talked himself out and he peeled the skin of his face off her latex legs and sat up. She gently wiped his face with her fingers. He was hers. William sneezed six times in a row.

"Careful, eight sneezes are the same an orgasm, so another two and I'll have to charge you."

"Eight sneezes are the same as an orgasm?" William asked, looking flabbergasted. "Well, I never knew that! I can sort of understand it though because…"

"Shut up," Jenny said and she pulled the boxes of chocolates towards her and opened one up. She offered it to him.

"No, you first, please," he said.

"I don't like them, remember? And I insist," she replied.

He looked at her stern face and obeyed. He took a chocolate and popped it in his mouth. He chewed it with enjoyment and she watched his jaw click and crush. What an oaf, she thought with love bubbling in her veins.

"Take another," she said.

"Oh no, I'm fine," he said.

"No. I insist."

He noted the serious set of her eyebrows and took another chocolate. She watched him eat this one.

"Take another five," she commanded. He paused. "William, in our relationship, I will only tell you to do something once. Your only concern in life from this point on is obeying the things I say. You will only get one chance to obey each of my commands. If that compliance is not immediate and total then you will suffer. Do you understand?"

"Yes, Mistress?"

"Good. Now take another five chocolates and eat them."

William took five chocolates and ate them.

"Now eat the entire box."

"Of course, Mistress."

"William, we both agree that you are revolting. Because I am a benevolent Goddess, I will redirect this revulsion back at you until you hurt. You will receive all of the punishment your heart has dreamed of. When you cannot stomach any more you may use our safe word which will be, "Liverpool Lime Street". Then – and only then - will I relent. Do you understand?"

"Yes, Goddess," William replied, with a smudge of chocolate around his mouth.

"Good – you've not quite finished that box have you."

"Yes, Mistress, look," he held up the box and showed that all that remained was the box and the plastic tray.

"I asked you to eat the entire box."

"I did Mistress – oh…" Understanding dawned on William's face and he took an exploratory bite of the cardboard box and chewed it up. Jenny watched as he ate first the box and then the plastic tray, she then pointed him towards the tower of boxes he'd brought with him and he swallowed.

Before the day was out William was admitted to hospital with theobromine poisoning and enjoyed his first, but by no means his last, stomach pumping. He'd never felt such love and such belonging. Neither had Jenny.

💎 💎 💎 💎 💎

Jenny couldn't help but run her fingers across the paintings in the study of Number 10 and marvel at the ridges of paint that made up the images – it was so clever. She knew some of the subjects of the paintings of course, but others just looked like a rogue's gallery of superior-looking arseholes. She licked her finger and traced it across the ankles of one former PM. Jenny wondered what all of the great and good from these pictures would say if they could see what was happening in the Prime Minister's study right now. She suspected more than a few of them would be queuing up for their turn.

"I'm ready," William said, on the verge of tears.

Jenny turned from the art on the walls and regarded William, stark naked apart from his long grey woollen socks. He was standing on the small meeting table in the middle of the office. She eyed his pale, thin legs and followed them to the dark fuzz of his pubic hair and his erect penis straining itself upwards in a manner that she'd never quite seen before. It stood nearly vertical and it seemed to pulse with a fullness. She looked closely at it and found it fascinating but revolting. She was reminded of a child in a classroom, their arm stretching upwards, hoping to attract the teacher's attention.

She took out her phone, pointed it at William and started to record. He'd been very specific that he'd wanted the process fully documented. And while "give the people what they want" wasn't Jenny's normal operating procedure, she was in Number 10 and so she would uphold her side of the agreement.

"Let's look at this filthy dog, shall we?" she said.

Slowly, she walked around the green topped desk and examined William from every angle, capturing on film the jaunt of his hip bones, the slightly sagging round of his buttocks and the shallow dip of his lower back. They had been together for more than ten years now, and she still loved him every bit as much as she had the first time she'd seen him distorted through the peephole, weighed down by all those boxes of chocolates and his inadequacies.

She smiled at the memory.

They had come so far. He had done everything she had ever asked of him and delivered on the promise of ultimate power. In the course of their relationship, he had been hospitalised on more than twenty occasions. To allay suspicion, she had even taught herself basic medical procedures, and thereafter she had stitched him up herself, wiped him down, pumped his stomach, retrieved items from inside him and so forth. He was the love of her life and he had made her the most powerful person in Britain. Quid pro quo.

"William, you've given me what I asked you for. So, it's only right that I give you what *you* have begged me for." His erection twitched as she said the words. From her pocket she pulled a yellow marigold glove and using her teeth she filmed herself pulling it tightly onto her right hand. She squeaked the rubber finger tips together.

She stood on one of the guest chairs in the office so she was level with his midriff. Then she took a firm hold on his erect penis and with a sudden brutal move, she yanked it down with all of her strength like it was the handle of a one-armed bandit. As it moved from vertical to horizontal there was a wet popping noise and she felt the resistance of his cock fail, but she continued to yank until it was pointing all the way down. For maximum effect, she raised it up and pulled it down again, but it was now perfectly limp. She adjusted her hand position and wrenched his foreskin back to its fullest extent, but she didn't stop when the frenulum offered a spirited resistance. Instead, she pushed it back harder until it tore and her fingers were nearly at the base of his penis.

"Done," Jenny declared, and stepped down off the chair. William's knees juddered underneath him as he stood on the table.

After a second, he screamed, his voice eventually hitting a rasping high D. As the pain shook through his body, he sank to his knees and automatically his hands came to his penis, although such was the pain that he couldn't quite bear to cup it, he simply used his hands to create a shield around it. Drawn by the howl, one of the parliamentary aides tentatively entered the room, her face etched with concern as she took in the scene. Jenny smiled as she watched the young woman try to compute what was going on, before backing out of the room with hollowed eyes and her mouth wide open, closing the door with a gentle click.

Jenny slipped off the marigold glove and threw it in the nearby bin

"Kobe!" she said as it hit the rim and fell on the floor. They had people to pick those things up for them now.

She put her phone away and squirted a puff of anti-bacterial foam onto her palms from a bottle on the Prime Minister's desk and watched him impassively as he writhed, trapped between ecstasy and despair. He had begged for this moment for many years, discussed the fantasy in such detail and now it had happened. A most generous gift from his loving wife. Maybe in another ten years she would touch it again if it hadn't fallen off by then. William's lips were moving and Jenny wasn't entirely sure, but she thought he might be praying. He was in fact reciting the stops of the Northern Line in order to delay the orgasm that he could feel building throughout his body. He wasn't sure if it was even possible that he could orgasm at this point – perhaps never again - but what a righteous moment of punishment.

"Right, now get dressed and let's go and tell the public how they should feel."

She straightened her jacket and reached into her pocket for a small plastic envelope. She removed a blue pill from the container and popped it in William's mouth.

"Swallow," she commanded and he automatically obeyed.

"Paracetamol?" he asked.

"No darling – Invictus – it keeps your head bloody but unbowed."

William's eyes dropped to his fractured penis and she experienced a ripple of joy from the fear on his face.

※ ※ ※ ※ ※

Not for the first time, Comrade Cho was regretting his height. His head was pressed against the roof of the missile warhead, so he had to kink his neck to the right in order to be able to fit inside. While he struggled to find anything like a comfortable position, he was being attended to by a gang of workers. One of them was strapping him in the seat, while another continued to screw the newly-installed seat to the floor. Simultaneously, a crew member was connecting a front-lying oxygen pack to his stomach and securing the tubing into the helmet of his high-tech flight suit. You could tell it was high-tech because it had an awful lot of pockets and zips. Cold, minty air reached Comrade Cho's face and he lifted his thumb up to the operative, who ignored him and carried on tightening other parts of his suit. While all this went on, another flight operative was explaining the instructions connected to the two buttons in his hands.

"Listen, this is important. Left button keep pressing. Always. Over and over. You do not stop. One…two…three…press. One…two…three…press. You…"

"One…two…three press."

"No, no! One…two…three…press. Got it?"

"One…two…three…press. Yes, got it."

"Not stop."

"No, not stop. One…two…three…press."

"This one," the tech nervously indicated the button in his right hand: "Do not press. Not until the end. You feel the landing, then press this button. Do not press the button before. You understand?"

"Don't press until arrival, yes," Comrade Cho replied. He wanted to ask about the explosion. Would he feel it? Could he survive it? He thought once again of his stupidity from earlier – telling the Supreme Commander that he had made a mistake! He was lucky not to be minced alive, but to have the chance to bring honour to his family name and advance the glory of the Republic was an added bonus that he hadn't dared hope for.

"What do you do with this button?" The tech indicated the left button.

"One…two…three…press."

"And this button."

"Don't press until I reach London."

"Questions?"

"They say that this missile was made of cardboard – is that true?"

The tech's face gave Comrade Cho the answer he needed. Yes, it was.

"No, no! It's North Korean missile casing substitute material. Very high quality of cardboard – weapons grade cardboard."

"And it will fly?"

"There are numerous reasons to think that it will. Questions have ended, our thanks to you Comrade Cho, you are a shining example to us all."

The tech gave the thumbs up to a camera which had been hastily fixed on the wall of the missile. A lightbulb next to it went green and the technicians swiftly finished their ministrations and started to file out of the entry hatch. Comrade Cho offered an embarrassed wave at the camera, while trying not to press the button in his right hand.

Watching the footage of Cho getting strapped into his seat, Kwon Hyun Gun toyed with his own large red button which was connected to an outdated dashboard. There were no computer monitors, just rows and rows of gauges and switches. Hyun Gun addressed the middle of the three cameras that were recording his actions on this historic occasion.

"I send this missile on behalf of the people of the North Korean Republic. It stabs at the heart of our enemies, who would see us blamed across the world for things that we have not done. As *The Art of War 2* tells us: 'If your enemy seeks to undermine your command, then this is an act of war. You must undermine their command with a bigger act of war. This is the way that peace will be avoided.' Countdown!" barked Hyun Gun, and a host of panicked faces surrounding him started to count down as they hadn't been primed for this starring role.

"Fifty, forty-nine, forty-eight…" they intoned. Hyun Gun looked confused about why the audience had started at such a high number. "Forty-five, forty-four, forty-three…"

"Go from ten," Hyun Gun whispered. As one, the team amended the count from ten…nine…eight…seven…six…five…four…three…two…one…*launch*. Hyun Gun flipped the little glass lid on the launch button and pressed it. Ten miles down the road a silo door bay slid open, accompanied by an orange spinning light and a klaxon. Comrade Cho felt the rumble of the engines, began to count to three and pressed the left button. On top of the missile a small red light flashed on and then off. One…two…three…press, flash. One…

two…three…press, flash. One…two…three…press, flash. Then all numbers were forced from his mind as he experienced multiple Gs of thrust and the gigantic missile powered out of the silo bay door.

💎 💎 💎 💎 💎

Jenny had demanded some army fatigues for William to wear for his first public comments as Prime Minister. The intention was that people would hear him saying that there was no reason to panic, but they would see that he was dressed for war and judge the situation on this instead. Fortunately, William had a knack of looking good in most clothes and so even though he'd never served in the military, he still looked authentic. Jenny just hoped that he wouldn't pass out. The timing of William's reward hadn't been ideal, but that was the deal that they had struck.

In the vast entrance hall of Downing Street, William fiddled with the tactical belt that Jenny had requested, and although this didn't quite disguise the Invictus-inspired bulge at the front of his trousers, it at least confused the eye. William hadn't really said much since he had received his reward but Jenny had noticed a thin beading of sweat coating his lip and twice his eyes had looped back in their sockets as if he was going over a switchback on a roller-coaster. Add to that he was walking like a cartoon villain trying to sneak up on a gang of plucky teen investigators and the overall effect wasn't exactly prime ministerial. Jenny decided that they wouldn't take questions from the press as had initially been planned and that it would be a short statement, a photo opportunity and then back into the safety of Number 10.

The famous black lacquered door was opened by two military policeman – further set dressing from Jenny – and suddenly they were striding out onto Britain's most famous street, hand-in-hand, to face the press. Cameras flashed and every single TV camera tracked them as they walked. Cries of "Let Us In!" rang out from the bottom of Downing Street as the crowd shook the gates hoping for access to a secret bunker. Over that noise came the barrage of questions from the journalists who had made it through the crowds to witness the emergence of the new Prime Minister.

"William – what's with the military uniform?"

"Prime Minister – are there missiles coming from North Korea?"

"Is Britain at war, Mr McCartney?"

Jenny was proud to see that William ignored them all and just focused on making it to the podium, where he could at least lean and take some weight off his trembling legs. Jenny hung back at what she felt was an appropriately respectful distance from the podium, but she could feel the desire to encroach fully. She wanted to straddle the podium and scream into the microphone – but there was time for that. She settled instead on emitting a wifely smile and an expression of rapt attention at her husband's brilliant words.

"My Britons…" William broke off and coughed to clear his throat. "Britons. This is aaaaah-aah bleak day in the storied pages of British history."

William had started to mumble and Jenny could see the press lean forward in the hope of catching a clearer recording of his words. Dictaphones were thrust as far forward as possible. William coughed and cleared his throat again and restarted very loudly, causing all the Dictaphones to retract and some of the cameramen to quickly remove their headphones.

"Our beloved Prime Minister has passed away, and our green and pleasant nation is facing dark and dangerous days. I shoulder the weight of the title of Prime Minister for you today, but I know that this is something that I am only guarbing, ahem, excuse me, guarding for the people, so that they can pass it on to whoever they deem worthy in due course."

Jenny allowed herself to breathe. He was hitting his stride, although she couldn't help but notice that he was slumping rather heavily on the podium. And perhaps listing a little.

"I need you-oooo, you, the courageous people of our nation, to endure what we will face together in the coming days. I, with the help of my wife Jenny, the professionals in the cabinet and the strength of God, will be the steady hand on the tiller, until our nation emerges into the sunlight once more. I would ask all of you to therefore remember three things: keep calm, carry on and be kind. Those vital instructions again: keep calm, carry on and be kind. At this time, I won't be taking questions."

Jenny quivered with delight as she stepped forward and reached for William's hand, which felt like it was carved from Spam.

"Keep smiling," she hissed through unmoving lips.

She had to admit, Tom had come through for them – that was a fine speech. It said precisely nothing of substance and allowed anyone listening to impose whatever meaning they wanted to on the speech. It also sounded authoritative and "be kind" was the perfect platitude to demand – after all, anyone who complained simply wasn't being kind, and wasn't that one of the three things they'd requested?

She saw the future unfolding in front of her. Build the panic. Delay a leadership vote. Stoke divisions. Cancel the general election. Blame everyone else. Reinforce William as de facto Prime Minister. Jab and move. Then, ultimately, foment a war against Fear. Win the war. Centralise power. Feed the people into the mincing machine and she would gladly lean on the handle. William looked pasty so she lifted him with the strength in her arm and squeezed his hand in hers until she felt the bones click together.

Once through the doors of Number 10, Tom was immediately jumping up at them like a housebound spaniel.

"It's true. Oh my God, it's true," he panted. "The North Koreans *have* launched a missile."

"But I thought you and Mike said it was all a mistake?" Jenny asked irritably.

"It *was* a mistake, but now they've done it for real – Hyun Gun's just announced it on state television and the missile is already being tracked on the BBC. Look!"

He held an iPad towards them and Jenny reached out and looked at the clip of the missile coursing up through the cloud cover with its red light winking in the darkness. Without her support, William slithered to the floor and placed his feverish cheek against the tiles. Actual war it was then, Jenny thought - that suited her just fine.

I'D MOVE THE CAPITAL TO BILLERICAY

"I'M JUST SAYING that if they move the capital when London is destroyed, then I think they should consider Billericay as the new seat of power for the United Kingdom. We've got evidence of people living there since the Bronze Age, it's where Gavin and Stacey were from and it's very close to London – all points in its favour as the new capital."

Martin drove the heels of his hands into his eyes to try and push past some of the exhaustion. On a day as momentous as this, couldn't people just marshal a brain cell or two to think before they spoke? Couldn't Sid find him anyone with a single valid point to make? He imagined exhaling a beautiful plume of cigar smoke all over the room. The fantasy made him salivate. The pouches must have worn off and they were getting a bit itchy, he'd ditch them during the next weather report.

"But you see, you've hit upon the issue there haven't you, Janet – it's *very close to London*, which if it were to become a radioactive wasteland, is probably the sort of thing that we would want to avoid. We're going to take a short break and we'll be back with your extended Big Talk show after the news and weather read today by Tony Kim and brought to you by Invictus tablets, for every pole emerging from a black pit."

Martin pushed his mic stand away and stretched in his chair which groaned nearly as much as he did. Charlotte made her way into the studio. She had a coffee in her hand and she passed it over to Martin who reached for it greedily. She held it slightly out of his reach.

"Not so fast, I need a promise that you'll catch up on the Invictus ad reads, I need two in the next hour."

"*Fine*, caffeinate me."

"And I want you to steer the gimps away from billionaire-bashing for the rest of the show. The compliance team texted to remind us that Talk Today is owned by a billionaire, who has a legendarily shit sense of humour. He's not going to appreciate his own radio station calling for him to be guillotined."

"I can't help it if people are pissed off, I'm going to sound like a corporate stooge if I'm cutting them off and both-sidesing the argument that billionaires aren't quite in it together with us."

"Martin, fuck, I don't care what you do. It's not going to be the least ethical thing that has come out of your mouth if you do stick up for the cash-rich, so just make like a good lap dog and talk down a few of the revolutionaries. That last one was basically a Maoist."

"I don't know what that means."

"Billionaires bully-bully-bully rah-rah-rah, we no get sacked."

"Weirdly, that I understand."

Charlotte relented, and Martin greedily reached out and slurped the coffee.

"Twenty seconds," Sid said through the studio speakers.

"I'm going to sit in again but don't throw to me too much, we're not a posse."

"You're not a posse? Got it."

"Billericay."

"Fucking Billericay, right?"

Martin downed the rest of the coffee and tipped the cup upside down on his head to prove that he'd finished it. He then shot for the bin, "Kobe!" he said, as the cup bounced off the wall and along the carpet. Charlotte pushed his mic stand back towards him and he centred it over his head.

"That was *Gimme Shelter* by the Stones. Welcome back to your Big Talk show, on a day that's had more twists and turns than an Agatha Christie novel in a tumble dryer," he said, shrugging at Charlotte. "So, we've now found that despite our new interim Prime Minister assuring us that there was no need to panic, no more than two minutes later it was confirmed that there was a missile – thus cementing his position as the holder of the fastest U-turn since Charlotte's last Tinder date saw her waiting outside the cinema. True story. We are now expecting the arrival of the missile in the next thirty minutes and our thoughts and prayers are with everyone in London at this time. Let's go to someone now who is actually in London – Doug, where are you mate?"

"I'm in Chelsea," came the voice of an elderly gentleman.

"And what do you want to talk about on your Big Talk show today then Doug?"

"I'm sorry, I'm a bit nervous."

"That's all right, Doug, I think it's fair to say we're all on edge."

"I just want to know what's going on? I can't keep up."

"I am sorry about that Doug – it's definitely been a difficult day to keep on top of, I'll do my best to summarise. There is a state of chaos in London at the moment because you have roughly 10 million people all searching for somewhere safe to shelter from a nuclear missile which was rumoured earlier today, then semi-denied by the new Prime Minister William McCartney and now has been confirmed."

"*New* Prime Minister?"

"*Hooo*, yes, previously the Deputy Prime Minister, he's standing in for Fenton Crossley who tragically died today in the Thames."

"Crossley's dead?"

"Yes, Doug, listen I am so sorry to be the bearer of all this bad news."

"In the Thames – did he drown?"

"No…his plane crashed in the Thames."

"The river?"

"Yes."

"So – there *is* a missile?"

"I'm sorry to say there is Doug. Do you have somewhere safe that you could shelter?"

"No. I've got a little dog and she doesn't like being out, so I couldn't go anyway. I'm…going to die here then."

"Ahhh Doug. We're all thinking and praying for you at this time. And your dog."

"What good will thinking and praying do?"

"Um, yes, that's a good question. I suppose it's something we've grown used to saying in the absence of actually being able to do any material good."

"Well, why not just shut up then?"

"Well, I suppose it's talk radio so people might get annoyed if I said nothing."

Charlotte mimed a throat-cutting gesture at Martin.

"There's a missile coming for me, and you're trying to protect me with gibberish notions of thoughts and prayers."

"Yes, I can see your point Doug – I'll certainly think more before I speak next time. Anything else you want to add?"

"No."

"Ok, thanks Doug and if I may – what's your dog's name?"

"Pikey."

"Woah, Doug! No! That's not a thing you can. No. Doug. No, no, no. Our sincere apologies there. I'm afraid there's been so much cultural learning in recent years and maybe that's bypassed Doug as it sometimes does with members of the older generation."

"I'm forty-eight."

"Really? Doug – rename your dog. Sid, give me someone else. Once again, our profound apologies to anyone offended by Doug's language."

"Karl, speak to me, I believe you're in London too – do you have somewhere safe you can shelter?"

"No mate, but I don't believe it's going down anyway."

"No? But the Prime Minister did sort of confirm it."

"He's not the Prime Minister, he's just a suit standing behind the suit. Did you see he had a stonk-on during his press conference as well?"

"We've seen some of this chatter on social media. Let's charitably suggest that he had a wardrobe malfunction, shall we?"

"Wardrobe, nothing. Man got wood; something was functioning."

"So, if you're not worried about the bomb, what do you want to talk about?"

"I'm just mad, fuming, that caller you had before."

"Again, I am sorry about the culturally insensitive language."

"No! I mean the stupid head saying about Billericay as the new capital. No chance. No way. If London is destroyed, we need to move parliament to Croydon."

LISTEN TO
THE SAFETY
LOBSTER, KIDS!

COCO RAN ACROSS the car park, following the ramps down and around until she came to the vehicle exit. There was no movement of cars in the car park, although there were a few people collecting things from their vehicles, or more likely looting things from other people's, given the shifty looks they gave Coco as she ran past. When she reached the ground floor, she realised there was no movement because a school minibus had crashed across the exit barriers, and the rest of the traffic had instantly been trapped inside. Coco considered the terror of the occupants. She saw children's car seats in the minibus and found tears welling in her eyes. Those poor children, they must be so scared. There was blood covering the dashboard, but any other trace of the driver and passengers was long gone.

A steady rain had started to fall and after a minute she shook her costume by the legs to try and rid herself of the water it was soaking up. Once again, she considered if she would fare better in the sports bra and briefs she had on underneath, but although the costume wasn't waterproof, it was at least warm. Away from Orange Street, the roads were somewhat quieter, but there was still a sense of urgency as groups of people jogged along with phones pressed to their ears. Others wore serious expressions on their faces and Coco found herself trying to mimic them to fit in.

She stopped next to a set of black metal railings that screened off steep stairs leading down to a basement flat. She went through the gate and down a couple of steps away from the bustling pavements and tried to think. She knew that even if there were bunkers in Whitehall, there were also a few hundred thousand people who were also intent on getting into them. With a thought for her little baby hand grenade, she couldn't face the horror of more crushes. A police motorbike siren wailed past the end of the road and Coco found herself looking to the sky again. She mentally shook herself and decided that her only hope was getting as far out of London as she possibly could in the time she had remaining.

Then Coco noticed that at the bottom of the stairs there was an old blue road bike. Unbelievably, it didn't appear to be chained to anything. Perhaps its owners were out of town? Maybe they were hoping that their basement flat would be subterranean enough to shelter them? Coco quickly padded down the rest of the steps and with a discreet check over her shoulder, she hefted the bike and cagily snuck back up the stairs, huffing with the effort. She stood the bike on the pavement, swung her foot over the crossbar with some difficulty – clearly the owner was taller than she was, but by standing on one of the pedals she managed to perch her bum on the sharp seat. Fortunately, her three months of pregnancy had prepped her to withstand all affronts to her nether regions. Every medical appointment she'd been to so far seemed to consist of a queue of people who wanted to probe her cervix with an array of implements and then give her their in-depth and uninvited opinion. This nearly always seemed to predict that her future contained a birth scene in line with *Alien*.

Coco launched the bike in the direction that her internal London compass told her was north and pedalled hard. She bumped off the kerb with a jolt that could have parted her unborn child's hair, almost causing her to topple over the handlebars. Gradually, she regained her balance, clicked down through the gears and slowly the pedalling became easier. She steered her way past stalled cars and deserted buses. As she turned left at the top of the road into Rupert Street, she heard someone calling behind her.

"HEY! Wait!"

Coco didn't look around but tucked her head down towards the handlebars and drove the pedals hard. She stood to give herself more power and by the time she hit Shaftesbury Avenue she was starting to build some pace. She braked slightly to avoid a young girl who stepped off the pavement next to her mum, and then felt the bike veer suddenly to the right, this time launching herself over the handlebars as she tried to correct the wobble. She broke her fall with her arm as she crashed into a yellow and blue plastic traffic bollard. She slid down and sprawled on the floor, a searing pain radiating from her upper thigh. She could only manage a weak "Hey!" as a man in grey joggers and a black t-shirt righted her bike, mounted it and started to pedal off.

"I'm sorry," he shouted over his shoulder.

"I farted on that seat!" she shouted at his back as he faded from view.

Coco pulled herself to her feet using the bollard. What she really, really wanted right at that very moment was to be sat in bed drinking hot chocolate and watching at least thirty consecutive episodes of *Below Deck*.

"You absolutely will not cry," she said to herself and her tear ducts seemed to get the message. She assessed her injuries. Her hands were still scraped and red from her earlier fall, but her latest tussle with gravity only seemed to have bruised her hip, thanks to the surprising softness of the bollard.

She knew she had to keep going, regardless of injuries, so she forced herself to limp across Shaftesbury Avenue and turned right and jogged into Great Windmill Street. The deep-fried smells of the looted McDonalds she ran past reminded her of how hungry she was, and she felt herself salivate as she thought once again of bed and the sachet of hot chocolate she had at home. She noticed a flash of luminous yellow across the road and as she looked again, she saw it was accompanied by a small man in a huge suit. The pair were scurrying along the street and seemed to be deep in discussion, or at least the smaller one was.

It was the pair from Orange Street. Cole and Bradford.

Cole was examining something on the floor and more or less pushing Bradford along. Even from twenty yards back she could tell that Bradford was complaining. They turned left just past a pub on the corner into an alley and Coco followed them but held back, watching them through the front and side windows of the pub. She didn't know why she was trailing them, other than the coincidence seemed to suggest that she should. At the bottom of the alley, she saw Cole smile widely as he examined something else on the floor. Coco made her way to the corner of the pub and peeked around the side. As she watched, Cole inserted something into the floor and pulled up a big triangular panel from the floor.

She watched as a soundless conversation played out between them. Bradford was looking aggrieved and kept patting Cole on the shoulder. He held his fist up for a bump, which Cole didn't provide. He said one word and Bradford examined the hatch with distaste. Cole said another word and Bradford sat by next to the hatch and tentatively started to climb down. Cole looked around and then followed Bradford down into the sewer. Coco wasn't sure why but she felt like there was something vulpine about Cole's face, like she was watching an Aesop's Fable unfold in front of her. As she watched, a hand reached up out of the tunnel and pulled the flaps of the hatch back into place with a loud clang.

Coco was stunned at the ingenuity.

It was so simple – in the sewers, they'd be able to avoid the crowds and the sort of people who would steal a bike from you. If they didn't make it across London in time, they would at least be underground, which must surely give them a sort of shelter? Coco ran over to where they had disappeared. On the ground were two hatches, and Coco decided that it was the larger of the two that they had used. The hatch had a waffle pattern on top and the rectangular grid seemed to be split into two triangular panels. Each panel had two black holes in them about the size of a pound coin. She dropped to the floor and tried to stare down through the holes. She thought she could see a ghost of light, but she couldn't be sure. She wriggled her finger into one of the holes and tried to heave it open, but it was thick metal and it barely moved.

Coco looked around in desperation. A few large industrial recycling bins were parked behind the pub and just next to those, a formation of black bins which belonged to the flats nearby. Without giving herself time to think of the grossness, Coco started flipping open the lids of the bins, releasing a stale cloud of bin bag odours. She switched to breathing through her mouth – a skill she'd mastered long ago working with seafood and bright lights. She searched through the bins, looking for anything that might help her open the sewer hatch. Would it be too much to ask that someone had recently thrown out their perfectly serviceable crowbar? Apparently, yes. She pulled out a string of fairy lights. She wasn't sure what they would do, but it seemed like it could be something. Another few minutes of searching through the bins yielded some shiny metal tubing, a coat hanger and the Christmas decorations.

She ran back to the hatch with her bounty and fed the metal tubing into the hole. To her startled relief, it was the perfect diameter to fit in the hole. When she'd fed in a few inches, she leaned back on the tube to try and lever the hatch open, and nearly fell when the hollow tube bent and snapped. She heard a wet clatter from below as half of the tube landed in the sewer. Undeterred, she stripped the bulbs from the string of lights. Once she had a few metres without any lights on them, she threaded the wire into the hole and fed it down until the next bulb left on the strip acted as a stopper. She then moved across to the other hole in the panel and turned the end of the wire coat-hanger over into a small hook. She straightened the rest of the wire and fed it into the other hole and started to fish around.

"Whit are ye daein? That's the council's," came a voice.

Coco looked up and saw a middle-aged man manoeuvring his mobility scooter closer to the hatch so he could get a good view of what she was up to.

"I'm from the council," Coco improvised as she continued to rummage for the dangling wire. She felt the hook brush the wire but then felt it drop. *Shit*.

"Aye? And why are ye dressed as a lobster?"

"I'm a safety lobster. I teach children about the dangers of playing in the sewers."

"Oh is that it, aye? Where's yer heid then? Hey? Safety lobster? Where's yer heid!"

"It's in the sewer! That's the danger I'm warning children about. Don't leave your lobster heid in a sewer. Now fuck off!" Coco screamed, as once again she felt the lights evade her hook.

"Aye, well, ye soond like yer fae the council noo," he admitted and beeped as he reversed his scooter.

Coco felt the coat-hanger hook the wire and she carefully teased it back towards her. She quickly pulled the wire through the other hole so she had a connection underneath the metal flap. By taking both sides of the wire and pulling as hard as she could the panel slowly started to rise. By leaning her entire weight backwards, the triangular section popped up. Coco sat by the side of the hatch and using a combination of her legs and her elbows she man-handled the other half of the hatch open, revealing a ladder just below. Coco clenched her fist in victory and shuffled over to the u-shaped metal rungs embedded in the wall. Fortunately, the torch on her battered phone was still working and she could see that the top rung was seaweed-slippery, so she made sure that she grabbed each rung firmly as she followed Cole and Bradford into the underworld.

💎 💎 💎 💎 💎

"PLEASE GOD NO!" Bradford shouted. "NO! NO! NO! NO! NO!"

"Shut up!" Cole replied, and drove his fist into Bradford's gut. Both the air and his resolve blew out of Bradford in a desperate wheeze. While he was sinking to his knees, Cole reached inside Bradford's jacket and relieved him of the black velvet bag. He patted him down and also pulled out Bradford's phones and the tactical knife.

"There's a decent blade on that. I'm going to keep it, I reckon. You were going to give it to me anyway, weren't you?"

Bradford still hadn't regained the ability to talk, so he simply exhaled in an annoyed manner to communicate his point.

"What did you think? Get me to take you through the sewer and then poke a few 'oles in me and escape on your own?"

"Noooo," said Bradford, his voice still raspy from the winding. "I saw a rat; I was protecting us."

"Yeah, you get rats down here," Cole replied with a smirk. "Now, how about you tell me how I get into that handy-dandy little bunker you've got lined up?"

"No," Bradford said defiantly.

"And what if I stab you and *keep* stabbing you, until you decide to tell me," Cole stared at the fine blade in the light of his phone's torch.

"What about my daughter?! She'll die without me."

"People don't mourn imaginary girls that much, old pal."

"She's not imaginary!"

"You're pushing it now. For me to believe you've got a little girl, I'd have to believe that someone would have sex with you and my imagination isn't that good. Now, how do you get in the bunker?"

"I won't tell you," Bradford said.

"Maybe Mother can help us sort this out," Cole said.

Bradford looked at the glint of madness on Cole's face and followed his eyeline towards the colossal fatberg.

"She's something, isn't she?" Cole said, gazing in awe at the silent, off-white blob. "We did some work on the junction back there a few months ago. Remember when it got baking and the Euros were on? We had a TV down here and a little beer fridge. When we got bored, we'd come and feed stuff into Mother."

"Please, I don't want to go in there," Bradford managed to utter in a pitiful voice.

"Oh, you're going in there. You can keep my ex-wife company!" Cole said with a laugh. "Nah, I'm only kidding. She's not in there. Go on, up you get." Cole poked at Bradford with his foot, but Bradford remained curled on the floor.

"Tell you what. Either you start climbing up in the next five seconds, or I'm going to stab you. One, two…" Cole punched the knife into Bradford's shoulder. Bradford's soprano shriek bounced around the tunnel, but Mother absorbed most of the shrill noise.

"Weird, innit? What she does to sound," said Cole, who tried to replicate the effect by yipping loudly several times. "You want the other shoulder doing, or are you getting in?"

Bradford whimpered and clutched the hand of his uninjured arm to the wound. It was only a few centimetres deep but a steady flow of blood oozed out of the gash.

"Up you go then."

Bradford sobbed. His shoulder was on fire, but even more painful was the frustration! He was Bradford Alderman VIIII, scion of the Alderman Retail Group! Since breakfast the litany of slights on his person had been building. He had been spurned – twice! The F1 had been egged. He had been punched – twice! He had been stabbed. Now, he was being forced into a sewer-clogging turd. Every man has his limits, and Bradford had reached his.

What Cole couldn't have known is that Bradford no longer had his knife, but he wasn't without a means of defence. During the work that he'd done with the psychic, through a combination of charm and bribery, he'd managed to extract the most vicious telepathic attack the guru knew. It had cost millions for the man to part with the knowledge; information which he'd made Bradford swear on an actual stack of Bibles that he would never tell another human soul. He'd even had to sign a contract to only use it in an absolute emergency. The time had arrived for Bradford to unsheathe The Psionic Blade.

"What's funny?" Cole asked, as Bradford smiled slyly and lifted two ramrod straight fingers to his temple and inhaled a galaxy of chi from the secret dimensions that the guru had explained were interconnected with ours: Cosmere and Arrakis. He focused the chi into a ball and mentally sculpted it into a wide, flat point. He gave the blade two deviously sharp points and aimed them directly at Cole's temples.

"BAKANA KANEMOCHI YARŌ!" Bradford screamed, recalling the sacred words he had been entrusted with, and as he did so he mentally thrust the dual-pronged weapon into Cole's face. He opened his eyes and looked at Cole's blank expression staring at him.

"Get in the fatberg, you muckhead," Cole said flatly.

Impossible! He should be witless! Could Cole know the secrets of Winter Shield? That protection had been the only reason that Bradford had been able to practice The Psionic Blade on the guru without leaving him befuddled. The guru had even shown Bradford one of the blade's victims, the poor man could only drool and stare out of the window. But had Cole somehow had lessons too? An audience with the guru alone cost upwards of £100,000. It seemed unlikely, but it was the only explanation.

At the prick of Cole's actual knife, Bradford turned hastily and regarded Mother. There she lay in all her fetid glory. Two metres wide, two metres high and log jammed tight against the side of the sewer wall. With a whimper he pushed a handhold into the congealed mass and started to climb. Although the fatberg looked crumbly from a distance, Bradford found that as he took hold of Mother, he got purchase easily. The dry outer crust gave way to a warmer and oilier core. Bradford created a foothold, feeling Mother embed herself under his toenails, inviting him to clamber up her side and feel her embrace. He gagged the entire way, as his fingers, knees and feet found the substance almost sentiently clammy to his touch. Soon he was fully astride the mighty beast, ducking his head to avoid the top of the tunnel.

He turned and looked at Cole, who was stood slack-jawed, marvelling at Bradford's progress.

"Please let me go now, you've had your fun, we can still make the bunker. We can go together!"

"It must be because you're so small," he said, his head to one side as he looked at Bradford on top of Mother, his foot in a clog of hair.

"What do you want now?" Bradford asked.

"What it's like?" Cole said, with a faraway expression on his face.

"It's horrible! Obviously, it's horrible! I'm on a fatberg. *Please* let me go. I did what you wanted."

"I think you should just wait there; it looks like you're already starting to sink a bit."

"Why don't you leave me here? All you need to get into the bunker is the phone, you've got everything you need but you have to be quick or they'll go without you."

"Yeah. I will in a minute," Cole said, still mesmerised by Bradford's plight. "Jump up and down a bit."

Bradford tentatively got to his feet in a crouch and jumped as much as the space allowed. He felt Mother shift underneath to accommodate him. First one foot sank down into the wretched mass. Then, as he shifted around, his knee fell into the crack, with his foot tucked behind him. The beastly white turd opened beneath him and Bradford found himself slipping in up to his waist. Then a deeper fissure opened and he sank to his shoulders, with his left arm tucked tight by his side. A stout grey rat with a long pink tail tripped lightly along the surface of the fatberg and scuttled across Bradford's back. Bradford tried to get it off by jerking at it with his head.

"I'm going to die," Bradford said plaintively. And as he said it, something within his soul cried out and he wailed a primal shriek of such force that it briefly snapped Cole out of his trance.

"HEEEEEEEELP MEEEEE!"

"Shut up, you numpty. There's no one here to help you," Cole said.

"Don't be too sure of that," Coco said as she pulled herself into the mouth of the tunnel. Her heroic reveal was spoiled slightly by the wet lobster costume making it nearly impossible for her to get to her feet. She realised she should have climbed up and then delivered her line. Unfortunately, real life didn't allow you to go again from the top of the scene. By the time she was on her feet, Cole was waiting with the knife in his hand. Coco reeled backwards when she saw it.

"Woah! Don't stab me, you mentalist, I'm pregnant! It's me, from earlier – I'm the lobster, remember?" Coco said, still struggling to her feet.

"Of course, I remember," Cole replied. "There haven't been that many lobsters at large today."

"Why don't you just let us go, eh?" Coco said in a soothing voice.

"Baby or no baby, I don't think I'll be letting him, or you, go anywhere."

"So, what are you going to do?" Coco asked hesitantly.

"Maybe I'll see if Mother's got room for one more. Why not? A mother in Mother? In for a penny, in for a pound," he mused. Suddenly, something cold and claggy splattered across the back of his head and he reached up in disgust to pull the decomposed remnants of a nappy from his head.

"Fuck you, yokel!" Bradford shouted as he sank even further.

Cole turned back to deal with the lobster. He looked with confusion as she tapped him on the head with what looked like a metal witch's wand. His last conscious thought was seeing the lightning emerge from the tip of the device and wondering if he would be turned into a frog. Then his head snapped back as fifty milliamps of current coursed through his brain and muscles, locking them into a series of convulsions. Then he went rigid and fell backwards into the shallow water of the tunnel. Coco looked with newfound respect at the Crustaystun in her hand. She would have used that on Red Steve and his dead tooth months ago if only she'd known. Then she looked around and realised that she was alone; Bradford had vanished completely.

THAT IS LITERALLY A PRETTY PENNY

MARGARET SLICED THE remaining section of the leftover duck bread into two pieces, giving Graham the mallard's share. She didn't think she would be able to eat much, but she thought she'd make an effort. She loaded the bread with the wafer-thin ham with the orange breadcrumb fringe (Ed Sheerham, Graham called it), iceberg lettuce and grated cheese mixed with light mayonnaise. As she was about to squeeze out a serving of the mayo, she caught herself and swapped it for the full-fat version at the back of the fridge. Cholesterol be damned.

In truth, Margaret was amazed at how calmly she was handling the end of the world. Of course, as a Christian, she'd thought about death, dying and rebirth most Sundays, but she'd always had a fairly benign conviction that everything would be all right. In church they had made a good case for the afterlife being enjoyable and she'd simply never conceived anything else. It was the thought of the cats suffering that pained her the most. And she couldn't help but feel cheated by the way her life had gone. Still, she had more than most and she forced herself to remember that.

She popped thirty of the sleeping pills out of the foil packet and formed them into a little mound, then, using the back of a soup spoon she leaned on the pile, crunching it around and squashing them over and over until all that was left was a yellow powder. Using the front of the spoon she scooped up the dust and deposited it into an egg cup. She took the egg cup and sandwiches over to the dining table and picked up the little remote control from its home in the dish on the windowsill and pressed the on and off buttons repeatedly. Upstairs in Graham's study, a custom neon sign saying "Live, Laugh, Logarithms" flashed off and on alerting Graham to lunch. She heard him stand, stretch and pad his way across the room, switch off the radio, emerge onto the landing, walk into the upstairs bathroom, wash his hands and then trot down the stairs.

As he entered the dining room he was rubbing his stomach in a pantomime of hunger.

"Greetings Chef! Pray tell, what is on the bill of fayre this day?" he said. It was always either this routine, or he would hold his hands together in prayer and say, "Rub-a-dub-dub, thanks for the grub, Amen." Many would say that he was a difficult man to love, but Margaret had an unusual capacity to foist love on extremely academic and emotionally incompetent men. Her father had trained that reflex into her. She sighed and smiled.

"It's sandwiches – baguette bread, ham and cheese."

"Ooh la la! Du pain, du vin, du Boursin."

"Oui."

"Ole! Multiple thanks Margaritte, it looks divine. Ooh, Ed Sheerham!"

They sat at the table and Graham took a long draught of the water that Margaret had filled for him.

"How's the water?" she asked.

"H2OK," he replied with a smile.

She looked at him with intent, and he noticed her just after he'd taken a large bite of his sandwich. He wiped at his mouth with a napkin and chewed in an exaggerated fashion.

"Sorry, I should have said, after you."

"No, I'm – Graham, what's happening?"

"Lunch?"

"No! I mean, do you even *know* what's happening? You must have heard the news. There's a missile!"

"Oh, that! They were talking about it on the radio. You're not worried, are you?"

"It's a nuclear missile! Yes, I'm scared!"

Graham put down his sandwich.

"Oh, Margaret, I'm sorry – I didn't think you'd be concerned."

Margaret's reeled in confusion. She started to speak several times but found that Graham's logic had robbed her of any sense.

"Why would you not think I was concerned?"

"*Well*, it all seems pretty unlikely don't you think?"

"Graham – Rash told everyone at work, he belongs to some sort of service that gives billionaires prior warning – it's real. There is a nuclear missile coming to London. He asked if I wanted to go to a bunker! Why did you think I asked you to keep the cats in?"

"I thought you might have heard there was a fox around?"

Once again Margaret tried to talk but the cumulative logic and energy needed to construct a sentence confronting such basic ideas thwarted her. Yes, she was scared of nuclear missiles. Yes, she thought he might be too. Instead, she took a bite of her own sandwich. The duck bread was lovely, not ideal for crowns, but dental problems could join the line of issues. Graham eyed her cautiously, bit his sandwich and then chomped on. They ate in frosty silence for a few minutes, before Margaret took a sip of water and tried again.

"Let's conduct a thought experiment," she said, and Graham looked momentarily hopeful - he was on much firmer ground with experiments, thought or otherwise. "If it was the end of the world, what would you want to do?"

"Do?"

"Yes - say? Do? You hear the five-minute warning – what is your next action?"

He bit at his top lip with his bottom teeth in little nibbles – a sure sign that he was giving the issue some genuine thought.

"Well – I'm assuming that you mean a four-minute warning – that was the primary form of alert that was reserved for notifying the public of a nuclear attack. Why four minutes? Well – it's because in earlier times – notably during the Cold War – this would have been the earliest that a missile could have been detected, confirmed and then broadcast to the public. Needless to say, methods of detection and global communications have improved since then. That being the case we might anticipate a forty-minute warning and indeed-"

"*Graham.*"

"Sorry. What do I do if I'm alerted to an imminent apocalypse?" He paused for thought and Margaret saw him glimpse briefly towards the stairs, to his study and his dissertation. Margaret knew – of course she knew - that he would choose his work.

"It's okay Graham – I won't make you say it. You'd go to the study."

"Well, yes. But I'd check on you and the cats first. I'm just so close Margaritte. I can feel the proof tickling me here." He pushed a finger into his head an inch above his ear. "It's there."

Margaret smiled. He was so much like her father that it was uncanny – a man of so much devotion that it was almost religious – but she'd never mastered the art of asking that some of that devotion be diverted towards her.

"Do you want to know what I would like to do, Graham? If I heard the five-minute warning?" She flashed him a stern look not to challenge her on the timing of warnings.

"No, please tell me."

Margaret took a breath and then the words came tumbling out.

"I would want to be held. As the bomb went off, I would want my body to be held. I would want to feel my lips on the lips of someone I loved as the world burst into flames. I would want that same feeling in my heart. I would want to be discovered by archaeologists in ten thousand years – an anonymous crust of a person, sealed to another in an act of love. I would want those future historians to be jealous of me – a dead, stone figure, but someone who was important, someone who knew and felt love. Burning, deadly, beautiful love. And Graham, I would want you. And I would want you to want me."

Margaret exhaled and felt herself deflate. There was a silence as Graham ran his finger around his plate and picked up the crumbs.

"I'm sure," he began at a slightly higher register than his normal voice. He coughed and looked to begin again, but instead he made another pass with his finger for the crumbs. "I want you to know that I enjoyed that sandwich. Thank you, Margaritte."

He picked up his plate and hers and the glasses and bussed them through to the kitchen. He walked stealthily past Margaret, almost tip-toeing towards the stairs.

"I almost poisoned our sandwiches, you know," Margaret said.

"What?" Graham turned to face her.

"When I was making our lunch, I wondered if it was the right thing to poison us with sleeping tablets. I thought it might be a kindness – for us to simply fall asleep and never wake up. The cats could have eaten our eyeballs. We've always said that they'd like that."

Margaret held up the egg cup with its deadly contents.

"Do you want some?"

"No!" said Graham aghast, as he shuffled back into the room. He knelt next to Margaret and gingerly took the egg cup from her and placed it on the table. Her heart beat fast at his proximity. *Curse love and the fools it makes of us.* "Honestly, I don't know why. I'm not scared. It's too absurd. All of this can't stop. The cats. Mathematics. People. Please don't eat that, it's not a peaceful death."

"So, what am I supposed to do, Graham? What can I do with this sadness?"

"I don't know," he said dolefully.

He turned his eyes back to the door, a hopeless addict drawn irrepressibly to his next fix.

"I have something for you," Margaret said. She retrieved one of her coins. She held out her hand and dropped one of the larger ones into Graham's palm. He held it in front of his face and turned it around with a mystified expression.

"A pretty penny," Margaret said. After more than two decades living with him, she knew that was the joke that he'd make. "If you're right and nothing happens with the missile, I want you to use it to set yourself up somewhere. You're free, Graham."

Margaret turned sharply and went back into the kitchen. Graham regarded her back and felt a vault of emotions open in his chest. He thought about pursuing her, but something stopped him. How could he be separate from Margaret? Was that possible? He tried to think of a time before her, but drew a blank. They had simply always been, as far as he was concerned. Glumly, he trod the centreline of the stairs. He went into the bathroom and washed his hands. He dried his hands on the towel and appreciated the smell of flowers and perfume that arose from the clean towels. He knew that he should tell Margaret that he valued the things she did. He understood that he should also tell her it wasn't just the towels that he appreciated – it was the order and the company and the life that she had woven around him. But knowing something and being able to express it wasn't the same thing at all.

LONDON BRIDGE IS FOR FALLING DOWN

LALLY BARGED THROUGH the crowd that was now filtering into the overcrowded Knightsbridge station. A pox on Colin and earnest communal singing. A pox on people. What was she thinking? There was no safety in sheltering in place, it was a pleasant fiction that these missiles could be survived in any way other than being in a bunker or by getting far, far away. The initial panic still hadn't left her, but the emotion was transmuting into fear and a stagnant pond of sadness. She stumbled blearily down past Harvey Nichols and turned right into Basil Street.

Lally fumbled for her phone and tapped on the Blacklane app. She needed to breathe and to cleanse herself from the chaos and that would be easier in the back of a climate-controlled Mercedes-Benz. When the app eventually loaded it showed a simple red box at the top of the welcome screen: Service Not Available.

Well, what the actual? Lally dismissed the notifications that were pinging onto her phone and pulled up the contacts app. Her finger wavered over a series of entries purposefully devoid of photos or names, which were simply numbered from #I to #XII. All morning she had been having no luck getting hold of #I and she knew for a fact that #V through to #IX would probably have her number blocked. They had never quite forgiven her for her drinking days, when she liked to pick up the phone in the small hours. It wasn't always good to talk.

#IV was tricky too – she might pick up, but she probably didn't have the clout to do anything of use. Lally needed the army, or at the very least the police. At this point she would settle for someone in a pointy hat on a horse with a regimental sword. She paused as she reached out to press the dial button. Come on, girl. You're in real trouble – isn't that when families are supposed to put rifts behind them and be there for each other? And what was the point of His Majesty's Service, if His Majesty couldn't summon a tank or two to drive his relatives around occasionally? She tapped #III, took a deep breath and held the phone to her ear.

"Fuck off, Eulalia," came a gruff voice and the phone went dead. So that answered that one.

Without giving herself time to think, she dialled #XII. Lally heard the line connect, but immediately all she could hear was a wash of static. A voice sounded faintly underneath the disturbance.

"You utter shit, you've got a fucking nerve suddenly finding my number. I hope you burn, you hom-" Lally hung up.

She immediately dialled #II, her best bet. It rang several times and then the same small voice and buzz of interference.

"Hey Lal, they're telling me not to pick up this call, so make it quick. Wait, Violet says she didn't get a chance to finish saying everything she wanted to, so can you fill in the blanks?"

Lally ignored him. At least now she knew that Violet was with #II. #XII had made the grade, so much for sororal loyalty. She checked the hip flask was empty. It was.

"Where are you? It sounds like you're being flushed down the toilet."

"I'm in a holly-cop. Can't say where."

Despite everything, Lally smiled at the use of the word, the best approximation she could make of the word helicopter at the age of four, since entered into the family vocabulary.

"J, I'm scared. I'm in Knightsbridge and I'm stuck – they must have told you more about what's going on. I mean good God!

What should I do? I tried to help in a tube station and they sang *Imagine* and it was awful…and now I don't know what to *do*! Send me a holly-cop, J. Please send me a holly-cop. Please, please, please, please, please."

"Are you *drunk*, Lal? Good grief. Lal! Shit, listen they're not going to let me speak any more. Just…take care of yourself, won't you?"

"That's easy for you to say when they've put you on a pissing helicopter and whirly-whisked you to safety. Just tell me what's happening!"

There was a scuffle and she heard a crack as the phone was passed over. A different voice came on the line - richer, more dismissive.

"Look, Eulalia," this voice, deeper and older – #I, himself. "Can you get this into your pickled fucking head – we have to draw the line somewhere. There has to be a cutoff. Don't you dare put your victim guilt bullshit on us. There's a line, whether you accept it or not. There is a line and you are on that side of it and we are on this side…"

Lally knew it. She accepted it, but it didn't mean that she didn't feel her soul detach from her body and float away like a balloon above a crying child. Here was the truth, finally: she wasn't one of them. Just as much as she wasn't one of the people.

"…best scenario is jump in a Blacklane and Foxtrot Oscar."

"At least tell me where you're going! Where should I go?"

"Don't worry, there's always a boat in the morning."

The line went dead. So, the cutoff was #I to #XII. No room for #XIII. She didn't want to think about whether they'd made room on the hollycop for #XIV, it wouldn't surprise her.

At least she knew her family were heading to the Isle of Man. "There's a boat in the morning" - the traditional Manx way of saying that you were welcome to fuck off if you so wanted. Lally remembered a summer in Milntown from childhood playing games of Paparazzi Chase. Running after #I and watching him fall and split his lip. He ran off and told on her, and the adults shunned her for the rest of the holiday because she had ruined the chance to take the family portrait. Lally's early adventures in being a pariah.

Shit, shit, shit, shit.

She stared at her phone and, with a bleak thud, realised there was no one left to call. There was no one to share this moment with, or to get drunk with, or to just hold onto. The human being that she was closest to was a woman called Eilidh, and she only knew her because she had occasionally borrowed her spaniel to take it for a walk. She found herself almost on the verge of calling her, but instead she sat down cross-legged on the pavement and cried. She bawled her eyes out. There was a cutoff and they were on that side and she was on this side. I hope you burn. Take care of yourself. There's a boat in the morning. The phrases queued up to play in her head.

Fuck the fucking family and their emotional constipation. It wasn't just the jewels that were guarded. She almost respected #III for telling her to fuck off, at least it was an emotional connection of sorts. It wasn't just money that made them like this, it was the illusion of importance. Millennia ago, the people had been told the King was chosen by God. Now the royals were just *Made In Chelsea* who happened to command a navy. There was no warmth. No honesty. No love. You couldn't speak your mind. You couldn't fall in love with anyone outside of a pool of candidates so pre-vetted that you knew their blood type before you said Hello. And all the affairs, the cheating, the deaths and the homosexuality were wafted away by that stupid fucking wave.

Lally sniffed her way to a standstill. She dug in the wax jacket's pocket and found the ancient golden box of Benson and Hedges, cued up one of the battered ciggies and lit the end. She inhaled deeply and let the smoke fumigate her brain. There had to be a way out. After quick-toking half of the cigarette, instead of feeling the inspiration she had been hoping for, she felt the light in her brain snuff out. There really wasn't any point. She couldn't escape. She couldn't get help. She had no one. She folded the ember of the B&H against the red-tiled wall of the building behind her and felt it burn the tip of her thumb.

If it were done when 'tis done, then 'twere well it were done quickly.

Lally got to her feet, unzipped the jacket and hung it on top of a roadwork barrier. Goodbye, Daddy. She turned to face east and started to walk. At the bottom of the street, she broke into a run.

💎 💎 💎 💎 💎

As she ran, Lally remembered that she still had her headphones hooked around her neck. She slipped them on and thumbed blindly at a playlist on Spotify. After a couple of skips, *What Can I Do If The Fire Goes Out* by Gang of Youths started playing and Lally listened to the relentless pounding of the drum and it made her feet move faster over the pavement. As the singer poured out his heart, yearning to know more, she found the alcohol in her blood levelling off and the fear rising again. She quickened her pace, looking for anywhere she could find booze. Down Pavilion Road, past the boutiques and chi-chi eateries that were her birthright.

The song segued into *Syke! Life Is Awesome!* and Lally watched it soundtrack furious Sloan Rangers abandoning their Land Rovers and screaming silently into mobile phones. She saw a crowd gathered outside the Saatchi Gallery, chanting about something, although the music in her ears blocked out whatever it might have been. A skip was on fire at the corner of Ellis Street and she briefly wondered how it came to be as she breezed through the grimy smoke. Mummy's prime command of Thou Shalt Not Be Fat and a succession of sinewy female PTs had left her with excellent cardio, so nearly a mile had fallen beneath her feet before she broke a sweat. She jogged past Maggie's grave and onwards to the river. She held up her hand to a Chelsea Pensioner she saw looking blankly out of his window. He saluted in return.

She kept the river to her right and slowed to a walk as she suddenly felt woozy from the odd combination of exercise and vodka. The wide pavement gave plenty of room for the people sensibly heading west, away from the seat of power. She found a newsagent which was inexplicably open and filled her hip flask with a bottle of Grant's vodka. The shop smelled richly of coriander and cigarettes. She asked the Indian shopkeeper if he wasn't going to close. He didn't answer, but looked at her curiously.

"The missile?" she explained.

"No, no missiles," he said and turned his hands up in apology.

Lally shrugged and made her way back onto the embankment to drink her vodka. Then, staggering slightly, she embraced the Thames' serpentine curves and let the sweep of the water push her into Westminster. Near College Garden, a policeman with a black machine gun shouted something in her face as she stumbled past but she pointed ruefully at the headphones. He continued to shout but she carried on with her swerving run until he was far behind her.

She sped past parliament, past the monuments and statues across Victoria Embankment. At the RAF memorial, Lally saluted. She paused her run and stood transfixed at Bazalgette's bust, inset into the wall, his coy expression and bushy moustache keeping his secrets close. She dallied by his statue and on a whim, she climbed up and planted a kiss right on his cold bronze face, and whispered that she would like the secret too. How do you do it, Joe? How do you just keep on taking shit from everyone? The bridges came and went: Waterloo, Blackfriars, Millennium, Southwark. Then she ran past a Fitness First and sprinted up twisting metal stairs and out onto London Bridge. She dropped her hip flask into an empty bin and breathed deeply, which only made her head spin faster.

"Clang bang," she said out loud. Her last words, just as stupid as her first.

She decided that she couldn't face Tower Bridge, it was too picture postcard. Instead, she crossed the gridlocked road and faced back towards Blackfriars. In her mind, this was proper London. London Bridge was for falling down. It was only a low barrier at the edge, so she placed her hands on the slick metal rail and hoisted herself up. She slowly got to her feet, found her balance and looked at the people scurrying across the bridge. No one was going to stop her. People had things to do today, people that they loved to get back to. Take care of yourself. She said goodbye to London and prepared to take one small step.

THE SOLUTION IS OBVIOUSLY TO STEAL A BOAT

AFTER LEAVING THE Pheasant, Greg's blood alcohol content was back up to the levels rarely found outside of wasps that had fallen into a pint of lager. To Greg's inebriated mind, this was a very pleasant state of affairs and he had decided that it was mission critical that he retain at least a moderate-to-heavy buzz until this whole thing was behind him. He'd dispensed with his suit jacket, rolled up his shirt sleeves and he was feeling a lot more in control.

Plus, he had a gun now.

People said a lot of negative things about guns, but they were peerlessly excellent for navigating large crowds. Greg's six-foot frame, his shambolic hair and the pint-powered glint in his eye would perhaps have been enough to keep the general public away from him anyway, but add in the gun and it was like watching a shark swim through a shoal of fish. No matter which way he turned, there was instantly space for him. He kept hearing, "He's got a gun!" which reminded him, hearteningly, that he had a gun. The people didn't need to know that it wasn't a real gun and that he'd simply taken it down from the wall of The Pheasant, removed the "BANG!" flag from the barrel and walked out onto the street. To them Greg was lunatic prime and, perhaps, at this point it wasn't far from the truth.

"Hello, B of the Bang, do you still need picking up?"

"Hello? Is that B of the Bang?" came a confused and alarmingly posh voice.

"Yes, yes, you've dialled the right number. You're trying to work out how to get away from these missiles, right?"

"Well, yes? I was supposed to be picked up on Trafalgar Square."

"Really, that's a new one, it's usually on the river. Anyway. If you still want saving, Greg is coming."

"And who is Greg?"

"Greg is me. I am Greg," Greg replied, hoping that it was true. "But listen, you're going to need to bring gold. Got that? You can't get on the rescue boat if you don't have gold."

"But I pay for your service!"

"Yeah, I know, we're all disappointed, but you see you've got two options – you can either submit a complaint to the ashen corpses of everyone working at Trading Standards in the nuclear wasteland that tomorrow will bring, or you can bring gold and go to the bunker. What do you fancy because I've got another three calls waiting."

"This is extortion."

"No, it's advanced supply and demand."

"I'll bring the gold."

"Excellent choice. Look out for a boat honking. If you're there, do the robot and I'll know you're one of mine."

"The what?"

"The robot - you know, the dance. I need to know you're one of mine, you see."

"But I don't know how to do the robot!"

"Ok, great, don't forget the gold!"

Greg had refined his sales pitch and as far as he could tell, he now had around twenty billionaires heading to various stops along the Thames to bring him those marvellous escape to the country tokens. If his maths was right, he was in line for the sort of payday that could see him break free of wage slavery.

"Look at it from my point of view," Greg chuntered to himself as he bounced down the shaky walkway heading to the Millbank Millennium Pier. "There has been an error. An egregious error. And you can't spell egregious without Greg. But none of this is Greg's fault! Greg said work on the green system. Sorry, the red system. Work on the red system – I was very clear. But they worked on the green. So now, people want a boat to take them to a bunker. And the first rule of showbiz is give the people what they want. But what is the flaw here? I don't have a boat. Or a bunker. But a bunker is next Greg's problem. A boat is this Greg's problem."

He paused to stop the slip-slopping of the walkway. Once enough of his equilibrium had returned, he continued to bound towards the river. At the bottom lay the angular dull box of the pier building. Greg stood momentarily puzzled wondering how to get into the building. He saw the steps leading down to the bottom section of the jetty and took them. Unfortunately, at the foot of the stairs, the path terminated in a pair of metal gates with a set of unashamedly barbaric spikes on the top. The gates were locked with a thick chain and the sort of padlock that could keep a bike safe in Central London. Greg briefly wondered if he could climb over, but decided that it would be safer to scout for alternatives.

Retracing his way back up the steps, Greg noticed that the roof of the pier ran alongside the walkway. He gave the structure a prod to verify its sturdiness, lobbed his rifle onto the makeshift platform and gingerly climbed after it. Once he'd reached the middle, he began to inch towards the edge, but found that the roof itself overhung the jetty some way and stood directly over the water. Spiderman would have made short work of the situation, but Greg was not Spiderman.

He scanned around and saw that the only boat docked on the jetty was one of the Uber catamarans, which was perfect for his needs. Greg calculated that it was about three or four metres away, with a slight drop onto the top level of the boat.

"You can absolutely do this," Greg opined.

"You're absolutely right," Greg agreed.

If he got a bit of a run-up, it would be possible to leap from one roof to the other. Then it would be a simple case of starting the boat, getting the people to a bunker, then totting up the gold he'd accrued and picking a country without an extradition treaty. He just had to make this jump. In his favour, he had watched hundreds of parkour videos on Instagram and he could picture the moves required in his head. Run. Spring. Leap. Roll. Present.

A little voice in his head pointed out that he was not particularly fit and that he had never done anything this gymnastically complex before. The voice started to detail the very real damage that could ensue. Greg wondered if maybe he could pick the padlock instead. With a rush of adrenaline he decided that what was needed was action, not thought and so he cut short his planning and backed up as far as he could go on the roof. He drew a few short, rapid breaths, danced on the balls of his feet and prepared to take off down the ten-metre runway.

"It's Terde time," Greg said, then the roof buckled beneath him.

As he collapsed through the ceiling and into the room below, he was grateful for a digital display board which broke his fall into two smaller, equally painful falls, although if he'd had the option, he decided that he wouldn't have put it directly under his spine.

"Oh, crap," he breathed as he gasped to try and coax some air into his lungs. He spun on the floor while repeatedly saying the word "crap" and as he rolled, he saw that he was in the ticket office. Job done. The display board that had broken his fall and possibly some of his vertebrae was showing a message that all sailings were cancelled until further notice. It also suggested he KEEP CALM, CARRY ON AND BE KIND. Greg wasn't sure how to apply this advice to his current circumstances.

Greg slowly got to his feet. His right leg was fizzing with turbocharged pins and needles. The ring finger on his left hand was crossed diagonally behind the other fingers. He grimaced and cautiously nudged at the wonky finger with his other hand. It was clearly dislocated at the base. Blessing his intoxicated numbness, he clutched the finger firmly and wiggled it with purpose, causing spasms of white-hot pain until there was a satisfying *click* and the bone found the socket. Greg felt a sheen of sweat on his brow and ran his arm across his forehead.

"Go Greg!" he said with a hoarse voice and he stooped to pick up his rifle.

The cabin's glass doors leading to the outside were shut. He examined them and saw that there was a latch at the top and bottom. He unlocked the top one and grimaced with the pain in his back and hand as he bent to unhook the bottom. He then pushed at the bar across the door which to his delight swung open freely. Slightly less delightful was the electronic beeping which began a second later. Greg looked around and saw a blinking red dot on the side of an alarm box.

Within moments, a pulsing klaxon began to blare. In a panic, Greg found the door to the back office and barged through the mercifully unlocked door. He snooped around the office, kicking chairs out of the way to look under desks and checking on noticeboards for any obvious PIN codes. He then realised that even though it was annoying, there was very little he could do about it. Plus, having seen the carnage across London, he had to assume that one more alarm would simply add to the thousands that were already blaring across the capital.

As he was leaving the office, his eyes were drawn to a large white metal cabinet with a cartoonishly unsubtle key symbol on the front.

"Bingo," he whispered as he opened the door and found thirty or more keys, each with a neat little label on it bearing the name of a ship. He peered out of the side window of the office and found that the Uber boat was called *Neptune's Desire*. He took the corresponding key from the box and jammed it into his pocket. He hobbled out of the ticket hall and down towards his vessel.

The boat was tied up at two points, front and back, or fore and aft, as he corrected himself. He started to unloop the thick rope at the front and threw it on board, repeated the process at the back and quickly stepped out onto the deck as the swift-moving current of the swollen Thames pulled the boat away from the jetty, and it rotated with the movement of the bloated river. Once on board, Greg was alarmed to see the riverbank sliding past with more speed than he'd anticipated. He hobbled around the outside of the boat as his back spasmed, looking for the driver's section. He imagined this would be indicated by the presence of a giant steering wheel and possibly the skeleton of a shark's jaw mounted on the wall, if his movie-based knowledge of the world held true.

Instead, *Neptune's Desire* was one of those featureless and barren modern constructions, all rounded beige plastic corners and smooth lines. It looked like a giant floating internet router. Inside there were rows of blue seats facing the front and a central pod containing a small café. At the sight of food, Greg discovered that he was famished, so he lifted the lid on a display case and stole a stale croissant, which he stuffed into his mouth. He then grabbed another and tucked it into his trouser pocket.

Finally, he found a set of stairs towards the rear of the boat which led up to an outdoor section. At the front was a dashboard and something that looked like it had fallen off a one-armed bandit. He scanned the system and found a keyhole with "Ignition" conveniently written above it. He plunged his stolen key home and turned it all the way round. Nothing happened. He promptly began to hit all of the buttons he could find and was rewarded with a flashing sequence of lights and then the faraway sound of an engine rumbling into life. He moved the metal handle back and forth and heard the lull and rise of the engine. *This must be go more, go less,* Greg surmised. *And this is go here, go there.*

"YOU BEAUTY!" Greg screamed with relief.

When he looked up, he saw that just ahead was the middle span of Lambeth Bridge. Greg screamed again and threw the steering wheel to the right, while simultaneously pushing the *go less* lever.

The water at the back of the boat churned and the nose of the boat spun to the right. *Neptune's Desire* narrowly squeaked past the nearest pillar and Greg exhaled with relief, but having barely escaped a collision, he was now crossing under the bridge where the arch was at its lowest point. He quickly calculated the angles of the approach, then turned and ran. He had just ducked down the steps when a horrible grinding noise rang out and the sound of shearing glass and metal filled the stairway. A shower of concrete and razor-sharp debris rained down on him as he covered his head.

Then, with a final *crunch* they were past the bridge and all he could see above him was the relentlessly shit London sky. Greg shook splinters of glass out of his hair and returned to the top deck. Most of the roof section around the top deck had been swept into the river, but the steering wheel and dashboard had survived. Greg laughed to himself, pulled the throttle forward slightly and pointed the boat into the middle of the channel. Once he was sure the next bridge was a decent distance away and there were no other boats within range, he scurried back down to the café where he crammed his pockets with another two croissants and a small bottle of red wine and a lager.

Back at the wheel, he spilled his bounty across the dashboard and set to work gnashing the cap off the wine bottle with his teeth. He reached inside his pocket and found the duty phone. He pointed the *Neptune's Desire* down river and took a big swallow of the cheap vino. He then pressed the green answer button.

"Hello, B of the Bang, how can I help you?"

THIRTY SECONDS TO MIDNIGHT (GMT)

THE BIGGEST PROBLEM with *Voyager* - the Prime Minister's state aircraft - was that it was currently in the Thames. In aerodynamic circles, this was considered the sort of fault that could keep it from flying for a number of days, or at least until the eels were removed from cockpit. Consequently, it wasn't a full-spec military-configured jet that William, Jenny and their makeshift cabinet of wonks found themselves boarding on their escape from London, but an EasyJet Airbus A319. The plane should have been packed with tourists and en-route to Tenerife, but instead it found itself pressed into service as the new UK's Prime Minister state aircraft.

When news had broken that North Korea had launched an Intercontinental Ballistic Missile towards London, Jenny had loaded William and whichever advisors were within reach into two helicopters and hot-footed it to London City Airport, nine miles away. With less than ten minutes to organise a plane, the best that Barry Comms, Tom and Mike Whittaker had managed to conjure up was the A319, which had been grounded along with all other passenger jets when Crossley's plane had crashed.

The plan was to circle Devon until the missile hit. Depending on fallout and blast radius they could then decide where to go next. This almost certainly would not be Billericay. The first eight rows of the plane's seats had been hastily unmounted and thrown out of the cabin doors and onto the runway. This had bought the team from Number 10 enough space to set up a desk for William and a green screen background, in case they needed to address the nation while they were in the air. The small space had also been rigged with two widescreen TVs which were showing the live footage BBC and Sky were broadcasting, showing the imminent arrival of the ICBM. The BBC's coverage had managed to find an angle that linked in the licence fee and Sky had hastily repurposed its migrant boats coverage team, and were streaming live from the seas around Dover where the missile was expected to make its entry into the country.

William was slumped behind his desk of state, emitting a guttural moan every time the plane hit turbulence. He looked like he was bordering on a fever, though occasionally there was a quixotic smile which quickly contorted back into his favoured grimace. Jenny had found time to change, and now her long auburn hair was flashing brilliantly against a dark green flight suit and combat boots. She was kneeling on a seat on Row J briefing a shellshocked panel of advisors.

"It's imperative we control the narrative," she said. "Yes, what is it, Barry?"

"Well, it's just that's what everyone says – "control the narrative", "lead the story" but you have to do a certain amount of reacting when countries fire nuclear missiles at you."

"Barry, go and get the drinks trolley and some peanuts. You're officially demoted to flight attendant."

"But-"

"Barry. Fuck. Off. Give the Prime Minister some gin, we might need him to look less broken soon."

Barry stood up and petulantly stomped off down the aisle in search of the refreshments cart, mumbling something about Jenny and targeted nuclear missiles under his breath.

"Tom, Mike, I want you on the phone calling anyone who isn't irradiated or in pieces. I want you telling them that William McCartney is on it. I don't even care what "it" is – I just want them saying that man's name over and over."

"Jenny – we appreciate that you want to take the lead, but we don't even know which broadcasters will still be on air."

"Well, find out! Get onto Radio Stoke, Chorley FM, Robin Hood TV. Speak to the Yank channels – they're not going to go offline. Send a bastard TikTok out. I don't care. When this missile lands it is the single most important second of our political lives and we need the media to be listening to us. William McCartney, the UK Prime Minister, says Keep Calm, Carry On and Be Kind."

The diminutive aircraft was buffeted by strong turbulence and everyone apart from Jenny grabbed onto headrests or armrests. Jenny regarded them scathingly.

"Come on gentlemen, let's display some gonads, shall we?"

"What about the Emergency Broadcast System?" Tom asked. "We can send text and live video to everyone's phones. We would just need to upload a message onto the system at the Cabinet Office."

"An emergency broadcast requires months of vetting! Parliament needs to approve the message. You can't just fire it up and start vlogging. It's not Twitch," Mike said caustically.

"That might be true if it wasn't wartime, Mike," Jenny replied. "In times of emergency it's only natural that we would take any and every available route to communicate with a terrified nation. We can't wait for parliament to hem and haw. William signs off on it – get it set up Tom."

Tom moved over to his bag and started pecking away at his laptop.

"Mike, I need a list of everyone who will support William's war. I want a united force of the world's nations pointing every weapon they have at Kwon Hyun Gun."

"Jenny, I'm sounding like Mister No Can Do here, but if parliament is destroyed then there's a chance that a decent number of the MPs will be toast too. There will be all manner of procedural hurdles to getting any kind of approval for a war."

"Mike, do you know why William looks like that?" Jenny asked. Mike looked over as Barry tried to pour a tiny bottle of gin into the Prime Minister. William registered them looking at him and raised sweaty fingers in salutation. Mike swallowed.

"I heard a rumour from one of the Number 10 secretaries," he admitted.

"Well, whatever you heard, it's true and more besides. What I want you to understand is that the normal rules have gone. Forever. From now until I tell you otherwise, the only word that matters, is *mine*. Now, tell me how we bypass this approval."

"Well…well…I suppose we don't need approval if we're not actually declaring a war, as such."

"What do you mean?" Jenny demanded.

"Well – you need approval from the Commons for a war, but what if it wasn't a war but more like a limited term, tactically focused episode…a special military operation?" Mike said, trying to conjure up a suitable term.

"Special military operation sounds too clinical; it needs heart and minds."

"A Global Harmony Adjustment?" Mike ventured.

"That makes me think we're going to release a charity single to end famine," Jenny said.

"How about a Tactical Tranquillity Insertion?" Tom suggested, looking up from his laptop.

"A TTI? I like it," Jenny said. "The tabloids will call it a Titty and that will be enough to distract half the nation."

"Incoming!" Barry shouted from further down the plane. Jenny, Mike and Tom rushed to the front of the plane to take in every pixel of the widescreens. William wasn't up to standing and joining them, but even he lifted his forehead from the desk and tried to focus on the televisions. Barry passed out miniatures from the drinks trolley and the Number 10 team all gathered together as the BBC and Sky synchronised their coverage.

"…we go now to join Carol Blanding on the cliffs of Dover…"

"Of course, Blanding is there at the end of the world," Tom grumbled.

"Thanks Adeema, huge apologies if you're hearing a lot of rushing noises, it is *exceptionally* blustery on these iconic clifftops. I'm happy to say that the tech geniuses have been at work and we've picked up the Intercontinental Ballistic Missile – or ICBM - on a separate feed and you should be able to see that on your screens now. We can now see the missile pass over a very rainy Calais and start its short twenty-one mile run across the English Channel. Here it is on its way to pass over the famous white cliffs and on towards London, where its current trajectory will take it."

"Thank you, Carol – what's the mood like there?"

"Well, Adeema – I have to say that these are some of the most unique circumstances I've ever reported from in over three decades of bringing live television to the people of Britain…"

"Oh, shut up, Blanding! You don't get to be the main character today," Tom snapped.

"…Amazingly, we're actually using some of Sky's bandwidth to bring you this report and we lent their team some gaffer tape – it really feels like that moment, so often eulogised, in the Second World War, where the two warring nations crept out of their trenches and turned No Man's Land into a football field on Christmas morning."

"It's nothing like that! Just tell us about the missile!" Barry cried.

"Thank you for that Carol – and you'll see on the screen that we've got some viewers' questions scrolling through and one that I've just seen is saying, "Why can't the RAF just shoot the missile down?" Any insights on that?"

"Yes, we've had a full statement from the MoD, who say that the UK has one of the best air defence systems in the world, but that unfortunately it can take up to a week to come online. They are adamant that any missiles which threaten our nation from next Sunday onwards will be dealt with promptly."

"Another question here from Graham in Reading who says, "As one of the BBC's LGBTQ+ viewers, do…"

Blanding turned away from the camera to face the white-capped seas behind her. Just visible in the distance was a tiny speck of fire that stood out against the clouds that blanketed the sky.

"Sorry to interrupt the studio, but this is it – we now have visual confirmation of the missile," a series of graphics appeared on the screen showing the missile's speed and a dotted line plotting its trajectory. "Yes, we can confirm we have contact. I repeat, contact. You can probably see the fiery dot streaking through the sky, casting a red pall on the sky surrounding it. To our colleagues in London, to our friends and relatives who are still in the city and its surrounds. Our thoughts and prayers are with you! It is here!"

💎 💎 💎 💎 💎

After over an hour strapped into the missile, Comrade Cho couldn't decide if the cramp in his legs or his fingers was worse. He was bitterly cold too. His body was awash with lactic acid and he could feel his calves and forearms seizing up.

But there was not long to go now.

"One…two…three…press," he mumbled to himself, still somewhat lost in the timings of his one job. He kept a watchful eye on the other hand, which grasped the detonator.

He felt the thrust of the rocket behind him. It had driven him insistently for the last hour and now he was so close to delivering his payload for the Fatherland. He just had to focus on the one… two…three…press for a few more minutes. The cramp in his left thumb was agonising, but he thought of his family and his nation and pressed the little red button. The light on top of the missile winked on and off again.

Comrade Cho consciously blinked away the exhaustion from his eyes as he felt a sudden disturbance in the movement of the missile.

A shudder seemed to ripple down the top and he assumed it was turbulence from the craft moving out over the sea. He rubbed his helmet's visor to try and rid it of the streaks of water that had started to drip in from the hole above his head. He looked up in shock and confirmed that there was indeed a large hole in the top of the rocket. He belatedly remembered to one…two…three…press and hoped he hadn't screwed anything up.

As he watched, another piece of the skin of the rocket flapped over and instantly disappeared into the sky behind him. Cho could now see the contours of the clouds through the hole. More of the rocket's outer skin began to rip as the aerodynamics of the rocket failed in front of his eyes. Air swept into the cockpit and yet more of the missile disintegrated. Comrade Cho could now see the frame of the rocket, as its semi-protective shell was dissolved by the rain shower he was passing through.

Shit! One…two…three…press.

Comrade Cho focused on what he could see beyond and he saw a dark stretch of waters with white caps swelling on the sea. He was so close.

One…two…three…press. Comrade Cho looked up at a sudden bright flash and realised that it was a light on top of the rocket. He One…two…three…pressed again and watched the light blink on and off. He didn't count this time, but simply pressed the button a few times to confirm his realisation that, for the last hour, he had painstakingly ensured that a small light flashed on and off at the top of this fake missile, in order to make it look more authentic and not like what it was: a large toilet roll tube with a torch on the top.

The noise and rush of the air streaming past him became nearly intolerable as his craft, now denuded of much of its outer skin, started to lose altitude. Comrade Cho looked up and saw a feature of the British landscape so iconic that even his restricted North Korean education enabled him to recognise: the White Cliffs of Dover.

Comrade Cho dropped his left-hand switch and swiftly concluded that if he'd been lied to about the function of that switch, then it was highly likely that his right-hand switch was probably decorative too. In a fit of pique, he flipped open the cap on top of the switch and clicked it. Of course, nothing happened. Cho laughed at the pointlessness of his mission and, by extension, his life. Then the 1,200kg of TNT and aluminium powder that were packed into the bottom two-thirds of the missile exploded.

💎 💎 💎 💎 💎

With a sudden flash of light and smoke, the BBC feed went dead. The Number 10 team stood with their mouths open as they scanned the other screen. The Sky footage had been filmed from a slightly more removed position and the camera jerked hastily to capture the blooming inferno that engulfed the front of the cliff. They had a perfect angle to broadcast the spot where Carol Blanding stood as it was consumed by the blast. The shockwave of the explosion reached the cameras and for a second all that the TV screen registered was the sky and a section of the billowing of a black cloud. The audio was cut entirely for a few seconds and then returned in full force with a sound that overshot the capacity of the mics and sounded like crumpling.

"It's going – get back!" a voice off-camera shouted and the camera view started to show a jerky retreat away from of the cliffs, and a mass of land slipping down into the sea below.

After a few seconds the primary instinct of the Sky cameraman – to always be pointing the camera at the interesting stuff – returned and there was a nauseating whip pan across the damp green field and a shot of a scene of very limited devastation came into focus. Just at the top of the cliff there was a raging fire with thick, dark clouds. As the picture settled, it appeared that only the very top of the cliff was scorched. Just beyond the fire, the body of Carol Blanding lay flat on the ground, smoking slightly.

Further up the field was another prone body of what looked like an astronaut struggling with his helmet. The camera zoomed in on them, and the blue and red bands and isolated red star of the North Korean flag were clearly visible on his uniform. Comrade Cho eventually managed to get to his feet and look around, clearly unsure of what was going on and where he was. He finally removed the cracked helmet and turned through 360 degrees. He focused briefly on the camera pointing at him, and set off in a limping run. Seemingly confused by the geography of where he was, Comrade Cho ran to the edge of the cliff and then downwards for several hundred feet before failing to continue his run on the tiny shingle beach below.

In the EasyJet there was a collective exhale, as the Number 10 team tried to compute what it was that they'd just witnessed.

"They fucked it up!" screamed Barry, who leapt in the air and pulled Mike into a hug and started to dance around. Tom pulled a tiny bottle of cava from the drinks trolley, ripped the foil off and sprayed it feebly around the cabin.

"And they got Blanding!" Tom blared, dancing in the aisle.

The three men held each other and jumped on the spot. Tom held out an arm to Jenny to try and link her in, but their excitement was brought to an abrupt halt when they caught sight of Jenny's face, which was set in a shrewd expression.

"Gentlemen, we are at war. Let us try and conduct ourselves with the dignity that the British people would expect of us during a TTI. Barry, I want you to do whatever you need to do to make it so that the Prime Minister doesn't look like he's recently won a shittest cadaver competition. Tom, chop-chop, we need to film the emergency broadcast. Mike, you get to make me a cup of tea."

"Jenny, what are you talking about," Mike said. "They messed it up, there's no more missiles."

"Mike, what I saw was an act of war against the British Isles and the violent destruction of one of Britain's most-treasured presenters.

This demands a global response. William agrees."

They all looked at William for confirmation, but he appeared to be unconscious.

"But…Jenny, they didn't really *do* anything,"

"They attacked England," Jenny insisted.

"At best they bruised Kent," Mike replied.

"And that's enough, Mike. Move the threat level to Critical And Then Some."

CREAM RISES, SHIT FLOATS

COCO FELT GUILTY. Cole's body lay at her feet, with the muscles in his lips and nose twitching involuntarily, making it look like he was doing a rabbit impression. She was *fairly* sure she hadn't irrevocably damaged him, but in any case, it wasn't him that she was feeling sorry for. Seeing the impact of the Crustaystun made her feel a swell of remorse for the lobsters. She could claim that she was just following orders, but Coco knew that her actions constituted a debt that she had to pay. She closed her eyes and swore an oath to King Glen that if her baby could escape from this madness and flourish then she would atone. She felt a shiver pass through her body.

"Get me out of here!" came a muffled voice from within the fatberg. Coco stopped disassociating and remembered where she was, and then wished she hadn't. The smell in the cramped tunnel was like a stilton that had been aged in a teenage boy's trainer.

"Can you get out?" she cried into the darkness.

"No! I'm stuck. Please, it's near my mouth!"

Coco gagged at the thought.

"Can't you climb up?"

"No! I'm just sinking in more. HELP!"

Coco couldn't contain it any longer and found the gagging she'd been doing suddenly erupt into a full vomit. She steadied herself and then recoiled as she noticed she was leaning on the fatberg for stability.

"I don't know how to get you out. What can I do?" she shouted.

"HERRMPPPPP!" came the tortured cry from inside the fatberg.

Coco cast around, wondering what she could do. She desperately surveyed the scene for any kind of tool that she could use, but there was nothing – just the prone form of Cole, who in the light thrown from his torch now seemed to be sleeping soundly on the brick floor of the tunnel with the trickle of sewer water diverting around him.

Coco could only see two possible ways to help. She could climb up on top of the fatberg and try to pull Bradford out, but that ran the risk of her falling in the same way and them both getting stuck. She also wasn't sure that she would be able to physically lift him out of the hole even if he was pint-sized. That left…

"Hold on, I'm coming through the front," she shouted.

The muffled noise she'd heard hadn't sounded like it was too far back – although with the echo from the tunnels, who knew how far back it had actually been. Despite every cell in her body telling her not to, she reached out her hand and tentatively forced it into the fatberg. While trying to look away, she reluctantly wiggled her fingers in further like a gynaecologist who hated their job. Her hand reached what felt like a piece of fabric, and she took hold of it and yanked it backwards. A shredded and bleached Jodrell Bank tea towel came out alongside a clump of the yellow-white tallow that surrounded it. As it fell, it unleashed a ripe whiff of musty ammonia. Coco wondered what her midwife would say if she could see her now. Given that she'd nearly had a coronary when Coco had told her she'd eaten a tin of tuna, she thought she might not approve. Coco's eyes landed on what she assumed was a human poo, nearly a foot long, mummified amid the white fat. She tried to stop her eyes from streaming and to force her retching back under control.

As she tugged and probed, she started to form a divot in the front of the fatberg. She ducked her head and reached inside the hollow she'd made and reached a clump of wet wipes and pulled them out.

Then a clot of plastic packaging. She scooped handfuls of the white globules from the fatberg and threw them behind her. As she dug her way inside, she got some leverage and caused a big slab of the material to break off. She stepped further inside and pushed upwards at the crusted roof of cack above her. With effort she managed to push it up a good distance, and as she let go it splintered off like a piece of arctic ice shelf and crumbled into the tunnel behind her, splattering the oblivious Cole.

As she pulled out yet another wadge of nappies in the centre, she felt something solid behind it – a body. She scrabbled at the outline of the form and gradually opened a hole where she could see the smeared and filthy form of Bradford. She could see that his mouth and nostrils were blocked with lardy discharge and she used a free hand to pinch them clear. As more of him became visible she could see his shirt was covered in blood and he seemed almost as pale as the goo around him. She let him tumble forwards through the gap and, taking him by the belt, she heaved him forwards. With a stuttering, slurping noise that reminded Coco of her work experience as a dental assistant, Bradford Alderman VIIII, scion of the Alderman Retail Group, was born again.

She yanked him over onto his back and then panicked as she looked at him – she didn't think his chest was moving, so she pulled his mouth open and started to unclog his mouth and realised that he had more of the fatberg lodged in his throat. Thanks to the adrenaline coursing through her and Bradford's childlike size, she managed to sit him up and hook her arms around his waist. She shifted her hands upwards until they sat under the protrusion of his ribs, then she summoned the last of her strength and hugged him violently, five times in succession.

"Come on!" she screamed in his ear, jerking his body again. She felt something in his position change and she realised that his feet had started to scramble underneath him. She focused all her power in her arms and she screamed as she gave one final heave.

Bradford rolled over on his front, and with his back arched and his mouth extended to its fullest he extruded a coil of matter, which fell with a *splash* into the water below them. His shoulders rose as he breathed in and in again. He fell back against the curved side of the tunnel and gasped greedily. Gradually, Bradford's face changed in hue from a white green, to pale and then a shock of colour formed in each of his cheeks.

"You've got something on your face, just there," Coco said, gesturing broadly at his head.

Bradford held a hand to his shoulder and gradually got to his feet, staring in amazement at the freshly excavated white turd.

Then he started kicking Cole.

"You! Piece! Of! Shit!" he shouted and with each word, he drove his bare foot into Cole's body. Coco moved backwards in alarm, but as Bradford's foot hovered in a stamp above Cole's head, she spoke.

"No. You can't."

Bradford seemed to notice Coco for the first time. He took in the filth of her arms and the spatters across her face and looked once again at the fatberg. Slowly, he returned his foot to the floor and instead spat a long string of saliva onto Cole's chest.

"You're not worth it."

Defeated, he slumped back down against the side of the tunnel. It looked like he wanted to have a good cry.

"Balenciaga," he said weakly.

"Got it in one," Coco replied. "Although I think it might need dry cleaning."

"You dug me out?"

"I did."

He looked around and seemed to be on the verge of saying something. Then he checked Cole over and pulled out the smudged black velvet bag. He reached inside, removed one of the gold coins and threw it over to her. He spotted the knife on the floor next to Cole's hands and quickly stowed it in his trouser pocket.

"That should cover the dry cleaning."

Coco caught the coin and saw more wealth than she had held in her entire life. Her net worth was now this gold coin, plus £9.98. Bradford had found his phones. One of them was smashed but he was holding the other aloft trying to get a signal.

"It doesn't cover it," Coco said, suddenly feeling bold.

"What?"

"The dry cleaning, the, erm, stress and mental anguish. I'm going to have to get a manicure with a pneumatic drill to clean out this crud."

With great effort, Bradford smiled. This one had spunk. Maybe she was the plus one he'd been looking for.

"Fine, you get all the gold, but I'm keeping all of the cocaine," he threw the entire velvet bag at her and she recalculated her net worth. Five gold coins plus £9.98. She didn't know how much gold was worth, but she felt confident that it was enough to get a pram. Her little hand-grenade now had a pram. The thought of her daughter, brought her back to earth.

"Shit! We need to get moving. Don't you need to get to your daughter?"

"My what?"

"Your daughter – you said that you had to get her at the Savoy?"

"I've missed it."

"It? What do you mean?"

"Look – you may as well know. I didn't tell this scum the exact truth…I don't have a daughter."

"What?"

"Don't get antsy, I didn't want him to take advantage of me, so I made up a story."

"And how's that worked out for you?" Coco asked pointedly.

"Badly! Okay? Really, really, really very badly indeed."

"So why did you need to get to the Savoy?"

"I had to meet someone. Someone who was going to help me. But I'm too late and I guess this is about as safe as we're going to get." He gestured at the tunnel as if trying to decide where he could mount a flat-screen TV.

"Who could help you?"

"You know *FDGE*, *Don't You Look*, and *Old Cream*?"

"The clothes shops?"

"Yes. The clothes shops. I own them. Well, my father…basically, I own them. I'm Bradford Alderman VIIII."

"You were going to get one of those bunker things, weren't you?"

"How do you know about those?"

"It was everywhere on social media, a man said something about… what was it *called*…B of the Bang?"

Bradford's eyes went wide. "That's right."

"Take me," Coco said. "I need to get into the bunker. I'm three months pregnant. *Please*, take me."

Bradford's eyes roved around Coco's body but he found it was harder to undress a lobster with your eyes than it was with normal female clothes, but he could imagine, he could see the black, lacy outlines of…

Bradford Alderman falls on his feet more often than a cat with another cat tied to its back, but who could really blame women for wanting to be with him and for men who want to behold his one-thousand-metre Golden Thumper? All who witness it, marvel at its glory!

…but, what was the point? They were too late.

"It doesn't make any difference. They will have gone by now."

"But you don't know that for sure, do you?" Coco said, getting to her feet. "You had to get to the Savoy, is that right? You can't be that late – maybe they waited for you? Maybe the missiles got destroyed. We have to try. The alternative is that we're going to die in here, next to that," she said.

Bradford looked at the ruptured fatberg and nodded – this was no place for an Alderman to die. His ancestors had died glorious deaths fighting with the Nazis and on ships at the hands of mutinous slaves. He wasn't going to die in excrement! He shoved himself to his filthy feet using the wall of the tunnel as support.

"We can but try," he said and started to limp towards the edge of the tunnel.

💎 💎 💎 💎 💎

With some trial-and-error Bradford and Coco followed the tunnels towards the Embankment. At points the water had become waist-deep. Coco had taken the opportunity to dunk her head fully under the water, preferring to risk the potential bacteria that the sewer water contained, versus the definite bacteria that was caked on her skin. Bradford was clearly a lech, so once more the idea of casting off the lobster costume had to be shelved.

Besides, she had started to wonder if her appearance and her journey was all part of penance from King Glen. She resolved to take her punishment on the chitin, even if it was soggy and beyond gross. As they trudged along the tunnels, Bradford alternated between checking whether the phone had reception and taking dabs of cocaine from his vial. He had offered Coco a bump, but she politely reminded him that Class A drugs were one of the things that the NHS tried to discourage expectant mothers from engaging in, along with salami. As they walked and the drugs took effect, he became more garrulous and chipper, until his recollection of the recent events saw him as a conquering hero and Coco as a bystander, who was fortunate to bear witness to his feats.

The tunnel started to dry out and before long it looked like the passageway's purpose changed. Thankfully, there was no more water; instead, the tunnels were now well lit and housed conduits of thick cables that ran in bundles along the walls. Coco took the opportunity to wring out her costume and thanked the Gods for the magical properties of polyester. The air passed from moist and pungent, to dry and stale. Occasionally, as they looked up, they could see the grates from the streets above. Coco could have cried when she felt the cool London air blowing from the grid only a few metres overhead. Never again would she complain about pollution or people emitting vape clouds in front of her. She promised to suck all of the above-ground goodness into her lungs.

They followed the tunnel until it terminated, not in slippy wall-mounted rungs, but a set of spiral stairs. Bradford held onto the handrail and followed the curve of the steps until it brought them into a small dark room. To one side of the room there was an old, dusty dashboard of switches and dials and a comfortable office chair. To the far side of the room, there was a thick wooden door with an old metal grill set at head height. The door was barred on their side with two heavy-looking bolts, which were driven into unyielding hasps.

"Where are we?" Bradford asked as Coco peered out of the grill.

"We're on the river. I think we're near Big Ben!"

Bradford excitedly pulled the bolts back and opened the door. They emerged into the dank drizzle of a miserable London afternoon. Coco shaded her eyes against the change in light and took deep breaths of beautiful air – never had it tasted so good. It smelled of pigeons and bus fumes, just as air should smell. As her eyes adjusted to the light, she took in Bradford's appearance and felt queasy all over again. His hair was matted, his shirt was wet with blood, cuts seeped from his bare feet, and a wet wipe clung to his suit jacket between the shoulder blades.

"You don't look much better," Bradford said, reading the judgement on her face. Her hair was tangled and slicked back from the water, and the general grime and filth made it seem like she was now wearing a woodlouse costume.

They made their way out onto the Embankment. Coco looked up at the Houses of Parliament and saw that they had emerged from just beneath the vast black statue of Boudicca with her hands in the air, as if imploring the House of Commons to do better. She wondered where everyone was – why wasn't it as rammed as it had been on Orange Street?

"It's ringing!" said Bradford, and he put his phone on speaker. Together they passed from hope to dismay, as the phone continued to ring and ring.

"It's not even going through to a voicemail," Bradford said dejectedly.

Coco gasped as her own sodden and cracked phone finally managed to load the BBC news site. She pored over the page of breaking alerts.

"Holy shit," she said as she tried to squeeze her mind around the day's news.

Bradford looked over her shoulder as she skimmed through the story about the missile landing in Dover.

"No! Not Carol!" Coco said in alarm.

"They said on the alert that there were seven missiles but three blew up. Take out that one and there must be another two on their way," said Bradford. Coco couldn't help examining the skies above. A cry caught in her throat. She would never be able to earn back the favour of King Glen. She would never get to spend her purse of gold. She would never meet her daughter.

"Hello, B of the Bang, how can I help you?" came a chipper voice.

Both Bradford and Coco stared at the voice emerging from the phone, then at each other.

"Hello? Hello? Is that a real person? Is that B of the Bang? This is Bradford Alderman VIIII, I am a *platinum* level customer."

"Oh, sorry mate, I've only got details on the system for Bradford Alderman the eighth and Bradford Alderman the tenth. Nothing on the computer about the ninth."

"What!" Bradford shrieked. "That's outrageous! I am real! I pay for platinum service!"

"Hahaha! I'm just messing with you. It's all good."

"Who is this? Who am I speaking with?" Bradford demanded.

"This is Greg. Greg the First."

"Please Greg," Coco butted in. "If you are with B of the Bang, we need picking up. We're on the Embankment, near Parliament."

"Right you are. I can pick you up," came the reply. Coco squealed in delight and Bradford heaved a sigh of relief.

"But you're going to need lots of gold…"

"What?" Bradford said. Coco instinctively felt in her pocket for the velvet bag and squeezed the contents tightly.

"Gold. Yeah, everything went to shit, so I'll pick you up, but you need to pay me gold."

"We have gold, please pick us up," Bradford said.

"How much gold have you got?" came the voice.

"I've got five coins," Coco said.

"Yeah, that'll do for one."

"Wait, that's my gold!" Bradford said.

"No, you gave it to me – when I saved your life remember?"

"Listen, that is my gold. You know it."

"Then why have I got it?"

"Because…because…" Bradford fumbled for a valid response.

"Awkward," came the voice from the phone.

"Would you take a card payment?" Bradford said. "I'm a billionaire. I can pay you ten million."

"No, I'm sticking to gold. Gold can't be traced or recalled."

"Bitcoin?" Bradford asked.

"Be serious."

"I have cocaine?"

"Listen, I'll be at the Savoy shortly – be there or be square. I'll bip the ship's horn. You'll have to do the robot when you hear it, so I know it's you."

"Listen to me, I am a platinum member!" Bradford said, but the man had gone.

Bradford looked at Coco and she wasn't sure what his expression denoted, but she definitely didn't like it. She started to walk quickly towards the Savoy. She then broke into a trot, then a run. Her sodden costume bounced along and the lobster arms kept flapping back and forth, but she thought of her daughter and the safety of the bunker she had secured and powered on. Bradford kept up as much as his bare feet would allow. He was too winded to say much, other than "Listen" and "Wait", but Coco kept upping her pace.

As they rounded the next bend on the river, they realised that there was a military cordon, which explained why the streets around parliament had been empty. A line of baffled soldiers and policemen watched as they ran back through the cordon and into the dense crowd they were keeping at bay. Despite how tightly the crowd was packed in, Coco and Bradford's putrid odour created a horrified partition which allowed them to race through unimpeded. Panting and red-faced, they ran past the looming spire of Cleopatra's Needle. Then they rounded the corner and broke into a rejuvenated sprint as they finally caught sight of the ramp that led down to the pier opposite the Savoy.

"There's the Savoy! This is it, isn't it?" Coco asked.

Bradford consulted his B of the Bang phone.

"I'll tell you if you give me back my gold," he said churlishly.

"No, you're all right, thanks," she said and hunched over to try and get rid of the stitch in her side.

"Look, you have to return that gold to me. I want it. It's mine. By right."

"No chance. You gave it to me for services rendered. That gold represents a fair day's pay for a fair day's work."

"£50,000 in gold for a bit of muck-raking is *not* a fair deal! You conned me. Do you even have a receipt?" Bradford asked.

"That's a great point, why don't you bring it up in small claims court and I'll tell you then."

"Look, you can't do this to me. I was going to ask you to join me as my plus one. Why can't you return the favour?"

"The man said that five gold coins was enough for one. I can't help you."

"But I want it!"

"You don't hear this often do you? *No*. I got that gold fairly and I can use it however I want. He said it was only enough for one. That *one* is me and my baby."

"Oh no, oh no no no…" Bradford turned and all of the day's frustration broke over him anew. The filth. The pain. The horrible humbling. He sniffed repeatedly. Then a sob emerged, and another. Then another. Soon Coco was treated to the unedifying spectacle of Bradford Alderman VIIII weeping. His face squeezed in on itself. Ropes of snot emerged from his nose and his arms hung outwards in the hope of a hug. Coco let him hang.

"Oh my, this is it, isn't it? It's so unfair! IT'S SO UNFAIR! IT'S SO FLIPPING, FUCKING, SHITTING UNFAIR!"

He shuffled forward to hold onto Coco, who recoiled as much as she could and tentatively patted him on the shoulder.

"My whole life has been unfair. Oh sure, I'm rich. I'm handsome. I've got cars and houses, but I don't have a daddy. I don't have my poppa. He hates me! He thinks I'm a fucking idiot."

"No," Coco said with as much encouragement as she could muster. "I'm sure he loves you."

"He doesn't! He thinks I'm a little shit. He said that to my face. He loves his island more than he loves me. He didn't even love me enough to get my name right! And now I'm going to die. I bet he's in a bunker with a hot little piece and a big bag of cocaine and I don't get to have any of that! I don't even get a bunker!"

On and on he wept. Coco didn't know how to console him, so she just patted him loosely on the head and made vague hushing noises, while she surreptitiously scanned the Thames for the rescue boat and willed it to arrive soon.

Eventually, Bradford's despair reached a welcome plateau. He took a calming breath and ran an arm beneath both nostrils.

Then he reached into his pocket.

"I'm sorry that it's come to this. I really am. I know you're pregnant and whatnot, but I'm going to have to mug you."

Coco looked at him ready to laugh, but then she realised that he was holding a knife. She had been so close to safety, but she didn't have any fight left in her. Her shoulders slumped.

"Come on, hand it over. Give me the gold."

She reached into her pocket and passed him the velvet bag. She couldn't quite bear to release her grip on it, but he tugged it from her grasp and smiled with relief.

"Not pleasant, but it's only right. I am a billionaire."

"Fuck off," was the only thing Coco could think to respond.

Looking over his head, she noticed a moped weaving through the traffic. About thirty metres down the road, it bumped heavily onto the pavement and revved towards them. It was driven by what appeared to be a very handsome Japanese man with jet black hair and aviator sunglasses. Behind him on the moped was a man in a navy pin-striped suit. Riding behind him was a beautiful woman in a white Dryrobe, her silver-blonde hair tucked into a half-shell helmet with a bullseye on the side. The woman was holding her phone in front of her as if tracking something. She looked up, spotted Coco and pointed to the driver who opened the moped's throttle. They jerked forwards and with five metres to go the woman pulled a long wooden tube from her back and levelled it as if it were a lance.

Bradford looked around at the sound of the engine and his face dropped.

"Oh God, no! Susie!"

He turned just in time to look down the barrel of the digeridoo, and Coco was treated to a hollow, melodic thump as it connected with Bradford's face. He was launched off his bare feet and came to rest near a bin. His nose looked like a blob of play-dough that someone was half-heartedly rolling into a toy sausage. Coco drew on all of her experience as a one-time dental assistant to diagnose that all of his front teeth were missing.

The moped screeched to a halt and the lady dismounted with grace. She took up the didgeridoo again and whacked Bradford in the testicles with another sonorous donk, then dropped the instrument on his chest.

The older man in the pin-striped suit took a piece of paper from his breast pocket and handed it to the woman, who screwed it into a ball, put it in her mouth, chewed it down and then spat it at Bradford.

"Next time you want to disappear, take the Airtag off your keys."

Bradford groaned in pain.

"And now, please feel free to shove your didgeridoo and your divorce right up your arsehole, you pointless stench!"

She gave Coco a cool, appraising look and proclaimed, "You're not even a hot yoga teacher."

Coco couldn't help but agree.

The woman mounted the moped again and the driver turned it sharply and the trio disappeared back into the traffic.

DO YOU THINK WE CAN BLAME NICOTINE WITHDRAWAL?

MARTIN LOOKED OUT into the control room, and seeing Charlotte was absent, he took a long pull on his vape under the desk. He then removed the bull clip from the mouth of a balloon he had stored there and forcefully exhaled his fumes into it, watching it inflate by another inch. It looked pretty full now, and he tentatively drummed the taut skin. He shrugged, replaced the bull clip and tucked the balloon back under his desk. He wafted his hands around in the air to dispel any fugitive particles. Charlotte entered the studio and stopped to sense the air like a snake. Martin transformed his energetic wafting into a double-handed wave.

"There she is! Hello Charlotte!"

"What's that smell?"

"I just opened these; it might be that – do you want one?" He threw her a boiled sweet and crunched one up in his own mouth. She rolled it mournfully in her fingers.

"No, I can't. I've got weigh-in on Thursday."

"The world's ending and you're still counting points?"

"The world isn't ending. North Korea are just having a bit of a mad one."

"Charlotte, they fired a missile at us!"

"They say it was a test."

"Yes, in the same way that any explosion of a bomb is an effective test of whether it works or not. Go *on*. Have a sweet. Satan won't care if you've got a bit of a muffin top going on."

"Fine. It's only a point per sweet," she unwrapped it and popped it in her mouth.

"There you go."

"Right – notes: I need one more Invictus live read and you're done with them. Also, compliance have been on again, saying you still have to push back much harder on the billionaires-bad narrative. They also want you to reiterate that officially, we're holding all reaction until we hear this emergency broadcast from Number 10, which we're expecting while you're on air. If it does go live then Sid will mix it in and you can do live reaction, punters, punters, punters, blah, blah. Tears, laughter, learning. Sony Awards all round. Got it?"

"Got it."

"Look, Martin. Keep the energy high for this last bit. We've survived so far, but this is big. Like we landed on Mars and found a shrine to Princess Diana sort of big. Okay? Keep the tone big and reverential. Don't flip out."

"For sure."

"I'm not sure why you're not giving me more shit, it's making me worried."

"I'm just aware of the stresses you're under and we're a team, aren't we? And there's no 'me' in team."

Charlotte looked confused. "No, but the letters are there."

"You make an excellent point."

"*Five seconds…*"

Charlotte snuck out and the light in the studio went green.

"That was *Black Hole Sun* by Soundgarden. Welcome back to the last half hour of your extended Big Talk show, where we're all coming to terms with the drama and, let's be honest, the fear that today has created. It's okay to be scared and to want today to be over. I know we tend to keep things pretty light here on the Big Talk show, but the whole team here wants you to know just how important you are to us. Whether you're one of the heroes of the NHS, or emergency services who are keeping this country going. One of our brave military men and women. Even if you're a regular nine-to-fiver like us, we want you to know how much you mean to us. We certainly hope you've been able to Keep Calm, Carry On and Be Kind today. Just a message from the heart there on your Big Talk show sponsored by Invictus, the drug that helps to make you the Master of your Fate, and the Captain of your Erection. Who have we got next, Sid?"

"Hello Martin, Gubi here from Luton. We spoke before in March, do you remember, Martin?"

"Gubi, of course I remember, how are you and what's on your mind?"

Martin made a lost and confused expression at the producer's booth and watched as Charlotte frantically scribbled something on an A4 pad and held it up to the control room window: *HE WAS THE ONE WHO HATED HIS NEIGHBOUR'S BABY*. She then held up another piece of paper: *HE'S AN IDIOT*.

"Well Martin, I just want to say that I know everything is going on today and it's been hard to keep up but I think we should remember Carol Blanding tonight and I had an idea. Do you remember how in Covid we used to bang them pots and pans for the hero nurses, didn't we – do you remember?"

"8pm every Wednesday, like clockwork. Possibly one of the stranger aspects of the pandemic, if you don't count those coin-operated centenarian captains doing laps of their garden."

"Yeah, well, I just want your listeners to know that at half past ten tonight I'm going onto my doorstep and banging a pan for Carol. I'd like to invite everyone to do it, especially if you're near me."

"Okay, that is probably a bit late, isn't it?"

"Well, if you do it at eight o'clock then people might think you're doing it for the NHS, so I'm going to do it at half ten instead. I'll do it every night from now on. I think it's a fitting way to remember her. If anyone sees me then feel free to join in and remember Carol. 10.30pm, for about fifteen minutes."

"Gubi, when we spoke before you were having a few problems with your neighbour's baby waking you up during the night. Was that right?"

"Yeah? So what?"

"So, I'm just wondering if your proposed tribute might not be a thinly veiled attempt to extract some late-night revenge using a fallen hero of British Broadcasting. Do you think that's what she would have wanted, Gubi?"

"No."

"So, shall we file this idea under B of the Bin?"

"Wish they would put the baby in the bin," Gubi replied in a mutter.

"We're going to move on! Line seven, what's on your mind?"

"It's Gavin from Leicester," the phone call was suddenly washed with jarring static and feedback.

"Woah, Gavin, I think you might need to switch your radio down. The producer could have told you that but I can only assume that she wants to deafen our listeners."

The squall of feedback died down.

"Sorry about that everyone."

"That's okay Gavin, how is your day going?"

"I've had better Martin; do you know what I mean?"

"I do, what's your take on it all?"

"I've got to say that the key thing is the conversation that you've been having about billionaires. They're just not right."

"And why do you think that, Gavin?" Martin asked, holding his hands up to Charlotte to show he couldn't help the calls he was given.

"It's too much power in the hands of one person. It highlights the failure of governments because what should happen is that when you get to a billion pounds, right, you should automatically forfeit every single further pound that you earn. It should all go to taxes, hospitals, schools, roads. Because do you know how many people that would upset? One person. And do you know how many people would benefit? Everyone. That looks a lot like democracy to me."

Charlotte stood close to the control room window and shook her head very clearly at Martin. She mimed scales being balanced.

"Well, now Gavin. There are two sides to this story, aren't there?" Martin said weakly.

"No, not really Martin. Did you know that the wealth of the richest one hundred people – just one hundred people – is more than the poorest four billion people on earth. That's not very balanced, is it?"

"Is that right? Yes, but, um, what about the wealth they create that trickles down?" Martin asked.

"It doesn't though, does it? They hoard wealth and use the power to protect themselves, which is easy when you only pay 3% income tax. That's not right, is it?"

"Oh, I don't know."

"You don't know, or you just don't have the nuts to share your opinion?"

"*Careful, that's bait,*" came Charlotte's warning in his headset.

"Ha! Well, that depends, if you're asking for the opinion of DJ Martin Pope, or the official position of your Big Talk show? I guess what you have to understand is that money creates power. If you have money you get to influence the shape of the world and the truth is that billionaires shape our world. And, *yes*, they shape it so that consequences are no longer relevant to them. They buy people. They choose what happens. And, ultimately, they use money to distract people like you and me, Gavin."

"*This isn't balance, you need to balance things Martin,*" came Charlotte's nervy voice in Martin's headset. He felt the need for nicotine wash over him in pulses. He really wanted a cigar. Or a vape. Or a big fat spliff. Or all of the above simultaneously.

"Yes, Martin! So, what are we going to do about it?" Gavin asked.

"*Don't!*" Charlotte shouted.

"Well, using power to control other people and to silence them is a form of bullying, isn't it Gavin – and what do we do with bullies?"

"Stand up to them?"

"Exactly, Gavin. Exactly."

"How though?"

"That's for you to decide. That's for all of us to decide. I tell you one thing though; I have never understood why being a billionaire isn't the most uncomfortable place in the world to be. We should stop looking at *The Times Rich List* as if it's some aspirational roster of brilliance and instead we should treat it like a hitlist…"

"YES, MATE!"

Charlotte was by now waving her arms over her head and shouting at Sid to cut the mic.

"I'll say this, yachts do sink, Gavin. Especially when the mechanic on minimum wage who maintains it doesn't quite tighten that bolt. Whoops!"

"*Martin, what the fuck are you doing? This is the end; you have to stop!*"

"Producer Charlotte is telling me to stop, but that's just another part of the control, isn't it? You see the Big Talk show goes out as part of Zaka Media and that's owned by a billionaire, so he calls the tunes. Literally, we get his shitty playlists. And on the fifth floor there's a whole team of lawyers who right now will be having a collective stroke about me saying this. But do you know what, Gavin? It may be the lack of nicotine in my system, or it may be the stupid number of hours I've been broadcasting for, but I am done. Mr Zaka can shove his job up his gold-plated arsehole. I quit."

There was an eerie sound of pulsing and alerts pinging on phones.

"*It's the Emergency Broadcast! Feeding it into the studio.*"

ALL ABOARD!

GREG FELT THE spray of the Thames on his face and decided that this was his favourite part of the day so far. Admittedly, it didn't have much in the way of competition, but idly steering the boat with the glories of London laid out to his port and starboard gave him an intuition that everything was going to be alright. His nausea was under control. The lump on his head was starting to go down and even his spine felt like it might not need surgery. Yes, there had been mistakes, but no one except the Prime Minister had died and maybe, just maybe, humanity could learn a thing or two from this day.

Greg was still working on what that lesson might be. He felt it could possibly be something about needing to look up from our phones every once in a while, and be kinder to each other. Whatever it was, he knew that when he managed to put the feeling into words, or paint it on a canvas, it would be a very beautiful sentiment indeed. He checked the strength of the recently finished bottle of lager he had liberated from the café down below and saw that it was 8%. Possibly his benevolent demeanour had something to do with that and the co-codamol he'd found in the first aid cupboard. But that didn't matter. Just right now though, life was good and he could breathe.

He pointed the boat towards the London Eye and on his approach, he realised he needn't have asked his customers to do the robot after all because even from a distance, the ultra-wealthy were obvious. They were tanned, beautifully coiffured and their veneered teeth gave off an eerily bright light, like those luminescent fish deep in the midnight zone. He pressed the button handily marked "Horn" and the *Neptune's Desire* gave a jaunty honk. A number of people on the pier snapped to attention and broke out into a self-conscious yet committed robot dance. For no reason other than it seemed like an incredible power to be able to abuse, Greg leant on the horn button several times and watched the billionaires dance for him. He gestured to the far end of the pier and his passengers made their way down.

He lined the front right quarter of the boat up with the dock and with a good distance to go, he cut the throttle so that the boat was barely crawling by the time it nudged into the jetty, although it docked hard enough that he heard a crunch and shouts of outrage from below. He quickly shut off the engine, slung his rifle over his shoulder and rushed woozily down the stairs. He hobbled to the back of the boat and with an effort he heaved the mooring line over the side.

He looked one-eyed at the position of the boat, which seemed wrong somehow. Greg puzzled and tried to work out what was going on. Then he noticed that in the time it had taken him to get below deck, the current had pushed the boat the full length of the jetty and his only option was to secure the rear rope to the point intended for the front. Boat driving was hard! He quickly wound it around the anchor point and leapt back aboard, just as the boat was starting to nose its way to the right of the dock like a dog pulling at a leash.

"Quick! Come on, B of the Bang crew! Get on board, let's go, let's go, let's go! Show me the gold, babies!"

The huddle of passengers hurried towards him in what was classically known as the basic mob formation. Fists were shaking, voices shouting, eyebrows furrowing. Greg had seen it all before. He had dealt with a number of B of the Bang's clients in the years he'd worked there and he'd never met a more pointlessly angry bunch of people. All of them had an axe to grind about something. Greg was pissed off with all of it. Here he was, going out of his way to rescue these ingrates and all they wanted to do was shout about how poor the service was and moan about everything. He was sick of it! The customers. The blame. The guilt! But this time it was different. This time he was armed.

"You're drunk!" came one accusation.

"What sort of rescue is this?" another moaned.

"Listen! This is the only rescue you're likely to get, and *yes*, maybe I have been upholding the fine seafaring tradition of taking a tot of high-strength lager, but that's none of your concern. I'm plenty sober enough to rescue you bunch of arseholes."

He unslung the rifle from his shoulder and brandished it in a way that he felt was meaningful.

"So, if you're a B of the Bang customer and you have your gold, welcome on board. If you want to complain to my manager, or get my details so your lawyers can sue me, then you can have that discussion with my rifle!"

The first passenger threw Greg his black velvet bag of coins, climbed over the side and headed inside to find a seat. Soon, they were all clamouring to hand over their money and claim their spot on Greg's ship of hope. Greg checked the bags and dropped them into his pockets, which started to sag dangerously after a few deposits.

"Come on! Come on! Move your arse!" he shouted at the last passenger making her way towards the boat. As she approached, Greg recognised her as Felicity Montgomery from *Monty's Mayday Loans*. She had been on every TV advert break for as long as he could remember offering quick cash to desperate people. Her hair was in its trademark extravagant whirl and her wrists were clogged with thick bracelets of diamonds. Her face was Botox locked in an expression of disdain and hooked over one arm was a large handbag which contained a white chihuahua. Greg screwed his eyes up in concentration until he concluded that the dog was, in fact, wearing thick glasses.

"Now wait just a minute," the woman berated in a firm Kent accent dripping with disdain. "You are *late*, you *smash into the jetty*, and *you are* shouting at me! Oh, and now you're pointing a rifle at me?"

"What's wrong with your dog?"

The woman looked confused that Greg had bypassed her complaints.

"What is wrong with my dog, Sir, is none of your concern. What is your concern is-"

"Everything on board this ship is my concern, *Monty*. I'm the captain of this vessel and I would be flouting entire pages of maritime law if I let a sick animal on board without knowing what was wrong with it."

"Ronan suffers from strabismus, if you must know."

Greg produced his mobile phone with a flourish. "OK Google, what is strabismus?"

His phone said nothing back to Greg because it was a Nokia 3210.

"Cross-eyed! He's cross-eyed! Ok?" The woman shrieked and lifted the dog's glasses. Sure enough, without his corrective goggles, one of his eyes went sliding off to look at the London Eye while the other remained fixed on Greg.

"I'll allow it," Greg said. "Gold please."

With a look of great displeasure, the woman handed over her velvet bag of gold, which he dropped into his trouser pocket, and just managed to stop them from falling down by quickly notching his belt tighter. She placed her handbag with Ronan inside on board and started to cross over onto the boat.

"Woah, hold up, Monty. You only paid the fare for one, do you have sufficient gold to cover your passage as well?"

"What are you talking about, you oaf! I gave you a bag of gold!"

"You gave me *one* bag of gold, but that paid for the first passenger, vis-à-vis Ronan. *You* need to pay another bag for your fare."

"Ronan is with me!"

"I'm afraid we operate on a policy of a fixed price per entity."

"I paid through the nose for this service and now you want me to pay again!"

"Listen, it's not your nose, so it's not your service. Why don't you give the office a call tomorrow and see if you can find anyone left who hasn't exploded."

"Fine, forget Ronan!" The woman reached for her bag.

Greg intervened. "Oh no, you see he's already on-board. If you took him off now, you'd have to pay a disembarkation fee."

"Which is what?"

"I'll check with the office but I'm pretty sure it's a bag of gold. Look, we can't hang about here all day. Tell you what, as a one-time offer, I'll let you work your passage. Grab that rope for us and cast off."

Monty looked affronted, and appeared to be on the verge of arguing the point but she cracked and made her way over to the mooring line and started examining how it came off. Greg shambled back inside, past several irate looking passengers. Ronan hopped out of his handbag and trailed along behind Greg.

"All right – find a seat, grab a coffee, just don't mill around where you can fall off, the seas are unpredictable today."

Greg noticed that Monty had managed to heft the rope from its anchor point on the dock and was struggling to carry it over to the ship, which continued to be pulled by the current. Seconds later, it was free of the jetty and heading towards a large black pole that jutted out of the water, which it hit with a crack.

Monty grasped that she was too late and would not be quick or agile enough to jump onto the back of the moving boat. She quickly calculated her position and concluded that her best bet was to stand on the dock and hold the rope – presumably hoping that through sheer force of will she would be able to halt the progress of the hundred-ton boat.

Instead, she was whipped viciously into the water in a frenzy of bubbles, rising to the surface after several seconds spluttering and waving. With a few kicks, she was able to grab hold of the posts that supported the jetty and started clambering over to a ladder.

"We'll pick you up on the way back!" Greg hollered to her.

"Hey! You can't just leave her there!" a young man said, standing to make his point. Greg turned and sought out the owner of the voice. He was a tall and exquisitely athletic man, with arms that were corded with muscles and tribal tattoos, which was unfortunate because Greg was really in the mood for hitting someone. He held his rifle across his chest.

"Listen, pal, you might have a Golden Ticket to Willy Wonka's factory, but that doesn't mean that you get everything you want. Some of you are going to be sucked into tubes of chocolate. That's just the way it is. Now, I have to concentrate on driving this boat, so the next person to interrupt me or talk near me will be shot. Does that seem fair?"

No one said anything and several people rushed for a seat.

"Excellent, so we understand each other. Now let Willy Wonka get back to his chocolate factory. Heel, Ronan!"

💎 💎 💎 💎 💎

In the absence of anything else to do while she awaited her rescue, Coco dragged Bradford's prone form to the top of the walkway and hunted around on the floor for his knife, which seemed to have vanished in the assault. She propped him up against a wall and briefly thought about staunching the flow of blood from his nose. Then she reflected that, balanced against his attempted mugging, it was reasonable to leave him to bleed to death. She mentally added Susie to King Glen on the List Of People Coco Owes A Debt To.

There weren't many boats on the Thames; Coco assumed that most of them had been used to escape. She stared at every passing ship. Most of them seemed to be military, and she kept hearing helicopters buzzing overhead. She tightened her grip on the gold in her pocket and felt soothed by it. It was a shame that she would only get to hold the gold for such a short space of time. When she peeked inside the bag, she couldn't help but feel a warmth emanating from the coins. It would have been nice to keep them, but it was an act of providence that she even had it in the first place, so she knew swapping the money for safety was the right thing to do.

She tried to replay the day so far, from starting her shift to arguing with Red Steve, then her random escape when she saw the video about the missile coming. Then there was that whole scene in the sewers, the horrors of which were still encrusted under her fingernails. She felt like she'd aged thirty years in a single day. Her back and legs ached from the miles that she'd covered around London and the various falls and bumps she'd picked up along the way. She just wanted to get to a place of safety. A place of safety with a really efficient nail brush. She checked her phone again but most of the stories revolved around the emergency broadcast that was due to come from Number 10.

Bradford jerked awake at her feet and shuffled back, holding his hands in front of his face.

"You're about ten minutes too late to flinch," Coco noted.

"Susie?"

"Long gone. Turned up, hit you with a didgeridoo, spat a piece of paper at you and ran. That happen to you often?"

"It was my wife and her lawyer. And my zen gardener."

"Why did she hit you with a didgeridoo?"

"My wife is not a supporter of the native arts," Bradford replied cryptically. "She's a narcissist anyway, she probably took something I said the wrong way, or interpreted it as a threat – she's always doing that. I'd leave her, but she keeps threatening to kill herself."

"She looked pretty sane."

"Oh, she's good at that. Convincing other people that I'm the problem. She did it with the twins and it looks like she's won you over too."

"Look, there is no winning me over. As soon as this boat gets here, I'm gone. You can sort yourself out."

Coco decided to put some distance between them and started to walk down the ramp to the jetty at the bottom.

Bradford winced as he got to his feet and hobbled after her as she followed the glass corridor down towards the jetty.

"I'm sorry, that was a misjudgement. I'm desperate. You have to see that!"

Coco turned at the sound of a faint tooting noise and she saw a listing Uber boat heading across the river towards them.

"Is that it?" Bradford said, voicing both of their thoughts.

"I thought it might be more of a military vessel, like a submarine or something."

As it approached, she could see that the top of the boat had been ripped off and there was a massive dent in the front that was emitting smoke. If she squinted, she could just make out a tall man at the controls waving at them both. His long shaggy hair was blowing semi-heroically in the wind as he beeped the ship's horn again. Coco remembered the instructions and ran down the final steps to the jetty and started to do the robot, which it transpired was considerably harder in a lobster costume. The man with the flyaway hair at the controls smiled broadly and kept honking, so Coco kept roboting. He punched his fist in the air and seemed to be having a great time.

"I...don't think...he's going to stop in time," Coco said in dawning realisation. Bradford looked up at the approaching vessel and tried to judge its path. It was definitely moving quite fast.

"Perhaps we should?" Bradford said, but Coco was already three steps ahead of him and had already started sprinting her way up the zig-zag walkway, heading back towards the safety of the pavement. Bradford saw the clipper boat about twenty metres away. He limped as fast as his injuries would allow, catching sight of Coco as she reached the top and turned to shout something to him. Bradford put his head down and ran as fast as he could. Through the walkways enclosed sides, he could see that the driver was now waving both arms to warn them that he hadn't quite judged the docking procedure correctly. Bradford ignored the pain that shot through his body, sprinted the last few metres and leapt at the top, just as the Uber Boat splintered its way through the deck and started to crush the passageway where Bradford had so recently been.

A grinding noise sounded behind them, and Bradford turned in time to see the ship swallow the entire jetty and watched as the twin points of the catamaran hulls crumpled directly into the wall. Through a miracle of physics, the destruction of the jetty served to take the speed out of the approach and brought the ship to an ear-splitting halt just in front of them. The street was a metre or so above the top of the Uber boat and the captain smiled at them.

"I saw you from over there!" he said, ignoring the state of his boat and the destruction that he'd caused. "I was hoping you'd be one of mine, but you're the first we've had in costume."

"It's Balenciaga," Bradford said.

"Are you B of the Bang?" Coco asked.

"Sort of, I'm Greg of the Bang, at your service."

"Hi Greg, I'm Coco," she said and wondered if the missile had actually already landed and this was all some odd purgatory.

Coco caught sight of the odd little chihuahua hopping by Greg's side, trying to get a view of what was going on. She had never seen a dog with goggles on before. "What's wrong with your dog?"

"Oh, that's Ronan, he's the ship's dog. He suffers from strabismus."

"Bless you," Coco said.

"It means cross-eyedness," Greg explained.

"Was he driving?" Coco asked.

"Ha! No. Sorry about that, that was all me. It's been that sort of a day!"

"What's wrong with you?" Greg asked, indicating Bradford's face and, more generally, his entire being.

"It's not been a great day for anyone," Coco remarked, before Bradford could launch into his tale of woe.

"No, agreed. Let me welcome you on board the *Neptune's Desire*. Now sailing for all those who have gold."

"Sorry to interrupt, but we're taking on water down here!" someone shouted up the stairs.

"Start bailing it out then!" Greg shouted back.

Coco took Greg's outstretched hand and stepped unsteadily onto the top deck of the ship. With a pained look, she handed over her bag of gold, which Greg assessed with a cursory shake before throwing it into a fire bucket on the deck floor, which had been hastily repurposed as the ship's gold repository. A large pile of sand sat by its side.

"Welcome on board. I'd advise staying up here in the captain's quarters, as rumour has it things are getting aquatic down there. Wow! Is that smell you? It's quite something."

Bradford coughed theatrically. Greg wiped his eyes and turned to him.

"And what about you, Young Frankenstein? Do you have- oh, you have my rifle."

Bradford grinned like a maniac and levelled the gun at Greg.

"That's right, I have your rifle. And I don't know if you've ever played Rock, Paper, Gun, but gun always wins! Now, as long as everyone is chilled, we're going to get along just fine and maybe people don't have to die."

"There's quite a lot of water!" the voice came again up the stairs.

"Bail it out then, shit-for-brains!" Bradford screamed, the mania of a trying day coming to the fore. "Now, what's going to happen is that we're going to make our way to the bunker and then me and Balenciaga here are going to make *you* dance like a robot for *our* pleasure. Honk!"

Greg looked at him quizzically.

"I'm honking! Do a robot! HONK! HONK!"

"Oh right, yeah, I'm not doing that. Because the one detail that you might want to figure into your plan is that that's not a real gun."

Bradford's face dropped as he assessed the gun in his hands.

"You're wrong, I know guns, this is a real gun," he said determinedly as if he was trying to convince the gun.

"Nope, do you know how I know it's not a real gun? Because I pulled out the flag that said "BANG!" from the end of it! And they don't *tend* to leave live firearms on the wall of a pub for any idiot to walk in and take. Now why don't *you* have a little think in your head and pick which side of the boat you want me to throw you off?"

"Yes! Do it! Kick his arse!" Coco shouted with glee.

Greg smiled and advanced towards Bradford, who yelped in fear.

"Get back! I'll fire!"

"Do it! Shoot me in the face!" Greg laughed. Bradford found his back pressed against the helm, he closed his eyes and squeezed the rifle's trigger.

There was a loud crack, and the bullet flew.

THE DUCHESS OF BERMONDSEY

MARGARET WAS ANGRY with God. Well, she was angry with Graham really, but she felt she had a much better chance of holding God to account.

Where are you? Was the only thing she could think to pray as she walked through Bermondsey. *Aren't you supposed to be walking with me? Don't I look at the footprints on the beach and you explain that you were carrying me all along?*

God kept his own counsel. Maybe she would have been better off talking to Graham, but he had made it clear that the only thing that would ever exist in his life was mathematics. Trains had displaced her in her father's mind, and numbers had done so in Graham's. She was finished being an emotional support animal. Didn't she deserve love? Regardless of how long she had to enjoy it – didn't she deserve to be treasured? *Well, God?*

Nothing.

It had taken her fifteen minutes to stomp to Southwark Cathedral from her house, through the familiar route that took her via the churchyard at St. Mary's and across the campus of Guy's Hospital, which seemed strangely calm. She thought briefly of the doctors and nurses and wondered how they were coping. People didn't stop being sick just because it was the end of the world. Had the medics abandoned their patients and made their way home? She couldn't blame them if they had.

At the steps leading down to the cathedral she paused and looked up at the Union Jack hanging damp and lifeless from the tower. It seemed fitting among the spires and folds of the lead-lined roof, which were damp with the day's mizzle. She thought of the hours she'd spent baking and eating mediocre cakes to pay for that roof. All for nothing.

She tried to head down the steps to the cathedral, aware that there was probably something inside that she could be doing to help that might distract her from how alone she felt. There was always duty waiting for her beyond those thick wooden doors. But it was like there was a magnetic force repelling her from the entrance. *Don't.* She just couldn't summon up the energy to descend, so she loitered at the top. Every so often she would turn around, walk in a loop to the nearby shops and try again, but still she couldn't bring herself to enter.

Fudge the cathedral cat came out and brushed past her legs, investigating what she was up to. She would have liked to believe that Fudge was an envoy of God, but she knew he was only interested because she was one of the rota of people who fed him, and Fudge was loyal first and foremost to his stomach. She scratched him behind his grizzled ear, turned away from the church again and tried to walk up to the bridge. Fudge deemed her insufficiently interesting to follow that far. She decided to cross the river and double-back to see if a bit of a run-up could get her over the cathedral's threshold.

For once, why can't you just make it clear what I should do?

The bridge was rammed. The traffic was static and she picked her way between cars and taxis that had been abandoned, sometimes with the doors left open as the occupants had fled on foot into the streets when the extent of the gridlock became apparent. She couldn't stop herself from closing the doors she passed to prevent the rain getting inside. Her feet seemed to be retracing her steps back to work. She wondered about walking past the office and seeing if anyone else had found themselves drawn back to work, but what was the point? What was the point of any of this? She didn't feel right at home. There was no one at work. She couldn't bring herself to go into church. Where was she supposed to be when it mattered?

She made it all the way across London Bridge and turned back on herself to walk with the greater flow of pedestrian traffic. Maybe she'd try the cathedral again, stroke Fudge one last time, make someone a cup of tea. She fell in behind a young woman with huge headphones perched on her ears. Margaret noticed her because she didn't seem to be wearing enough and she was weaving slightly. The day was turning colder and her thin arms were bare against the rain even though she had a tracksuit top tied around her waist. Her blonde hair was plastered to the sides of her head, but she seemed oblivious.

The woman pushed her headphones off and dropped them without a care onto the floor. Margaret stooped to pick them up. By the time she stood up the woman had placed her hands on the blocks of the side of the bridge and stepped up. She was putting her feet onto the metal rail on the barrier before Margaret even realised what was happening. The rest of the foot traffic on the bridge instinctively rerouted to avoid the drama. Margaret knew she had to say something immediately, but her mind drew a blank, so she just voiced the first words that came into her head.

"You're not allowed to do that here!" she shouted.

Another pedestrian bumped into her and she was buffeted closer to the young woman on the wall. "You're not allowed to do that here. Not today."

The woman coughed out a wry laugh. "Yes, today."

Margaret didn't give herself time to think. "No. You can't do it because who knows what's next?"

"Missiles. Deaths."

"Please just stay with me for a minute. I'm Margaret, what's your name?" Margaret noticed that a small bubble had formed around her as people dodged past, keen to avoid this drama and get on with their own.

"It doesn't matter," the woman said.

"I'd like to know," Margaret said kindly. "Please?"

"Lilly," the woman replied without emotion.

"Lilly? Well, Lilly it sounds like you've had a tough day. Well, of course you have. We all have. Stupid thing to say. But I'm here for you, you know. Do you want to talk for a bit?"

"I don't think so. I think I just want to step forward." She shifted her feet and Margaret wondered if she would have the strength to hold her if she could grab her legs.

"Okay! How about I talk and you listen? Would that be okay, Lilly?" Margaret babbled on, trying desperately to think of what she could say to bring the girl back. "I've not had a good day. Not at all. 'Dear Diary, it's not been a good day.' And I'm in love with my lodger. I am. I'm in love with my lodger. Isn't that silly? Who falls in love with their lodger?"

"Why don't you tell him?" Lally asked, while still looking out over the Thames.

"I made him a sandwich and thought he might do something, but he just went back up to his study. I made a fool of myself is what I did. I thought I'd go to church but I can't go in and now I'm here talking to you." Margaret tried not to think of the egg cup full of crushed sleeping tablets back at home. That had been a moment of madness. And didn't that give her all the more right to say that the girl was better off coming back down? That everyone was better off here, no matter what mess they were in. There was always hope, but it gets buried sometimes.

"Lodger is a funny word," said Lally. Margaret recognised for the first time that the woman was drunk.

"Lilly, I don't want to bible bash, but you have to know that there is someone who loves you very much for who you are, right now. There's no expectations, there's nothing, but just someone who sees every bit of you and loves you infinitely."

"Margaret, you do know the world is ending, don't you? We're at the G of the Bang."

"Yes. I do. I'm sorry about that. It had such potential."

Lally laughed. "It really did, didn't it?"

"It still might. I don't know what's going to happen, but we have to hope don't we? Isn't that the strength of humans – we just keep going. Even if you don't believe in God, you have to hope because things can change in a moment, in the twinkling of an eye, at the last trumpet - the King of Kings promises us that."

"This isn't your fault, Margaret. I've just had enough of Kings."

The young woman took a step forward.

Time stretched and Margaret saw the scene unfold in clear, stark photos. A pigeon speeding under the bridge, cutting low over the dirty water, the colours on its breast like the mallard's. Her own fingers stretching too slowly towards the three white lines on the woman's tracksuit bottoms.

Then a noise. *Pfffft*, followed by a piercing crack, and she was no longer stepping off the bridge. Margaret watched as she was folded backwards on herself, careening towards the pavement. A spray of blood settled on the concrete, and people screamed, dropped to a crouch and dived on the floor as they connected the blood and the falling woman with the shot still ringing in the air.

Lally came to rest on the metal ridge, with her standing leg tucked underneath her. She grunted and started to slide forwards off the bridge. Margaret instinctively reached out again and gripped her fingers into the woman's left arm. Her fingers dug deep into the flesh and she thought for a horrible second that the girl's rain-slicked skin would slide through her grasp, but she threw her other arm around her neck and heaved. Lally slithered onto the pavement into Margaret's arms.

※ ※ ※ ※ ※

By this point in the day, the emergency services weren't even answering calls that came in. Margaret waited with 999 ringing on speakerphone until a message eventually played, saying: "If your emergency is life-threatening then you are advised to get someone to take you to the nearest Accident and Emergency. You can also find first aid advice on the NHS website." It then gave a recorded list of the hospitals that remained open. Guy's hospital wasn't one of them to Margaret's chagrin. Something about the routine frustration of waiting on hold, allowed Margaret to calm herself and the trembles that had run across her body since the bridge, gradually came under control.

She couldn't remember how she had done it, but in the immediate aftermath of the incident Margaret had half-dragged, half-carried the semi-conscious woman into the Cathedral, leaving splatters of blood across London Bridge. Lally had started to come around as they entered the building, with its stained-glass windows somehow conjuring an ethereal glow out of the dull light outside. The pews were full, with a reverent congregation kneeling and praying their way to the end. It hadn't stayed sombre for long as Lally started to scream with shock and confusion as to why she had gone from London Bridge to a church — and why she was covered in blood. She raised her fingers to the burning gouge in the side of her head and saw the blood on her fingers. Then she really started to scream.

Margaret had bundled her into the cathedral office and retrieved an ancient medical kit from a tall cupboard.

"What happened?" Lally croaked, as Margaret pushed her into the Dean's battered wingback chair and quickly draped an old towel over it to prevent it getting stained.

"I don't know!" Margaret said. "I think you were shot."

"Shot?" Lally repeated incredulously, and her hand came up to the wound on the side of her head. She grimaced as she lightly traced the furrow from her temple to above her ear.

"Why would someone shoot me?"

"I don't know. The bleeding is slowing but let me clean this up a bit."

"Was anyone else shot?"

"No, just one shot. Just as you – hold still."

Margaret busied herself with laying out items from the medical kit, most of which seemed to have expired in 2015.

"Do you have anything to drink?" Lally asked in a shaky voice. In the closeness of the warm office, Margaret heard that she had a refined accent and pegged her as being a Sloane of some sort.

"I don't think so," she said.

"No communion wine? Isn't this a house of God?"

"Well, yes, but that's for communion."

"I'll take communion."

Margaret worked her way through the logic for a second and then went through a door at the side of the office into the church store. She flicked the light on. Inside there were various boxes and piles of papers lining the shelves – along with four entire shelves of colouring books for the hordes of young people who never seemed to arrive. At the bottom of one of the shelves was a large white box with nine bottles of sacramental wine. She took a bottle out and blew a cobweb off it as she brought it back to the office. She handed the bottle to Lally, who sat the bottle in between her legs and unscrewed the cap, while Margaret looked again at the cut in her hairline.

"I'm sure this is from a bullet. It needs stitches, really."

"Can you patch it up for now?"

"I'll do my best," she said and looked among the medical items for some sterile gauze, wipes and tape. Lally grabbed two mugs from the desk and nearly filled them with wine.

"The blood of Christ," she offered by way of a toast.

"That's sacrilegious," Margaret said.

"I'll apologise in person later."

"This might sting," Margaret said as she tried to wipe any debris out of the cut on her head. Lally hissed through her teeth as she did it. "I know, I know – be brave."

She pressed down hard with a bandage and kept the pressure on her head while trying to think of a way to hold it in place. Eventually, she conceded that for now, it was more important to keep the pressure on and ended up winding a long cream bandage around and around Lally's head.

"I was shot as I tried to kill myself," Lally stated, experimenting with voicing the situation out loud. As she let the words settle, she laughed to herself.

"All done, your majesty," Margaret stood back, and a dark expression flashed across Lally's face.

"Sorry – I just meant – look in the mirror you'll see what I mean."

The girl got up and turned towards the mirror Margaret pointed at on the office wall. She examined her face and picked at a fleck of blood. On top of her head sat a white crepe bandage crown.

"Your majesty," Lally smiled and curtseyed.

She turned and sat abruptly in the chair, then lapsed into a thoughtful silence.

"You haven't touched your mug of blood," Lally observed.

"No, it might be a bit early for me."

Lally finished her wine in one go, sloshed more in and drank it down again.

"You should go slow with that-"

"Wouldn't want a sore head in the morning," Lally said and Margaret smiled. "What are you going to do about your lodger?"

Margaret sighed and started to fold the remaining bandages back into the medical kit. Lally thought how sad it was that someone could be so tired and beautiful. She squinted at Margaret and saw the goodness shining out of her in long embers of silver light.

"You remember that? I don't know. I think that might be one of the few situations that would be improved by a nuclear explosion."

"Why can't he see what he has in you? You're an angel."

"I'm not…I don't think I'm comfortable talking about this. It's personal. Not just that, it's complicated. We've lived together for decades. We do everything together. We are together. We're just not together."

"You mean sex?"

"Good grief, no. But someone to hold me. Someone to physically acknowledge I exist. Oh, what does it matter? The blood of Christ," she said by way of a toast and drank from her mug.

"Blood of Christ," Lally returned and finished her mug. The alcohol was warming and hopeful. She had been shot, but there was wine. She laughed to herself again. This might take some getting used to. "If you think men are bad, you should try being a lesbian."

"Ah, right."

"Don't worry, that wasn't a recruitment pitch. I just mean. I…don't know what I mean."

"Lilly, are you going to be okay? Do you want to talk about what happened on the bridge?"

"I do not."

"There is a reason why we were there together. I was supposed to be in here, but I couldn't face it, so I crossed the bridge – and then you were there. I think God put me there for you."

"And then that same God also shot me in the head?"

"I'm not saying it's a conventional miracle, but that bullet saved your life. That has to mean something. You have a purpose."

"Does it though? With everything that's happened today, are you still clinging to meaning and happy endings?"

"Maybe. If we keep hoping. I have something for you," Margaret said and put her mug of communion wine down and went in search of her handbag. She returned moments later with a coin in her hand and passed it over to Lally. It was a glorious, shining sun of a coin. Lally hefted it in her hand and turned it over and saw the face of her grandmother turning the other cheek. As she passed it over Margaret felt an openness in her chest like she was breathing eucalyptus oil in steam. All the coins were gone.

"What's this for?"

"It's for you. It's real gold. You can do what you want with it; keep it, sell it."

"But the missile?"

"Who knows what happens with the missile. Maybe it comes, maybe it doesn't. Maybe we live, maybe we die. That was always going to be the case. For now, all we can do is hope, and I believe that where there is God, there is hope."

"I can't accept this," Lally said.

"You have to, I insist."

Lally sat in silence and drained the last drops from her mug of wine.

"Do you want some more?"

"No, I'm good, thanks," she said, still staring at the coin and turning it over, end-to-end in her hands.

Margaret assessed the girl sitting in the chair.

"You don't half look familiar, you know?" Margaret said.

"People say I look a lot like the Queen, but only when I do this," Lally replied and turned to show Margaret her profile.

"Ha! That's uncanny," Margaret said with a deep chuckle that made Lally smile too.

"Weird, isn't it? I keep wondering if there's a way I can make money off it, pose for knock-off stamps or something. I just need a business model. Margaret, thank you for this and…for everything. I'll find a way to pay you back. Maybe when I ascend to my throne of bandages, I'll make you the Duchess of Bermondsey."

"Throw dominion over ducks into the package and you've got a deal."

"Fine, you get ducks, but I keep the swans. I'm gonna need them swans."

"Naturally. Just keep being you. It's hard to see it sometimes, but that's enough."

Margaret leaned over and very gently kissed the young woman on the head and smoothed her hair backwards.

"Go well, Lilly."

"Thank you, Duchess," Lally replied and got shakily to her feet, the gold coin pressed tight in her palm.

OH, NO! NO NO NO NO!

THE PRIME MINISTER'S Jaguar XJ Sentinel was fitted with a red, white and blue leather interior, which was very much to Fenton Crossley's taste, just as much as it was not to Jenny's. She was stationed in one of the two large rear seats, which hugged the passenger tightly. In front of her was a pull-down mini desk and a colour screen in the back of the headrest. William was hunched in a foetal position to her right, Tom was in the front tapping away on his phone, next to a close protection officer behind the wheel. The car hit a pothole the approximate size and depth of a paddling pool, sending a shock through the entire vehicle. William bounced in his seat and emitted a groan that sounded like he was auditioning for Obvious Ghost #2 in a low-budget horror.

"Fuck me blind! Did you just drive into a tube station? I felt that in my uterus. Tom, more painkillers."

Tom passed over a sheet of ibuprofen. Jenny popped several from the foil and pushed them into William's mouth.

"Swallow and then shut up," she commanded, and William meekly dry-swallowed the pills.

Suddenly, the screen in front of Jenny started to flash around the sides and then just the audio from the QVC channel started playing. The presenters were talking about a pair of gardening boots which could rake leaves.

"What's this? I didn't switch this on?"

"Sorry Ma'am, must have been the bump. It's a bit temperamental. You can use the control and switch it off," the driver said.

Jenny fiddled with the controls but she couldn't stop the presenters explaining that raking while you walked around your garden was also excellent cardio. Jenny pulled the screen off the headrest and threw it at Tom, where it fizzed quietly and then died.

"Where are we on the emergency broadcast?"

"Erm, yes, still going. I'm writing it up now and then I'll edit the video we shot. It's going to be pretty basic; I've only got iMovie on my phone."

"Doesn't matter, make it syrupy. Black and white photos of children and pensioners. War bad, Britain good. Tom, confirm that you heard that correctly and you're not going to do it the other way around."

"War bad, Britain good," Tom repeated.

"Excellent. And what do we need to do to get it live?"

"I'm in contact with the IT operative who sends the alerts. She said it's as simple as giving her the text and video when we're in the Cabinet Office."

"And that automatically hits phones across the country?"

"Yes, ma'am, immediately."

"Ok, get Mike to check over the text when he's done rounding up global support. Tell him the brief on the text is bleakness and despair without any concrete details that we can be held to account on. Things are dark, but Britain is a light in the sea of something something and absolutely not a place where fuckwits wear boots to rake their gardens. The key point is that the normal order no longer applies and during this unprecedented time in our history, we will be in power until we choose not to be. Hit the word "stability" a lot."

"Yes. Bit of an update there," Tom said with an attempt at brightness. "Mike messaged and asked me to tell you that he's very grateful for the opportunity, but he's decided to take a step back from the current administration. Barry too. I also can't get hold of any of the others."

Jenny's nostrils flared and she pursed her lips. She looked out of the window at the outriders who were speeding them back towards Westminster. She wondered if the rumour was true that there were a series of roads under London dug by billionaires for billionaires. The Roman roads. She'd have to have MI6 brief her on that. It wasn't as implausible as some of the information she'd already unearthed about what the money got up to when they weren't buying football teams so they could experience a sliver of what it was like to be actually liked. This was what intrigued Jenny most about what William had given her – the access to information. It was why the only way they would ever take this power away from her would be by prying it from the rigid fingers of her booby-trapped corpse.

"Good riddance to bad rubbish. I have William, what else do I need? Driver, we need to make some secure calls. I'm assuming that this acme of British engineering can do that, or do you need to stop and unspool the string for the yoghurt pots?"

"Yes, ma'am, you can make calls on your screen, just tap Home, then Calls, then Send Call, then Yes, Yes, choose the name of who you want to call and then press Execute."

"Simplicity itself," Jenny said and then twisted William's ear so it was facing her. "Lazarus, I need you back from the dead, sit up and look like an international statesman for one minute. We still need significant people on our side, so I want you to look adorably brave but wounded, like one of those baby seals getting thrown in the air by the orcas. Do you understand?"

William grunted.

"Close enough," Jenny said and tapped the screen in front of him several times, while he sneezed and righted himself in his seat. He smiled experimentally at her and Jenny noted how much he looked like a balloon two weeks after a party. He would have to do.

"Who designed this system?" Jenny asked. Finally, the screen changed to reflect the fact that a call was in progress. William's face filled the screen and Jenny recoiled. A woman's face appeared in the smaller screen and under the scrutiny William managed to look passably human.

"Speak, William," Jenny hissed.

"Good day to you, this is William McCartney, Prime Minister of the United Kingdom of Great Britain and Northern Ireland, I need to speak with…Jenny, who do I need?"

"The President," Jenny supplied.

"Hold for POTUS," came the reply. The image shifted and instantly the face of an imperious black woman appeared on screen. She was smiling at the camera as a make-up lady administered powder to her face.

"Bill, sorry about the multitask, I'm doing an address in two minutes. Listen, I want you to know that the whole American public was devastated to hear about Fenton's death. What a guy. Remind me to tell you about the maple syrup thing at Bilderberg last year. *Hooo*, boy, we laughed. What do you need?"

"Madam President, the United Kingdom has traditionally stood shoulder-to-shoulder with the United States…"

"Bill, I've got 40 seconds, skip the prologue."

Off-screen, Jenny mimed an explosion and then a sad face.

"The missile has made us sad, um, as a country…" William began unsteadily, and he looked at Jenny for further advice.

"Bill, here's a suggestion: we both know there's a power-behind-the-throne situation going on, so why don't you just point me at her?" William gratefully reached forward and tilted the screen so it was facing Jenny, who composed herself.

"Jennifer," the President said coolly. Jenny realised that she still hadn't forgiven her for the London diplomatic tour two years before, when POTUS was a lowly House Minority Leader and Jenny a mere MP's wife. They had been bundled off to tour an artisan gin distillery near

Camden Lock with all the other women. The day *may* have ended with the two women arm-wrestling. Jenny had won, but a spirited debate rumbled on afterwards about the permissibility of biting in the contest.

"Martha. We need you to condemn the attack on British soil and say that the entire American military stands ready to honour our long-standing status as comrades."

"Can't do it. They're saying it was a test and the markets prefer that take. And "comrades" is punchy. You're more like an old, incontinent cat that we can't bring ourselves to cull, but maybe you've started to notice that we're not feeding you as much as we should lately."

"So, the special relationship isn't that important to you? Five Eyes isn't that important to you?"

"Jenny, Five Guys is more important to me. Come on. You know the only reason we still have a military presence over there is because of the cheeses. And even then, we have Wisconsin."

"So, you won't help?"

"Of course I will Jenny! I'm sending you thoughts," the President held up one middle finger to the camera. "And prayers," then the other. She bared her teeth and mimed little bites at the camera. The feed cut out. Jenny didn't pause to reflect, she tapped at the screen again and pointed it back at William as it rang.

"This time just get straight to the point and ask for a show of solidarity," Jenny said as a large woman filled the screen and then moved back into focus after adjusting the position of the camera.

"William?" she said in a thick French accent.

"Sélène, the United Kingdom has been attacked and we want the EU to offer a statement to show solidarity."

"Oh, but of course! I was just writing something on that matter as you called. Let me read you what I've got so far and you can tell me what you think," she cleared her throat and picked up a piece of paper from her desk and moved her glasses down from her chic grey hair to her nose.

"Ok, so far I have: ha ha, haha ha ahhha hahaha, ha ha ha aha, hahahahahaha,"

The screen went dark. *Nul points*, indeed.

"Should I get the First Minister of Wales on the line?" William asked.

"We need the titans of the globe to come to our aid William, not someone whose chief export is whimsical dragon tea towels."

"The Scottish?"

"I'll ignore that, William. Tom, I hope this broadcast is the most powerful drama since *Threads*, but without the funny bits where Sheffield is on fire."

※ ※ ※ ※ ※

By the time they returned to Westminster, the Great Panic was in full swing, as the public continued to search for a way inside the cordon that the army and police had created and then into the mythical bunkers beyond. Naturally, there were bunkers in Westminster, but none that would house members of the public in the event of a crisis. As they walked up the steps of the Cabinet Office building Tom was fussing about finishing his masterpiece while he was on the move.

"Shit! I'm going to have to send this to you Jenny, my phone is running out of battery."

"Fine, WhatsApp it," Jenny replied.

"Okay, coming through now."

Jenny saw the notification ping and threw her phone back at Tom and gestured for him to get on with it. They crossed through one of the offices where there was still a hum of activity. None of these hard-working patriots had left their post when their country needed them, Jenny noted with a hint of pride. Admittedly, the doors were locked and there were armed police stopping them from going anywhere, but it was still good to see. Jenny followed Tom with William limping behind holding onto the close protection officer. As the workers noticed it was the Prime Minister crossing their floor they stood out of a mixture of curiosity and duty. The Number 10 team marched towards a small corner office with glass walls daubed with writing and complex technical drawings. Sat behind the desk of the corner office was a beautiful, young woman in a white short-sleeved blouse.

"Prime Minister, it's an honour to see you on the IT floor."

"It's a pleasure to be here-" William broke off to sneeze four times and Jenny watched as he made a note of something on his phone. "Excuse me, allergies are…"

"We don't have time for a meet and greet," Jenny interrupted. "We need to get this message out on the emergency broadcast system now. As in right this second."

"Ahh, right – that's impossible I'm afraid," the woman said and shrugged an apology.

"But when we spoke…" Tom began in a panic.

"Yes, I said that it was *theoretically* possible, I didn't say we *would* do it. You need access to the EAS, which naturally we do have, but you also need authorisation from the Cabinet Office, which we can't get as we're at Critical. There are different rules at Severe."

"Ok, William: give your authorisation," said Jenny.

"I give you my authorisation."

"That's certainly important, Sir, but it's still not possible."

"We don't have time for this, did you know that our nation is under attack. Britons have been killed?"

"*A* Briton," the admin corrected, but then quailed under Jenny's glare.

"Muscles – I'm guessing you carry a gun?" Jenny said, addressing the close protection officer William was leaning on.

"Yes, ma'am."

"Okay – madam, I'm going to give you to the count of five to send this message or I will command William to command this man to shoot you."

She threw her phone to the admin this time, who fluffed the catch and then hurried to fetch it from under the table.

"I can't! I'm not allowed!"

"William?"

"Do the thing she said," William mumbled, and the officer drew his weapon and levelled it at the admin, who suddenly looked very awake and invested in the conversation.

"One."

"I can't! It's more than my job's worth!"

"More than your life's worth? Two. Three. Four. F-"

"Fine! I'll send it!" the admin spluttered and she started to shuffle things around on her desk. She checked the phone and muttered "iPhone" under her breath. She connected a cable from Jenny's phone to the computer and made a few mouse clicks. She typed furiously on her computer causing the keyboard to jump on her desk. Then her finger hovered over the mouse.

"I won't press it. If you want it sending then click this," she said to Tom, who was closest to her. Tom looked at Jenny for reassurance.

"Do I have to?"

"William," Jenny said.

"Man," William said. The officer turned his weapon on Tom, who shut his eyes and jabbed his finger. There was a pause of no more than five seconds and then throughout the building they heard the chirping of notifications, vibrations and a digital klaxon sound. They looked out over the IT floor and watched as the workers reached for their phones.

※ ※ ※ ※ ※

Martin was still feeling amped by his Comrade Braveheart rant, so the vibrating and pinging that sounded out would have left him feeling deflated, if he hadn't been so perturbed by the oddness of hearing phones in a studio. It was beaten into everyone in radio that phones were set to silent at all times. He had literally beaten work experience students to make this point. So, to hear not just one but a volley of alerts sounding out was eerie.

"Martin, you need to react – read the alert and tell people what's going on."

Martin collected himself and looked at his screen to get himself up to speed.

"As you can probably hear, the emergency alert from the government has arrived. I can read you the full text and there's a video. It starts: People of Great Britain: this is a dark, dark hour for our country. We have lost our leader and our shores are under attack. Your countrymen have died today as a result of this monstrous act. We will not take these affronts on our national security lightly. Under the strong guidance of William McCartney, parliament is already setting our course. Understand that this will require a very flexible approach to governance and we must be flexible in the course of action the country is forced to take, but know that all choices are being made by the McCartney leadership with you and your loved ones' best interests in mind. God Save The King. God Save The Country. God Save The Prime Minister."

"Wow, powerful stuff and clearly there are phenomenal pressures on this very fresh government. I'm now going to play the video and you should be able to hear the audio – we are also live streaming the footage across our social media channels and on our website."

Martin pressed play.

"Ok. It appears that the video has been recorded in one of the offices at Number 10. There is no sound but it appears there is a man, and he's standing on a desk."

The video rolled onwards. Martin's eyes opened wider.

"Keep going, not everyone can see – tell them what's happening," Charlotte commanded.

"There, uh, there's a man. It seems that it's the new Prime Minister and he's, um. He has a…His, um."

"Let's look at this filthy dog, shall we?" came a woman's voice. "William, you've given me what I asked for. So, it's only right that I give you what *you* have begged me for, Mr Prime Minister." There was the unmistakable sound of a marigold glove being snapped into place.

"Oh no," Martin said. "No no no no."

His jaw dropped, his eyes bugged and as the video continued, he recoiled so hard in his chair that his movement was accompanied by the sound of a popping balloon. After a second the sprinklers in the studio sent forth a spray of water. Martin barely even noticed.

DANCE AND DRINK AND SCREW

LALLY LEFT THE Cathedral with her head humming with adrenaline, alcohol and possibilities. As she ran her tongue around her teeth, she felt a rough patch at the front, where she'd chipped a tooth. Her back was stiff and her bandaged head was throbbing like a cartoon thumb hit with a hammer. Every window she passed, she checked her reflection trying to see if blood was running down her neck. There was a thin red line in the middle of the bandages, but otherwise, Margaret seemed to have done a good job of patching her up. She had no idea where she was going or what she was going to do next, so she settled for following her feet deeper into Bermondsey.

As she walked, Margaret's advice tumbled through her mind. It shouldn't be such a difficult thing to be yourself, but Lally knew that she had no idea who she was now. Lally is dead, long live...who? What would be so wrong if she moved to Southend became a piano teacher, raised a clowder of cats and swam naked in the sea every day? That felt like a good future. Would that be her being herself?

Lally felt the gold coin in her tracksuit pocket and continued to turn it over and over. On one side lay royalty, on the other a strong woman in charge of her own destiny. Lally hobbled up some stairs holding onto the handrail. Further down the road she saw a flat square car park, which gave way to a low-slung pub called The Flower Pot.

It was squat like a shoebox but the lights were on inside the pub and Lally could see coloured lights shining through the window's mottled glass, like stained glass in reverse. She could hear someone murdering *New York, New York* on the karaoke. She leaned on a post box to listen as the song finished, and the music was replaced by cheers and applause. She felt a bit dizzy and flushed, her hand reached to her collar and she gave herself an inch to breath. She looked at the red gloss of the post box to try and ground herself. Daddy had often joked that this was the real family business. Spreading bitchy gossip, business circulars and £10 notes in a birthday card from an aunt that you never saw. Lally closed her eyes.

"What can I get you?"

"A pint of lager and a triple vodka please."

Lally wasn't entirely surprised that she was now in The Flower Pot. She thought she could hear her Granny sigh with disappointment.

"Drinking again, Lally? What about service and duty?"

"Fuck off, Granny," Lally said out loud.

"Sorry?" the barman said in shock.

"Oh sorry, I'm a bit confused."

"It'll be the bang on the head," the barman said.

"How did you know about that?"

He pointed in the mirror that ran behind the bar and Lally saw her bandage crown astride her head.

"Oh yeah," she said smiling.

He passed her the drinks and she sipped a few centimetres off the pint, then tipped the vodkas in on top. The barman didn't even blink.

"£28 please."

Lally held out her card.

"Oh – all the payment networks are down, so it's cash only. Is that a problem?" he asked, looking like he was preparing to reclaim the drinks.

"No, no, wait. Can I pay with this?" Lally held out the gold coin. The barman looked at it and held it up to the light.

"You can't see through it," she said. "It's real."

"Yeah, but what is it?" he asked.

"I don't know. It's gold."

"*Tina*! Do we take gold as payment?" the barman shouted to someone in the kitchen. A young woman with olive skin, dark black hair and a perilously low-cut top came out drying her hands on a tea towel. She took the coin from the barman and held it up to the light.

"You can't see through it," he advised.

"Which piggy bank did you smash to get this?"

"It's all I've got," said Lally said, feeling stupid.

"Wait up," said Tina, and took a photo of the coin with her phone, before pasting the image into Google. Her eyes grew wide as she read. "This is worth about ten grand!"

"Is it?" Lally said.

"Are you sure you want to pay with this? I'm not going to give you change," said Tina, looking at Lally with suspicion. "You can have credit with the rest."

"Credit? How much?" Lally pressed.

"A grand?"

"Two," Lally countered.

"One and a half – final offer. I'll need your bank card in case this turns out to be made of chocolate."

"Deal. Stick the credit behind the bar. Serve until it runs out."

"Right you are!" The barman said breaking into a grin. He took a small hammer and donged the side of a brass bell above the bar. "Drinks on this lady."

An appreciative cheer went up, and suddenly Lally was surrounded by well-wishers and people pushing past her to get their orders in. She felt irrelevant and essential at the same time.

"Thank you very much for the drink. Do you want to come and sit with us?" A young woman in a shiny V-necked white top and white leggings asked Lally. Her hair was pulled back in a severe ponytail, which widened her eyes and made her seem like she was staring.

"That would be nice – thank you."

"We're just at that one in the corner, with the baby on it. I'll get a drink and come over."

Lally looked up and saw a sofa area with a baby in a car seat propped up on the table. "Go and grab a seat, if he squeals just ignore him. Same for his dad."

Lally took her vodka-powered pint over to the table and looked at the baby who was chewing on some car keys. His cheeks were the red of a drunk's nose and Lally could see the individual capillaries snaking their way across the surface of his skin. The baby looked at her incuriously as he gummed the car keys and his saliva worked its way inside the buttons.

"Hi, how are you?" Lally asked the baby.

The baby didn't say anything – babies could be like that sometimes. Lally sat down and looked around the pub. Everyone was at the bar and Lally noticed the first few coming away with triple pints wedged in their hands and bottles of wine under their arms. Good on them, Lally thought.

Her tablemates returned. The girl introduced herself as Kay and her boyfriend, Kieron, a tall, balding man with massive oily black nails.

"Cheers for the pints," he said. "I got three, hope that's ok."

"You didn't fancy champagne then?" Lally asked.

"Can't stand it, makes me wheezy."

"Last time we had prosecco, Bertie arrived nine months later. Probably best we steer clear," Kay explained. "Anyway, thanks, Your Highness."

Lally looked shocked and then remembered, "Oh, the bandage."

"Well, yeah, but you are that Eulalia, aren't you?"

"Oh, I'm not used to being recognised."

"It's okay, I won't say anything. Don't freak out but I had a phase where I loved all your dresses when you were about fifteen." Kay unplugged Bertie from his seat and then shuffled him onto her lap and latched him onto her breast. Lally tried her best to find the ceiling tiles fascinating.

"The chintzy ones? God, I hated them."

"Well, I was about eight at the time, so I'm not saying I knew much about anything. Why are you spending the end of the world here then? Shouldn't you be in one of those bunkers for the billionaires?"

"Long story," Lally started to reply. "Actually, no it's not. I'm not royal enough. They all went to the Isle of Man and left me here."

"In Bermondsey?" Kay asked with confusion.

"In London. On my own."

"Oh, shit. That's bleak."

"There has to be a cut-off point somewhere," Lally repeated, realising how cruel that sounded when she said it out loud. She didn't deserve that, even if she'd made mistakes in the past.

"So, I tried to help out on the streets because I thought that's what my granny would do, but I messed that up. Then I tried to kill myself but I got shot. Then someone gave me a gold coin. Now I'm here. So, it's not a long story, it's just an odd story and I'm not sure what it means."

"You got shot?" Kieron said in disbelief.

"It's a bandage not a fashion statement," Lally said pointing at her head.

"I was going to ask," Kieron said. "You look like one of those kids from the old comics. Did you get stitches?"

"Kieron, shut up – it's not nice to ask about injuries. Sorry ma'am."

"Please, Lally is fine."

"That's messed up. Are you okay?" Kay said.

Lally really tried to think about the answer. She was physically more hurt than she'd ever been. She felt abandoned. She felt confused. But there was something else underneath those feelings straining to be heard. She had first noticed it when she was sat with Margaret.

"And next up we've got Kieron and Kay – come on up and sing us a song!" the DJ said and Kieron beamed.

"We're on!" he said.

"I told you not to put us down, you dick! I just started feeding," Kay said. "Go on, Your Highness – you go up."

"Me?"

"Yeah, go on, you'll be great – it's only for a laugh."

Lally looked up and saw that some of the people in the pub were staring expectantly over towards their table. Kieron was standing up and waving at people who had started to applaud. Somehow, Lally found her legs straightening and she stood up too – the applause grew into cheers when people realised that their bandaged benefactor was going to be taking the mic.

"I'm not a good singer though," Lally said to Kay.

"You can't be as shit as Kieron," Kay said. "He's tone deaf. I mean that genuinely."

Lally looked at Kieron who was holding out his hand to her. She held up a finger and downed her pint, which just brought more cheers, so by the time she wobbled towards the karaoke there was a tumult of noise. Then, as the alcohol began to dance in her head, she found herself at the front of a two-metre-square stage crammed with karaoke equipment and mic stands. Kieron handed her a mic and she took it. He turned to the crowd and shouted, "HAVE IT!" Lally smiled as she watched the place go even crazier.

"Kieron, what are we singing?"

"Dunno – what do you want?"

"*Don't Stop Me Now?*"

"It's already been done," he replied. "Hold up, I've got a good one."

He whispered in the karaoke man's ear and he pressed some buttons on his laptop. Instantly, a pokey synth and tambourine started up and the cheers grew as people recognised the intro.

"She came from Greece, she had a thirst for olives…" Kieron began erroneously, even though the words were clearly displayed on the screen in front of them. He barged undaunted to the front of the stage and posed like an angular lamp. Lally danced back-up, but as the vodkas and lager started to unwind her spine, she found that the mic was ever closer to her mouth – as the chorus came in, suddenly she was screaming how she wanted to be like the common people, she wanted to live like them. She wanted to sleep with them. She wanted to see what they could do.

The song ended and another began. Then the emergency broadcast landed on everyone's phones and the evening dissolved into madness. What could you do when you'd just been sexted by the Prime Minister? Lally embraced the chaos. Pints were pressed into her hand. Shots of absinthe were consumed. Someone had pills. The music got louder. There was dancing and sweating. And burning in her heart she saw an unending, golden bond with the other people in the room and beyond them to the people in every room. She loved them and they loved her. Even when word went round that she was Eulalia, that weird one from the royals. No one actually seemed to care much. At some point she gave in to the requests, took the mic and answered any and every question that they had about The Firm. Yes, he could sweat. Definitely not the father. Literally more of a Nazi than Hitler.

The doors were locked and the pub became a single unit of humanity, sealed off and perfect, containing all that was important in life: alcohol, crisps and people. Then Lally was in the small alleyway at the back of the pub, drunker than hell, gasping in the cold night air with the warmth of Tina's body pressed to hers. There, hidden amongst the common people, Lally found something surprising hiding beneath the pain of the day. A delicate little thread of happiness, so thin that you could barely see it, but held up close it was bright and colourful. The night blurred into the morning and Lally allowed herself to start to wonder where that thread might lead if she followed it.

THE KELLY CRITERION

MARGARET WAS STACKING chairs in the cathedral. Although some worshipers were still dotted around the church pews, she had been asked to clear the extra chairs from one of the aisles. As she picked up another of the plastic chairs she reflected on the journey of her faith, and decided that stacking chairs had played more of a role than she would have anticipated. She knew that each person was called to perform different tasks for the Lord, she just didn't know that the Lord would want her to get her finger trapped between moulded plastic furniture quite so often.

Things were quieter in the cathedral now. Prayers had been offered. Hymns had been sung. Fudge had been fed and was now curled up, sleeping on a hassock. As the evening had worn on, people had gradually trailed away. The general confusion of earlier giving way to a sort of watchful waiting. It turns out that after relentless hours of terror the brain simply starts to accept that the world may or may not end, but maybe we should have something to eat anyway? Who knew what was really going on, maybe the emergency broadcast would help people to get the bottom of things. Perhaps there had been secret negotiations between the governments? Maybe God had performed another miracle like the bullet he'd sent for Lilly? Margaret knew only one thing: if she lived another sixty years, she would never be more surprised.

She slid the stack of chairs closer to the wall and trapped her entire right hand this time.

"Ow! Shhhhugar!" she hissed, sliding her hand out from the wall and shaking it to release the pain. She pressed it to her lips and squeaked her mouth against it, unsure of what else to do.

A strong hand gripped her left shoulder and another took her injured hand. A man's hand, pale skin with faint dark hair. She spun in shock and stared straight into Graham's chest.

"Graham?"

Graham said nothing, but caught her hand again between his two larger hands and brought it to his face. He was so close. Closer than he had ever been before, and Margaret caught a trace of a woody aftershave, which she thought might be the one that she'd bought him for Christmas several years ago. With immaculate gentleness he lifted her hand to his lips, then brushed it against first his left cheek and then the right. Margaret felt the slight rough of the day's stubble. Graham then pressed her fingers against his lips – not quite a kiss, more like a promise. Margaret's mind reeled.

Is this the end, God? She heard God snort with laughter.

Margaret was vaguely aware of phones ringing and loud notifications echoing around the Cathedral. Graham drew her towards him with a strength that she'd never experienced, but had sometimes thought about. Then, his arms were around her back, pulling her further into him. He inhaled her hair deeply and gradually drew a line with his nose down the side of her face. He brushed the hair from her neck and greedily pressed his lips to the naked skin.

Margaret felt something in her stomach drop and was reminded of the bumps – a series of bridges that her father would take great pleasure in speeding over, leaving all his passengers fighting to hold onto their lunches. But not Margaret – she loved the feeling. A pit of uncertainty and delight mixing in her stomach. As Graham's lips worked their way along her jawline and finally found her lips, she felt the same delirious abandon. Her hands rose involuntarily as if in worship and she thought that if her mouth wasn't occupied then she might have finally been able to speak in tongues.

Here then, was love, joy, warmth, answers.

"I've switched the boiler off, Margaret," came a voice from the other side of the transept and then, "Oh, I beg your pardon."

Margaret felt herself recalled to the spaceship; her interstellar fantasy prematurely ended. She focused her eyes and saw Paul the Dean stood near the vestry, clearly uttering a prayer that God smite him to avoid the awkwardness of the moment. Margaret didn't know what to say. She wasn't entirely sure she still knew English. Fortunately, Graham spoke for her.

"Sorry Paul – Margaret's not herself – she's just considering whether she'll marry me," Graham said. Margaret's mouth opened and closed with no words emerging. Yep, English word not work now.

"Oh, good show – dare I ask what the verdict is Margaret?" the Dean asked.

"Yes?" she replied.

"I say, that's terrific. Well done, Margaret. And you, Graham. Well dones all round."

"Thank you, Paul."

"Right, best leave you to it, I mean – leave you to…leave you two together. I'm going to leave you two together. Goodbye." Paul walked off, shaking his head to himself.

Graham lifted his hands to her face and kissed her again on the lips.

"Graham, what's going on?"

"It was that coin you gave me," Graham said in a hushed voice. "I couldn't stop looking at it on my desk. Britannia kept staring at me and I just found that I couldn't concentrate. She was very insistent."

"What happened?"

"I started thinking about the Kelly Criterion. That's a formula that you can use to help you make decisions about odds. It's a fascinating branch of mathematics. I realised I could use it to tell me what I should do."

Margaret could sense a long explanation incoming and moved to head Graham off.

"So, you did a great big long calculation to decide whether you wanted to marry me?"

"No, I started to and then I saw that it was simpler than that – I just had to toss the coin. Heads I would tell you how I felt. Tails, I wouldn't."

"And you got heads?"

"No. I dropped the coin behind the radiator, but I realised that I really wanted it to be heads, so here I am."

※ ※ ※ ※ ※

Margaret assumed that they must have made it home because they were suddenly back in the dining room, where they had shared meals and their lives for so long. She couldn't think how she had got there and she wouldn't have been surprised to learn she'd floated back, sealed in a neon bubble of happiness. By the time she came to rest on the edge of the dining room table, her face felt joyously warm and flushed from what she could only describe as snogging. She had snogged. She had snogged Graham. And if that wasn't incredible enough, somehow he turned out to be the best kisser that she'd ever, ever imagined. She'd kissed men before, but it had been a very long time – but now here she was: snogging. Graham raised his face from hers and lifted his eyebrows in question.

"What? Oh," Margaret said and couldn't help but laugh. "Where are the cats?"

"Upstairs, safe."

Graham kissed her again and she felt like the pale-yellow bubbles rising up the side of a champagne flute, her insides sparkling. Rashid would have been pleased to see that the smile had returned to her eyes. Graham reached behind her and swept the table free of the doilies and the place mats.

Next door, Terry's prized display of miniature trucks that was mounted on his wall started to shake. Terry turned up the radio as someone prattled on about nothing. He turned in dismay as a 1937 Model 73 was rattled off the shelf and fell onto the floor. This was it; the end was coming. He lit his pipe. He couldn't help hoping that his wife Janet wasn't in his section of the afterlife, because she'd give him an eternity of grief for letting her garden go to weeds.

The Colonel raised his head from the duvet and cocked it to one side. Mitsi stared out of the window and watched a woman walking down the street against the streetlights. She yawned; this had been a boring inside-sort-of-day. Hopefully tomorrow would be better.

PSSST...
I HAVE
A BUNKER

COCO WAS DOING her best to steer the *Neptune's Desire* in the tight circle that Bradford had demanded, and given that her previous nautical experience was sitting in a rented pedalo when she was five, she felt she was doing a decent job. Bradford had commanded Greg to sit on the floor with Ronan restrained on his lap, and Greg felt that he and Ronan were doing a decent job of that. Ronan had taken the measure of the situation and was emitting a primal growl and baring his teeth simultaneously at Bradford and at a spot several metres to his right. Bradford was stalking back and forth across the bridge, switching between wild gesticulation and pointing the rifle at Greg, Coco, the sky, bridges and Ronan.

Bradford had reached the zenith of his mania. Anyone who has spent time with a cocaine enthusiast will recognise it as the point where the person's ego spews from their mouth like magma from a volcano. All bystanders can do is to hope that they don't asphyxiate in the pyroclastic flow of hubris. Bradford's eyes were bulging in their sockets and a gummy white spittle had gathered at the corners of his mouth. Between the broken nose, the missing teeth and the remnants of fatberg on his clothes and hair, it was fair to say that he wasn't looking his best. Trent and Alexandra would have had notes. But he was certainly full of joie de vivre after the bullet had nearly pierced Greg's ear and disappeared into the sky.

"...Project Focus Pull is go! Go! Go! You've got to pump it up! Don't you know, pump it up! Do you hear that Pops? Thinking you've got one over on me? You haven't! You haven't got it anymore old man! You're going down. Down in the ground! I am The Bradford! You put me in the shit and I will emerge smelling of Chanel. Actually, Pops, I'm sorry, you're not going down in the ground. Sorry, I didn't mean that. No one needs the car wash now, do they? Not me! But, you two! I warned you two! I told you I would do it! Do you remember? I said I would do that and then I did it. You said shoot me and I did and now you know who has the power! I shot my first giraffe with one of these. You can't make mince with Bradford Alderman VIIII. I am the scion of the Alderman Retail Group! I have the testicles of a gorilla – literally, they're in my study. Try and lay Bradford Alderman VIIII low with didgeridoo or fist, see what happens. He will rise again like the Phoenix of myth and set fire to your face! I am bigger than any of this. I am *more* than any of this! I have a thirty-thousand-metre Golden Thumper! It will shower you with victory! You want a victory shower from the Golden Thumper? Form a queue! Who's the psychic guru now, Sensei Steve? Huh, Sensei Steve…"

Despite the fact that he'd nearly shot him in the face, Greg quite liked this guy's vibe, much of which seemed to emanate from the cocaine vial that he kept dipping his finger into and rubbing across his gums. He'd initially tried snorting, but the squashed tomato that now passed for Bradford's nose had decreed that none shall pass. Bradford paused to twitch his jaw from side to side, as if trying to make it crack and then he experimentally opened and closed it several times before bringing his frothing monologue to a close.

"…And now I own you and this boat!" Bradford concluded, and seemed to remember that he was holding people hostage and aimed the rifle at Greg once more.

Greg tried to make himself as small as possible and scooted Ronan behind his back in case the rifle decided to misfire again.

"Look, *again*, I'm sorry I said I'd throw you off the boat. Can I just say that it seems like it's been a trying day all round," Greg replied.

"Please, just keep calm Bradford. I'm sorry I said he should kick your arse. But please can I steer somewhere other than in a circle? I think I'm going to be sick," Coco said in soothing tones. Once more the boat alternated between views of the Royal Festival Hall, Cleopatra's Needle and then back towards the Royal Festival Hall. It appeared that the baby wasn't going to be much of a sailor.

"Oh, I will be calm. I will be oil on water. I will be baby rabbits massaged in a woodland setting. I will be an entire windchime orchestra. Just give me what I want: give me the bunker," he said and clicked his jaw at them for emphasis.

"Right, about that…" Greg began wishing he had more lager to hand.

He had a sense of things unravelling fast, and he had to admit that things hadn't been particularly ravelled up to that point. As he looked at his bucket of gold, he felt a nibble of regret that it was all slipping away. It would have been lovely to escape to the country and just be still for a bit, but there was also a sense of relief that he could finally unburden himself.

"…there isn't a bunker," he said.

"What?" Coco and Bradford said in unison.

"Explain now!" Bradford screamed and pushed the barrel of the rifle into Greg's face.

"There is no bunker," Greg confirmed quickly. "…but, I *do* work for B of the Bang, but I'm not an operative, I'm the legal compliance officer. I do training. And forms. But mostly I sit in my office and hope no one talks to me."

"What do you mean there's no bunker? What about the missiles? What did I give you my gold for if there's no bunker?" Coco asked.

"Well, you see, here's the thing," Greg explained.

And as carefully as he could, only skipping over some casual arson and putting a more positive slant on what was essentially dognapping, Greg explained the thing. Greg explained that, through *very* little fault of his own, he'd been caught up in a teensy little fiction which had snowballed. Namely, that there weren't any missiles heading for London and that it was all a training exercise that had gone wrong. He explained how it was all Serge's fault. Stupid, stupid Serge and his inability to know the difference between the live red system and the green test system. No, sorry, the other way around. Red was for learners, that was how you remembered.

He explained that when he'd seen the chaos that had erupted, it felt like that moment in *Fawlty Towers* where Basil pushes Manuel back into the kitchen that's on fire. It was like that, but with nuclear missiles. Bradford hadn't seen *Fawlty Towers*, so Greg searched around for another comparison, which eluded him, so he just said that he felt trapped in a bad situation and that somehow it had been easier to lean into the fantasy and procure a boat and pick people up, rather than just staying in the pub, drinking lager and waiting for the whole thing to blow over. Like in *Shaun of the Dead*? Coco asked – but Bradford hadn't seen that either.

"I don't know, it just seemed like everything was already waiting to explode, like we'd been rehearsing the anxiety for too long and London just wanted to do it for real. Does that make sense?"

"Yes," said Coco emphatically.

"No," said Bradford emphatically.

"And B of the Bang," Greg continued – his explanation coming to an end – "It's not a *scam* precisely. Part of my job is ensuring that legally we're never technically *lying* about how we can help our customers, but a sizeable part of the company's business model is built on the idea that if the apocalypse does happen, then customers will probably be too busy exploding to register a complaint. So, things like bunkers they just photoshop and put in the brochures. And they don't technically, well, exist."

Coco could only suppress a laugh. This whole day. This dumpster fire of a day. The hellscape that London had become in a matter of minutes, was all just a result of a workplace whoopsie. It was playing the wrong video for the presentation. It was leaving the document detailing everyone's wages on the photocopier. It was hitting "Reply All" rather than just "Reply." After a suffocating pause, Coco threw her head back and cackled. Greg looked at her wholesome pixie face and the jiggling of her lobster legs and something in the mania of her delightful laughter made him laugh too. When her laughter had peaked, she found enough breath to talk.

"Ohhh. You big lunk, Greg!" she said with mock anger. "Destroying the world with a training exercise!"

"Grrrrr! Silly old Serge!" Greg said, trying to play along, but allocating the blame where he felt it rightly belonged. "How dare you bring the Western world to its knees with your incompetence!"

Coco laughed even more and Greg smiled. Ronan barked so that he could get in on the act.

"Trillions in damages!" Coco said through tears of mirth. "Actual deaths! I electrocuted a man in a sewer!"

"You're a very naughty boy, Serge! HR will hear about this!" Greg laughed trying to stay on top of all these shifting feelings. Was… was he going to be okay? Could he just Serge his way out of this?

A gunshot interrupted his moment of hope and brought silence back to the bridge. While they had been chatting, Bradford's keen analytical brain had parsed what Greg was telling him and he had reached the only logical conclusion.

"Do I look like an idiot?" Bradford said.

Greg looked at him. He looked like one of Santa's elves had been brutalised at work and escaped via a series of septic tanks and boxing rings. Greg decided that it would be smarter to treat the question as if it was rhetorical.

"I know what you're up to," Bradford said wagging his finger and he looked at Greg as if pushing him to admit something. "You too, you naughty girl," he said to Coco.

"Do you?" asked Greg, who was now quite keen to know what he was up to.

"Who was it, eh? One of the race-you-to-a-trillion boys? Some hedge fund cuck?"

"I don't know what that is," Greg said.

"You almost had me!" Bradford shouted out loud, as if he was addressing a hidden camera. "It's genius. Buy up all the bunkers when the shit hits the fan and tell everyone else that they're full? Send an expendable idiot out to sow chaos and confusion? That is priceless. It's something I would have thought of myself, but you forgot *one little thing*. I am Bradford Alderman VIIII, the scion of the Alderman Retail Group!"

"What's going on?" asked Greg, wishing that they could rewind to when Coco had been laughing.

"I especially like the little detail with the bucket of gold. And the lobster? Little honey trap, eh? Clever, but it won't wash. So, here's what's going to happen. Here's what we're going to do: I am going to go to the toilet and I am going to boof the rest of this." He shook the little vial in a blur. "And when I get back, we *will* be on our way to the bunker, or I *will* shoot you in the face, then I *will* shoot you in the face, then I *will* shoot the weird dog in the face. Do you hear that? Are we clear?"

Bradford abruptly left the bridge. When he was gone, Greg scrambled across to Ronan tucked him under his arm and grabbed the bucket of gold.

"We have to go! Come with me."

"Go where?"

"We can swim for it."

"With a bucket full of gold and a dog? I'm three months pregnant!"

"Oh, mazel tov! Okay. We'll scuttle the ship then, or we can hit him on the head with the bucket when he gets back? I don't know – think!"

"*No*, no more killing," Coco said emphatically.

"More killing?" Greg said, looking confused, but time was too short for him to explore this further. "Look, you have to believe me. I was being serious, I don't know what he's talking about, I don't work in secret for any billionaires. I'm just a mid-level idiot. I'm in way over my head and I absolutely do not have a bunker."

"Were you serious about the missiles? The news said that one had landed in Kent."

"Did they? What the fuck is going on?"

"I don't know! But there was definitely a missile from North Korea, the new Prime Minister is making an emergency broadcast."

"This is all news to me!"

"Where have you been?"

"I've been busy rounding up billionaires! You have to trust me: it's all bullshit, it's all a mistake. It's all Serge - and to a lesser extent – Meg. There are no missiles."

"But there's no bunker either?"

"Exactly! And now we're going to get shot because the world is not ending."

"So, let me get this straight - you had no actual plan?"

"I had a plan! Get all the gold and then something would happen and then I could escape to the country!"

"And you were leaving the "something would happen" bit intentionally vague? You had no plan for if anyone demanded a bunker?"

"The bunker was next Greg's problem!"

"Here I come, ready or not!" came Bradford's voice up the stairs.

Coco looked out across London. She had to admit that Greg had a point on one thing. It *did* feel like all of this was primed and ready to go. Like for once, it felt like all the anxiety had a reason. All the stress of life, the bullshit of work and -

"I have a bunker," Coco stated in a flash of inspiration. "It's not perfect and we may still get shot, but I want all of the gold," Coco hissed as they heard Bradford making his way up the steps.

"All of it!? No way! Fifty-fifty?" Greg yelped.

"Is my offer better than getting shot in the head?" Coco countered.

"He's going to shoot you too, remember! And what about if he kills Ronan?" Greg asked, and quickly held up the dog and made a pathetic face at Coco. "I have to do puppy eyes for him."

"Seventy-thirty, final offer," Coco said.

"Deal."

"So, are you ready to stop this little game?" Bradford asked as he reached the top step and saw his captives shaking hands.

"You win, you get your bunker," Greg said.

The journey to Hammersmith didn't take long. Coco thrashed the engines and Greg and Ronan marvelled at the huge wake trailing behind the boat. The *Neptune's Desire's* engines started making an abrasive noise and as they approached their destination a smell of smoke filled the boat and started to snake up the stairs. Coco pulled the lobster costume up around her mouth and pushed the throttle even harder. Not much further.

A few minutes after they chugged under Putney Bridge, Coco heard something snap and then a series of thuds coming from down below. The steering went slack in her hand and when she turned the wheel from side-to-side it made no difference to their course.

"Hold on to something!" shouted Coco, and she pushed the throttle to the very top, urging the failing engines to get them to the shore. As they approached the shallows, they could hear the bottom of the boat dragging against the silt of the river bank. Then the boat mounted the mudbank at the edge of the river before pitching over to the right. Down below, they heard their passengers scream and the sound of breaking glass.

Coco, Greg and Bradford spilled to the side of the bridge. Greg reached out and caught Coco as she tumbled past him. She noticed the bucket of gold teetering on its edge and lunged to stop it from tumbling overboard, just catching it in time.

"Okay, where are we going?" Bradford demanded.

"Right. Yes. We're going to the bunker. Well, first of all we need to get everyone off the boat. That's the first step. I will then lead you to it."

Greg noticed Coco struggling to pick up the bucket of gold.

"Allow me. You shouldn't be lifting things like that in your condition," he said.

"I shouldn't be doing any of this in my condition," Coco said gesturing broadly at everything.

Bradford shot the rifle into the air to refocus the attention.

"Enough with those coins – they don't matter!" he shouted and he pushed the bucket out of Greg's hands. Greg and Coco watched in horror as the bucket landed and spilled across the deck. The contents slid across the bridge until every coin slipped through the railings and into the muddy water below.

"My gold!" Greg shouted as he rushed to watch the last flickers of the coins as they blinked beneath the churning surface.

"Our gold!" Coco interjected.

"Oh, boo hoo," Bradford shouted. "You need to realise that what you want doesn't matter, the only thing that matters, is what *I* want. And *I* want my bunker!"

Greg's shoulders slumped in defeat. There would be no gold for him. There was no escape to the country. He scooped Ronan up and led the way down the stairs. They followed the other passengers who had already jumped off the side of the ship into the knee-deep sludge of the riverbank. Greg held out his hand for Coco to hold as she dropped down. Bradford waited until last and then dropped into the mire.

The passengers trudged up to the edge of the bank and began to climb slowly up a ladder set into the side. They clambered onto the pavement and together they watched the *Neptune's Desire* succumb to fire from the engines. Greg and Coco stood next to each other in their mutual cocoon of misery.

"I had the gold for longer, so I'm feeling this moment more keenly," Greg said.

"What's the bloody point, all I want is to be at home drinking hot chocolate and watching Below Deck," she said in dismay.

"Don't leave me!" Greg said, a note of panic in his voice. "You need to help me! I'm not competent like you."

Coco didn't say it, but she felt a warm glow from someone describing her as competent. If he could have seen her just a few hours ago trying to tip over the lobster tank, he might have felt differently.

"You're not entirely incompetent," Coco replied and Greg felt a warm glow. If she could have seen him just a few hours ago setting his office on fire, she might have felt differently.

"Come on, chop-chop! Bunker time!" shouted Bradford, and he jabbed Greg in the back, making him jump.

"Ow! My spine!" Greg whined. "Okay! Come on, let's get to your precious bunker!" A small cheer went up from the billionaires.

"It's this way!" he said, and started to march off into the streets of Hammersmith.

Coco coughed pointedly. Greg looked at her questioningly.

"But there's a shortcut this way! Come on!"

The evacuees from *Neptune's Desire* fell into line, with Greg, Coco and Ronan at the front, followed by Bradford with the gun trained on them to ensure there was no funny stuff. He kept up a running commentary of his brilliance for anyone who was bothered to listen. Behind him, a crocodile line of London's richest people, whose lives had passed from smooth and luxurious to fraught and terrifying in a single day. All thanks to their proximity to Greg.

Greg led them like a tour guide, holding his hand in the air for them to follow and listened for Coco's whispered prompts on directions. The streets were quieter here than they were in the capital and soon Coco brought them to a halt outside two large metal gates, marked by a garish sign overhead proudly proclaiming this to be *London's Best Subterranean Alien Escape Room*.

"4808," she hissed to Greg as his finger hovered blankly over a control pad set into the side of the gates. He tapped in the code and waited for the gates to do something. This was the only bit of her quickly-conjured plan that Coco hadn't had time to think through. Her ex-employer had passed into liquidation with startling rapidity, so she knew that the escape room would be empty, but would the power still be on?

She sighed with relief as the gates swung inwards, revealing a small courtyard populated with cardboard cutouts of the Shmerms, the alien race that Coco had spent several months of her weekends portraying for minimum wage and that most-loathed currency: exposure. The Shmerms looked a lot like lobsters, but they were green and had guns. It didn't look much like a state-of-the-art nuclear bunker.

"What's this all about?" Bradford said gesturing to the decorations as the gates closed behind them, sealing them away from Hammersmith.

"It's the bunker?" Greg said – looking to Coco for confirmation.

"Don't you think that's clever?" Coco asked. "Hiding a nuclear bunker in plain sight and concealing it as an alien-themed escape room! I suppose you did that so that it was easily accessible, but wouldn't be over-run in the event of an apocalypse?" Coco said.

"Yes. That's what we did," Greg replied.

Bradford looked sceptical. Then after a moment's analysis he nodded and said, "Yes, it's clever. It's like I wrote in *The Art of War 2*: 'Sometimes when you want to hide something, the best way to hide it is not to hide it at all.'"

"I think that's where they got the idea," Greg said and Bradford nodded in appreciation. The band moved into the wide entrance hall and Coco subtly pointed a finger towards the stairwell in the corner, which led down to the old underground tunnel. As they filed down the dark stairs, lit by ankle-level mood lighting, their descent triggered some pre-recorded audio which boomed out from the PA along with an injection of dry ice.

"The Shmerms were a peace-loving race who valued co-operation and friendship above all else, until the day space junk from earth entered their atmosphere and destroyed their home world of Kronth – leaving them with a thirst for vengeance and a passion for recycling! Now it's time for you to pit your wits against the Shmerms and learn about the value of the world around you!"

"Ignore that! Ignore that!" Greg shouted. "It's all part of the subterfuge."

An inflatable Shmerm suddenly inflated behind a plastic rock to their left and Bradford screamed and fired the rifle at it. In the confined space the bullet ricocheted off several surfaces. Ronan started to yip wildly and a number of the older billionaires held their hands to their chests.

"Quick! I can hear the sirens!" Coco screamed, employing every minute of her dramatic training. The panic spread across the group and they pushed through a series of double doors. Coco led them down through the escape room's various stages. They ran straight through where the Shmerms attack and the customers had to sort recycling to repel them. Then they careened into the final set of the experience – the holding cells where the Shmerms were incarcerated, providing you could solve the final riddle in time (the answer to the riddle was "recycling").

"Get in a bunker!" yelled Coco, and the billionaires all fought for the right to get in the cells first. With a great deal of pushing and shoving they found themselves seven to a cell, squinting in the dim emergency lighting at their new cellmates.

"Here come the missiles! Everyone get down!" Coco screamed and Greg slammed the doors shut, while Coco locked the doors.

The faces of the billionaires peered through the tiny glass panels on the doors and Greg shouted: "Everyone! Keep your eyes closed for at least the next ten minutes, the lights will be blinding. We are going to seal the outer blast doors and engage the…um…"

"…shield generators!" Coco finished, barely holding back her laughter.

"Yes. Those. May God have mercy on our souls."

A hush fell over the holding cells as the billionaires shrunk into the corners of the cramped cells and covered their faces. Greg held out a hand to indicate that Coco should lead the way and she walked back to the stairwell. Ronan bumped between them as they took the stairs upwards, back into the light.

YOU GET A TRIDENT! YOU GET A TRIDENT! EVERYONE GETS A TRIDENT!

THE FLAT ABOVE Number 10 looked as if it had been decorated by a demented aunt with an unlimited kitsch budget. There were well-padded floral sofas, intricate patterned carpets showing imps and faeries frolicking, and across every flat surface there were tiny white porcelain figures of animals in repose, kind-faced women with children at their feet and shepherds tending their flocks.

In the flat's main bathroom, William was horrified to find that even the toilet hadn't escaped the bechintzing and it sported a floral-patterned seat cover. William couldn't quite square this campiness with Crossley's reputation as the prime shagger-in-chief. With utmost care, he undid his belt and winced pre-emptively as he thumbed the button of his camo trousers open, panting while he slowly pulled his y-fronts past his swollen, subjugated member.

"Oooooohhh, no, no, no," he whispered, and when he dared to look down, he was dismayed to see that his penis had been swapped for a black pudding. He tried to point it at the toilet, but he started to fade into unconsciousness when he brushed his fingers against it and so he just settled for being in the same room as the toilet and let his urine stream away. He eventually found that if he leaned against the wall, gravity dangled his broken appendage over the water.

He had to admit that Jenny had done an absolutely first-rate job. His pink font of woe wouldn't bother him anymore. The relief was tremendous.

He counted the seconds of the stream and using the algorithm that he had refined since his teenage years, he adjusted the average for the current player at-bat. He did a single fart, which he chalked up as a maiden over. The game was coming to a thrilling conclusion, he was delighted to say. If this was to be the last series he ever played then it couldn't have gone out on a better game. He sneezed and awarded the single. It was so close!

With careful effort, he re-trousered himself. Then with a hobble he returned to the lounge area where Jenny had taken the single armchair in the room. William made his way to her side and carefully perched on one of its arms. He noticed that Tom, their only remaining advisor, couldn't meet his eyes after seeing the emergency broadcast. That was fine. He had to assume he was going to get this a lot now people knew what he and Jenny were really like. He found that he didn't really care. He was very happy to fade into the background and let Jenny get on with things – that was what she was good at after all.

"It's over. We've got to walk this back. We could claim it was a deep fake released by the North Koreans," Tom was saying to Jenny. "William could resign and let the party decide who to replace him with. You then go and hide in the Highlands for a decade or two. That's the only way that you can come out of this with anything like respect."

"Respect? Who wants respect? Power is the only thing that matters."

"What did I miss?" William said. Jenny turned to stare at him with shock.

"Don't loom over me, get on the floor."

William nodded meekly and curled up in a ball next to the armchair. There was a KitKat wrapper under the frilly skirting of the chair. William would quite like a KitKat, but he knew now was not the time to reach out for the plate of biscuits on the table.

"For crying out loud! Don't make him sit on the floor, he's the leader of the country! William – have a shred of dignity, man!" Tom said appalled.

"Tom, we've been in power for several hours now. Do you not think that I've used at least some of that time to read your MI6 file? If you continue to kink-shame me and my husband, then I'll see to it that the details of how that girl at Oxford came to be in a coma gets to her parents. Would that work for you?"

"That's blackmail!" Tom spluttered.

"Yes. Of course it is. I find it remarkable that you chucklefucks don't seem to have cottoned onto the fact that we're not pretending. We're not playing at leaders. We are the leaders and we will be until we choose not to be."

"Jenny, this is ridiculous – it's not democratic."

"Tom – I love democracy, but democracy is a stick that the people beg to be hit with."

"But there will be reports and investigations. You can't escape the consequences of what you've done today."

"Tom, you simply do not have the imagination to understand what I can do and what this nation will let me get away with. You're not thinking big enough."

"I didn't mean to hurt her," Tom said in a small voice.

"Oh, I know that, Tom. Accidents happen, plus it's not been all bad for her, has it? She gets to blow into that little straw anytime she wants to go somewhere. That looks like fun." Tom's face became paler. "I don't blame you, Tom. But also, I don't need you, you're excused."

"And...you won't mention anything about..."

"Just like your uni chum, I won't blink a word."

William heard feet shuffling again and then a door closing.

"You can get up William, everyone's gone."

William stood up and wasn't sure where his Mistress might want him to go, so he just stood mutely by her awaiting a command.

"Take a seat Will, I'm tired. It's been a busy day, I'm out of commands for now."

William perched carefully on the sofa. He noticed that the hairs on his arms were standing on end. Experience had taught him that Jenny was at her most dangerous when she seemed human. He looked at her and, for once, she looked almost vulnerable, rather than the Amazonian that he so often saw her as.

"It's been a big day, hasn't it?" she asked.

"Yes, Mistress."

"Refer to me as Jenny until I tell you otherwise."

"Yes, Jenny."

"This place is incredible, isn't it? What the fuck was Crossley thinking when he decorated?"

"There's a chintzy cover on the toilet seat," William informed her and Jenny nodded.

"It's like a Nanna's Paradise, isn't it? Tell me William, do you think we've reached the end of the line? Do you agree with Tom and all those turncoats?"

Jenny's flame red hair seemed muted, as if she was somehow in the process of being doused. It made William feel something that he hadn't experienced much in their relationship: protective. Of course, he always wanted to look out for his Mistress's needs but there was nothing that *he* could do to protect *her*. She was stainless steel. He was wafer-thin ham.

"I don't think so, Jenny."

"You don't?"

"If I may?"

"You don't need permission to speak, William."

"Jenny, you've been everything to me since we met. I've never wanted another. Just because we're in power now, that's not changed. I don't want or need anyone else. And if you're still with me, then what do we have to fear?"

Jenny smiled, really smiled – as if it was beaming out of her soul – and stood up from the armchair. William was pleased to see that some of the colour was returning to her face. She walked over to the big sofa and thumped down next to him which caused a rip of pain to shoot through his genitals.

"Ooh, still a bit tender?"

"Yes, it is rather."

"We really did a number on it didn't we?"

"I'll say!" William said happily. Jenny reached into his pocket and took out his mobile phone.

"Give me your finger," she commanded and William held out his hand. Jenny unlocked his phone and pulled up the Trident app. She tapped on it.

"*Please give voice authorisation to access the Trident programme,*"

"William?"

"Hm, oh okay – William McCartney, Prime Minister."

"*Voice authorisation accepted, connecting.*"

On the app a video connection was established of a broad and muscular man in a blue uniform. He was sitting at a small desk in what looked like quite a cramped and poorly lit room.

"Good afternoon, this is Major Ground of HMS Vigilant, please repeat the authorisation code that you can see on the top of your app now."

"181B49-actual," said Jenny.

"Please confirm the code."

Jenny repeated it.

"Ma'am, I accept your authorisation and I have visual confirmation that I am speaking with Prime Minister William McCartney and his wife, Jenny McCartney."

"We thank you for your confirmation. We need you to prepare to launch."

"Ma'am?"

"Do you need a confirmation code?"

"No, but ma'am – has this…been approved?"

"Can you see the Prime Minister here, Captain Ground?"

"Yes, ma'am."

"Then I think you have your orders. Goodbye."

She clicked on the red phone icon and the image of the General winked off.

Jenny thumbed her way through to the next stage of launching. The app was asking her where she wanted the warheads to be sent.

"What do you think, Bill? I'm thinking we could jam one or two up Martha's skirt and send a couple to butter Sélène's baguettes. And maybe we should spare a thought for Pinky and the Wibbles over on the Isle of Man. What do you think?"

"We can't do this," William said in a faint voice.

"I beg your pardon?"

"We can't start a nuclear war for no reason."

"William – it's not for no reason – they killed Carol Blanding, remember?"

"That's not an act of war Jenny, it's just Carol Blanding."

"I'm sorry William, but it's happening," Jenny closed her eyes and finished scattering the pins across the map on the phone's screen. "There, that looks good to me."

The app screen changed and a red "LAUNCH" button appeared on the screen next to a green "ABORT" button.

"We can't Jenny," William said, and with a distinct sadness he held out his left hand in front of her and slowly revolved his wedding ring around, so that the black opal faced away from him and the small diamond glinted upwards once more. Jenny gasped.

"No, William, we can! Don't you see - *the chaos is the way*. We have to lean into it. Deflect. Confuse. Start more fires. Always start more fires! The second we stop, we die."

"Liverpool Lime Street."

Jenny's face fell and her hand came up to her mouth in shock.

"You're using the safeword?"

"I am."

"But you've *never* used the safe word."

"I know."

"Even when I made you squat on all of those bottles."

William winced at the memory.

"It turns out that getting what you want isn't always the best thing. I know you want the power, my angel, but there will be other ways."

Jenny looked crestfallen. Her bottom lip turned over and she looked at William with big doe eyes.

"No, Jenny, that won't work: Liverpool Lime Street. Cancel the missiles and give me the phone."

"Fine! I'll figure something else out. It was nice to finally find your boundary. It took longer than I imagined."

William watched as Jenny clicked the little X by each of the missiles she had primed. Jenny pouted and William laughed. She passed the phone over to him and as she did so her thumb pressed the red rectangle that read: *LAUNCH*. The phone emitted an obliging missile launch sound effect, and William took it from her in horror. He watched the screen helplessly as a notification pinged up to inform him that his missile would be delivered in… *five*…minutes.

"Whoops! But it was just *one*," Jenny said and bit the tip of her index finger between her front teeth. "Naughty Jenny."

William continued to stare at his phone, his face aghast as he saw where the missile was due to fall.

TIME GENTLEMEN, PLEASE

JUST AS THE billionaires were settling into their subterranean safehold, Lally was finishing her final song on the karaoke. By this point her voice was a hoarse rasp and she was so entirely drunk that her eyes had shut several minutes ago and she didn't notice that she was singing *Red Red Wine* to the backing track of *Like a Prayer*. No one in The Flower Pot minded. Most of the patrons were lying on the scarred leather sofas, either snoring loudly or swaying along to the music in the room, or the music inside their heads.

Lally abruptly concluded and after a beat of silence she heard one person clapping. Her eyes opened and tried to focus on the room. She felt a tickle of excitement like she was coming up, as if she was being ushered into a new dream.

"Thank you, you've been a beautiful audience."

She missed the step and stumbled off the stage, just righting herself before she walked into a column. The backing track cycled onto the next tune, Johnny Cash's cover of *Hurt*. It was Kay who was clapping. She was feeding the baby again. Lally had forgot his name. She staggered over and plonked herself down on the sofa, causing the baby to noisily disengage from the breast and look at Lally as if he was scandalised. Kay put her boob away and sat the baby up.

"*Bertie*," Lally said.

"That's right. The one and only Bertie Mason. Do you want to hold?"

Lally wanted to object, but holding babies was pretty much in the job description for royals. Lally took him, stunned as she always was with babies, at the denseness of this parcel – he felt solid and valuable like the gold. She stood him on her legs and tipped her head to one side feeling with relief how much the alcohol had numbed the pain from the wound.

"He's small," Lally said. Kay laughed.

"Babies generally are. Do you not want kids?"

"I'll tell you a secret, Kay. Shhhh! I'm not much for the whole man-sex thing."

"Ha! You don't have to do the whole man-sex thing you know. There are sperm clinics."

"Can you imagine it? A Princess getting IVF from some random commoner. The Firm would explode into a trillion, gabillion pieces." Lally laughed at the thought. It would be hilarious. Maybe, baby.

Bertie held out his hand towards Lally's face and gripped her lips and mushed them together with great force, whilst simultaneously unleashing a ripper of a belch.

"Bertie, no," Kay said barely able to keep her eyes open any more.

"Ishhfiiii," Lally said. "Hessssgoodilikehim."

A brilliant light consumed the room. Lally looked to the main room's big lampshade in discomfort, but saw that it wasn't the source. A spectacular dawn, a transcendent, phosphorescent blaze was swallowing the room whole in a blessing of white. Bertie relinquished his grip on Lally's face and turned to the window. Lally watched as Bertie was consumed with the light, became the light, and then diminished back into a regular human baby.

Lally turned to see if anyone else had witnessed it, but everyone was on their phones, or sleeping. She nudged Kay who was resting her eyes.

"I need to home," Lally said and passed Bertie back to Kay.

Kay leaned over and kissed her on the cheek and then pulled her into a tight embrace with Bertie caught in-between them. She whispered urgently into Lally's ear.

"You're not shit like the rest of them, you know. Just be you and it'll come good. We do karaoke here every fortnight and you're always welcome. I think Tina would like to see you again," Kay said and smiled teasingly as Lally's cheeks tinted red.

Lally smiled and stood up. She wanted a shower, an Irn Bru and a long think about what the future looked like. She didn't know the answer but she felt that maybe there was a future for her after all. That felt like enough of a victory for today. She waved at Bertie. Bertie didn't wave back.

💎 💎 💎 💎 💎

Margaret pulled the duvet up to her chin and stared at Graham, who was staring back at her. She was finding it hard not to be self-conscious of her nakedness, even though there were no more secrets that she had to share after the last few hours.

"Graham?"

"Yes?"

"Why did you never do anything about us before?"

"Good question."

He let the words slip into silence and continued to stare at her with a smile on his lips.

"Yes. Well – what's the answer?"

"Oh, right. Yes. I didn't know how you felt. I knew I loved you and I didn't want to risk getting thrown out. There was a time when I could have said something but it passed and then it was gone."

"How could you not know how I felt?"

"Well, you never said anything."

"What about earlier?"

"I thought you were just being emotional because of the missile."

Margaret shut her eyes. He was a genius, but he was also a total and complete idiot. She made a mental note that she had to remember that for the future. She leaned her head against Graham's chest. She smiled to herself with the bright joy that she had found, right where it had always been. Today was going to be a big day, they had a wedding to plan.

A silence settled on the room; Margaret and Graham closed their eyes. In a minute they claimed the shared simple victory of sleep. They were far away in slumber when the room lit with an eerie brightness that didn't want to cease and threatened to bleach everything into nothingness with its primal greed. The cats were the only ones awake to witness the light bleed in around the edge of the room's thick curtains and then recede almost apologetically. Soon, the cats fell asleep too.

💎 💎 💎 💎 💎

Bradford Alderman VIIII, scion of the Alderman Retail Group, sat on the wire-framed prison bed with a Lord on one side and a hedge fund cry-baby on the other. The bed wasn't designed for so much weight so it bowed in the middle leading the other men to lean in on him. Another thirty minutes and it would be his turn on the orange crate.

He thought briefly about his twins and reached out to them.

"I'm fine, don't worry about me," he told them.

His fingers pinched along the ridge of where his nose used to be and discovered only a painful mush. He would have to find a way to get it reset. He wasn't going to go through the rest of his life looking like he'd actually played rugby at school. Screw Susie. She might have won the battle, but he had won the war. *He* was safe from the blast and the radiation. He visualised her dying moments being frozen in a number of painful positions. Hands raised to shelter her face. Good. Clutching at her chest. Yes, nice. Arms, legs and head blown clean off her torso. Ooh, perfect.

He imagined that in the future, when they gave the all-clear, he might be able to find her body somewhere, flash-fried in stricken stasis. He pictured himself throwing a single white rose at her crispy charcoal remains. Or perhaps she would have been instantaneously cast as a shadow on the floor. That would be cool too. He saw himself throw a single white rose at the shadow. Yes, that was ideal.

There was still cocaine in his system, and he could feel his jaw urgently clenching and unclenching. He wanted to say something to his cell-mates about all the thoughts in his head, but they'd recently reached a consensus that he wasn't allowed to speak. He still had the rifle, but he was fairly sure that there was only one or two bullets left in the magazine. It was good to hold it all the same – who knew how valuable a working weapon would be in the nuclear wasteland. It was a shame that he'd lost the knife, but that couldn't be helped and, regardless, he was alive! Bradford Alderman VIIII was alive and loving life! He had made it to the bunker against all the odds and he would be alive for decades to come! He couldn't contain the joy any longer and he whooped until the hedge fund manager told him to shut up.

Bradford didn't care – he wanted to whoop, so he whooped and whooped and whooped. He added another thought to *The Art Of War 3* working file in his head – "Know yourself and you will win all the battles. Especially if you have a gun and, especially even more so, if you are a winner." Bradford jiggled himself into a more comfortable position on the bed and knew that it was over.

"I win!" he screamed.

"I win!"

💎 💎 💎 💎 💎

Greg, Coco and Ronan were on their way to buy a lobster. Greg was trying to navigate them towards a fish market without admitting that he didn't really know where he was. Coco wasn't sure if the fish markets would be open today, but she wanted to try – she had a promise to keep to a king. Greg felt that this was enough of an explanation and settled into a comfortable walking pace alongside her. As they sidled along, he noticed with alarm that he recognised a jazz club down a side street and felt a pang of déjà vu. He swept the street looking for any angry cats who might give him away.

London wasn't at its best. Cars were smouldering, street signs and windows had been smashed, and people sat dazed in shop doorways as gales of litter blew along the streets. As he walked proudly alongside Coco, Greg decided the best course of action would be to abandon all attempts to understand what had happened and how he had arrived at this point. Somehow, he was going lobster shopping with a beautiful pregnant woman who also happened to be dressed like a lobster. It also appeared that he owned a dog now. Yes, he had briefly held and then lost unknown amount of wealth, but for once he didn't feel poor. He didn't want to ask in case he messed it up, but he thought that he might be on a date.

"You know, if we *do* rescue a lobster together then I should take your number, so I can call and we can discuss schooling options and the like. I heard a podcast about Montessori and that sounds good. Here's my card," Greg said and fished in his battered wallet for a business card, which he handed to Coco.

"*Greg Terde?*" Coco read aloud.

"Yes. I'm Greg Terde. Hello."

"Seriously?" Coco asked, and Greg felt the familiar burn of nominative disgrace. He considered explaining that Terde was a distinguished name with French heritage. He could explain that it could possibly be pronounced *Taird*, but what was the point? He had briefly dared to hope that Coco might have been different.

Coco extended her hand towards him.

"Nice to meet you, Greg Terde. I'm Coco. Coco Butt."

"Coco Butt? Seriously?" Greg asked.

"A Butt Never Lies. It's on the family crest," she replied.

They both monitored the other's face for a sign of teasing or belittlement. There was a shared sense that they had each had enough of belittlement. Whatever the future brought, they would only focus on enlargement. That would be their thing.

Greg caught a flash of light and stooped to inspect something glittering on the pavement. Lying on the floor were two gemstones, each about the size of a broad bean. The myriad faces on the jewel shone and darkened from different angles. He held them up and examined them against the light in the sky, a light which suddenly flared and burned through the clouds and stained the heavens.

"Wow, that's bright," Greg said and shielded his eyes. They pushed in behind a bus shelter. Coco tucked herself into Greg's side and Greg felt his arm instinctively drop around her to keep her and the baby safe. Coco couldn't say why, but it felt like for the first time that she was in exactly the right place.

"What *was* that?" she asked, as the light in the sky retreated behind the cloud cover and faded far into the distance.

"I have no idea," Greg replied. But deep down they both knew.

💎 💎 💎 💎 💎

Jenny made a cup of tea and sat with her bare feet on the coffee table, glued to the Trident app on William's phone. William stood by the window of the flat and looked to the sky in anticipation. Jenny had already started planning what they would say in their next press conference. Deep fakes. Rogue submarine commanders. North Korean hacking. It didn't really matter. She knew what they needed to do now, was ensure no one ever had time to fully digest the last thing because they were too busy reacting to the new thing. An endless series of dead cats, thwacked on the table. One atrocity after another. It was how modern politics worked and she felt her profession had prepared her for it beautifully.

At the window, William watched the sky over North West London growing brilliant white. He looked up and felt it tickle his eyes. He tried not to imagine how bright it was on the Isle of Man right now. He sneezed. One. Two. Three. Four. Five. Six. Seven sneezes. He stared again at the waning white radiance in the sky and willed that elusive eighth sneeze to emerge that would take the title for England.

💎 💎 💎 💎 💎

It had been some minutes since the light had scorched the sky and nothing more had happened, so Greg, Coco and Ronan had continued on their way to the fish market, the two gemstones clicking together in Greg's pocket.

"Hold up," Greg said, as they approached a traffic light and he caught Coco's hand to stop her from stepping out into the road.

"Why?"

"Wait until the light's red," he explained.

Coco looked at the gridlocked road.

"I think we'll be fine to cross," she said and then she checked the lights. "Besides – it is red."

Greg looked at the traffic lights, "Is it? Don't judge me but I'm not great with colours. After you then, Miss Butt."

"You're too kind, Mr Terde."

The fish market was just over the road and some of the lights were coming on, so it looked like it might be open after all.

"We should get something to feed the billionaires while we're here," Greg said. Coco looked at him.

"Or…we could not?" she suggested.

"Now. That's an interesting thought," Greg said. "We should give that some serious consideration."

THE END.

EPILOGUE: THE GREATEST TREASURES ARE FORMED UNDER THE HEAVIEST PRESSURES

WHEN ANGELINA BIRD was shredded into a novelty mince by Fenton Crossley's jet, her possessions, along with every molecule of her being were caught by a mild north westerly wind measuring around ten knots, according to the Met Office. The plane's engine was spinning at approximately 9,000 RPM, which meant that in the few seconds that she was inside the jet, Angelina was struck at least thirty times by the forty fan blades and then again by the hundreds of turbine and compressor blades inside. Consequently, Angelina herself left the rear of the engine as a fine mist, which was blown across Stratford and East Ham. Somewhat improbably, one of her shoes survived entirely intact and fell heel first, embedding itself in the roof of a conservatory in Mill Meads.

The diamonds were a different story.

In the first place, these were protected by the flight case. They were also protected to a lesser extent by the small canvas bags that Bird had swept them into when she transferred them from the safe. The wind had less of an influence on the drop radius of the diamonds, but approximately speaking, they were ejected in the shape of a cone stretching from the A114 in Forest Gate to the A1205 in Mile End. Approximately five billion pounds of diamonds dropping across several of London's lowest income areas. Although it was not the strict dictionary definition, it was absolutely an example of trickle-down economics.

Rupak was one of the beneficiaries of this windfall. He had started his shift delivering food at 9am the night before. By 3am the cold was down to his bones and he was starting to have fantasies about his girlfriend and his bed. For Rupak, the best part of the day was the thirty minute overlap where he had finished his night of work and he would arrive home with any of the food that customers had spurned. He would place the reject food in their part of the fridge and lock it. He would then quietly tiptoe past the sleeping forms of his flatmates to the ladder which took him up to the mezzanine level. There he would shrug out of his jacket and trousers and slide like an icicle into bed alongside Mia. He would feel his body absorb her warmth and the gentle sweet smell of the bed. The simple, routine joy of his nightly reprieve made up for every cab that had tried to kill him, every customer who shouted in his face - and occasionally tried to kill him - and every pound that his employer leeched off his pay for 'admin charges'.

He actually saw the flash of Angelina entering the jet out of the corner of his eye. In part, he registered it because he thought it might have been a speed camera flashing, and he was hoping that the thick gel he'd bought from eBay was really as effective as it claimed at making his number plate unreadable. He was heading north with a container full of kebabs and chips for a high rise off Jansen Road. Occasionally at traffic lights the hot cumin scent escaped from his insulated bag and he would unzip the container and huff the smell as a placebo for eating actual food.

At the light he felt a splatter of rain hit his helmet and he cursed British weather. He was twenty-four and already he swore that when it rained his knees would ache and his ankles swell. He often had a vision of a road so dry that a stiff wind brushed up a cloud of dust. He thought about walking barefoot on a beach that burned the soles of his feet. He saw Mia sitting in a hammock in the shade. A car behind him beeped him back to the sodden asphalt of the city.

The drop was sketchy and involved him climbing several flights of stairs. He rang on the door and heard the disordered thud of footsteps – he guessed stoned, but would settle for not-crazy. The young man who opened the flat door was dishevelled and zoned out. He looked catatonic, but his blue scrubs suggested that he was simply an exhausted junior doctor summoning food from the apps because he couldn't handle the idea of expending non-existent energy on cooking. The young man yawned for the entire time that Rupak was unpacking his food.

"Two kebabs, one chips, and a side salad - there you go," Rupak said and smiled. "Long night?"

"What day is it?" the man asked, seemingly without irony.

"Monday."

"Good grief."

"Well, enjoy your food," Rupak said and smiled again. The man held out his hand and a pound coin dropped from his hand into Rupak's upturned palm. His smile warmed.

"That's very kind – thank you."

"It's a shit tip, sorry it's all the change I've got."

"It's much appreciated," Rupak said sincerely, and slid the pound coin into his trousers as he collected his delivery box and turned.

"By the way, you've got some red on the back of your hat thing," the doctor said through another yawn as he shut the door.

Rupak skipped down the stairs and stowed his box on the back of his moped. He took his helmet off and turned it round, and sure enough, there was a slight red spray across the back of his helmet. It looked like blood. He searched in his box for the wipes that he used to clean up the boxes if they spilled and swiped it across the surface. He shuddered and dropped the soiled wipes in the bin, and tried to figure out where that could have come from. He'd heard of another driver hitting a pigeon before, but that had been at the front and it wasn't as if it had escaped his notice as he'd steered into the side of a bus shelter when it happened.

Rupak felt around his neck and head to see if he was bleeding, but there was no evidence that it had come from him. He looked up and wondered if it had come from above. He bristled again slightly and got back on his bike, before tapping the app to show he was on the way to the next drop off. A bungalow five minutes around the corner; a regular and another guaranteed quid. It all added up, especially when it was money that no one could see. As he rode along London's slick streets, he didn't feel the weight of the five diamonds nestled in his hood. Throughout his journey, from kebab drop-off to pizza delivery, his hood remained slack on his back. It billowed once or twice as he rounded a corner, but the diamonds only snuck deeper into the folds of the fabric.

Then, finally, Rupak was home. He had five hours of sleep to look forward to, provided his flatmates could avoid waking him up when they got up for work at seven. But none of that mattered as he ascended the metal ladder and ducked into his bed platform. Mia was there and for the next thirty minutes, he was the richest person in London, with food waiting in the fridge and a warm woman snuggled next to him. At the foot of the mattress, his coat sat discarded, concealing the unimaginable wealth. Rupak stretched his aching muscles and felt happy with his life.

MY SINCERE THANKS AND LOVE TO

Jon Barnsley
Laura Brown
Mia Caven
Fraser Clenehan
Richard, Katie, Olivia and Sophie Deakin
Victoria Feargrieve
Julie Gibson and all of www.theendoftheworldreadingclub.com
Ciarra and Hayden Havon
Emma Jones
Pippa Lambert
Michelle Lile
Wolfgang McFarlane
Lauren McMenemy
Craig Morris
Fay and Joe Roe
Martin Stevens
James, Ruth, George
and Lucy Pierpoint
Pete Sant
Emma, Harry, Frank, Matilda
and Quinn Shanahan
Clare and Chris Sheard
Mark Tanner
Lee Teste
Michael Walsh
Anji Warden
Gemma Whitford
Yolander Yeo

The billionaires who helped me with research, even when they heard what the book was about.

Cover photo credits (Pexels) Engin Akyurt,
Katarzyna Modrzejewska (lobster) coloured by Andrew Shanahan.
Other images from Shutterstock and charity shop magazines.

I WILL LITERARILY KILL YOU

Several of the names in this book were provided by my readers who donated their names to save me from thinking of fictitious ones, something I find strangely hard to do. The deal is that they lend me their name and I find ways to feature or kill them in my writing.

You can join them. Sign up for free at www.iwillliterarilykillyou.com

Lauren Crossley
Ryan Patrick Kaye
Eilidh Miller
William Monroe
Jennifer Morgan
Chris Morton
Tabitha Montaner
Felicity O'Keeffe
Angelina Warden
Mia Raquel Wilson

OTHER FICTION BY ANDREW SHANAHAN

Novels:
Before and After
Flesh and Blood

Short Stories:
In the Room
I Want You To Write A Letter

SAY HELLO

Website – www.helloshan.co.uk
TikTok – www.tiktok.com/@shaniswriting
Facebook – www.facebook.com/shaniswriting

If you have questions about my writing or anything you want to share, please feel free to get in touch.

As an indie author it makes a huge difference to me if you're able to review my books on Amazon, Goodreads, social media, or to recommend it to that colleague or friend who might enjoy it. If you hated the book, recommend it to that dude who creeps you out, I won't tell.

Finally, I'm always happy to do readings for people, libraries, schools or book clubs - online or in person.

**THANK
YOU
FOR
READING.**

Printed in Great Britain
by Amazon